Heavy is the de

RIVER
OF
SHADOWS

UNDERWORLD GODS #1

KARINA HALLE

GLOSSARY AND PRONOUNCIATION

Tuonela (too-oh-nella)
Realm or Land of the Dead. It is a large island that floats between worlds, with varied geography and terrain. The recently deceased travel via the River of Shadows to the City of Death where they are divided into factions (Amaranthus, the Golden Mean, and Inmost) and admitted into the afterlife. Outside the City of Death, Gods, Goddesses, spirits, shamans, and the dead who have escaped the city can be found.

Tuoni (too-oh-nee)
The God of Death, otherwise called Death, and King of Tuonela who rules over the realm from his castle at Shadow's End.

Louhi (low-hee)
Ex-wife of Death's, former Goddess, half-demon daughter of Rangaista.

Loviatar (low-vee-ah-tar)
The Lesser Goddess of Death and Death's Daughter. Her job is to ferry the dead down the River of Shadows to the City of Death, a role she shares with her brother Tuonen.

Tuonen (too-oh-nen)
The Lesser God of Death and Death's Son. He shares ferrying duties with his sister Loviatar. Tuonen is also a lord in the City of Death and helps oversee things in the afterlife.

Sarvi (sar-vih)
Short for Yksisarvinen, Sarvi is a relic from the times of the Old Gods and originally from another world. Sarvi is a unicorn with bat-like wings that died a long time ago and is composed of skin and bone. Sentient, Sarvi is able to communicate telepathically. While he is a loyal and refined servant to Death, he is also vicious, violent and bloodthirsty by nature, as all unicorns are.

Ilmarinen (ill-mar-ee-nen)
Louhi's consort, the demigod shaman whom she left Death for. He lives with Louhi in their castle by the Star Swamps.

Eero (ay-ro)
A powerful shaman from Northern Finland.

Väinämöinen (vah-ee-nah-moy-nen)
Death's past adversary and legendary shaman who became a Finnish folk-hero. Väinämöinen has supposedly been dead for centuries.

Ukko (oo-koh)
A supreme God and the father of Tuoni, Ahto, Ilmatar, husband to Akka.

Akka (ah-ka)
A supreme Goddess, wife to Ukko, and the mother of Tuoni, Ahto, Ilmatar.

Ilmatar (ill-mah-tar)
Goddess of the Air, sister to Tuoni and Ahto.

Vellamo (vell-ah-mo)
Goddess of the Deep, wife of Ahto. Protector of mermaids. Vellamo can be found in the Great Inland Sea.

Ahto (ah-to)
God of the Oceans and Seas, husband of Vellamo, brother of Tuoni & Ilmatar.

Kuutar (koo-tar)
Goddess of the Moon, Mother of Stars, protector of sea creatures.

Päivätär (pah-ee-vah-tar)
Goddess of the Sun, protector of birds.

Kalma (kahl-ma)
God of Graves and Tuoni's right-hand man and advisor.

Surma (soor-mah)
A relic from the days of the Old Gods and the personification of killing.

Raila (ray-lah)
Hanna's personal Deadmaiden.

Pyry (pee-ree)
Deadmaiden. Head cook and gardener of Shadow's End.

Harma (har-mah)
Deadmaiden. Head of the Shadow's End servants.

Tapio (tah-pee-oh)
God of the Forest.

Tellervo (tell-air-voh)
Lesser Goddess of the Forest and daughter of Tapio.

Hiisi (hee-si)
Demons and goblins of Tuonela, spawns of Rangaista.

Rangaista (ran-gais-tah)
A powerful demon and Old God, father of Louhi.

Liekkiö (lehk-kio)
The spirits of murdered children who haunt the Leikkio Plains. They are made of bones and burn eternally.

Vipunen (vee-pooh-nen)
An unseen giant who lives in the Caves of Vipunen near Shadow's End. The most ancient and wise being in Tuonela from before the time of the Old Gods.

PLAYLIST

Scan the code
(or search for River of Shadows)

"Immigrant Song" – Trent Reznor, Atticus Ross, Karen O

"Dead Skin Mask" – Slayer

"Sin" – Nine Inch Nails

"The Beginning of the End" – (+++) Crosses

"Gatekeeper" – Torii Wolf

"Castle" – Halsey

"You've Seen the Butcher" – Deftones

"Meet Your Master" – Nine Inch Nails

"Welcome to My World" – Depeche Mode

"Doing it to Death" – The Kills

"Blk Stallion" – (+++) Crosses

"Goddess" – Banks

"I am not a woman, I'm a god" – Halsey

"Various Methods of Escape" – Nine Inch Nails

"Last Cup of Sorrow" – Faith No More

"Death's Head Tattoo" – Mark Lanegan Band

"This Link is Dead" – Deftones

"Master of Puppets" – Metallica

"Bone House" – The Dead Weather

"Should Be Higher" – Depeche Mode

"Welcome Oblivion" – How to Destroy Angels

"Die by the Drop" - The Dead Weather

"Born to Die" - Lana Del Rey

"Death Bell" - (+++) Crosses

"King for a Day" - Faith No More

"Nocturne" - Mark Lanegan Band

"Gods & Monsters" - Lana Del Rey

"Phantom Bride" - Deftones

"Surprise, You're Dead!" - Faith No More

"Lantern Room" - Torii Wolf

"The Epilogue" - (+++) Crosses

"This Place is Death" - Deftones

INTRODUCTION

River of Shadows is the first book in the Underworld Gods series and is based on Finnish Mythology. I have dual citizenship with Canada and Finland and have always been fascinated with the lesser-known mythology of my mother's side (my father was Norwegian, and while I love Norse mythology, it's certainly not obscure). Finnish mythology is dark, gruesome, and disturbing, all things that call to my deviant little soul, but there's also an undercurrent of heart built into the myths and folklore, especially when it comes to Tuoni (Death) and his family. Usually underworld rulers in mythology do their job alone, but Tuoni does it alongside his family members, with each of them having their own role. I liked the fact that ruling the dead is a family affair.

All that said, I have taken various liberties with the mythology and the Kalevala, the famous epic of Finland, so for some more astute Finns you may find that some names have been changed to avoid confusion, or characters have been added. Any mistakes in the Finnish language are mine (I ran them past my mother, but I won't throw her under the bus if they aren't correct because I am sure she was tired of me).

CONTENT WARNING

This is a dark fantasy adult romance that ends on a cliffhanger. It contains mature themes such as graphic sex, language, captive situations, violence, and dub con. While this book belongs in the **dark fantasy** sub-genre—and sensitive readers should heed the warnings—it is **not** dark enough to be considered a dark romance.

For my father, Sven Halle – Until we meet again

CHAPTER ONE

THE ARRIVAL

"We come from the land of the ice and snow, where the midnight sun and the hot springs flow," Robert Plant sings through my noise-canceling headphones as the plane begins its descent. My music choice was certainly apt since there's nothing but ice and snow for *miles*. I don't even see the town of Ivalo, let alone the airport where we're supposed to be landing shortly. There're just low rolling hills of white until they blend in with the monotone sky, like we're flying into nothingness.

A flutter of panic forms in my chest and I immediately grip my armrest, my eyes pinching shut. I'm lucky no one's seated next to me on this Finnair flight from Helsinki up to Lapland because I've been riding the Hot Mess Express the whole time. One minute, tears are streaming down my face, lost in grief and regret over my father, the next I'm having a full-on panic attack, wondering what the hell I'm doing, flying to not only Finland, but the remote north of the country, all by myself. I'm no stranger to taking flights alone—it's a part of my job— but this time it's different. My mother refused to come to my father's funeral, and I'm an only child, which means I have to carry the burden without any support. I've never even been to a funeral before.

At least I've been to Finland, though this is my first time in Lapland. I was actually born in the town of Savonlinna, but my mother left my father when I was only six years old, ushering me off to California. I don't remember much of my childhood in Finland, and my only other visits were every other summer when growing up. My father fought long and hard to see me when he could, and I later learned that it was only when he threatened my mother with a custody battle that she relented and let me visit.

Suddenly a memory floods my mind, making my heart feel waterlogged. I had been staying with my father at his lakeside cottage where he lived, having just come in from a refreshing near midnight swim. Despite the hour, the sun was still shining, as it does in the summer months, and the air was thick with dragonflies that buzzed about on kaleidoscope wings, nipping at the mosquitos.

I walked along the dock, a towel draped around me, wet footprints in my wake, wondering where my father had gone, when suddenly he appeared in the doorway to the cottage.

Only he was pretending to be someone else. Santa Claus.

My father is…*was* one of those people, like Leslie Neilson or Christopher Lloyd, who always looked old with his prematurely white hair and beard, so he suited the role perfectly. He stood there in the waning golden light of the summer sun, dressed in the red velvet Santa suit, a sack full of toys beside him.

I was about eight or nine years old, old enough to not

believe in Santa Claus anymore. And even if I had, it would have given me a major pause to have Santa come visit during the summer. But I know from the letters my father would write me (my mother didn't let us talk on the phone very often), that he missed having me around at Christmas, especially since Finland is Santa's home, and so I played along happily, reveling in his attention, and the toys and treats of course.

My chest grows warm at the memory, and yet there's a sharp pinch between my ribs. That's how it's been ever since I got the phone call that my father had died. Every moment I feel like I'm torn between two worlds: the world where my father is still alive and my life can carry on as usual, and the world where my father is dead and my life has changed irrevocably, never to be the same.

It was my father's colleague, Noora, who had made the call a week ago. She told me that my father had gone for a walk in the woods and somehow became disoriented. A search party found him the next day, coated in ice and snow. Dead.

The news didn't seem real at the time. To be honest, it still doesn't. It feels like those two worlds are still intermingling with each other, and I keep being bounced around and I never know where I'll land. Sometimes I just wish that the grief would set like cement, because the moments where the reality crashes upon me can be too difficult to bear. I'd rather be stuck in the thick of it, all the time, as real and raw as possible, as if I could get the pain over with.

People assumed that because I rarely saw or spoke to my father that we didn't have a close relationship, but the strange thing is that, despite the distance, I felt closer to him than my mother. It's like we had our own silent language, or some kind of magnetic tie between us that kept us connected throughout my life. I always felt him with me, felt his love, even when we were technically estranged.

That's the part that hurts the most, though. After high school, when my mother moved to Seattle with her now-husband George, and I was still in LA, I thought about going to Finland. I thought about asking if my father would come to LA. I thought these things, but along with the thoughts of *I should stop eating so many donuts* and *I don't need to watch Howl's Moving Castle again*, and *I certainly don't need another succulent for the patio*, they never came to fruition. I just thought them and moved on, making the mistake of thinking there was plenty of time. I decided that a year from now, when I turned twenty-five, that's when I'd finally take a vacation from work and go and see my father. I thought that's when I'd start making him—my family—a priority.

I never thought he'd die. Not now, frankly not ever. He didn't seem the type, and if you'd met him you'd know. My father was like an unstoppable force. He was the life of the party, popular to the bone, full of life and zest. People loved him and he loved people. My father had this way of making you believe in magic, in that anything in the world was possible, and that you could be anything you wanted to be.

And now he's…gone.

There has to be a mistake, I think to myself as the plane slams down onto the runway. I grip the armrests tighter, warily glancing out the window at the snow that's blowing across the slice of bare pavement on the runway.

We bump along for a while and finally come to a stop.

I let out the breath I was holding as the flight attendant starts speaking in Finnish, so fast that I can't understand a word of it. I have a very rudimentary grasp of the language from what my father taught me as a child, and I'll admit it was only because Finnish inspired Tolkien's Elvish language that made me stay interested in it.

It doesn't take long for me to exit the plane, considering how small it is and it was only half-full to begin with, February being Lapland's off-season. I still have to wait for my carry-on bag though, since they made me check it because of the diminutive overhead bins, and it's while I'm waiting at baggage claim in what must be the world's tiniest airport that I feel a burst of cold at my back.

For a moment I'm disoriented, dizzy, and the skin on my scalp prickles.

I turn around to see a middle-aged woman staring at me, short, with a graying blonde bob and round, weathered cheeks that shine like apples. She's smiling, though her dark eyes aren't.

"Welcome to *Sampi*," the woman says to me in a thick accent, and though I've never met her before, I immediately know it's Noora. In fact, I can hear her name being sung in my head, as if from a robin on a branch, and I have to blink a few times to right myself. Jet lag is no joke.

"Sampi?" I repeat. Dear god, don't tell me I got on the wrong flight.

"It's what we Sami people call Lapland," she says. Then she extends her hand, like an afterthought. "I'm Noora. But you already knew that. I'm sorry we couldn't have met under better circumstances. You meant the world to your father. There wasn't a day where he didn't talk about his dear Hanna."

Don't cry, don't cry.

I shake her hand briefly and manage to hold myself together, only because I'm still a bit confused.

"How did you know what flight I was on?"

Noora gives a half-smile. "You said you'd be here for the funeral tomorrow, and there's not many flights coming up here. Lucky guess." She reaches out and tugs at my black wool coat. "This might be fashionable, but this won't keep you warm."

I'm about to point out that she's dressed only in a thick wool sweater herself, but decide to keep my mouth shut.

"Your father told me that you work for a clothing company," she says, her attention still fixed on me, those dark eyes of hers sharp as tacks. "Something to do with the internet."

"Social media," I tell her, raising my chin slightly. I'm 5'10" and Noora is a lot shorter than me, but whenever I have to explain my job I feel like I'm suddenly very small. The minute someone hears that I'm in fashion, and then hears that I'm in social media, they tend to make an assumption about me pretty fast. "Social media manager," I add. "It's basically how we do all advertising and marketing these days."

She nods and finally looks away to the baggage carousel, breaking eye contact. I feel a strange rush of relief, like I can breathe again. "I told your father we could use someone like you for the resort, but he always brushed me off, saying that the right people would find the place. He was right, in the end." She lifts her arm and points as my rose-gold hardcover suitcase appears on the belt. "There it is."

This time I don't have to ask how she knew. Not many rose-gold suitcases up here.

I stride over to the carousel and pick up my bag, taking a moment to gather my thoughts. I've always been someone who can pick up on vibes (my father used to call me an empath, my mother says I'm "too damn sensitive") and Noora has vibes up the wazoo. But she did take the time to meet me here, and perhaps the strange energy I'm getting off her might be because she's grieving as much as I am. My father moved up north to open his resort five years ago, and though I'd never heard him mention Noora, it's possible they were really close, maybe in ways I don't want to imagine.

I remind myself to stop making judgments and assumptions and roll the bag over to her.

"Good," she says with approval. "I will drive you to the resort now."

"Oh." I pause, gathering my coat collar. "But the funeral isn't until tomorrow."

"Yes," she says patiently. "But you are staying at the resort."

It's not a request, it's an order. I shake my head. "I booked and paid for a hotel room in town already. I won't get a refund if I cancel."

She gives me a placating smile. "You will get a refund. I know all the hotels here. Don't worry about it." She pauses, light brows furrowing. "I must say I was disappointed when I didn't see you book a room at the resort." Then she turns and heads over to the doors to the outside, a marching-like walk.

"I know," I admit after a moment, following after her. "I guess because it didn't show up on the hotel booking site I use.

Creature of habit."

That's not the total truth though. I'd always wanted to stay at my father's wellness resort, even before it started getting some recognition amongst the travel influencers who stumbled upon it in their quest for something new. But the idea of finally staying there, only to have him gone, felt wrong to me in ways I can't really explain. Like it was easier to just stay elsewhere, put a bit of distance in, as if that's going to make any of this hurt less.

We walk through the automatic doors to the outside and the air is a slap to the face, freezing my lungs. It's cold as hell, with snow covering every inch of land, including the sidewalks, and cars are making fresh tracks on the road. I'm cursing myself for not bringing a parka. I'm also wishing my luggage had skis attached to the wheels.

"So your mother isn't coming," Noora notes as we walk to the parking lot and I drag the luggage through the snow drifts.

I shake my head, trying to ward off the anger that sparks inside me. Noora told me she had called my mother before she called me. As soon as I got the news about my father, I texted my best friend Michelle first, then told my roommate Jenny. There was a lot of crying and drinking shots of bourbon in shock.

I didn't actually call my mother until the next morning. I knew that Noora had told her, but Noora had never told my mother that she was calling me. Which meant my mother had no idea I knew my father was dead and she sat on that fucking information for twenty-four hours. Maybe even more, had I not called her.

And, fuck. Even if I wasn't an empath I could have picked up on her vibes loud and clear over the phone. She thought it was good that he was dead.

So no, my mother isn't coming to the funeral.

"I'm sure it would be too hard for her," I say, but from my meek voice, I know that Noora won't believe me. I don't believe me either. It's all bullshit.

But Noora just nods as we head toward a small red hatchback. Once inside the car, I'm met with a plethora of smells, a lot of them familiar like sage and palo santo, the rest earthy, bitter, and cloying. Because my legs are long they're crammed up against the glovebox and I have to wrestle with the seat control until it slams back.

Noora looks over me with amusement, and for once I see it reach her dark eyes. "Just like your father," she comments. "He was tall too. Is your mother the same?"

I shake my head and scoff. "She's five two and a delicate little flower." And boy, she never lets me forget it either.

Noora makes a low *hmmmm* noise and starts the car, fiddling with the heat. The controls were set low, which strikes me as odd, but maybe the cold isn't a problem for her. She's only wearing a sweater, after all.

"We have no use for delicate people up here," she says stiffly. "They don't survive very long. Sorry, I'll have the heat on in a moment." The car backs up and then rolls across the parking lot, the tires on snow making a pleasing crunching sound. "Your father told me you used to be a dancer."

"Yes," I say, the bitterness in the air now settling on my tongue. "Unfortunately, you have to be a delicate flower in dance and there was a point where I couldn't do that anymore." In other words, dance was everything to me, and especially to my mother. But the extremes I went to so I could remain lithe and airy and light eventually took their toll on my body and mind. "But then I discovered martial arts. Capoeira. It's from Brazil. Combines dancing and fighting."

Noora takes her eyes off the road to look at me. "He never mentioned that."

I shrug. I'm not competitive. My heart can't take anything competitive anymore, not after what I went through. It's just a hobby. After high school I realized if I couldn't be accepted in dance anymore, then I wanted to do something else to keep my body moving. I started building muscle, lifting weights, and it just came naturally to me. I used to do a little tae kwon do for a while, even arnis, but capoeira is what stuck.

Noora's vibe shifts a little. Like this information concerns her. Perhaps she's old-fashioned and doesn't believe girls should fight. She'd get along with my mother with that view.

I flash her a placating smile. "Don't worry, I'm not going to go beating up anyone at Papa's funeral." She gives me a stiff smile and I immediately feel awkward. I look around the car. "So what's the smell?"

"Do you like it?" she asks.

Not really. "Smells like sage." *And like rotting corpses*, I add in my head and the accurate thought makes me shiver. I pull my coat closer around me, my cold hands shoved in my pockets. I've always been morbid, but I don't need these thoughts before my father's funeral.

"Sage, palo santo, lavender, myrrh and *sieni*. Mushrooms."

"Didn't know dried mushrooms smell like that."

"These ones are special."

Aren't all mushrooms special? I think. If I actually had a social life in high school maybe I'd know what dried mushrooms smell like.

I turn my attention to the scenery passing by the window. Like the view from the airplane, the land is made up of pine trees and snow, with a few low rolling hills thrown into the mix. I have a feeling we're driving past lakes and rivers, but the thick snow covers them and makes everything look the same.

It's such the opposite of Los Angeles that I'm suddenly hit with a pang of fear, like I'm on the edge of the earth, close to falling off into infinity, and I feel precariously placed. In my mind I'm looking at the globe and I can see the little dot where I am and there's just nothing above me at all except ice and snow forever.

Not only that, but I've barely seen any cars on this highway and I realize I don't know Noora at all. I'm about to pull out my phone and check for reception, maybe send Jenny a text even though I have no idea what time it is back home, when the skin on my spine starts to crawl. I have the most awful, unsettling feeling that if I look at Noora right now, that I won't see Noora at all. That I'll see some smiling demonic creature. In fact, out of the corner of my eye, I swear I see a pair of horns, no, *antlers*, growing from the top of her head.

I immediately close my eyes and take in a deep breath. *Jet lag*, I tell myself. *Grief and jet lag. Hell of a combo.*

"Are you alright?" Noora asks.

I nod, pressing my lips together, keeping my eyes closed.

"Just really tired all of a sudden."

"Why don't you sleep? The resort is another forty-five minutes away."

Hell no, I'm not sleeping now, I think, resting my head against the frozen window.

But then the car engine suddenly turns off and I hear Noora say, "We're here."

My eyes snap open and I sit upright in my seat. We're parked in front of a low rustic building, the roof piled high with snow, a forest surrounding it, the branches glittering in the waning sun like icing sugar.

What the hell?

I blink and shake my head. "What happened? I literally just closed my eyes."

"You fell asleep," she says. "Come on, let's get you to your room so you can go to bed."

My brain feels like a train that's slowly pulling out of the station as I try to make sense of how time has passed so quickly. "You're not supposed to sleep the first day you arrive, not until night. Otherwise you'll never get over your jet lag," I tell her, my tongue feeling thick.

"It'll be night in an hour," she says in a no-nonsense voice. She gets out of the car and opens up the trunk, pulling out my suitcase. I stare at the log-building, at the intricately carved sign that says "Wilderness Hotel" over it, smoke rising from the chimney. I guess this is it. This is what my dad worked so hard for.

Like clockwork, I feel hot tears behind my eyes and I take in a sharp, shaking breath trying to ward them off. I don't want to cry in front of Noora. I feel like I can't let myself be vulnerable in front of her.

I get out of the car, the air even colder here, but bracingly fresh, peppered with the smell of pine and woodsmoke. There are only four other cars in the parking lot.

"I guess it's not very busy right now," I observe, walking somewhat unsteadily over to Noora, holding my hand out for my suitcase.

"Shoulder season," she says, keeping the suitcase away. "We only have one guest at the moment. You relax, Eero will take care of your bag."

I'm about to ask who Eero is when the door to the hotel opens and a tall, robust man with a long gray beard appears in the frame. For a moment I swear I'm staring at my dad, except this man looks older, and somehow crueler. I know that's an odd thing to glean from someone's looks, but it's all in his eyes. Once again, my vibe radar is going off the rails.

He walks over to us and gives me a wide smile, taking the suitcase from Noora. He's wearing a reindeer fur vest over a snowsuit, and a white and red knitted cap that stands tall on his head, ear flaps hanging by his cheeks. At least he seems more appropriately dressed.

"Nice to meet you, Hanna," he says in a deep voice. "I'm Eero. I was a good friend of your father's. We are *so* glad you are here."

I can only muster a half-smile. I know I might seem rude and stand-offish, but I just can't shake the weird feeling.

He exchanges a look with Noora that I can't read, and they head toward the hotel.

"As you know, the premise of the hotel is that guests can stay in little wilderness cabins in the woods and by the lake, all perfectly placed for watching the northern lights," Noora says as we walk down the path to the hotel entrance. "But we figured it would be better if you stayed in one of the rooms in the main lodge here. That way you won't feel so alone. I imagine with your jet lag and your grief, all of this must feel quite confusing by now." She glances at me over her shoulder. "Tomorrow morning I'll give you a tour. For now, you rest."

Suddenly I'm too tired to protest. Eero opens the door and leads us into the hotel, the air smelling of butter, cinnamon, and cardamom, my stomach rumbling in response. The lobby is wonderfully rustic with the log cabin walls, woven tapestries and paintings, numerous chandeliers made of reindeer and moose antlers hanging from the ceiling with flickering candles in them. I know that was one hundred percent the aesthetic choice of my father.

I look around and catch a glance of a dining room, lounge and kitchen before they lead me upstairs to my room, located down a narrow hallway.

Eero opens the door and places my bag beside the bed. I step inside, quickly taking it in. The room is simple, with birch walls and fur curtains, though it smells just like Noora's car.

"We'll see you in the morning," Noora says to me as they start to leave.

"Wait," I spin around, and she pauses in the doorway. "It's only three in the afternoon. Where are you going?"

"You need your sleep," Eero says, not answering my question at all.

Then he closes the door.

I stare at it for a moment, part of me almost expecting it to lock from the outside. But, of course, it doesn't.

I walk over to the window and peer outside. I'm looking right onto the parking lot which gives me a bit of comfort for some reason. Even though they seem hell-bent on me going to sleep right now, I'm grateful they put me in here instead of out in the forest. I already feel thoroughly creeped out, and for no reason at all.

I decide to lie down on the bed to test it out. It's a queen and quite firm, but my body immediately relaxes into it.

I should unpack and then maybe find Noora, see if I can get something to eat. Text Michelle and Jenny and my mom and let them know I…

But the thought starts to drift away.

My eyes close.

My eyes open.

Darkness.

Complete and total darkness.

For a moment I think I'm dead, then I see a green light above me blink on and off and I realize it's a smoke detector.

I fumble for my phone and it's in my pocket. I'm still wearing my damn coat.

I bring it out and turn it on. The time is ten p.m., the light bright, making me wince, and the photo I have of my father and me as the screen wallpaper makes me want to burst into tears.

I manage to hold it together and shine the light around the room until I see the bedside lamp and switch it on.

Well I just totally passed the fuck out, didn't I? This is exactly why I wanted to stay awake as long as possible. Now I'm wide awake when everyone else is going to sleep.

I sigh and get up. Use the washroom, splash some water on my face, then my rumbling stomach tells me I need to get something to eat. Even though I'm sure Noora and Eero are asleep (and I have no idea if they live at the hotel or elsewhere), maybe I can help myself to something in the kitchen.

I leave my room and walk down the stairs to the main level, heading toward the kitchen. I'm almost there when I notice another room, just past the dining room and lounge. While there are only a few lights on in the hotel, and it's eerily quiet and empty, I can see flickering candles dancing on the walls, hear the soft sound of music. The music itself is strange and becoming, like choir voices and low tribal drumming.

I walk toward it, feeling the need to be quiet for some reason, then stop.

There's a casket in the room, lit by candles on either side, chairs lined up on either side of the room.

Oh my god.

This is where the funeral is being held.

I swallow hard as I walk into the room, my eyes drawn to the casket. Beside it is a blown-up picture of my father's face, some smiling moment out in the sun when he was younger, and that's when it hits me. I mean it really hits me, like I'm in the middle of train tracks and for once I don't see the locomotive coming.

Tears spring to my eyes and I'm frozen, stunned by the immensity of it all, of the fact that life will keep going on without my dad in it and how fucking unfair that is.

I don't even notice that my knees are buckling and I'm collapsing into the ground. I don't even notice the strangled cry that's ripped from my throat, filling the empty room. I don't notice anything but the devastatingly cold and hard realization that my father is gone.

He's gone.

He's really gone.

He's dead and he's not coming back.

But it can't be true. It just can't. Why do I still feel him within my heart, why do I still feel that connection?

Because you're delusional, a voice in my head says.

But it just can't be true. People like my father, they just don't die. They're the type that live forever. They're the ones that defy the odds. They're larger than life, larger than death. My father can't be living on this planet one minute, drinking coffee and listening to bird song, having the sun on his face and then… not. You can't just stop *being*. You can't stop what has started. How dare God take him like this, to just decide my dad's time was enough?

It's not enough. It's never enough.

"Papa," I cry out, my voice breaking and echoing in my ears. I sound like a child, I feel like a child. Oh god, I would do anything to be a child again, to go back, to be with him. I want to be young again, I want to do this over again and get it right this time, I want to tell my mother that I'm not leaving him, that I'm staying with him.

"I want to go back," I whisper hoarsely, my face buried in my hands. "I want to go back to when I was your little girl. I want another chance. I don't…I can't move on like this. Not in this world. Not without you."

But the room gives nothing. All there is is the casket at the end and my father's wonderful smiling face beside it and all I feel is so much despair and sorrow and regret, a deeper cut than bone deep.

A cut that will never ever heal.

A scar for all my life.

Right in the heart of me.

I stay on the floor of the room for what could be minutes, might be hours. It's hard to tell when I'm jet-lagged. Eventually though, I stagger to my feet, leaning on the chairs to push myself up.

I know I should turn around, go to my room, maybe cry my eyes out until I fall asleep again. But I can't. I know my father is gone and yet I feel that if I turn my back on the casket, I'm turning my back on him. That I'm abandoning all I have left of him, his cold dead body.

But it's still him. It's still his.

And I'm here.

So I find my strength and I walk down the aisle. The closer I get to the casket, the more I realize how beautiful it is. Made of some tree with a lot of knotted "eyes," and intricate carvings all over, showing reindeer and trees, eagles and swans. Beneath and to the sides of the casket are the floral arrangements, pine boughs, and various berries all strung together with red and silver ribbons.

I run my hands over the casket, wishing I could feel his energy come from inside. But dead people don't give off energy. I'll never feel that again from him.

Open it, a voice in my head says. *You'll regret it if you don't.*

I swallow hard. I've been debating this last week whether to look at my father's body. On one hand, I don't want the memories of him tarnished. I want to remember him alive and full of life. On the other hand, I need closure, badly. And if he was found frozen, well, how bad can he really look?

So I place my fingers along the bottom of the lid.

Lift it up.

And stare directly into an empty casket.

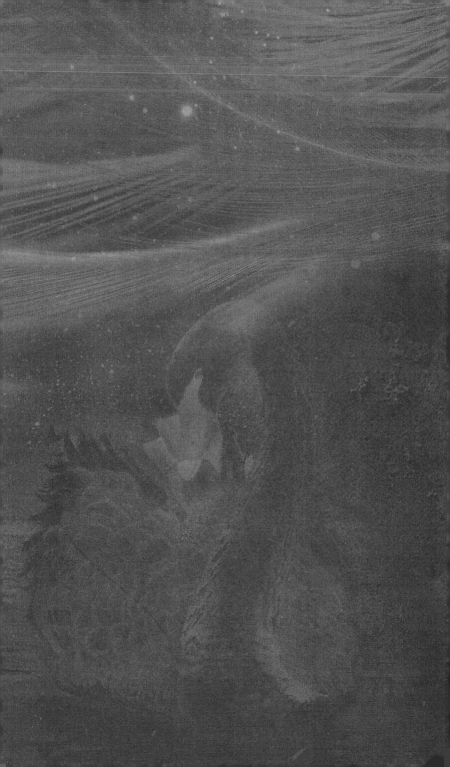

CHAPTER TWO

THE FUNERAL

What the fuck?

I stare at the empty coffin, bewildered, then push the lid up further, quickly glancing down the end, then putting my arm inside, frantically feeling around.

There's nothing.

It's fucking *empty*.

What the hell is going on?!

A flush of hope warms my chest, the idea that perhaps my father isn't dead after all. But then none of this makes any sense. They would have had *a* body at some point—where did *that* body go?

"You need to leave."

I gasp loudly and whirl around, but the room is empty. Where the hell did that voice just come from?

I turn back in time to see the casket lid slowly lowering and, standing behind it, the tall slim shadow of a man.

I gasp again, taking a step backward, just as the shadow comes forward into the candlelight. The light of the flames flickers against his face, revealing a young man with floppy red hair and sky-blue eyes, his cheekbones high with alabaster skin and ruddy cheeks, making him look eternally youthful, his age hard to pin down. He's dressed in all black, except for a string of spotted feathers tied around his wrist.

"Who are you?" I ask, pressing my fingers harder into my chest as if to keep my heart from jumping out.

"You need to leave," he says again, his eyes briefly going over my shoulder to the doorway and back to me, shimmering in intensity. "*Now*."

I shake my head, having no idea what this crazy stranger is saying. "What? No. I'm staying here at the hotel. My dad is supposed to be in this casket. It's his funeral tomorrow. I'm Hanna—"

"Heikkinen," he interjects with my last name. "I know who you are. But please, listen to me, you have to leave this place right now, before it's too late."

I hate how slow my brain is, that nothing is making sense, let alone this stranger who literally just appeared before me out of the shadows and is telling me what to do. "I'm not going anywhere. You know what happened to my father? To Torben Heikkinen? Is he really dead? Please tell me he isn't dead."

The man is breathing hard now, his eyes keep flitting to the door. I look over my shoulder quickly but it's still just the two of us in the room. Two of us and an empty casket. "I know the truth about your father," the man says, his eyes taking on a feverish gleam. "And I can take you to him, if you come with me right now."

He reaches for my arm and I rip it away from him.

"I'm not going anywhere with you!" I cry out, stumbling

back a few feet. "I just want to know where my father's body is! Tell me where it is!"

The man shakes his head, putting his finger to his lips. "Please, don't wake them."

"Don't wake who? I want to wake up everyone!" I roar, throwing my arms out. "I don't know who you are! For all I know, you've broken in here and stolen his body!"

"Please, Hanna," he says.

"Don't call me that! You don't know me."

"I know of you. Very well." He licks his lips quickly, pupils growing as small as pin pricks. "Your father spoke of you all the time. Every day we'd work together, he would tell me everything about you. I know that you were a dancer, that now you do martial arts, and it suits you even better. That you work in fashion. That you live in a house in North Hollywood, but that's nothing like the actual Hollywood, and you have a housemate who has a hair salon in the garage. That you used to write your father letters and draw little nature scenes with each one, a magic forest."

"Stop," I whisper. Everything inside me is shaking. How does he know all this? "You can't…how do you know all this?"

"Because I was close to your father," he says, his voice rising with a hint of bitterness. "Maybe as close as you were to him. And when I tell you I know where he is, you have to believe me, and you have to leave this place while you can."

"Is he…alive?"

I hold my breath as my hope, my desperate hope, seems to float in the air between us.

His thin, dark brows come together. "He might not be

dead."

I stare at him in disbelief, my hope transforming to anger. "What the fuck is that even supposed to mean? You know what, I don't care. Maybe you knew him, maybe you found out that information because you murdered him yourself, I don't know, but I'm done. I'm going to get help."

The fact that he thinks I'm going to leave this hotel with him, a creepy stranger, just because he knows some facts about me, just because he can't give me a straight answer about my father…

I turn around to head for the door when I stop.

Eero is standing in the doorway. The sight of him gives me a pause, my spine prickling. He's dressed head-to-toe in what looks like reindeer fur and bearskin, and there's a string of bones and canine teeth around his neck. Hardly bedtime attire.

"What's going on in here?" he asks in a booming voice. He's staring over my head at the mystery man. "Rasmus. What are you doing here this late?"

Ah, his name is Rasmus. Suits him.

"My father's body is gone," I say to Eero, trying to summon the strength and anger I had seconds ago with Rasmus, but now my voice is coming out quiet and unsure. I gesture to the casket behind me, but I don't turn around. For some reason I'm afraid to break eye contact. "I just wanted a look at him and he's gone. Go and look. He's not in there. The casket is *empty*."

Eero doesn't move. Instead he gives me a close-lipped smile while his eyes shine in the light. "It's been a long day, Hanna. Perhaps it's best if you go to your room."

"Eero," Rasmus says in a pleading voice. "Why not tell her

the truth? She's Torben's daughter after all."

"What truth?" I ask. "What fucking truth? Please, one of you just tell me what the hell is going on." I feel like I'm being led in circles and getting dizzier as I go.

"You need your rest," Eero says, taking a step toward me.

"No." I swallow and move backward instinctively. "I do not need any more rest. I need answers. My father is supposed to be in that casket, it's his funeral tomorrow. I'm not going anywhere until you tell me what's happening!" I can't help but yell that last part, my words echoing in the room.

"Your father is dead, my dear," he says to me after a moment. "And he's in that casket. I guarantee it. Just go and look and you'll see him again."

I keep my eyes glued to him. I don't move. I feel like turning around would be a mistake and I can't explain why.

"What's happening in here?" I hear Noora's voice, and it brings me just a smidge of comfort as she appears behind Eero.

"She thinks her father isn't in the casket," Eero says, but he's not taking his eyes off me either. In fact, the more he stares at me, the harder it is for me to get my thoughts in order.

"Oh dear," Noora says. "Hanna, you look like you've seen a ghost. I know how it can be. Death. It's so…final. It's hard for mortal brains to comprehend."

I gesture to the casket again while keeping my eyes on them. "Noora. Go and look for me. Please. He's not in there. I'm not hallucinating. And then that guy just showed up out of nowhere. He says he knows where my father is."

Noora doesn't even glance at Rasmus. "Oh don't mind him. He was your father's apprentice. Seems he can't let go of him either. So terribly sad. I feel for both of you."

I sense Rasmus' presence still behind me but he's staying silent. There's a dark, cold feeling in my stomach like I've swallowed a pit of ice. "Apprentice? Apprentice of what? Hotel management?" As far as I know, my father didn't even run the hotel, he was just behind the concept, one of the owners.

"Noora, why don't you go take a look," Eero says in a patient tone and nods at the casket. "Just to give our dear Hanna peace of mind."

Noora gives me a tight smile and walks past me, the air smelling like rot, so much so that I nearly start gagging.

Don't look, I tell myself. *Keep your eyes on Eero.*

Eero gives me a half-smile in response, something more sly than anything, like he heard my thoughts and he knows I'm going to lose. Lose what? I don't know. That pit of ice in my stomach grows sharper.

I hear Noora chuckle softly from behind me. "Oh, Hanna. He is in here, looking so peaceful. He is at peace now, don't you understand? Come look."

Eero holds my gaze as I start to waver.

"Really?" I ask. "Rasmus?" I add, wanting to hear it from him. "Is he really in there?"

But there's only silence. Why isn't Rasmus saying anything? He was so hell-bent on getting me out of here and now he's just gone mute.

"He's at peace, so you need your own peace," Noora says. "Come see, Hanna. Come see your dear father."

I can barely swallow the lump in my throat. My entire body feels like shaking uncontrollably and I can't stop it.

I turn around, breaking eye contact with Eero, a freeing sensation entering my body, and blink. Rasmus is gone. Like, he's completely disappeared. But before I can even point that out, how that's even possible, I see Noora peering over the casket.

And I see my father in that casket.

My mouth drops open, hit with both bewilderment at how fucked up my mind must be to have not seen him before, to utter gut-kicking sadness.

It's *him*.

"Papa!" I cry out and run toward the casket, Noora stepping out of the way.

Tears automatically stream down my face as I stare down at my father's lifeless body. It's him, it's really him. From his white beard, to his hooked nose which he always used to call his beak, to the stubborn crease between his white brows, like he's frowning his way through death…

"Papa," I say again, the word coming out raw and broken and I feel like the grief I thought I knew, the grief I thought I was making friends with, that was setting like cement, has changed once again. It's deeper now, potent, and ripping my soul apart into tiny little pieces that will never come back together.

I want to touch him but I'm afraid he'll be cold, that he won't feel like him. I lean over his face, trying to memorize the details. It had been so long since I'd seen him and yet he looks the exact same. Like he hasn't aged at all. Like he's not even dead, just resting, just sleeping.

"I love you," I whisper to him, and the tears fall from my face, splashing onto his skin. "I'm sorry I never said it enough.

I should have said it more. I should have called more, I should have been more present, I should have been with you as soon as I was able to and I'm sorry. I'm so sorry I kept putting it off. Putting you last. I thought we had more time. I really thought we had more time and we…we don't. We didn't. Now you're gone. You're gone."

More tears fall from my eyes, landing on his face. With shaking hands, I reach to wipe it off his cheek but before I do, his skin seems to move beneath the droplet. I pause, staring wide-eyed. His skin seems to warp and shimmer, becoming translucent, and I swear I can see something underneath.

Something *moving*.

Something like…another face.

I shake my head, as if trying to right it, because I have to be hallucinating again, I have to be.

But then something shifts, and my father's nose appears to disintegrate before my eyes, turning black, like it's rotting off.

His eyes open.

He stares right at me.

A scream chokes inside my throat.

Because it's not my father's eyes.

These are Rasmus' eyes.

"Run!" Rasmus's voice comes out through my father's open mouth, now turning black like rotting sludge, his teeth falling out.

I scream. Pure panic courses through me and I turn to run, because it feels like the only thing to do. This isn't my father, I don't know what this is, but I have to get far, far away from here.

But Noora is right there behind me, her body pressed

against mine, and she's grabbing me in a chokehold before I can even turn, her arm pressing in hard against my windpipe.

I can't breathe. I start to struggle. For an older lady, she has the strength of a beast, and her smell is becoming even more pungent, and for a moment I feel this sensation to give up, almost like there's another voice inside me, one that doesn't belong to me, telling me it's all over.

But then I manage to push through it and I remember who I am and what I can do, and all my training comes flooding back. It's basic self-defense and I'm jabbing my elbow back, striking her where I can. It doesn't loosen her grip as much as I hoped, but she does let out a groan, shifting, and I take the opportunity to quickly widen my stance and flip her over my head.

She goes summersaulting over on top of the casket, knocking it off the stand, and for a moment I'm horrified as my father's body starts to slide out, but that horror stops when I realize it's now Rasmus, scrambling to his feet.

"Run outside!" he yells at me, trying to push off Noora who is trying to drag him down.

I whip around and see Eero coming at me. He's a big man and his eyes are so black that there's no iris, and I don't know if it's my mind or something else that's making me believe he has claws on his outstretched hands and horns starting to poke through his hair, but I drop low and spin forward off my hands, sliding under him as he tries to make a grab for me.

Claws just scrape along the back of my scalp, slicing off a strand of hair, and then I'm up again and running out of the room, through the lounge, past the dining room. I want to scream in horror, scream for help, but I don't think anyone is going to help me now.

As I round the bend to the lobby, I can feel Eero's presence behind me, getting closer and closer, but I don't dare turn around and look. I'm almost at the front doors when I suddenly feel a flash of intense cold at my back, as if a door opened behind me, and in the reflection of the glass I see a white wall, as if the air in the lobby frosted over.

My hands strike the door and I push it open and I keep running, the sub-zero temperatures causing my breath to freeze in my lungs, my eyes to burn. Thankfully I'm wearing boots, but I'm just in a sweater, my coat left back in my room, and I'll freeze to death soon if I don't find shelter or someone to help me.

My first thought is of the cars in the parking lot, maybe I'll get lucky and find the keys in one of them, drive off to safety, wherever that is. Fuck, I don't even know where I really am.

I reach into my pocket to grab my phone to see if I have enough reception to call the police—no bars—and hear the hotel door slam shut behind me and suddenly Rasmus is at my side, grabbing my arm and pulling me along into the knee-high snow, away from the parking lot.

"This way," he says, his legs moving preternaturally fast.

I look over my shoulder at the hotel, expecting Eero and Noora to come running out after us, but there's no one there.

"What happened in there?" I cry out.

"I stopped them," he says gruffly.

How? I want to ask. Did he kill them? I try to pull back and slow down, pointing at the parking lot. "Where are we going, shouldn't we try and steal a car?"

He shakes his head firmly and continues to pull me along. I'm nearly stumbling as I go, the snow getting higher and higher, filling my boots. "We wouldn't get very far," he says. "I have to take you to see your father."

"I don't understand!" I'd tear my hair out if the adrenaline wasn't propelling me forward. "Where is he? Why were you in the casket? What were they trying to do to me?"

"Plenty of time to answer those questions later," he says. He glances over his shoulder and frowns. "They'll be out any minute now."

I guess he didn't kill them. I look behind me again but immediately eat shit, falling right into a snowbank, snow sinking into my sweater and jeans. Rasmus hooks his arms under me and pulls me up like I weigh nothing at all.

"Almost there," he says. "You can do it."

My mind seems to empty out, the cold finally getting to me. I have this vague sensation that I'll die soon if I don't get inside somewhere, if I don't get warm, and that death wouldn't be such a bad thing.

"Fight it!" Rasmus barks at me. "Don't let them in your head!"

Don't let who in my head? I don't even know who we're running from. I don't even know where I am. Who I am.

My sight starts to turn gray at the edges.

"Fuck," Rasmus says. "Hold on."

The lights from the hotel fade away, like they're being snuffed out, and everything is turning black. I'm falling for a moment and then I'm being lifted up in the air. Carried. I hear the rasp of Rasmus' breath in the cold air, his legs as they plow through the snow.

Then, somewhere in the distance I hear. "Rasmus! Hanna!"

The voice doesn't even sound human. It's sinister and macabre and strikes fear in the deepest part of my soul.

Hanna. That's my name. I'm Hanna.

I'm…trying to survive.

I gasp, as if just being pulled from drowning, and open my eyes to find myself being placed on a low, two-person sleigh, blankets piled high around me.

A sleigh attached to a fucking *reindeer*.

I stare at the animal for a moment and it turns its head, staring right back at me with brown liquid eyes, as if wondering who I am.

Holy shit.

"Sulo!" Rasmus says to the reindeer as he pulls up several blankets and animal hides from behind me and starts draping them over me. "Go!"

The reindeer starts running, the sleigh tugged through the snow until it finds the tracks left from before. Rasmus tries to steady himself while keeping me as warm as possible, but no matter how many blankets he puts on me, I don't feel any warmer. I'm iced to the bone.

"Where are we going?" I ask, teeth chattering. I want to point out how nuts it is that a reindeer-pulled sleigh was his preferred escape vehicle over a car, but Sulo is really picking up the pace and we're gliding along deeper into the pine forest. I look over my shoulder at the hotel and I barely make out the lights at all. I certainly don't hear or see either of them.

I'm just heading off into the darkness with a stranger and

a reindeer.

Once again I'm hit with a wave of fatigue, but this time I don't think it's anyone in my head. The adrenaline is starting to wear off.

"We're going somewhere safe," Rasmus says. "Your father's house."

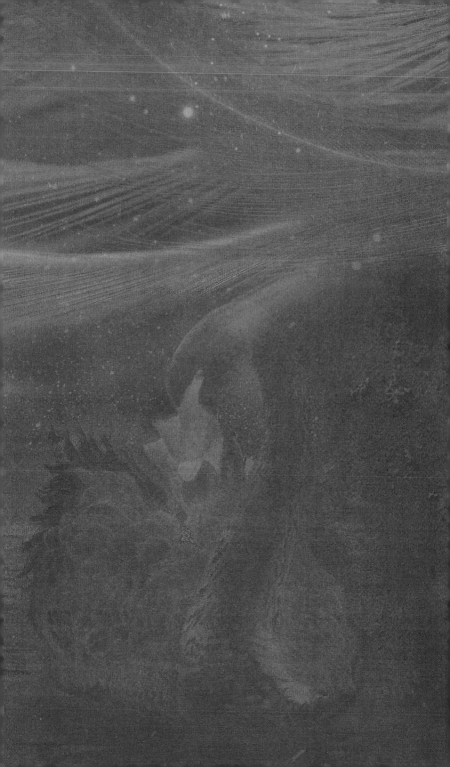

CHAPTER THREE

THE COTTAGE

I wake up to the smell of fresh cedar, cardamom, and baker's yeast. For a moment I'm back at my father's cottage on the lake, when I used to wake up in my tiny room with the heavy wool quilts at the foot of the bed, simple watercolor paintings of flowers on the walls, and smell the tinctures he was preparing for the day, along with the *pulla* bread he'd make me for breakfast. It's a nostalgic smell, one that makes me want to curl up under the covers and go back to sleep again, content.

But when my fingers pull on the covers, I realize I have no idea where I really am, and all the strange and horrific images from last night come crashing into me.

I gasp and sit straight up, nearly hitting myself on a low log beam from a slanted ceiling. I'm in an attic of sorts, weak gray light coming in through the small windows at either side of the house, ice and snow at the corners of the frames.

"Are you awake?" I hear a voice from downstairs and it takes me a moment to place it. Names flip through my head until I find one that makes sense.

Rasmus. That voice belongs to Rasmus.

But who the fuck is Rasmus and the what the hell happened to me?

I start to pull off the covers but something makes me stop and stare. There's such a familiar feeling to them in my hands, such a sentimental weight. I stare at them in the dim light, taking in the blue and red pattern of snowflakes and squares, then look at the rest of the blankets that are all folded at the foot of the bed, and fuck…I'm not imaging things. These are the same blankets I had as a child, growing up in the house in Savonlinna, and then later at my father's cottage. These are *his* blankets.

I throw them back and am relieved that I'm still wearing my jeans and sweater, then get out of bed, careful not to hit my head on the low ceiling, go over to the ladder and poke my head over the open space. The soothing smell of butter, sugar and cardamom comes floating up, along with cozying warmth.

I go down the wood ladder and find myself in a small living area with an even smaller kitchen just beyond it. Everything about this place is both familiar and strange, making me uneasy and yet comforted. The knotted walls house many rough-hewn shelves made from birch bark. On them are an assortment of books, both leather-bound and hardcovers, as well as worn booklets with tattered covers, held together with loops of golden twine. Crystals of all sizes and colors are peppered between the books alongside tiny glass jars stuffed with herbs, and wooden cups with feathers, twigs and paintbrushes sticking out. Above is an impressive reindeer-antler chandelier that dwarfs the place, and across from me is a roaring crackling fire. I spy the mantle above it with framed photos, and am about to walk over to it to get a closer look when Rasmus says, "Good morning."

I whirl around to see him in the kitchen, which I swear was empty a moment ago. He's pulling a tray of buns out of the oven, the warm smell of spices filling the room. I stand there and stare at him for a moment, trying to wrap my head around the weirdly domestic scene.

"Where am I?" I ask.

He nods at the mantle. "As I said last night…"

I turn and go over to the pictures. There, in tarnished gold and silver frames, are pictures of my father. One of them he's with Rasmus beneath the northern lights with a bottle of vodka in hand, in another he's standing in front of the hotel, looking proud. But all the rest of the photos are of me. Some are of the two of us, like the self-timer he took of us when he was dressed as Santa Claus, but the rest are just of me. There's me at a dance recital when I was eight, there's me in Swan Lake when I was sixteen—the last recital I would do—an elaborate headdress of swan feathers on my head. There's me at Venice Beach with Jenny, another one of me joking around at work. I have no idea where he got all these, then I realize they're all on paper. He must have printed them out from my Instagram account.

"Papa," I whisper, a lump forming in my throat. I pick up the photo of the two of us on the dock. "You did all this?"

"I told you he talked about you all the time," Rasmus says from behind me. "I know you don't know me from Adam, but that's why it feels like I know you. Here."

I twist around and he's handing me a ceramic plate with a chip out of it, a warm bun on top. "You need to eat. It's pulla.

KARINA HALLE

I'm sure you've had it before," he says before he walks back to the kitchen. "Your father's recipe, by the way."

I eye the bun stuffed with cinnamon and cardamom, sprinkled with big shiny hunks of pearl sugar. My stomach growls ravenously. There's a slight chance that Rasmus is trying to poison me, but if he wanted to kill me he could have just left me behind with Noora and Eero.

At the thought of them I shudder. It's enough to squash my appetite. I take the plate over to the couch and sit down, watching as Rasmus tidies the kitchen.

"So," I begin, trying to form my thoughts and keep the panic at bay. "I hate to be blunt, but now that I'm awake and apparently in one piece, you need to tell me just what the fuck is going on here. Because I can't tell if last night was a jet-lag infused nightmare or not, but either way you have a lot of explaining to do."

Rasmus sighs and then comes over to me, holding two mugs of something hot and places them on the tree-trunk coffee table in front of me.

"What's that?" I ask, nodding at the mug.

He raises a brow. "I'm not poisoning you, if that's what you're worried about." He sits down on a leather armchair. "It's pine needle tea."

I peer down in the mug to see a few pine needles floating as well as a couple of tiny flower buds. They're dusky pink in color, yet when I move the mug and the water jostles, the flowers look gold, like they've been painted with a metallic sheen.

"And the flowers?"

He takes a sip of his tea and then smiles. "Frost flowers."

"What are frost flowers?"

"You ask a lot of questions."

I stare at him for a moment. "Can you fucking blame me?"

"You swear a lot too. Your father didn't mention that."

I ignore that. "Tell me where he is. Then tell me why we're in his house. Tell me how you're his apprentice. Then tell me what the fuck Eero and Noora wanted. In that order."

He lets out another low sigh, tapping his fingers on the leather armrests. "I'll tell you everything. And it will be the truth. But I need you to drink your tea first."

I stiffen, eyeing the tea for a moment. "Why?" I ask hesitantly.

"Because it will open your heart and mind. What I'm about to tell you will be hard to believe at first, but it's imperative that you believe. The tea will help."

"How do I know this tea isn't going to make me forget everything you say?"

He chuckles, looking positively boyish, and I'm briefly trying to place his age again. He could be eighteen. He could be in his mid-thirties. He might even be in his eighties since he just used the word *imperative*. "There's another tea for that. And I don't want you to forget a single word. I'm going to need you to remember. The truth will serve as fuel."

I stare at him to go on, my patience already threadbare.

He stares right back until I relent. I pick up the tea and have a tepid sip. It's hot, but not scalding, and the fragrant scent of the pines seems to wake me up. The tea itself tastes like sugared lemons, and before I know it I've finished the whole thing.

He clears his throat. "Good." Then he looks into my eyes,

so deep that I feel like I'm being pushed back into the couch cushions, my body melting. "Hanna, your father was dying of cancer."

I didn't expect him to say that. The words are sharp and cold and they seem to puncture the air.

"What?"

He grimaces. "He didn't want to tell you. He didn't want to tell anyone. Only I knew. Eventually Eero and Noora figured it out, but he didn't want them to know either."

It feels like I have a vice placed over my heart, the pressure coming slow and painful. "What kind of cancer?" God, why didn't he at least tell me?

"I don't know, he never said. He did go to a doctor in town. They gave him six months."

"And how long ago was that?" my voice shakes as I speak.

"Six months ago."

I try to take in the information but it's not sinking in. Not sure if this tea is working since it just doesn't seem real. How could my dad have had cancer?

"So he wasn't found frozen in the woods?" I ask absently.

"He wasn't found *at all*," Rasmus says.

I look at him sharply. "The body in the casket."

"There was no body. You know that. Noora and Eero, they made you see it afterward. They put me in there as a base, and built your hallucination on top of it. I tried to stop them but sometimes, when they work together…"

I press my fingers into my temple, as if to keep my brain from unraveling. "Built my hallucination?"

He gives me a steady look before taking a sip of his tea,

swallowing with deliberation. "Okay. Here we go." He clears his throat. "Eero and Noora are powerful shamans. Eero most of all. I'm a shaman as well, as was your father. That's why I was his apprentice. He was teaching me. The entire resort was founded in the hopes that one day the Sami people, and other indigenous peoples around the world, could come visit and practice their beliefs in private, in a learning environment. There was a time where the shaman here had to travel to Brazil, into rainforest communities, or to the Southwest of the United States, to the Navajo tribes, in order to practice without judgment or persecution. Your father's idea was that there would be no need for running away. That we could find peace here."

My father was a *shaman*? Somehow that isn't surprising. Maybe the tea is working after all. Still, I say, "I can't believe he kept all of that from me." I hate how fragile that makes me feel. He didn't trust me enough with the news of his diagnosis, nor did he let me in on the whole shaman thing.

"How long was he…practicing?" I ask awkwardly.

"Since long before you were born."

Now I'm surprised. "He's been a shaman my whole life!?" I exclaim.

Rasmus nods firmly. "A very powerful one. I was lucky he agreed to take me on. I've been training with him since I was ten."

"And how old are you?"

"Thirty," he says. "Don't let my boyish good looks deceive you."

Now I understand Rasmus' involvement. He's been with my father for twenty years, a couple of years before my mother moved me to California.

"I must have seen you when I was younger," I tell him, trying to think of any older boys who might have been hanging around our cottage.

He shakes his head. "Your father was very discreet. He did everything he could to keep it a secret."

"So my mom never knew?"

Rasmus gives another tight smile. Oh, of course she knew. That's why she left him. That's why she did all she could to stop me from having contact with him, even though it didn't work in the end.

"Look, we will have plenty of time to talk about this," Rasmus says. "But I believe time is of the essence. Eero and Noora will be here soon."

Their names bring me back to the present. "So if my father's body was never found, why did they tell me he died of exposure after getting lost in the woods? Why not tell me he had cancer? Why put on an elaborate fake funeral?"

And why the hell did they seem to want to kill me last night?

"Because they don't want you to discover where he really went."

I blink, growing more confused by the second. "Well? Where did he really go?"

"*Tuonela*," he says after a beat, a darkness coming over his eyes.

"And where is that?"

"It's the Land of the Dead."

Another slow blink from me. I almost laugh. "I hate to tell

you this, but that tea isn't working. It almost sounded like you said the Land of the Dead."

Rasmus' eyes remain stone-cold serious. "Tuonela is the place where the dead go after they die. It's accessible only through a few shamanic portals within the Arctic Circle, and one of those happens to be close to here. Your father went there, hoping to either barter with Death in order to have more life, or to break into the Library of the Veils at Shadow's End and find a specific spell."

I can only stare. Learning that my father was a powerful secret shaman his whole life is one thing, but *this*, whatever the hell this is, is on a whole other level entirely.

I clear my throat and start picking at the pulla on the coffee table. "Let's just pretend for a second that everything you said has made perfect sense, and that you didn't just talk about something tantamount to Frodo strolling into Mordor."

"Tolkien was very inspired by Finnish folklore," he points out.

"Yes, I know," I say impatiently. "So again, let's say this is all real. That my father traveled to another realm to go barter with…Death? Like, the Grim Reaper?"

He nods.

"And how exactly does one barter with Death? Does my father have something he could trade him?"

"Trades happen all the time between the mortals and the Gods."

Wow. I didn't think he'd have an answer to that. Especially not *that* answer.

"Fine," I say slowly. "So he's gone there to do that, go to a library, get a spell to live longer. What the hell does any of that have to do with Eero and Noora?"

"They're afraid you'll go into Tuonela in search of your father. That you'll gain power and wisdom yourself, *and* that you'll bring him back, possibly with immortality."

"And you?"

"And I'm hoping that's exactly what you will do."

I take a bite of the pulla and try to think, the delicious taste distracting me for a moment. Rasmus must be in shock. I do believe my father was a shaman and that the two were very close, that perhaps Rasmus looked to him as a father figure. If that's the case, that could explain why he's not handling his death very well. And I don't think I am either, considering I'm sitting here in this remote cabin and entertaining all this nonsense with such calmness.

"You realize you sound crazy," I tell him after a moment.

"I know," he says softly. "And I know that there's nothing I can really do to make you believe me…unless you see it for yourself."

I swallow down the pulla and get to my feet, walking over to the window which nearly vibrates with the sub-zero temperatures. Outside is a fresh blanket of snow covering the boughs of the pine tree. In the distance is a small shelter with two reindeer outside munching on hay that's been scattered about. One of them must have been our transportation last night.

"Those your reindeer?" I ask without turning around.

"Your father's," he says.

Another secret my father kept from me. I would have *loved*

to know he had reindeer.

I absently run my fingers over the frozen glass. "So what happened to Eero and Noora last night? How did you stop them? Why didn't they come after us?"

"If I told you, you wouldn't believe me," he says.

He's right about that.

"What were they planning on doing to me?" I ask.

"They were going to kill you. Probably sacrifice you."

My heart thumps in my chest. I slowly turn around to look at him. He's bringing a big pot out of the fridge, seeming unbothered by what he just said.

"I'm sorry...they were going to *sacrifice* me? Why?" I mean, Jesus.

"Shaman won't take lives for no reason at all. They'd make use out of your death. Even the bad shamans operate around this code, and they are bad shamans. Please don't think we're all like this. Almost all of us operate on peaceful magic and coexisting in nature."

I don't fucking believe this. "I need to call the cops," I say, bringing my phone out of my pocket. The battery is running low, and like before, there's no reception. I quickly scroll through to the wi-fi, but nothing is showing up. I know I should have a million notifications from Jenny, Michelle, from the store's Instagram account, from work itself even though they promised I was on bereavement leave. But nothing has come through.

"And say what to them exactly?"

I growl in frustration and shove the phone back in my jeans before throwing my arms out. "I don't fucking know! Two crazy shaman people faked my father's death and then tried to attack me and make me into a human sacrifice for who knows what. I can't stay here." I march on over to him. "You have to bring me to town."

He lights the stove with a long match before placing the pot over it and gives me a curious look. "Is that really what you want?"

I look at him like he has two heads. "What do you think?"

He shrugs. "I would have thought you'd do anything to save your father."

Well that felt like a slap to the face. "No. That's not fair. That's not fair at all. You know I would do anything for him. But not…nothing you told me is real."

"But if you could pretend it was," he says, "like how you were humoring me earlier. Pretend it was. Would you still do anything for Torben? Would you go to the Realm of the Dead, as Eero and Noora fear you will?"

"And do what?"

"Find him. Save your father."

"But if he's…" I don't know how to reason with nonsense. "Can I save him? Is he still alive? Can I bring him back?"

"That's the question, isn't it?"

Rasmus suddenly reaches out for my ears and I take a step back, putting my hands over them.

"What are you doing?" I whisper. "Don't touch me."

"Your earrings," he says, looking mildly rebuked. "Your father gave you those. When you were eighteen, right?"

I run my fingers over the small stud earrings. They feel frozen to touch, though they've always felt cold.

"Yeah," I say uneasily. My father sent them to me in the

mail as a birthday present. I haven't taken them off since.

"Do you know what stone that is?" he asks, and then walks off into the living room.

"I don't know," I say. Actually, I collect stones and crystals, and it's always bothered me that I could never figure out what the earrings were made from. In the end I just assumed green-colored cubic zirconia and called it a day.

He pulls a large crystal off a shelf and comes over to me, holding it out. At first glance it resembles a fist-sized chunk of quartz, a translucent glowing green in color, the same color as my earrings. Then the green starts to shift, turning purple, then blue, while tiny sparkles form and disappear. The crystal seems alive.

"Your earrings are from this," he says. "The aurora stone. Very, very rare. Your father brought it back from his travels once. It is said that if you give the stone to someone else, the aurora will always be inside, as long as you are both alive. He took the other piece of this stone with him. This is what tells me he's still alive."

He places it in my hand. It's shockingly heavy, cold, and almost feels sentient, like there's a universe inside of it. My ears start to grow warm, a strange buzzing sensation running through my lobes and down my neck.

"So now that we know he's alive, for now," Rasmus continues, his voice deepening, "are you still willing to do anything for him?" He takes a step closer to me. "Hanna, are you willing to go to the Land of the Dead?"

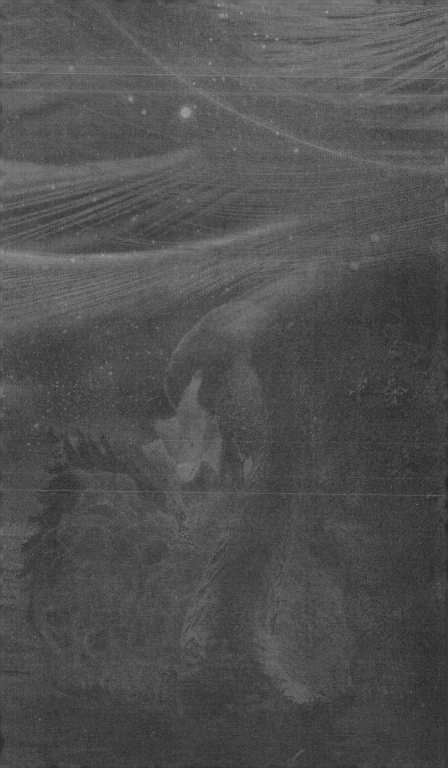

CHAPTER FOUR

THE WATERFALL

I turn the stone over in my hands, mesmerized by the changing light. It really is like holding the northern lights in your hands.

"Yes," I say, transfixed by the stone. Then some sense comes into my head. "And by the Land of the Dead, you mean the police, because that's exactly what my father would expect me to do. And he'd want me to go *now*."

Rasmus exhales loudly and gestures to the pot. "I was going to heat up some *hapankaalikeitto*, that's sour cabbage soup. It's not a close journey to anywhere. You need to get your strength up. Then we'll set out. I promise."

I sigh, and while Rasmus attends to the soup again, I go back into the living room. I gently place the aurora stone on a shelf and start going through everything I can get my hands on, from journals to field diaries and photobooks. Maybe there's something in them that the police will want, some type of evidence. I don't even know what exactly I'm going to say to them, but I'll say whatever it takes so that I get them to pick up my passport and luggage from the hotel, and then tell them that my father's body is missing and his funeral was faked. There's a tiny little voice in my head that tells me that maybe Eero and Noora have gotten to the cops and they won't be on my side, but that's just paranoia brought on by all the delusional nonsense I've been subjected to for the last twenty-hour hours.

So far though, the notebooks aren't providing me with much I can use. There are decades worth of my father's work in here, jotted down in tiny handwriting. It's all in Finnish, so I have no idea what it says, but occasionally there will either be some piece of dried foliage taped to the page, or a quick sketch of an animal. Except the animals aren't quite right, like he's sketching them in a decomposing form, half-skin, half-bones. I flip through page after page of a reindeer, a raven, a bear, a wolf, a fox, an eagle, an elk, and even what looks like a dinosaur, all of them drawn in various states of decay. What puts my teeth on edge is the fact that none of them are drawn in death. They're all alert or moving, and if they happened to have an eyeball intact, the eye looks gleaming and alive.

Papa, that's creepy, I think and quickly shut the book. *What else are you hiding?*

I pick up the one next to it, one of those ones meant for painting, with the thick textured pages, and tentatively open it, expecting to see more half-dead creatures.

And I do. On the first page there are three white reindeer. One is mostly bone, a standing skeleton with molting antlers, the others are intact but with milky eyes. They're standing in front of a river, black as ink, and there are ripples on the surface that make me think there are large snakes slithering just below. There's something so visceral about the image, like he's captured a moment in real time, like there's life in the painting, and if I stared at it long enough I could enter it.

I had no idea my father could paint so well, and all from his imagination.

With some effort, I flip the page to see another breathtaking image, this one of a forest quite similar to the one outside this cabin, with another river, only this one is light blue and iced over. At the end is a frozen waterfall, at least fifty feet high, and I swear the water is gleaming like a million crystals, like he's used metallic paint.

Along the river is a sign with an arrow pointing at the waterfall.

Underneath the sign my dad has scribbled "*Tytär, älä tule luokseni.*"

Tytär sounds familiar to me, but I'm not sure what it means. I close the book, feeling a little unsteady on my feet.

"Soup is ready, if you want to join me," Rasmus says, gesturing to the tiny circular table by the door.

I nod and go sit down. Rasmus brings me a bowl of steaming hot burgundy soup, some sour cream in the middle, and a cup of coffee. I eat two huge bowls, the sour cabbage strangely addictive, and drink three cups of coffee, while Rasmus stays mostly silent, his focus on his food and thankfully not me, slurping away. I used to eat like a bird, but part of my recovery was to embrace the messiness of food.

As soon as the meal is done, I wash the dishes, feeling bizarrely domestic, and Rasmus starts gathering things from all around the cottage, throwing them in a leather backpack that has seen better days, then brings out clothes from a closet and starts laying them on the couch.

"What's all this?" I ask, wiping my hands on an embroidered dish towel.

"Can't go anywhere if you're just wearing that," he says, pointing at me. He then shoves a long black coat in my hands. It's leather but there's shearling inside and along the wide collar and when I bury my nose into it, it smells like my dad.

I close my eyes for a moment as my heart aches for him.

"There's no way this will fit," I tell Rasmus, but I put it on and somehow it fits perfectly, cozy without being bulky.

"I think he's had that since the 70's," Rasmus says with a smile. "He was a lot slimmer then." Then he hands me a black scarf and a pair of black-and-white mittens and a matching knit cap with flaps over the ears, similar to the Sami traditional dress.

At first I think it's overkill, but when we step outside to fetch the reindeer, I immediately know how life-saving these clothes are. I pull up the scarf over my mouth and nose, the air biting at my exposed skin, and watch as Rasmus gets the reindeer attached to the sleigh.

"Ladies first," he says when he's done, having made quick work of it.

I sit down on the animal pelts he just laid out on the sleigh, then he gets down beside me and says an encouraging word or two to the reindeer. It starts to trot, pulling us through the snow with a jerk.

"You don't even have any reins," I point out as the sleigh glides along under the snow-frosted trees. "How are you steering him?"

"Sulo is a *she*," he says, "hence why she still has antlers at this time of year. And we have a connection."

"Is this a shaman thing?" I ask.

He gives me a wry smile. "You have a lot to learn."

He says it in a jovial way but his words strike deep. My father was a shaman. All this time and he had this whole other life, one he never let me be a part of. Why didn't he trust me? He knew I wouldn't think it odd, or any less of him. Hell, he knew I was a bit woo-woo myself with all my crystals and tarot decks and whatnot (I mean, I mostly have the tarot decks because I like the artwork, I don't actually know how to use them well).

And yet, it was all kept from me. Why?

What hurts even more is the fact that I may never get an answer to that question. For all that Rasmus has been talking about my father being alive somewhere fantastical, I can't help but cling to the idea. I don't believe in a Land of the Dead, no matter how powerful a shaman my father was, but part of me hopes that Rasmus is at least partially right. That my father is still alive and out in the world somewhere, and it's just a matter of time before he pops up.

But that's what people think when their loved ones die, isn't it? They keep thinking it's only temporary. That they're gone, in the other room, maybe at work, or on vacation. That they're just *away* and they'll be back at some point. Maybe that's how you get through death, by telling yourself your father will pick up the phone, and that if he doesn't that he'll call you back soon, and so in the back of your mind, at the back of your heart, you're just *waiting*. Waiting for them to return and for life to go back to normal again. The idea that they're never coming back is...

it's more than unbearable. It goes against everything you've ever known.

My father was a true constant in my life, even when he was far away. He was always there. That's all that I've known. That's all I can accept. I've never had someone just vanish off the face of the planet—everyone always comes back in some way.

But maybe not this time, I think to myself. I shut my eyes to the tears.

I don't know if it was the food, all the stress, or the fresh air and rocking motion of the sleigh, but I seem to doze off for a bit. When I come to, the sleigh has stopped and I expect to find myself in a strip mall parking lot or something like that.

Instead, we're still in the forest.

I look around to see Rasmus getting off the sleigh and patting the reindeer who is snorting, stamping its hooves, and looking restless.

"What's happening?" I ask.

"We have to walk the rest," Rasmus says to me. He reaches into the sleigh and grabs his backpack, shrugging it on over his coat, then reaches for my hand.

"What? Why? Where are we?"

"A place where Sula won't go any further."

"How far from the police station are we?" I ask.

"We only have to walk a bit," he says, gesturing impatiently with his hand again.

I sigh and let him help me out of the sleigh.

Once on my feet, I gasp at the sight ahead of us.

I'm standing in my father's painting. While I don't see a sign, I see an ice-blue river that's frosted over, coming from a frozen waterfall in the distance. It's at least fifty feet high, caught in mid-cascade over a cliff dotted with dead trees.

"My father painted this," I whisper in awe.

"Yes, I know."

"He called this…Tytär, älä tule luokseni."

A tight look comes across his face and he nods, then turns his attention back to the reindeer. He says something in a quick, hushed tone while stroking its nose and the reindeer snorts again, before backing up with the sleigh. Like on a dime, it turns and runs away, snow flying in the sleigh's wake.

"What the hell!" I yell. "Where is he going?!"

"*She*," he corrects me again, adjusting the backpack on his shoulder. "And she is going home."

"She's not going to wait for us?"

He stares at me for a moment as light snowflakes begin to fall. "You're not coming back this way, you said so yourself."

"Okay, so how are *you* going to get back home?"

He shrugs. "It doesn't really matter now. Come on."

He starts to walk off, skirting along the edge of the frozen river. The snow is falling faster and sticking to his shoulders.

I look behind me, but the reindeer is long gone and the tracks it left in the snow have already disappeared. I truly am in the middle of fucking nowhere and I have no choice but to follow Rasmus.

I grumble and then start after him. "I'm starting to believe this isn't the way to town," I tell him. "I mean, we're heading toward a frozen waterfall and a cliff. I'm starting to think this isn't the way to anywhere."

Rasmus doesn't say anything.

"So, what did the painting say?" I ask, trudging through the snow behind him. "What did my father write at the bottom? When was he here?"

"All the questions again."

I run a few feet and grab his arm, pulling him to a stop. It's harder than it looks. He may be tall and skinny, but he's built solidly, like a tree with roots.

"What did it say?" I repeat.

He rubs his lips together and then looks off to the waterfall. "It says...Daughter, don't come for me."

Then he pulls out of my grasp and keeps walking.

Daughter, don't come for me?

"What does that mean?" I ask, jogging after him again. "That was directed to me. How did he know I'd be reading his journal, his diaries? How did he know?"

"I'm sure he wrote it in a lot of places, knowing someday you'd find out he was gone, knowing someday you would be right here, in this very place, about to go after him."

"In this very place?" I repeat.

Rasmus stops and nods at the frozen waterfall. We're right next to it now and I can see the darkness behind it, feel all that empty space. There's a cave or a passage back there behind the solid ice curtain, and the wind that's blowing out of it smells like mint and I swear I hear a low murmur, like a crowd of people.

And then I hear it.

I hear *him*.

I hear my father's voice, airy and breathless, like a forgotten whisper. "Hanna, don't come for me. Please. Just let me go."

My heart sinks, my eyes going wide. I try to swallow but can't.

"Papa!" I cry out softly at the cave, tears freezing on my lashes.

But there's nothing in return. Just this mint-scented wind, that's sometimes ice cold and sometimes furnace hot and sounds like another world, another life is hidden in the depths.

"Was that you?" I ask Rasmus. "Was that some trick you did with your voice?"

He gives his head a firm shake. "No. I wouldn't have told you to stay behind. I need you to do this, Hanna. I can't go and get Torben alone. You have to be with me."

No. No, this is still all crazy talk, still all nonsense, still all a fairy tale and make-believe.

"I just…I want to go home," I say faintly.

Rasmus stares at me.

"And I want my father back." My voice is louder now.

He sighs and looks at me with melancholy eyes. "You can't have both. Which one do you want more?"

Of course there's only one answer. "I want my father back."

Oh god, Papa, I want you back.

He gives me a quick smile. "Okay. Then we keep walking."

He starts again, heading to the cliff face and walking alongside it until he disappears behind the iced veil of the waterfall.

"Rasmus?" I call out after him. No response. Even the wind seems to have stopped. All is eerily calm. I look behind me, but there's just the frozen river and the snow and the trees and there's nothing but silence. Rasmus had lied to me, told me he was taking me to town, when he was really taking me here. He's unreliable and untrustworthy, but there's shit-all I can do about that now.

My father doesn't want me to save him.

And so I will.

I take in a deep breath and go behind the waterfall.

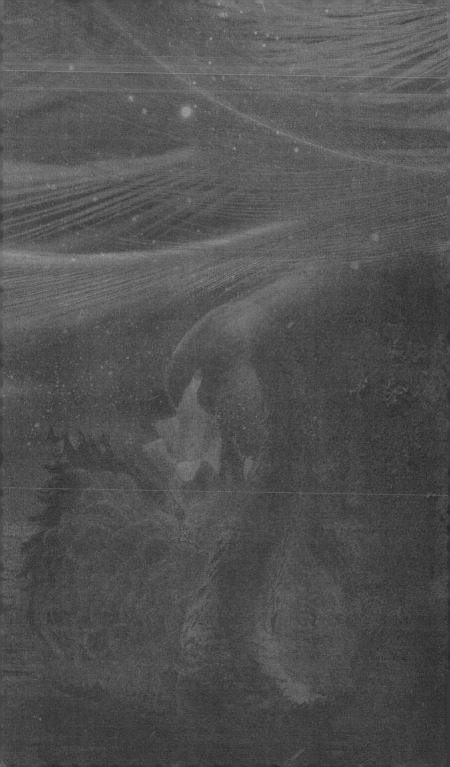

CHAPTER FIVE

THE RIVER OF SHADOWS

I t's dark in the cave.

Silent.

I stop walking and listen, trying to pick up on the sound of Rasmus' footsteps or his breathing, but there's nothing. The air is horribly cold and still, though it smells faintly of mint.

"Rasmus?" I say, and my voice bounces off the walls of the cave, almost making me jump. "I'm not going to walk blindly into a dark cave alone. Where are you?"

There's no reply. Not at first. Then, as I'm turning around, ready to head back the way I came in, the iced wall of the frozen waterfall glowing faintly from the outside light, I hear a whisper.

"Don't talk," Rasmus says, voice so low that I nearly miss it.

I open my mouth to say something, to do the opposite of what he just told me, when he quickly adds, "Just walk forward." He pauses, and I hear him take a shaking breath in the darkness. "Don't. Make. A. Sound."

Considering I don't know where I am and he does, I press my lips together firmly and slowly start walking toward where his voice came from, holding out my hands as I go in case I run into something.

"I can see you," he whispers. "A few more feet. I'm reaching for you."

Suddenly I feel his hand against mine, warmth amidst the cold, and he's grasping it tight. I nearly gasp but manage to keep quiet as he pulls me along gently.

Beneath our feet, the snow and ice has faded away to what feels like a floor of hard-packed dirt, and the further forward into the cave we walk, the warmer it gets. Eventually the sound of our footfalls disappears and I can tell the walls are coming in around us, as if we're now in a tunnel.

I'm lucky as hell that I'm not even slightly claustrophobic because I think I'd be losing my mind about now. Even so, I'm doing everything I can not to think about the fact that I'm walking blindly through a black tunnel to who knows where.

The Land of the Dead? No. I still don't believe in it, still don't believe that's where Rasmus is taking me. Maybe it's a clever moniker, perhaps when we pop out at the end of this tunnel (that so far, has no light at the end of it), we'll end up in Russia. But we aren't going to be stumbling around some underworld looking for my father.

Rasmus squeezes my hand and slows his pace so that I'm pressed up against his back. With his other hand he reaches back and pushes against my hip, moving me over so that I'm directly behind him and from the change in the air, I know that the walls of the tunnel are close now. Really close. I keep closing my eyes and opening them hoping that they'll adjust to the darkness better, but no matter what I do I only see a black void.

I think I've been doing pretty good about keeping my cool

so far, but my heart is thundering in my chest so hard and so fast I'm afraid that maybe I could die from fright.

There's a faint rustling sound right in front of me, I think of Rasmus' coat rubbing against the tunnel walls, his shoulders are broader than mine, and we slow down even further.

Suddenly my ears pop and it feels like we're walking through something, like the air has thickened and we have to really push to keep going forward. It's like walking through glue.

Then, just as quickly as it appeared, it's gone, and we're nearly falling forward. In the black, I'm beginning to make out the outline of Rasmus in front of me and when I look around him I see a faint gray light at the end of the tunnel.

My heart leaps. Thank god.

Rasmus starts walking faster now, his grip on my hand even tighter than before, and I have a feeling I still have to be quiet.

The opening to the tunnel gets wider and wider but no matter how hard I stare, I can't decipher what I'm looking at. It's like all that's outside is this gray mist, no shapes or structures.

It isn't until we're standing at the mouth of it that I finally see where we've ended up. In front of us is a pebbled beach that's coated with a light dusting of snow, the stones pitch-black, shiny and smooth. Beyond that, a line of dark water laps at the shore before being obscured by thick fog.

I step out onto the beach and look around in awe. The cave is set into tall slick cliffs that reach up into the sky until the mist swallows them. The beach itself is only a few yards long, just a patch of pebbles protruding out into the water. Everything else fades away into the fog and it feels like we're standing on the edge of the world.

Goosebumps erupt over my skin, even beneath the layers of clothing. But we're not at the edge of the world, right?

I look over at Rasmus who walks toward the water, the tips of his boots getting wet. He reaches out into nothing and then the mist clears just enough to reveal an iron pole sticking out from the water with a large iron bell at the end. Rasmus reaches into the water and pulls out a shining rock, then whacks the stone against the bell, the note ringing out loud and eerily low, and I watch in confusion as the water starts rippling outward into the mist, as if the bell is sending soundwaves.

So much for not being able to make a sound. "Why did you do that?" I ask Rasmus. "Where are we? Russia?"

He throws the stone back into the mist where I hear it land with a splash, then turns to me with the most intense look in his eyes. He reaches out and grabs my shoulders with his gloved hands, squeezing them. "You did a good job in there by not making a noise, but I'm going to need you to humor me for a bit longer. This next part is especially important."

I frown. "Why, what's happening?"

"There will be a boat coming through that mist any minute now—"

"A boat!?"

"Yes. We will be getting on that boat and I want you to play along with everything I tell Loviatar."

"Who the hell is Loviatar?"

"She's the ferryman," he says in a low voice. "She'll be taking us across, but only if she thinks we're dead. If she can't be fooled, then we'll be lucky if we can find our way back without her killing us."

I stare at him, my mouth dropping open. "I'm sorry, *what*!?"

"Only shamans are able to trick her, and I'll do what I can to make her see us as dead, but you have to go along with it or the spell won't work and the magic will be ruined."

This isn't happening. I can't even form the words, let alone wrap my head around the nonsense he's spouting. There's something seriously wrong with this man-child.

"You want me to…pretend I'm dead? So that you can put a spell on a ferrywoman, so she'll give us a ride to…?"

"Just keep your mouth shut for a little longer is all I'm asking," he says. "I've tricked her before but I was alone. Got as far as the Gorge of Despair before my luck ran out. Don't want to go through that again."

"You've done this before?" I ask in surprise, but then I raise my mitted hand and shake my head to shut myself up. No. I can't entertain any of this right now. For every question I ask, I'm not getting any reasonable answers in return.

Suddenly Rasmus stiffens. His hands drop from my shoulders and he turns around in time to see the shape of a boat appearing in the mist, someone standing at the bow with what looks to be a paddle.

"She's here," he whispers. Then he stands beside me, back straight, chin up.

Meanwhile I'm holding my breath as the boat becomes clearer. It's shaped like a small Viking ship, long and narrow and low to the waterline, the name *Norfinn* etched on the side. At the bow stands a slim, tall woman with incredibly long pale blonde hair that billows behind her like a cape. She's wearing a flimsy dress that looks like it's made of gold silk and tulle and I absently wonder if she's frozen.

But that's not what has my attention, what has my blood running cold.

It's the massive deer skull she's wearing as a mask.

God. It is a mask…isn't it?

The boat glides forward until it runs aground on the pebbles, the sound of them scraping the iron hull sounds like nails on a chalkboard and I want to cover my ears, but something tells me that wouldn't be a good idea.

The ferrywoman puts down the paddle and then reaches down and picks up a thick silver sword, at least four feet long with a blade bigger than my forearm. She raises it in front of her like it weighs nothing at all.

"Who goes there?" she asks, her voice light and almost… bored.

Fuck, please let this be some epic LARPing gone wrong. That would explain *a lot*.

"My name is Seppo," Rasmus says. He puts his hand on my shoulder. "This is my girlfriend Ephemera. We followed the light."

Seppo? Girlfriend? Ephemera?

I can't see the girl's eyes beneath the deer skull, but I can feel them just the same as she stares at us, not moving, not saying anything. Beside me Rasmus practically radiates with energy, a strange sort of warmth that I can feel, like standing next to a heater, and for a moment I really do believe he's conjuring something.

Finally, she lowers the sword and gestures to the boat with it. "All right. You may come aboard."

I exhale softly. Well that was easy.

Rasmus nods and walks through the ankle-deep water, hoisting himself up over the side of the boat and onto the deck. He stands up and offers me his hand, beckoning me to do the same.

I can't take my eyes away from the deer skull woman, even though I know I should.

"Ephemera," Rasmus says to me firmly. "Come on. You have to accept it."

Accept what? Oh right. Death.

I swallow uneasily and then slosh through the water, grateful that I used waterproofing spray on my boots before the trip, then give Rasmus my hands as he hauls me up onto the boat. Like the rest of the ship, the deck is made of iron.

"You can sit there," the girl says, nodding at a low iron bench in the middle of the boat as she slides her sword into the thin leather belt she has around her tiny waist. It looks comically large there, but she's picking up the paddle and wielding it like she's got nothing larger than a butter knife at her side.

She walks with the paddle down to the back of the boat and starts to steer, turning us away from the shore and back into the mist.

With our backs to her, I sneak a glance at Rasmus. I have a million questions, but the warning look in his eyes tells me I need to stay quiet.

"How old are you two?" the girl asks. "Not that it matters, but I don't receive many young people. How did you die? You look fine to me."

"Alcohol poisoning," Rasmus answers without missing a beat.

"Both of you at the same time? Must have been a hell of a party."

A hell of a party. The fact that she used that phrase is a clear sign that this is some sort of LARPing costume game. Maybe Rasmus created all of this himself in order to cope with my father's death, I have no idea. If he wanted it more believable, he should have had this woman talk in more stilted, old-timey English. And why is she speaking English anyway, shouldn't she be speaking in Finnish?

Part of me wants to call him out on his bluff. Say something. He said we could die if she found out this was all a ruse, but I mean we wouldn't really die, would we? Maybe I'd be stabbed with that sword that's probably from a movie props department and is made of foil paper or something.

But the other part of me wants to play along and see just how far this will go. I'm not sure why, but that part is winning.

"The journey isn't too long," she says, as if we'd just asked. "A few days, give or take."

I'm glad she can't see my eyes widening. A few *days* of this?

Rasmus clears his throat. "Where are you taking us?"

"To the City of Death," she says nonchalantly. "Where you will spend eternity. But, you know, my father likes people to really *earn* their place in the City. So I can't promise I'll get you there in one piece, though I'll try my best. It's just things have been a bit, uh, volatile lately, with the Stragglers having a bit of an uprising and talk of the Old Gods waking up. But you don't have to worry about that once you're in the City. You'll be untouchable."

That was quite the speech. I gently kick Rasmus with my

boot, wanting him to ask more questions.

"The City of Death…" he says carefully.

"Yes," she says. "You know I've never actually been? Only my father and his right-hand men can go. Even my fucking *brother* can go, and he's useless. Anyway, jokes on them, they don't know that I sneak out to the Upper World every now and then. Once I spent a whole summer in Paris and they never even knew. Winters in Copenhagen. New York in autumn. I absolutely adore where all you mortals live." She pauses and I can feel her energy at my back. "Hey. Girlie. What was your name again?"

Oh fuck. I turn my head and look at her over my shoulder. "Ephemera."

"Neat name," she says. "Doesn't that mean like scrapbooking junk?" Then she lets go of the paddle and places her hands on either side of the skull. "Can I ask you something? Am I intimidating at all?"

I swallow hard. "Yes."

"Is that why you're scared?"

Am I scared? I must be. I nod.

"Good. I'm supposed to be scary. I'm supposed to intimidate everyone I give a ride to, something about how it makes them behave. But honestly, if they don't behave, it's their loss. I'm ferrying you to your afterlife and you don't want to get in the way of that, believe me."

Rasmus clears his throat. "Has anyone tried to?"

"Oh yeah," she says with an exaggerated sigh. "The shamans are the worst. They're always finding their way here through one of their portals, poking around for magic plants or buying spells from some of the less honorable Gods before heading back to the Upper World. And sometimes there's a recently deceased person who decides they'd rather be running around the Hiisi Forest instead of having their allotted afterlife, but that's not a fate I would choose for myself. I usually let them go."

"Usually?" Rasmus asks.

"It depends on my mood." I can almost hear her smiling beneath the mask, and once again I'm praying that it really is a mask and not her actual face. "Anyway, the name's Loviatar but you can call me Lovia. Oh look, I can see land."

I turn my attention back around to see low white hills poking through the mist and the water narrowing until it becomes a river, the water black as ink and flowing quickly inland. The hills are barren, save for a few low bushes scattered about, bright red berries appearing on the branches like drops of blood.

"You'll have to excuse me, I like to pretend I'm a safari guide," Lovia says to us before clearing her throat. "As you can see on the right we have frost berries just ripe for the picking. The crimson berries are found all over Tuonela, but proliferate in the Frozen Void because both the white reindeer and the ice deer have learned the berries are poisonous."

Her words are strangely familiar. The frost berries sound similar to the frost flowers I had in my tea, while the white reindeer remind me of the painting my father did. Then again, my father painted that waterfall and that ended up being real. What if the white reindeer are too?

"Ah, we are in luck," Lovia says from behind us. "There's a snow fox just to your left."

I look in that direction and see a small white fox sitting on an icy riverbank watching us float past, its fluffy tail curled up around its body. At first it's cute...until I get a closer look. Its eyes are completely black, with no whites showing, and when it flicks its tail, I see bones where its furry legs should be. It's only then that I realize it doesn't even have eyes at all, and what I'm looking at are empty sockets.

Oh hell no.

I gasp in horror, unable to help myself, my hand reaching over for Rasmus.

"I know, he's super cute isn't he?" Lovia says. "I used to have names for them all, but I forget things all the time. I think that one's name was Socket, though."

Rasmus squeezes my hand back in an attempt to be comforting, but I'm starting to feel like we've graduated from elaborate cosplaying to a full-on bad acid trip. I mean, what I just saw can't be real, can it?

None of this is real, I tell myself, closing my eyes. *None of this is real. There're a million explanations to be had but you're not in the Land of the Dead.*

And yet repeating that to myself is starting to lose its hold on me, like reality is slowly losing its grip.

Oh god, I wish I had my Ativan.

"Ah, there's the herd I was looking for," Lovia chatters on. "The one at the front, that's Celes. You can ride her sometimes, if she's feeling charitable."

I reluctantly open my eyes to see a herd of white reindeer standing by a few golden pink flowers, delicately plucking off the petals and chewing. The one that Lovia is talking about looks majestic with ice-blue eyes and a thick white coat. But her antlers are like twisted branches, like she has a tree growing out of her head, and the rest of the reindeer match the ones my father painted in his sketchbook—half skeleton, with a milky white gaze. On one of them I can see straight through her ribs and to the snow on the other side.

Oh god. Okay. Okay. *Now* I'm really tripping.

And the flowers that the reindeer are eating, they look exactly like the frost flowers in my tea.

I glance at Rasmus, my eyes narrowed.

You fucking drugged me, I think venomously.

He glances at me and gives me a look like, *no I didn't*.

I stare at him for a moment, wondering how he knew what I was thinking.

Okay, fine. What number am I thinking of? I ask in my head, knowing he can't actually read my mind. For me, it's thirty-seven, my lucky number.

He smirks at me. Then moves his hand. I glance down to see him show me three fingers, then seven.

Lucky guess. It has to be a lucky guess.

"Hmmm, unfortunately I don't think we have anything much more to look at for a bit," Lovia says, oblivious to the weird mental games we're playing. "The Frozen Void is pretty much as the name says, though I briefly lived with my mother in an ice castle nearby, back when my parents first separated. But that would be a few days walk and I have to get you to the City on time. Why don't you two just sit back and relax?"

Relax? Oh, there's no relaxing to be had here. Instead I keep playing the numbers game in my head with Rasmus, asking him again and again to keep guessing what numbers I'm thinking of.

And again and again, he keeps getting them right.

I keep making excuses as I go, but by the time he's gotten twenty-five right in a row, I have to give up.

I concede.

Rasmus can apparently read my mind.

I take that fact and put it in the mental file folder that contains the information that my father was a shaman, that I saw my father in the casket who then transformed into Rasmus, that Noora and Eero tried to attack me, that my father painted a frozen waterfall with a message to not come after him, that I ended up going behind that waterfall and ended up in a tunnel that led to a land of mist, that I've seen my share of living dead animals, that there's a young deer woman with a giant sword at her hip and dressed in nothing but a gold dress wielding this iron boat down an ink black river who is pointing out the local wildlife like she's Steve Irwin's apprentice.

And that the point of all of this, is that we're supposed to go to the City of Death and find my father.

I'm starting to get the very disturbing feeling that this might be fucking real.

Suddenly the boat slows and I look behind me to see Lovia holding her oar straight in the water, bringing us to a stop.

"Don't worry," she says, catching my gaze. "Routine stop. It's just the gatekeepers. The swans of Tuonela. We have to pass through them and then we're onto the Great Inland Sea."

"Oh fuck," Rasmus mutters under his breath.

My eyes go wide. Oh fuck? Rasmus is saying *oh fuck*?

Lovia walks along the deck past us to the bow. "Well hello

there," she says to someone, her attention focused on the river. "I haven't seen you in a long time. Checking up on me?" There's a bitter tone to her voice.

Rasmus! I yell at him in my head. *Why did you say oh fuck? What are the gatekeepers? Are they actually swans?*

Suddenly there's a flapping sound and even Lovia shrieks as two swans fly onto the boat, one black, one white, coming up each side of the ship.

They aren't your average swans, I know that much. They're about the size of a small pony and they're focused on the two of us with beady dark eyes. I immediately know they're sentient and it's the most disconcerting feeling in the world.

"What do they want?" Rasmus asks Lovia as the swans start walking toward us, their webbed feet shaking the deck as they come. Despite playing the lead in Swan Lake, I've had a healthy fear of these birds all my life. They're nasty, and these ones have beaks that could bite my hand clean off.

"They're just checking to see if you're really dead," Lovia says in an irritated voice. "They've been around since the Old Gods, back when this place was *Kaaos*. Or in your words, Hell."

The white swan stops right in front of me, while the black swan stops in front of Rasmus. They both stare at us, and when I mean stare at us, I mean I can feel them poking around inside my head, inside my very soul.

Suddenly the white one opens its mouth at me, showcasing a long skinny tongue and a row of razor-sharp shark's teeth and starts screaming like a fucking banshee, this awful voice that's both human and not.

"No!" Lovia yells above the swan's scream. "No, they're

dead! They wouldn't lie to me!"

Now the black swan is screaming in unison, the awful, chilling sounds filling the air and Lovia is violently shaking her head. "No," she says. "They're dead." She looks to me and Rasmus. "You're dead right? Please tell me you're dead."

Rasmus has been keeping his eye on the swan but the moment he looks up and meets Lovia's eyes, her face falls in disappointment. Well, for a second anyway. Then it quickly morphs into anger.

"You guys lied? You lied?! Well, fuck you both," Lovia snarls at us, pulling out her sword. "Have at them then."

The swans come for us at once, teeth snapping, wings flapping.

There's no time to think.

As the white swan leaps at me, I jump up on the bench then dive over its head, just clearing its outstretched beak in a move that never would have been possible before, no matter how much training I had. Before I can mull that over though, my body keeps going, and I summersault across the deck in time to see Lovia swinging her sword at me. I duck and dive out of the way of the sword as it hits the iron deck with a *clank*, then push up with my hands so that my boots connect with Lovia's stomach. I watch in amazement as I kick Lovia right off the side of the boat, the giant sword clattering to the deck, her body hitting the water with a splash.

"Hanna, behind you!" Rasmus screams.

I don't even have to look. I pick up the sword, heavy as hell, and turn with it swinging out. With a long low arc, the sword cuts through the air, chopping off the head of the white swan, which goes flying off the boat and into the water. The rest of the body falls to the deck in a heavy thunk before I kick it off the boat.

Rasmus is bleeding from the hands and head, but the black swan stops attacking him enough to turn its attention to me. It sees the decapitated white swan and starts screaming, a pitiful sound.

I almost feel bad for it, enough that I lower the sword.

"Hanna!" Rasmus yells. "It will kill us both and we can't die here. Believe me, there would be no coming back."

I swallow hard, making a split-second decision, and before the swan can launch itself at me, I take the sword and stab it right in the heart.

It screams again, a sound that I think will haunt my dreams for years to come.

I stare at it, then at the sword in my hands, then kick the dead swan overboard. I look over my shoulder to see if Lovia is still in the water, or swimming after the boat, but I don't see anything but the ink black river. We're picking up speed now, the current moving fast, and the white frozen hills are speeding past even without anyone paddling. The water shouldn't even be flowing this way, but obviously nothing here makes sense.

"Well," Rasmus says slowly, getting to his feet with a groan. "I don't think I've seen anyone kill the swans of Tuonela before. So that's something."

"A good thing, right?" I ask him, taking off my knit cap, feeling unbearably hot all of a sudden. I don't know how I did any of those moves, let alone while wearing a mound of clothing.

"We're alive," Rasmus says with a sigh. "So that's a good

thing." He gives me a stiff smile. "But if we were hoping to get to your father without anyone knowing, well that opportunity went away with Death's daughter when you kicked her off the boat."

I blink. "Death's daughter? You mean Loviatar's father…"

"Is *Death*," Rasmus finishes. "You bested his daughter and you killed his swans. He's going to be pissed."

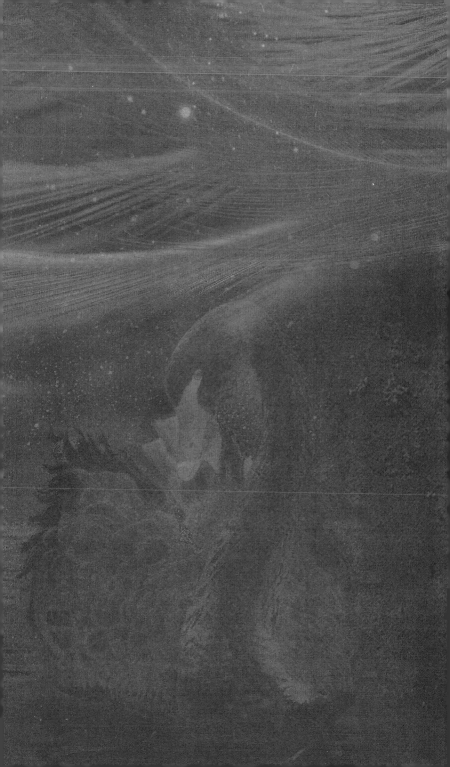

CHAPTER SIX

THE GREAT INLAND SEA

"**S**o what do we do now?" I ask Rasmus, who is standing at the bow of the iron boat. We've been stewing in silence for the last few minutes while the enormity of his words began to sink in, the black river taking us along at a clip while the riverbanks get further and further apart. "I just kicked Death's daughter off her own boat, then slaughtered his two swans, and now Death is going to know we're here…somehow."

Rasmus gives me a dirty look over his shoulder. "Do you hear yourself? Even after all you've seen, you're still acting like this is a joke."

"A joke!" I exclaim. "I may be struggling to understand what's happening but none of this is a fucking joke."

He grumbles and fishes out a handkerchief from his coat pocket and dabs it at the clotting wounds the swan left on his forehead, wincing. "You could have believed me from the start. I told you about Tuonela. I told you all of this was real. It took you almost dying before you started to take any of this seriously."

"Can you blame me?! What kind of person would I be if I

just believed what you were saying about my father going off to the Land of the Dead?"

"An open-minded one," he says tiredly, sounding disappointed. "Your father assured me you were open-minded."

"Yeah! I am! I have crystals that give me good energy! I believe in my horoscope half the time, and I think the Ancient Egyptians were in cahoots with aliens. But even the most open-minded person has their limits, and this was my limit."

"Even after seeing your father in the casket morph into me?"

I shrug, trying to get my thoughts in order. So much has changed and so fast. "I don't know. I was hallucinating! I was grieving and jet-lagged! For all I know I still might be hallucinating, or at the very least in some awful, fantastical dream."

Rasmus turns around and storms over to me, reaching for my hair and giving it a sharp yank.

"Ow!" I cry out, trying to move back. I like a good-hair pulling in the bedroom, but not this. "What the fuck is your problem, pulling my hair like a schoolyard bully?"

"That hurt, right?" he says, narrowing his eyes. "That's your proof right now that you're not dreaming."

"Jesus," I swear. "There are other ways to make a point."

"And anyway, how do you explain this?" he says, reaching down to pick up Loviatar's silver sword at my feet. His hand curls around the handle but as much as he pulls, he can barely lift it up. "This is what this sword weighs. A lot."

With a grunt he tries to pass it to me. I take it from him, the handle cold even through my mittens, expecting it to be ridiculously heavy now, and yet in my hand it feels as light as it did earlier. I pick it up with ease.

"See! How the hell are you able to do that?" Rasmus asks me, and if I'm not mistaken, there's bitterness to his words. "I've never been able to take Loviatar's sword from her. And yet you not only kicked her clear off the boat, but you killed the swans with it, which also shouldn't have been possible."

"Don't tell me the murder swans were supposed to be immortal," I mumble, staring at the sword. Up close, I see the handle is covered with detailed skulls, bones and filigree, looking both beautiful and macabre, just as Lovia looked herself. "Look, I don't know why I'm able to use it. And for the record, I've never been able to fight like that before either. My training is pretty basic. I don't compete, it's just a form of exercise that's fun and makes me feel empowered. For some reason my body just isn't obeying the law of physics or gravity here. Neither is this river, by the way. Shouldn't we be flowing in the opposite direction?"

"It's taking us where we need to go," Rasmus says after a moment. "And unfortunately, we'll be heading into the Great Inland Sea without Loviatar's protection."

I raise the sword up, almost slicing off Rasmus' ear, which garners another dirty look from him. I don't know what it is about redheads, but they can cast a dirty look like no one else. "I have her sword," I tell him. "That has to count for something. And protection against what? More murder swans?"

Rasmus walks back to the bow. I follow, bringing the sword with me. I'm getting used to having it already.

In front of us the river is opening up into a big black sea of nothing, and in moments all land disappears, covered by mist as heavy clouds set in and a light snow begins to fall. I can't tell if we're close to shore or not, but it doesn't feel like it. It's creepy as hell and it's getting darker by the minute, like we're fast-forwarding into twilight.

"Maybe we need to start paddling or steering?" I ask.

Rasmus shakes his head. "The River of Shadows will keep us on course, the current is running beneath us. This boat only goes to the City of Death and back to Death's Landing where we were picked up. I've tried to take it elsewhere in this sea before, but it would always right itself."

"If you've been here before, how did you get past Lovia? Were there no swans?"

"Lovia is forgetful, if you couldn't tell. When I'm using a spell, I can make her see whatever she wants. I made sure to disguise myself well from the last time I fooled her."

"And me?"

"I left you as you," he says.

"Great. So if she survives and complains to her father, he'll know exactly who to look for."

He gives me a shy smile. "You're going to stick out anyway. Not many pretty girls in the Land of the Dead. Though you do have an ethereal, fairy-like quality to your face. Perhaps they might think you're a Goddess." He lets out an awkward cough and looks back to the blackened sea. "Anyway, there were no swans the last few times I've been here. They were the original gatekeepers, before Death took over and became God of the Underworld and created the City of Death. Actually, it's one swan split into two, or three, or however many different versions of itself it wants to be."

"And I killed it," I say, feeling bad again despite everything.

"It's not dead," he says. "It is immortal, like you guessed. A God. The Swan of Tuonela will come back in a few days' time, probably hell-bent on vengeance, so if we're still alive, we have that to look forward to."

"And Lovia?"

"She's a Goddess. You couldn't kill her if you tried. Only Death himself can kill the Gods. I think it's one reason why he lets so many of them live here. So he can keep an eye on them. His ex-wife in particular."

Lovia had said something about them being separated but I wasn't really paying attention at the time since it's been nothing but information overload. "Death has an ex-wife? How fucking modern."

Rasmus shrugs, brushing some snow off his shoulder. "I guess. She's a demon though. Well, half a demon. The marriage was arranged by her father, Rangaista, a demon who used to rule Tuonela back in the times of the Old Gods, as a way to keep that blood in the new ruling family." A warm, sentimental look passes over his eyes and he smiles softly. "I'll tell you, your father was obsessed with all of this stuff. He loved trying to figure out the complicated family trees and politics of this land. But it's all a bit soap opera to me."

I almost laugh. My father loved history, and all history around the world is more than a little soap opera-ish. I wouldn't expect the Land of the Dead to be any different.

"So if that doesn't interest you, then what brought you to this place more than once?" I ask. "It's not exactly a walk in the park."

"Eternal life," Rasmus says simply, a snowflake getting stuck in his hair. "Immortality. I like finding spells here and new magic and herbs to bring back home, but I can't pretend my goal isn't power in the end. The power to live forever. Isn't that what everyone wants? Including your father?"

I swallow thickly, the idea of immortality and talk of power making me uneasy. "Do you know for sure my father wanted to be immortal? Maybe he just wanted to live a little longer."

"Maybe. But I won't pretend that's not what I'm here for."

"I thought you were here to help me rescue my father," I say slowly, squinting at him.

His face remains blank, with boyish innocence I'm starting to second guess. "I am. Don't forget he's like a father to me too. I'd do anything to help him."

I want to believe that. "So you're not going to toss us to the side to try and get some magic to make you immortal?"

He lifts his shoulder. "I promise I will not toss either of you aside. My mission here is clear—bring home Torben Heikkinen. But one day, I will be back. Each time I'm here, I get a little closer, I make a few more allies. If I can get into the Library of the Veils and then my hands on the Book of Runes, then I'll be set. They say that some magic, in the right shaman's hands, can rival the power of a God's."

A greedy look settles across his blue eyes and for the first time since we set foot in this place, I'm a little wary of him.

Don't let your guard down, I tell myself.

But at that, his eyes crinkle at the corners and I know he

just heard my thoughts. Fucking *hate* that.

I take in a deep breath. "Do you really think my father is still alive?"

He twists around and reaches into the front pocket of his mahogany leather backpack and pulls out the aurora stone, which is still gleaming in various electric hues of green and purple. Actually, it's shining even brighter than it was back in the cabin, like it's plugged into an electrical socket. "He's still alive," Rasmus says. Then he raises the stone in the air. "Watch this."

The snow that's been falling suddenly changes color, mimicking the color of the stone. Glowing flakes of green, purple, blue and pink start landing on our coats, creating a frosted rainbow on the deck.

I laugh at the sight, reverting to the sense of awe and wonder I had as a child, when everything new was magical. Rasmus is laughing too, the uneasiness between us being buried by the glimmering multicolored snow.

I take off a mitt, wanting to feel the snow in my hand. A yellow-pink flake lands on my palm, shining like a little firefly. It warms up as it stays on my skin, but it doesn't melt, it just sits there shimmering, and my eyes focus on how delicate and intricate it is, how perfectly every angle comes together to create a work of art.

I'm about to remark on nature being amazing—in every world it seems—when suddenly there's a loud *splash* from behind us.

I gasp and whirl around as Rasmus quickly puts the stone

back in the backpack. He quietly walks down the deck and I follow. The snow is still falling in different colors, making it slippery beneath my boots.

The sea is choppier now, and even with the snow, the light is like eternal twilight. It's hard to see anything between the wake and the waves but even so, Rasmus is on edge.

"Hanna," he says to me in a low, quiet voice as he keeps his gaze glued to the surface. "You've got the sword, right?"

"Yes, why?" I move it over to my bare hand and grip the handle. It's shockingly cold against my skin, enough that I feel fused to it.

Suddenly something pelts me on the head from above, like a small stone.

"What the fuck?" I look up as another object gets me right on the forehead with a quiet splintering sound before falling to the deck. I peer down to see a couple small bones attached to a skull about the size of my pinky finger. I take my sword and touch it with the tip of the blade just as I'm pelted again.

I look over at Rasmus to see him hold out his hand. A tiny skeleton falls from the sky and lands in it, then jumps off his hand and onto the deck, as if alive.

"Oh my god," I cry out softly. "Is that a…frog?"

More of the tiny frog skeletons begin to fall from the sky, some of them pinging off my sword, others hitting the deck. Most of the bones shatter on impact but some manage to hop away and off the boat, into the water.

It's another magical yet macabre thing but Rasmus doesn't look in awe as he did with the snow. His mouth is set in a grim line. "She's here," he says dourly.

From his tone I know that whoever *she* is isn't good. "Loviatar?" I ask, almost hopefully. I actually liked the deer skull daughter of Death. You know, before she wanted to kill us.

He gives his head a firm shake. "I won't speak her name yet."

So…Voldermorta? I think, just as the water off the left and right sides of the boat splash simultaneously, droplets flying on the deck. A chill runs down my spine and I grip the sword tighter.

"What's in the water, Rasmus?"

He doesn't say anything. Now a bigger splash comes from behind us, and I whirl around to see something dark, long and shiny pass over the surface and disappear below.

Oh god.

Oh god.

Giant sea snake serpent thingy.

Right under our boat.

"Rasmus," I repeat, my voice going several octaves higher. "Tell me what's in the water."

Suddenly the boat shudders and rocks and the both of us stumble, knocked off-balance.

"If anything comes on the ship, hack away!" Rasmus yells at me as he reaches into his coat and pulls out a necklace with a blue stone at the end, wrapping his fist around it.

Anything? I think and something from underneath rams the bottom, causing me to go flying into the railing. I grip it hard, staring over the edge at the black water, terrified to see what's below.

Thump, thump.

I whirl around to see two giant black tentacles come over

the side of the boat and slam into the deck, shaking us violently.

Okay. So *this* is what's in the water. Jesus, they're bigger than my torso. How fucking huge is the Cthulhu beneath us? Enough to swallow this boat whole?

"Hanna!" Rasmus warns from behind me.

I blink and spring into action. I run down the deck, sliding on the snow but managing to keep my balance, sword raised in the air. There's a part of me that's watching all of this from far away that's laughing at the sight of me turned into some kind of Finnish warrior princess about to tackle some Lovecraftian monster, and there's another part, the larger part, that has to shove all bewilderment and disbelief aside in order to survive.

With two quick swipes, I slice the blade of the sword against tentacle one and tentacle two, severing them until they're flopping on the deck. As easy as cutting into sashimi, albeit at a sushi restaurant for giants.

At that, the boat vibrates so hard that I feel it in my fillings, and giant bubbles burst in the water around us, followed by an ear-piercing shriek that sounds from the depths. In all directions at least twenty tentacles come rising out of the water, and if that isn't bad enough, half of them have snake heads at the end. Their mouths open, fangs bared, tongues forked.

"Holy shit," I swear under my breath. "Now what?"

I expect Rasmus to say something—*do* something—but he's chanting something over and over again in Finnish, almost like he's singing from his throat, his hand clasped over the stone, his eyes pinched shut. The snowflakes are no longer multicolored but they're falling fast, covering him in a thin layer.

"Rasmus!" I yell at him. "I can't do this alone! What the hell is this thing?"

The water in front of the bow of the ship begins to break up, waves sloshing, and I see a giant head begin to emerge from below the surface. At first I think it's another snake head, but then I see white hair matted against a narrow skull and then the monster rises up and up and…

My screams echo off the iron hull.

This creature is about twenty-feet tall, maybe thirty, and at first glance I'm sure it's like a giant woman, but I can't be sure. She has the low-hanging breasts and torso of a woman, but her thighs taper off into something reptilian, splitting into tentacles and snakes. Her face is flat and gray, with snake eyes set off to the far sides, no nose, and in the middle is a wide circular mouth lined with multiple rows of razor-sharp teeth that remind me of a giant lamprey. Black leeches cover her waxy skin and there's a long flickering forked tongue sticking right out of her throat.

It's the most disgusting and terrifying thing I've ever seen.

"The Devouress," Rasmus says in a raspy voice before continuing his chanting.

I stare at him in horror. "And you're not going to do anything?"

He ignores me.

But The Devouress doesn't.

Her mouth starts to spin like a vortex of teeth and she spits onto the deck of the boat, right in front of me. I barely have time to get over how gross that was before the hunk of saliva starts moving and shifting, dividing and dividing until it becomes hundreds of translucent snakes, all slithering toward me at increasing speed.

I scream again and start wielding my sword, chopping a few in half before they all overtake me and I'm being pushed back to the deck, failing, struggling beneath the slimy writhing bodies.

This is it. This is how it ends. Indiana Jones' worst nightmare.

Then the snakes scatter and one thick strong tentacle grabs me by the waist, wrapping around me and lifting me high off the boat, squeezing my ribs like a python until I'm sure my bones are being pulverized. I drop the sword on the deck and open my mouth to scream, but air is choked out of my lungs and I can't breathe, can't get a single gulp of air in.

No, *this* is how it ends.

The Devouress lets out a high-pitched scream, it's breath hot and smelling of decaying fish as it blasts me, and I manage to see Rasmus down below throw his arms out to the sides, as if he's some sort of savior leading a church proceeding on the boat.

While The Devouress screeches, squeezing me to death the water behind her begins to whirl and stir, and just like that the tentacle lets me go as if it's suddenly bored of me.

I scream again and fall straight down into the sea, the water shockingly cold as my body sinks fast below the surface. I try to keep my mouth shut, to stop from breathing in, and I know I have to get rid of my coat and my boots if I want to swim to the surface.

Suddenly hands wrap around my ankles, around my legs, my wrists and arms. I start flailing, kicking, trying to swim free, and it's so black I can't see a thing. I don't know who or what's holding me down, but I know they mean to drown me in these depths.

Oh god, oh god. *Now* I'm really going to die.

A strangely beautiful tone, similar to whale song, erupts all around me and through the black I see glowing bubbles rising to the surface all around me, and I realize I've been completely disoriented, thinking the hands were bringing me down to the inky depths when really they're trying to pull me up.

The singing intensifies, vibrating in my bones, and the glowing bubbles grow brighter and brighter as if the water has come alive with phosphorescence. Once, in Cabo, I went swimming in the ocean at night, the water having come alive with it and glowing, but that experience doesn't even hold a candle to what's happening now.

And through the streams of glowing bubbles, I'm starting to see flashes of female faces, beautiful faces, then flowing hair, and iridescent scales that shine coral, pearl, and sky-blue.

Suddenly I'm breaking through the surface, gasping for air, the boat Norfinn a few yards away. I can't see Rasmus, but I also can't see The Devouress either. Instead there's a bright white light coming from the bow.

The hands are still holding me up underwater, supporting me, and one by one five heads break the surface and smile at me. Five mesmerizingly beautiful women with hair the color of turquoise, and snow, of lilac, gold, and fire.

Mermaids. Fucking *mermaids.*

I'm not sure I even have the strength to be surprised anymore. If there are murder swans and lady lamprey serpents, why not mermaids? At least these ones seemed to have saved my life, contrary to all the legends and myths about them being man-killers.

They don't say anything and their rueful singing has stopped but they swim me over to the side of the boat where I yell, "Rasmus! A little help!"

His head appears over the side, a wide smile breaking across his face.

"You're alive!"

"Thanks to the mermaids," I tell him. "Mermaids!"

"I was hoping they'd show," he says, holding out his arms and leaning over, grabbing me by the elbows and pulling me up. The mermaids give me a bit of a boost, a pair of hands going to my butt and pushing me until I'm falling over the side, sprawled on my back on the deck.

I take in a deep breath and then move my head to the side to see a woman standing at the bow, glowing with incandescent light. Her skin is pale, ageless, while her eyes are bright blue and hint at eons past. She has a tall headdress on that resembles a bishop's hat made of pearls and scales, and fishbones that flow over the rest of her body like a dress, with giant shimmering clamshells at her shoulders.

Who the hell is *this*?

"Hanna," Rasmus says to me, gesturing to the woman with reverence. "This is Vellamo, Goddess of the Sea."

The woman turns her attention to me, and there's an overwhelming sense of grace and power coming from her. She's so still in her movements and yet she's staring at me so deeply, it's scaring the hell out of me. I didn't even think I had anything left in me to be scared.

"Hanna," Vellamo says in a calm, deep voice. "Rasmus has summoned me and my mermaids for protection. Do you promise to fulfill your end of the bargain?"

I swallow, pushing myself on my elbows. "It depends. I'm not giving up my firstborn or anything, am I?"

She doesn't smile.

"Rasmus has promised me a golden dress made of moonsilk from Kuutar." She pauses and her eyes go to him now, and I swear I see them flare with icy anger. "However, the last time I did Rasmus a favor, he never got me the dress, nor anything else in return." Rasmus looks away uneasily. She brings her penetrating gaze back at me. "I'm hoping that with you on this journey, you will help him fulfill his promise. After all, you now owe me, too."

"Not until you escort us all the way to land," Rasmus says quickly, as if he's seriously bossing a Goddess around. "So we can be back on the River of Shadows and on our way."

"I will do as promised," Vellamo says in that low monotone voice. "But if you don't fulfill your end, then next time The Devouress will swallow you whole and I'll feed your bones to my mermaids. Understood?"

"Understood," Rasmus and I say in unison.

"Very well," Vellamo says. "Then on your way back, when you've gotten your father, make sure to leave the dress on the banks before the Frozen Void begins."

"Wait, you know about my father?" I ask, getting to my feet and struggling. All the wet clothing weighs a ton.

Vellamo nods curtly. "Rasmus has informed me of your quest."

"And you're not going to try and stop us?"

A tiny smile teases the corner of her full white lips before disappearing. "I have no reason to stop you. I am the Goddess of the Sea. What mortals do is none of my concern, not in this world, at any rate. But what is my brother's problem is rarely my problem."

"Your brother?" I ask.

"Brother by law," she says, raising her chin. "My husband is Ahto, God of the Oceans, brother of Tuoni."

"Tuoni?"

"Death," she says with a hiss.

Then she turns around and, in a flash of pearls, she disappears over the edge of the boat, landing in the water with barely a splash.

So Death has a first name. That almost makes him more personable.

Almost.

I look at Rasmus, brows raised. "Is that what you were doing while I was battling sea snakes and serpents and nearly drowning?"

"I was summoning," he says, tucking his necklace back in his coat. "Just because you can wave a sword around doesn't mean I'm useless."

There's an edge over that last word, like it's a sore spot for him.

"I never said you were useless," I tell him.

"Whatever," he says, walking toward the bow where Vellamo disappeared. "The mermaids have our ship surrounded. They'll protect us until the river begins again."

I walk over and stand beside him. The night has fully descended now, and though there is some mist lingering in places above the black water, stars are beginning to peek through in the velvet sky. Below them, the water shifts as iridescent bubbles form the shapes of mermaids, our underwater escorts, and mirrors the stars above.

I don't know if it's sheer exhaustion or almost dying several times today or a new kind of jet lag from getting to this world, but I feel tears starting to creep up on me. Everything is so scary and so beautiful and I wish I had my father to share it with me. I wish he was here right now more than anything.

"She didn't seem surprised that we're going for my father," I say through a sniffle. "She at least didn't tell us he was dead."

"He's not dead," Rasmus says quietly. "You know this."

I swallow hard and wipe away a tear with the heel of my palm. "I don't know what to believe anymore. I don't even know where I am. I don't even know who I am."

"You're Hanna Heikkinen," Rasmus says to me. He reaches over and brushes a strand of wet hair behind my ear. "And you're pretty incredible."

I feel my cheeks flush, feeling anything but. "I'm not incredible. I'm not anything. I'm just trying to get my father back."

"Because you love him that much. Isn't *that* what's incredible?"

I take in a deep breath and we both lapse into silence. I think that over as the ship sails through the night.

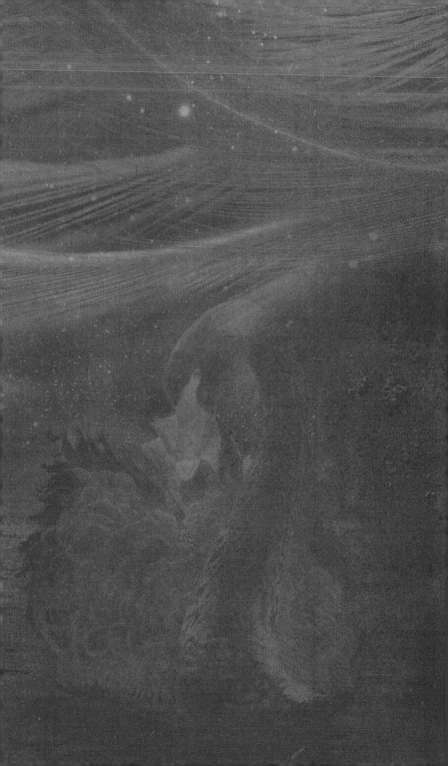

CHAPTER SEVEN

THE HIISI FOREST

A loud scraping sound wakes me up. For a moment, I have no idea where I am and then I feel it. I feel all the awful things at once, from the hard iron deck I've fallen asleep on, to the wet, frozen clothes covering my body, to my sore, aching muscles, to the fact that I haven't gotten to pee in a really long time.

With a groan I lift up my head to see Rasmus on his feet, looking over the bow.

"Where are we?" I ask groggily.

"You were given safe passage across the Great Inland Sea," a low, calm voice fills the air. Vellamo. So none of that was a dream.

I push myself up and get to my feet, staggering slightly in my heavy wet coat. I feel awful, but the sight of Vellamo is distracting enough.

She's standing on a snowy bank, her long ice-blue dress seeming to melt into it, so I can't quite tell where she ends and the snow begins. Her headdress is even more spectacular than the one I saw before, with fishbones and pearls sticking out of her crown like feathers, and a giant clamshell in the middle. Her ethereal gown is wet, moving over her body like sentient water, clinging to every curve, while silver and gold hermit crabs glide over her like moving jewelry. Two octopus rest on her shoulders, becoming one with the dress and finishing the look.

She's glowing as she was last night, lit from within, but in the dim light of this misty morning, it's more subdued.

The iron boat has lodged itself on the bank, right beside the River of Shadows, which cuts a dark flowing path through the frosted land, disappearing into the fog. Behind us is the wide expanse of the dark sea. I shudder and make a point to not look back there, as if The Devouress will come back for what she's lost.

"We will fulfill our promise," Rasmus says to Vellamo, grabbing his backpack and jumping over the side of the boat and into the shallow water with a splash.

"Where are you going?" I ask him as he wades through the dark river until it's waist-high. He doesn't answer me but he reaches into the water as if pulling down his pants.

"Here fishy, fishy," he says in a sing-song voice with a strange smirk on his face.

I look at Vellamo, my brows raised. "What is he doing?"

Vellamo keeps her intense gaze on me, her irises flashing through different shades of blue. "He is occupied." She walks to the water's edge so she's standing in front of the hull. "And it is just as well. I need to ask a favor from you."

"Okay," I tell her. I want to look at Rasmus to see what's happening, but I'm ensnared in her gaze. "I'll do whatever it is that I can."

"Very well. A long time ago, Tuoni took one of my mermaids to keep as a pet. At least, that's why I assume he took her. For all I know, she might be dead. Being with Death often ends that way. When you go to Shadow's End, if you happen to come across a mermaid, please do what you can to free her."

"You think that's where my father is? Shadow's End?"

She nods slowly. "I know that's where he is. And he's alive. I may not be an omnipotent God, but I do have contacts throughout the land. We all do. And it makes the news when a powerful shaman such as Torben has been captured."

I try to swallow the brick in my throat. "He's been captured?"

She gives me a patient look. "Don't tell me you thought you'd find your father waltzing around collecting magic? Shamans come here with a goal in mind. They either achieve it or they don't, but their intention is always to return back to the Land of the Living. I don't know if your father ever found what he was looking for, but I do know that Death found him first. He is being kept at Shadow's End as a prisoner."

I put my hands over my mouth in horror. "Oh my god."

"Yes. And you're lucky that the God of Death is so mercurial. It is only by chance and perhaps boredom that your father is still alive." She pauses as she studies me closely. "You are most peculiar for a mortal, do you know that? I can sense a power inside you that I rarely see outside of a God."

I'm having a hard time believing that. "What kind of power?"

"I don't know," she says after a moment. "It appears inconsistent, like it is just waking up. But it does seem to be fueled by love. Which is why I think you might have a shot at saving your father, so as long as you're willing to sacrifice all that you have and all that you are. Including your life."

"I'll do anything," I whisper, my mouth going dry.

Her thin blue brow raises. "You say that. But you won't know the truth of it until the time comes."

Suddenly Rasmus lets out a loud moan and both Vellamo and I look over to him. He's still in the water and his hands are fisted into the hair of a mermaid as her head bobs beneath the surface.

"Oh my god," I exclaim. "Is he…getting a blow job from a mermaid?"

"Mermaids are fascinated with mortals," Vellamo explains dryly as she looks back to me. "As are most Gods. If you ever can, I would use that to your advantage."

My cheeks go hot and I look away. I have to admit, there's something thrilling about the voyeuristic aspect of it all, not to mention the whole mermaid thing, which would fit nicely in the monster erotica I read when I need a helping hand, but seeing Rasmus at any stage of sexual activity is just plain gross.

"If you're finished, we must be on our way," Vellamo says curtly to him.

He gives us a sheepish look and then zips up his pants before sloshing back onto shore, the mermaid swimming away. "Sorry. That one always likes me for some reason."

"Now you're all wet," I tell him. "I hardly think that was worth it."

Vellamo just shakes her head and holds her hands out, gesturing for me to put my hands in them. Her palms are covered in shimmery designs, like henna but in fish scales and pearls.

"Wait, what's happening?" I ask.

"You're to continue your journey on foot," she says, gesturing again. "As I told Rasmus, you'll never get a chance to dry and warm up if you stay on the boat, and I can't offer you protection on the river. Just stay on the banks but don't stray far into the forest either. The Hiisi control it." She nods at the sword at my feet. "And bring your sword in case you run into any Stragglers. With it you should be able to handle them with ease. If you can't, Rasmus can always call on Tapio, God of the Forest. Like me, he doesn't mind doing mortals a few favors, but he may want something in return."

I try to suck up each bit of information she gives me but it just goes over my head, and I look over at Rasmus who has stopped at the highest point of the snowy river bank. Beyond him I just see mist, no forest, nothing.

"Don't forget the sword," Vellamo says, her voice getting impatient.

I nod and pick it up. I throw it and the sword goes sailing through the air like a silver bird, stabbing the snow perfectly. Then I place my hands in Vellamo's, her touch cold and almost electrical, and she lifts me up out of the boat, placing me on the pebbled shore.

"I will return the boat to Loviatar," Vellamo says, gracefully climbing into the vessel. "I owe her a favor."

Then the mermaids surface around the iron ship and push it off the shore until it's floating freely. They turn it around and the ship starts to move across the sea. Vellamo raises her hand in a subtle wave and then turns her attention to the bow as they get further and further away, disappearing into the mist.

Then I turn around to face Rasmus. "What the hell is your problem?" I ask.

"Me?"

"Getting your dick sucked by a mermaid," I sneer at him, stomping through the snow to my sword. "Right in front of me, I might add."

He shrugs, looking pleased as punch. "What do you care?"

I roll my eyes, my hand tightening around the sword's handle. "I care that I didn't want to see that. If I had an annoying younger brother, I could imagine it would be the same."

He frowns, his lip curling in a snarl. "I'm older than you."

"It's hard to tell sometimes." I say that simply, enough to raise his hackles.

He continues to glare at me, then turns and starts walking along the riverbank. "Come on. Vellamo is right. We need to make a fire, get warm and dry, then have something to eat."

Brush my teeth, take a warm shower, put on deodorant, I continue wistfully in my head, trudging after him. *Get a fresh change of clothes, slap on some moisturizer, do my hair.*

We walk for a while—time seems too fluid here to keep track of—and eventually we come to a stop by a thicket of birch trees. As we walked, the land became less barren, with shrubs and bushes populating the low hills, eventually leading to scattered trees that look extra creepy in the ever-present mist, their bare branches skeletal. The snow has faded away too, only leaving a light dusting, like walking in icing sugar.

"This will do," he says, putting his backpack down in the middle of the birch trees, moss covering the ground. "Can you go and find some flame ferns? They look like regular ferns. Just don't touch the mushrooms."

We hadn't been speaking to each other for the walk and now I'm a bit wary of him sending me out into the forest alone to go collect some ferns.

"Are the mushrooms poisonous?" I ask.

"No, but they are sleeping. You don't want them to wake up." He turns his back to me and starts rummaging through his stuff. "Just don't go far and bring your sword, just in case."

I sigh, having not let go of my sword for a moment, and walk beyond the stand of birch trees, their knotted eyes on the white bark seeming to follow my every move.

"Fuck this place," I mutter under my breath. I'm cold, tired, hungry, a little scared, and I have to be afraid of waking up sentient mushrooms now. I have to wonder how they would cause any harm but I'm not about to find out.

Once I'm far enough away from Rasmus, I lower my pants and pee on a bare patch of ground, hoping I don't wake up some sentient rock that's napping or something, shuddering as I pull my wet jeans back on. So gross.

I'm already feeling a little disoriented, the forest seeming to press in on me from all directions. Here the birch gives away to towering cedars and pine, with ferns and flowers peppered amongst the moss and rocks. Though the air is still cold, the snow is gone and everything is green.

"Rasmus?" I call out uneasily, afraid that I'm lost already.

"Yeah?" he answers, the sound coming from the trees behind me, the opposite way I thought I came.

"Just checking!" I yell back. Something tells me I shouldn't yell much in the forest, so I quickly go about collecting as many ferns as I can. There's nothing about them that seems to warrant the name "flame fern." In fact, they look similar to the ones I've seen growing in the Pacific Northwest. I've gathered as much as I can when I finally notice the mushrooms. They're of all shapes and sizes, including the classic toadstools with the red caps and white dots, growing at the base of cedar trees and on fallen logs. At home they'd probably kill you or get you high as fuck, though here it would be the former.

Thankfully they seem to be asleep and the more I stare at them, the more they seem to move, like they're all breathing in unison.

Okay, creepy as fuck. Time to move on.

I head back in the direction of Rasmus' voice and luckily I'm back at camp in no time. He's been busy, creating beds out of piles of moss and placing cairns of stones around the moss, like he's creating a giant circle, with a few fallen logs in the very middle.

"Are these the right ferns?" I ask, holding them out. "Because it's all I found."

His eyes light up. "Perfect," he says, taking them from me. He places most of them in the logs and branches, then hands me a few. "Here, stuff them in between the stones I've laid out."

I do as he says, then join him in the middle when he brings a pack of matches out of his backpack and lights one. He drops the match on top of the ferns in the fire pit and it immediately goes up in flames, enough that I have to jump back.

"Whoa!" I cry out, the heat fanning my face.

"Watch," he says and grabs my arm. "And stay still."

One part of the fire starts to reach higher in the sky right above us and I want to step back, but Rasmus holds me in place. It slowly starts to curve over us, creating an arc of fire that has me both terrified and mesmerized, the flames so close to our heads. Then the reaching tip of the flame makes contact with one of the fern-stuffed cairns and it lights itself on fire, creating another arc of fire that connects each cairn to each other until all the ferns around us are lit.

The flames then retreat back to a manageable size, the show over.

"Flame ferns," Rasmus says, clapping his hands together. "One of my favorite things about this place. I've brought them back to our world, but they aren't flammable at all. Here they only burn if they've been cut or taken up from the ground, and the fire it creates will only ignite other flame ferns. Watch."

He suddenly puts his hand straight into the fire and I gasp as he removes it completely unharmed, his sleeve untouched. "It's hot enough but it's no danger. You try it."

"I don't know…" I muse. Rasmus made it look safe, but every human instinct tells you *not* to put yourself in a fire.

"Chicken?" Rasmus goads.

I exhale shakily and square my shoulders. "Fine."

I stick my hand out, palm down, and slowly move it into the flames. It's hot at first, tickling the undersides of my fingers like burning feathers, but it doesn't hurt at all.

"Oh man, this can't be good for you," I tell him, unable to take my eyes off my entire hand now fully engulfed by the flames.

"See," he says. "Now take it out."

I remove my hand.

Except the flames are now growing from my fingertips, as if I was made of a flame fern.

"Um!" I yelp, waving my hand around, the flames not going out. "What the fuck?"

Rasmus just stares at me, dumbfounded, the flames reflected in his eyes.

"How are you doing that?" he whispers harshly. "That shouldn't be possible."

"Well it is! A little help? What the hell should I do!?"

He just shakes his head. If anything, he looks a little pissed off.

I grumble at him and go over to a cedar, trying to wipe it off on the rough strips of bark, but the flames don't go out, and they stay lit when I try smothering it on the moss and in the dirt. The fire isn't hurting me, and from the looks of it my skin isn't burned, but still, I don't want to be a walking flamethrower.

Finally I just inhale deeply and blow on my hand.

And as if they're a bunch of birthday candles, all the flames go out at once.

"Holy shit," I say breathlessly, examining my hand up close. It looks the same as always. If anything it looks smoother, like my skin just got exfoliated.

"Is your nail polish flammable?" Rasmus asks.

"I'm not wearing any," I say, wiggling my fingers at him.

"I don't understand," he says, turning his back to me and going through his bag. "It's never done that with me."

"Well maybe I'm just that special," I say jokingly. "Or maybe I just have the feminine touch."

He grunts in response and brings out a tiny teapot and two wood carved cups from his backpack. I'm not sure why he's grumpy again, you'd think getting a blow job from a mermaid would cure all your woes for a long time.

But as Rasmus starts preparing dinner, or lunch, whatever time it is, he seems to get in a better mood. I suppose the idea of having actual food when you're starving will do that to you.

Since it's not as cold anymore, I take our coats and boots and lay them out around the fire and between the cairns so that they'll dry, then I scooch myself onto the moss right beside the fire. Too bad the whole lighting my hand on fire can't be a party trick I can try back home.

Dinner is as mundane and practical as it comes—cans of corned beef, a packet of chicken-flavored potato chips, a few oranges, and a Cliff bar for dessert, but nothing has ever tasted so good. I know reading *The Lion, The Witch and the Wardrobe* when I was young made me think fantasy worlds were full of Turkish Delight, but the reality is oatmeal cookie energy bars taste just as heavenly.

After dinner, Rasmus disappears into the forest for a few minutes and when he returns he has a handful of cedar needles and some gooey white substance which he places in the diffuser in the teapot.

"Cedar sap," he explains. "It will help your body and mind heal. It might make you a bit sleepy though, and your sleep will be deep and restorative."

"So *now* you're drugging me," I say.

"Drugging us both," he says. "Unlike you, I didn't sleep last night. I watched over you instead."

I have to admit, I'm rather touched. "And if danger comes for us in the night?"

"We'll spring into action, feeling better than before," he says.

While the tea steeps he takes a stick and starts poking at the fire and my mind finally has a chance to slow down and wander, going over everything that's happened. There's been so much I feel like I haven't had a chance to catch my breath.

"Vellamo seemed pretty forgiving," I tell him, holding my hands out in front of the fire. "You know, considering you've dicked her around before."

He raises a shoulder and pokes the stick in the fire. "Gods and shamans have a complicated relationship. On one hand, we're always getting under their skin in our quest to gain power. On the other hand…we believe in them."

"What do you mean?"

"I mean that when humans first began to walk the earth, the Gods made themselves known. It didn't take a lot of faith to know that the Goddess of the Sea was real when you saw her rise from the deep. People believed in them and worshipped them and you didn't have to be a priest or a shaman to do that. But in time, more and more people were born, scattered around the globe, and most of the Gods stayed the same. Outnumbered. So some people saw the Gods, others didn't, and those that didn't found it hard to believe in them. Over time, they lost their faith, their belief, and the Gods lost their power in the Upper World, in our world. They stayed here in the Underworld. The shamans, which includes witches and wizards, never lost that belief and remain the one true link between the worlds." He pauses. "Except for Death."

"No?"

He gives me a tight smile. "No one has ever lost their belief in Death."

I wrap my arms around my knees, hugging them tight. "Have you ever met him?"

He shakes his head. "No. I've heard stories, of course. That he always has to wear gloves because if he touches you, you'll die. And that his face is a skull and he wears a cloak and he eats babies for breakfast."

"Let me guess, rides a skeleton horse?"

"Skeleton unicorn," he corrects me with a smile, my eyes going wide. "And it's an ugly, nasty, bloodsucking beast. Those horns are dangerous."

"A unicorn? Seriously? What about dragons?"

He laughs. "No dragons. But there are a few species of dinosaurs wandering about."

"Dinosaurs!" I exclaim. "You got to be kidding me."

"What, so dragons and unicorns you'll totally believe but dinosaurs, creatures that literally did exist on our planet, are far-fetched?"

He's got a point. "Well, since dinosaurs are real, what are mermaids and unicorns doing here?"

"This is the Underworld for all the worlds. Not just our own. There are other worlds out there with creatures you can't even imagine. This place is your best bet for seeing them. Eero once told me he saw an alien."

I frown. "You talked to Eero?"

"Well, yeah. We all live or work at the resort."

"I don't understand. If Eero was my father's business partner, then why did he want to prevent me from rescuing my father, and, dare I say, try to kill me?"

"Jealousy," Rasmus says. "He didn't want your father to become more powerful than him."

"So how powerful is Eero?"

A dark look comes over his eyes. "Enough that he's been reincarnated his whole life. The closest a shaman has gotten to eternal life, but not close enough. Not for him, anyway. Rumor has it that he's actually the legendary shaman Väinämöinen, who is the hero of Finland's national epic, the Kalevala."

Shit. That's pretty big.

"You know, I wanted to become Eero's apprentice," Rasmus admits quietly, voice hushed with shame. He picks up the tea pot and pours the hot, fragrant liquid into the wood cups. "But I'm glad he turned me away. Your father is a good man, Hanna. One of the best. If it had been Eero teaching me…"

I study him in the firelight and for the first time I feel like I'm really seeing Rasmus. A contradiction. A boy on one hand, a man on the other. Someone who wants to be good, someone who craves the ability to be bad. Someone happy with something as simple as flame ferns, someone who wants all the power in the universe.

He looks at me as he passes me my tea. "What are you thinking about?" he asks warily.

"You mean you don't know?" I ask as I take a sip. The tea smells invigorating, like a cedar forest on a crisp snowy day, and tastes just as good.

His brows come together. "No. I can't pick up on your thoughts anymore."

Good, I think, though I hide my smile behind the cup.

CHAPTER EIGHT

THE TRADE

A rustling sound wakes me up. My eyes fly open, the towering birch tree branches coming into focus overhead, low clouds behind them. It's daylight. Another gray morning. And I know I'm not alone.

I sit up and gasp.

There's a woman with long copper-red hair crouched down, her back to me, rifling through Rasmus' backpack.

The woman jumps, startled, and whirls around with preternatural grace.

"I'm sorry," she says in a breathy voice. "I thought you were sleeping."

I stare at her slack-jawed for a moment. Her bright green eyes, pale skin, and dress made of leaves, flowers and twigs make her look fairy-like, as do the small smooth antlers growing out of her head.

"Who are you?" I ask, my heart pounding like a jackhammer. "Where's Rasmus?"

She shakes her head, eyes impossibly big. I look down at her hands and see she's clutching a Cliff bar, the sight of something so plastic and mundane in the hands of something earthy and ethereal is throwing my mind into a tizzy.

"The trees told me he needed help," she says. "He may have been trying to summon my father, Tapio. I'm his daughter, Tellervo, but you can call me Telly." She points off into the forest with the Cliff bar. "I came from there, but I didn't see or smell your friend. He is mortal, is he not?"

"Yes." I say, sitting up straighter, my back killing me from having passed out on the forest floor like I did. "A shaman."

"I figured," she says. "Not many mortals believe in the Gods enough to call on us. I do hope he's all right."

"Well, considering he left his backpack behind, I don't think he was planning on running out on me," I say, easing up to my feet.

"That would be your first thought?" Telly asks, getting to her feet as well. She's nearly as tall as I am. "Doesn't sound like much of a friend."

"He's helping me find my father," I tell her. "We're heading to Shadow's End."

Telly shudders. "I don't think you want to do that."

"It's where my father is imprisoned."

She nods slowly, her brows furrowing comically. "And I suppose your father isn't a God, is he?"

"No. Another shaman."

All this time I'm talking to Telly, I've been thinking that Rasmus is off taking a shit in the woods and will be back soon, but there's a creeping, hollow feeling in my chest that says he might actually be in trouble.

"I'm sorry," I say to her as I notice her stuff the Cliff bar into a satchel made of moss attached to her hip, "but did you say the *trees* told you he was in trouble?"

She nods. "The birch have eyes to see and mouths to whisper." She clears her throat, a flush appearing on her cheeks. "But of course being a Goddess of the Forest helps."

"We've already met Vellamo," I tell her, and her eyes brighten appreciatively. "She said that if we ever needed help, Rasmus would summon your father...Tapio, was it?"

"Yes, Tapio. My father might have heard him, he might not. But I was out in the aspen grove when the trees said to come here. So I'm afraid this might be the best you can get. Do you want me to help you find him?"

I look around the campsite. Everything looks as it did last night, though the flame ferns have burned down to nothing. It seems like he's coming right back and I know the best thing to do in these situations is just to stay put (I got lost in LAX when I was eight and that's all I remember from the ordeal).

"What do you think?" I ask her.

"About what?" She looks puzzled.

"What I should do?

"I guess it helps to know your name."

"Oh, I'm sorry," I say, feeling flustered. I don't feel appropriate shaking the hand of a Goddess, so I do a half bow, half curtsey thing that's totally awkward. "I'm Hanna."

And Telly does the awkward curtsey bow right back to me in earnest. "Pleased to meet you. So you want to know where your supposed friend Rasmus is and you're not sure whether to go find him or stay where you are?"

I nod.

She taps her delicate fingers against her chin in thought. "Hmmm. Well, if you were another Goddess, I would tell you not to worry because no matter what he's probably fine. But since you're mortal and he's mortal, and the trees told me he was in trouble, well, I'm definitely going to set out after him. If you choose to, that's up to you."

I don't even have to think. I grab the backpack and swing it on, then pick up the sword and give Telly a determined nod. "Lead the way."

Telly takes me through the forest, past the cedar grove where I collected the flame ferns, through mossy glens of red berries and bushes of purple and blue hydrangeas, along rows of tall pine trees whose trunks resemble iron, and where vibrant orange poppies grow in the underbrush.

At some point I let her know that Vellamo said we shouldn't stray far from the river, but Telly pays me no mind and keeps going.

Finally she comes to a stop in an old growth forest, where a babbling brook runs beneath the relics of dead cedars, the trunks split open and charred like they've all been decimated by lightning.

"You get any big storms here?" I whisper to her as she looks around. Whispering seems appropriate in this place.

Her expressive face looks incredulous. "Yes. Depending on Death's mood."

"What do you mean?"

"You didn't know his moods control the weather in Tuonela?" she asks so solemnly that I feel like a real idiot.

I decide to embrace my mortal idiot status. "I did not. In

fact, I don't know much."

She looks me up and down with those innocent eyes. "I can see that," she says, but it's hard to take offense. She starts walking again and I'm right behind her, the dead forest giving me the creeps.

"That's why it's always cloudy," she goes on. "Because he's always in a foul mood. The only time the sky clears is when he's either happy, which is never, when he's drunk, which is sometimes, or when he's asleep. Hence why you can usually see the moon and stars and planets at night. There are a few times each year where we'll get a few days of sunshine and clear nights in a row, but my father says that's when Death is on a *bender*. I believe that's a mortal term that means drinking alcohol for too many days in a row and acting foolish."

"Sounds lovely," I mumble.

"Who? Death or my father?"

"I was being sarcastic," I quickly point out. "About Death. I'm sure your father truly is a lovely man. Um, I mean God."

She shoots me a charming smile over her shoulder. "Thank you. He is. And your father must be too, if you're going after him. I would do the same." She pauses. "And Death, well, everyone has an opinion about him. He does rule this land after all, and the other Gods don't always agree with him. But I think he's just misunderstood."

My brows go up. "You think Death is misunderstood?"

She nods. "Yes. He's just doing his job. And to hear my father talk about it, things were much worse here before Death came along. People had died, of course, but there was no proper afterlife. They called it *Kaaos*. There was no justice, no rhyme or reason to anything, just pain." She shivers, her red hair rippling down her back. "The Old Gods just wanted the mortals to suffer."

Telly suddenly stops and I nearly run into her back. She slowly holds her finger to her lips and holds still. I do the same, trying not to breathe, listening.

Then I hear it.

In the distance, behind the charred trees, is a sound that can only be described as both giggling and snarling. Gurgling, maybe, but with sinister tones. Either way it makes every single hair on my body stand on end, my bones vibrating with uneasiness.

"*Hiisi,*" Telly says in a low voice. Then she raises her chin and yells into the forest, "Come out, come out, I know you're there. I have a mortal under my protection, so there's no use trying anything."

The gurgling noise gets high-pitched and at any moment I expect Gollum to come out from behind the cedars.

Instead, a small sickly green creature with large black eyes, no nose, and a line of teeth comes crawling out on all fours, ram-like horns curling back from a bald head. So it's not Gollum, but it's pretty damn close. For a brief moment I'm wondering if Tolkien actually did stumble upon Tuonela at some point, but then the creature hisses at us and my mind goes blank with fear.

"I'm Goddess of the Forest," Telly says to me, not taking her eyes off the creature. "But this is the Hiisi, and this part of the forest is allotted to them. I don't interfere with their games and torture, and they leave my family alone. They know we can take it all back from them at any moment."

The Hiisi thing lets out a snarl and comes bounding toward us, only to stop a few feet away. At this close distance, it's a lot more disgusting than I originally thought, with its skin peeling away in slices like the cedar trunks, black fungus collecting on its long fingers and toes, and a row of branches poking out of its spine. Gooey centipedes slither from its ears to its mouth to its eyes and then back again and it takes everything in me not to vomit up the corned beef from last night.

Telly doesn't seem bothered. She crosses her arms. "We shall be out of your way in a moment, if only you'd tell us if you've seen a mortal. A shaman, to be more precise."

The Hiisi opens its mouth and big, thick black flies come crawling out, taking flight and coming right for us.

Before I can both scream and run, Telly puts her palm out flat and the flies land in it. Then she makes a fist over them and opens her palm and tiny little glowing pink dragonflies fly off into the sky, having been transformed.

"Well?" Telly asks, impatiently.

The Hiisi snarls something else, saliva going everywhere, then eventually nods its gruesome head in the direction we were walking.

"I see," Telly says gravely. She eyes me with trepidation. "The Hiisi says that Rasmus went that way."

"Was he alone?" I ask.

Telly looks back to the Hiisi but it just shakes its head before turning its back to us and scampering away into the forest.

"Come on, we better hurry if we want to save your friend."

We keep walking. Along the way there are groves of roses where metallic gold bees swarm, sweet-water marshes where silver loons dive for sparkling fish, white deer with their fawns resting in meadows of roses, and large black owls swooping above the willows, but for all the fantastical, beautiful sights, all I can think about is getting Rasmus back. I can't rescue my father without him. I don't know the way to Shadow's End, I don't know what will kill you here and what won't. I like Telly a lot, but I don't know how loyal she is, or if she can even leave the forest.

I'm pondering all of this in a flurry of agonizing thoughts, the grip on my sword growing tighter and tighter, when suddenly the forest begins to open up. The green fades to brown, the leaves are dying on the branches and in front of us appears a long flat desert beneath an oppressively low cloud-covered sky. All is silent except for a chilling wail that sounds from the distance. It's both human and not, and I'm pretty sure it's not Rasmus.

Telly and I come to a stop by a few fallen willows, their leaves dead, the water gone long ago. Beyond this point there is nothing.

"Where are we now?" I ask her.

"The Liekkiö Plains," she says. "And as far as I will go."

I knew this was coming. "You can't leave the forest?"

"I can," she says slowly. "But I don't think it's wise. I would be no use in this situation. You're the one that they want, the one they've been waiting for."

I blink at her. "The one that who's been waiting for?"

She points out at the desert. "Death."

I stare again. It's so dry and desolate out there that I can't imagine a single living thing ever setting foot on it, and the way that the sun glows through the mist, creating a land of orange haze, is strangely disturbing. Seems a place that death would lurk at every corner, literally and figuratively.

But then the mist starts to clear a little, as if helping with a dramatic entrance, and I can see shadowy figures emerging from the orange haze, three men on horseback and one man on foot.

The closer they get, the faster my heart races, until they come to a stop about fifty feet away. When Rasmus told me that Death rode a unicorn, for some reason I was expecting a gorgeous, serene, magical-looking creature, even though Rasmus had told me otherwise. But now that I see it in person, the sight of it makes my skin crawl. Their versions of unicorns are big, moose-sized, and like so many of the animals in this world, mostly skin and bones. Their horns look made of metal, three or four feet long, protruding from a boney skull, and spooky, watchful eyes that vary in shades of black, white, or pale blue.

The unicorn in the middle is the largest, black as a moonless night, and sitting atop him is Death. While the other two men are equally scary, they don't hold a candle to this guy. He makes the unicorn look small beneath him, which is no easy feat, and everything he's wearing is both luxurious and sinister, from the elaborate spikes on his armored shoulders, to his metal gloves, to his iron boots. Underneath the dark velvet hood of his cape his face is in shadows.

But despite all that he looks like, it's what he *feels* like, even from way over there. I know it's Death because I *know* it's Death. I think if anyone, human or not, were to be in his presence, they would react with fear, with panic, with a deep primal urge to run far, far away. Even now, even though I knew I might have to face him, let alone see him, I'm terrified to the bone with the unwavering sensation that I'm going to die.

I don't think many get to look Death in the face and live to talk about it.

Of course, the others beside him are frightening as hell too, with their skull faces, hoods, and zombiecorns that paw the dry earth impatiently—they just pale in comparison on the *holy fuck* scale.

Then there's Rasmus. He's off to the side, chains around his hands, attached to Death. Even though Rasmus is tall, he looks short compared to the others, and his wiry build seems weak. Too weak. He meets my eyes and I expect to see something pleading in them, like he's asking for my help, or maybe embarrassment at getting caught. But I can't read him at all.

"There you are," Death booms. His voice is unlike any I've heard before, rich and baritone, like the low bass behind a gloomy melody, and yet there's a rasp to it, a huskiness that would sound sexy on anyone else but him. "Thank you for bringing her here, Tellervo. Make sure to pass my thanks on to your father. I enjoyed the black grouse the forest provided the other day."

I gasp and turn to look at the Forest Goddess. The traitor!

But Tellervo's green eyes are wide, like she's surprised he said that, and when she looks at me for just a second, I see bewilderment in them.

She clears her throat. "I will do so," she says to Death and then quickly turns, avoiding my stare, and walks back into the forest. Now I don't know if she brought me here on purpose or if Death is just toying with me, but there will be no relying on her anymore.

I'm on my own.

I tighten my grip on the sword.

Death notices. I can't even see his eyes but I know that he sees every single thing that I'm doing. I'm wondering if he's like Rasmus, and can hear my thoughts as well.

Fuck you, you fucking fuck, I think, hoping he can.

He doesn't show any reaction, just adjusts his position on the unicorn.

"Do you know who I am?" he asks me, voice like sinister silk.

I don't say anything. The sword pulsates against my palm, as if it's trying to give me energy, or I'm trying to give it energy. I'll take what I can get.

"Because I know who you are, Hanna Heikkinen," he goes on. "And I know your father quite well too."

I stiffen, my blood running cold.

Papa!

"Ah," he says, after observing my face. "I figured that's why you were here. Your friend Rasmus wouldn't tell me much, even when we tortured him. But I knew."

My stomach twists and I look at Rasmus. He seems okay, maybe a bit dusty and tired, but otherwise like he was just yesterday. Maybe it was a mental torture thing, or the box of pain from *Dune*.

"And I can understand why you're so angry," Death adds. "I'd be angry too if my father was dying and didn't tell me. Then again, my father is a God and yours…very much isn't. He's barely even a shaman. Just a pathetic excuse for an old wizard."

"Fuck you," I snarl at him, unable to keep quiet.

Death chuckles. "Finally, she speaks!" He claps his armored hands together, the metal clanging, setting my teeth on edge. "The fairy speaks. Apparently she can hear as well. So let me tell you something, mortal one, while I have your attention. I'm angry too, perhaps as angry as you are. You see, I had heard a rumor that seemed outlandish, that you had kicked my dear daughter Lovia off her boat, stolen her sword, and then proceeded to murder the sacred Swan of Tuonela with it. I laughed it off at first, but now that I see Lovia's sword in your hand, I'm starting to think the rumors might be true."

I press my lips together, not saying a word, just in case I incriminate myself.

Death studies me, his eyes burning beneath the shadow of his hood. "Are you trying to take the Fifth Amendment? Don't you know that what works as law in the Upper World, doesn't work down here? Our laws are very, very different. They're tailored to me. And what I want, what I decide, changes from day to day."

He tilts his head to look over at Rasmus, and in the orange misty glow I see the gleam of his forehead. It's dark, like metallic tourmaline or some other polished black rock. A black skull.

I don't think. I just act. Like my body knows what to do before I do.

Perhaps Vellamo was right and my power is just waking up.

I squeeze the sword, feeling energy flow through me, and while Death is momentarily preoccupied with Rasmus, I start running across the desert toward Death, sword raised in the air.

I will kill him.

I get about ten feet before Death's hand shoots out and suddenly the sword is ripped right from my grasp. The sword goes flying through the air and in seconds the handle slams into Death's armored palm, his fingers curling around it.

I come to a stop, dust flying around me, watching in horror, my weapon gone.

"Did you know I forged this sword?" Death says, staring down at it in his hand. "One of my many talents. My hands might be deadly, but I assure you they are especially skilled where it counts." His voice gets huskier over those last words, dragging them out in such a way that I can't help but think he's being sexually suggestive.

"It's not magic though," he goes on, casually sliding the sword into a sheath on his thigh. "Just the power of magnets and a little starstone."

Death looks to the guy on his right. "What do you say, Kalma? How should we round the fairy up? Chase her onto the plains where the Liekkiö will get her? Take her by force? Perhaps torture her boyfriend a little more until she gives herself up? She seems the type to doing something as stupid as self-sacrifice."

"A chase is always entertaining," Kalma says good-naturedly.

"I prefer the torture," the guy on the other side of Death says in a ragged, squeaky voice, raising his skeleton hand, strips of skin hanging off.

I look at Rasmus. I want to save him, but at this point I have no idea how. I have no sword, I have nothing.

But there's something in Rasmus' gaze that burns. A fire that says he's not giving up, that he's going to fight.

"Hanna," Rasmus says in an even tone. "Remember I said I'd tell you what I did to Eero and Noora at the resort? What if I showed you instead?"

My brain quickly scrolls back. The real world feels like ages ago. Maybe it was. I remember running through the hotel and seeing a wall of ice behind me and that was it.

But Rasmus wasn't really asking me a question. He was telling me to start running.

I nod at him and then turn on my heel and start running into the forest. I hear this loud cracking sound, followed by a whoosh, which sounds like breaking ice and blasting snow, and when I look over my shoulder, I see a wall of ice where Death and his henchmen were, and Rasmus is running free. The iron shackles are around his wrists, but the iron chain has snapped in two where the ice sliced into it.

"What did you do?" I yell at him as he's quickly gaining speed at an alarming rate. "Why didn't you do that earlier?!"

He doesn't say anything. In fact, he doesn't even look at me. His focus is on the backpack I left behind in the dust. He runs right to it, picks it up, and then keeps running until he catches up and then passes me, booking it through the forest, leaping over fallen logs, ducking under branches as if he just powered up like Super Mario.

And just like that, I don't see him anymore.

He's gone.

And he has the backpack.

"Rasmus!" I yell, trying to run faster, not understanding

what just happened. Rasmus could have used that Iceman thing during the swan attack, or The Devouress attack, and he could have already escaped from the chains. Maybe his magic had to warm up or something, or he was waiting for the right circumstances, or—

The ground drops beneath me.

I'm falling.

I scream for a moment and then I stop, as if caught in mid-air.

Then I realize I *am* in mid-air, suspended.

I just ran off a cliff, right into a giant spiderweb that must stretch thirty feet across a rocky chasm. I'm on my stomach, the sticky webs strung across my face, staring at a babbling brook forty feet down that's half hidden by ferns.

Oh god. This isn't good. This really isn't good.

I groan and try to push myself up onto my back but it's impossible. I can barely lift my head off the web, the silky threads sticking to my face until they finally snap back into place.

Okay, don't panic. Don't panic. Just because you're in a giant spider's web, doesn't mean there's going to be a giant spider. I mean the web might be huge but the spider could be small. Or maybe it's like a family of small spiders. Oh god, no, that's worse. Don't think about that. Don't think about anything, just calmly get up, and climb out onto the cliff.

I take in a deep breath and try to push myself up. It's like doing pushups while being attached to the ground. Every single muscle in my arms and back are straining to the max, causing me to shake, the threads refusing to yield.

"I wouldn't do that if I were you," a rich low voice says from above me, now horrifically familiar.

I pause, still shaking, trying to swallow.

"And why not?" I manage to say.

"Because," Death says smoothly, "you're trembling. I must admit I'm impressed by your strength. You may have the face of an angelic fairy but you're built like a warrior, and even I can admire that. But you're also painfully stupid."

"Excuse me?" I exclaim, though I immediately regret it. This isn't the time to be insulted.

"You don't even know me and yet I already get under your skin," Death says. "Don't know what that says about me, but I think I like it. At any rate, you're stupid because you've obviously never seen a spider web before. Even in your world they work the same. The spider waits in the corner for the prey to fall on the web and then once it's caught, the vibrations from the prey's struggles are what alert the spider to come and feed. In this case, it's a wrathspider, which has earned its moniker for reasons you will soon find out."

Oh my god.

I have to get out of here.

I go back to pushing myself up, but the web shakes even more and out of the corner of my eye I see something gigantic and black step onto the web. It's not Death—he's somewhere on the cliff behind me—but it's dark as sin and about the size of a fucking hippo.

Not including the eight thick legs which stretch out from it like oars.

Fuck! I swear. No, no, no, no. This can't be it, this can't be how I die. Not here, not now, not so close to finding my father.

Not by a giant spider.

"I'll make a bargain with you!" I cry out.

Death sighs, and though I can't see him, I feel like he's bored. "I'm tired of bargains, to be honest. The more that I make, the more this world tilts off-balance. Eventually there will be a reckoning."

"I don't give a fuck about your reckoning," I spit out, feeling the web shake now as the spider gets closer in my line of sight. "I want you to free my father."

Death laughs dryly. "I figured. And so what's your bargain?"

"Me for him," I tell him without hesitation. "You save me from this spider, you take me as your prisoner, you let my father go."

Silence falls. The web continues to vibrate.

"Or," he muses, "I could just let you die. Do you know what happens when a not-dead mortal dies here?"

"I've been told," I say, my voice trembling now, the fear starting to eat me alive.

"I could just let you die," he goes on. "And keep your father. And maybe one day when I tire of his company, I'll bring him here and feed him to my new spider friend and you both will share the same fate."

"No!" I scream, tears rushing to my eyes. "Please! I will do anything. Anything you wish, anything at all, just let my father go. You don't even have to save my life, let me die here, but please let my father go."

Another weighty pause. My heart is pounding so hard that I can't tell if it's shaking the web or the spider that's slowly getting closer, its massive shape starting to block out the light.

"You would really do anything for him?" he asks carefully.

"Yes!" I cry out adamantly. I knew from the beginning that if my father was in this situation, where he was taken by Death and still alive, that I would trade my life for his. I would trade my soul. I would take his place and let Death do his worst to me.

"I promise you, I will do anything you want. I will endure anything you wish. I will cook you meals and clean your house, or you can chain me up in your basement, keep me in a cage, you can torture me, have your way with me, give me to others, make me your bride, treat me like a dog, beat me, spit on me, I don't care. I will do it all, if you just let him go."

The spider is almost on me now. I see a glint of fangs, about as long as my forearm, and my spine starts to prickle at the nauseating thought of getting stabbed there.

"*Please*," I add pitifully.

"Hmmph," Death says slowly, too fucking slowly. "A trade."

Fuck. I'm going to die. This is it.

"You did list off a lot of things, some of which aren't relevant, some which are intriguing," he continues. "I really don't like the idea of letting a shaman go, though. It's not good for them to have too much power. You saw what happened to your redheaded boyfriend."

He's not my boyfriend! I think and then almost laugh, because this is probably going to be my last thought before I die.

The spider is right above me now. I manage to turn my head to finally look at it, getting a glance of its leg and the five iron claws at the end. Of course this thing has claws, made of iron no less.

It stops and rears up on its back legs like a horror-show horse, the fangs glinting, and hundreds of red eyes gleaming like balloons of blood.

Hell.

Death sighs dramatically. "Fine."

There's a pause, a swooshing sound, and then the web violently shakes. The spider crashes to the sticky threads, one of its giant hairy legs narrowly missing me, and I realize that Death jumped on top of it.

The spider immediately goes still, dying instantly.

I crane my head up to look at Death as he gets off the spider like he's dismounting a horse, and makes a show of putting one of his armored gloves back on his hand, and for a brief second I see his bare skin, which is covered in lines of pulsing silver.

Then he walks over to me, balancing gracefully on the web. He looms over my body, his figure larger than life, his cape black and flowing behind him, hate burning in the depths of his unseen eyes, and I realize that perhaps it would have been better had the spider ended me.

I'm about to find myself on another web, Death lurking in the shadows, waiting for me to tremble.

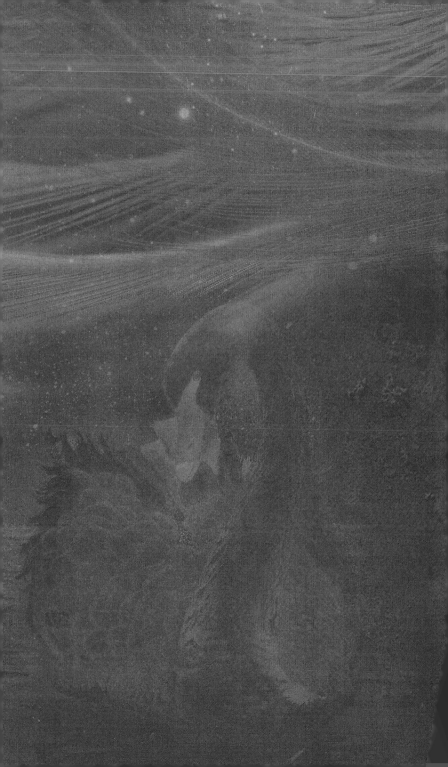

CHAPTER NINE

THE LIEKKIÖ PLAINS

Death reaches down and grabs me by the elbow, hauling me to my feet, my skin screaming in pain as the web stretches and pulls and finally lets go. It feels like half my flesh goes with it.

I nearly fall back into his arms and it's then that I realize how fucking huge Death is. He's at least a foot taller than me, which makes him what, close to seven feet? And his hand is the size of my head, and I don't think that's because of the fancy metal gauntlets.

"Having second thoughts, fairy girl?" he asks and before I can answer, lifts me up so that I'm thrown over his shoulder, like a caveman would do to a kidnapped bride.

I don't bother with the fist-pounding and kicking theatrics since I did sign up for this moments ago in exchange for my father's life, and there's also the fact that logically I can't walk on the spiderweb without sticking to it.

Once we're on solid ground again and away from the cliff's edge, he puts me down and I get a whiff of his smell. I expected Death to smell like, well, death. Decay. Rot. Everything vile and disgusting. But for whatever reason, he actually smells pleasant. It's deep in tone and hard to place, maybe sandalwood and… smoke? A bonfire with really good wood? Something like that.

"Are you smelling me?" he asks, a hint of amusement in his gruff voice.

I glance up at him, wishing that at such close range that I could see more of his face. His hood does such a great job of keeping his features in shadow; I wonder if it's part magic.

Then again, I don't think he has any features. If he really is just a black, shiny skull, then no wonder I can't see anything.

But then, when he turns ever so slightly, I see a flash of white where his eyes should be. It's hard to tell if it is a trick of the light or not.

"You smell vile," I tell him.

"Good," he says simply. "I take a bath every day but when you fill the tub with bat's blood, the smell is bound to rub off on you."

I still. Oh my god. I can't tell if he's joking.

"Now," he goes on, reaching into a pocket inside his hood, "that we've made an agreement, struck a bargain, we still have to get you back to my home at Shadow's End."

"Is this the place you bathe in bat's blood?"

"Where I *what*?" he asks. Pauses. "Yes. As will you." He pulls out an iron collar from his coat, attached to a long chain. I have no idea where he's keeping all these things, it's like Mary Poppins' purse in there. "And as I was saying, in order to make sure you uphold your part of the bargain and won't try something foolish again like escaping and nearly going to Oblivion, I need to keep you on a leash. Literally. This belongs to my hound,

Rauta. And before you take credit for this, because I do recall you listing *treat me like a dog* as one of the perks in owning you, I had planned this already."

I don't move as he places the cold iron collar around my neck, fastening it with a loud click that sounds like a jail door closing.

"There," he says, sounding proud, and I can feel the intensity in his gaze as he looks me over, even though I can't see it. "I must say, it looks rather good on you. Like you're some wild fairy who's been finally caught and tamed."

I'll never be tamed, is a thought I have but what I say is, "Do you have fairies here?"

"Not exactly," he says. "There's no Tinkerbell."

"Tinkerbell?" I repeat. "No mention of fae folk, or sprites, or any of the other myths and legends from around the world that are most likely real, but Tinkerbell? From Peter Pan? A *Disney cartoon?*"

The air between us changes. Goes cold, goes...dead. Like there's no life left in it and I'm starting to think I can't even breathe and—

"I've only read the book," he says gruffly. "Now, come along and let me cross something else off that list."

He starts walking, yanking at the chain and I fall to the ground, skinning my knees open on a rock, my jeans ripping.

"Fuck," I grumble, swallowing the pain, but he just pulls at the leash again until I'm on all fours, my palms digging into the ground.

"Treat me like a dog," Death says, mimicking my voice. "Humiliate me. Do you feel humiliated yet, fairy? Because I'm just getting started."

"Fuck you!" I snarl, and before he pulls the chain again, I fight back. I push up off my hands, doing a summersault and landing on my feet right beside him, the chain noisily going slack between us.

Death's shadowed face stares down at me. "Look at you fly, little bird." There's a hint of awe in his voice. "You're just full of surprises, aren't you?"

"It's easy to be surprised when you don't know a thing about the person."

"You think I don't know you, Hanna Heikkinen?" He starts walking and I quickly follow before he pulls me along again. "Well, I suppose I only know what's written down in the Book of Souls. Your father wouldn't tell me a thing. The man truly wanted to protect you…and look at what you've gone and done. It's going to break his damn heart when he finds out what you've sacrificed, that you've traded your life for his. Do you really think he's going to live a good life now, even with his cancer cured, if he knows that his dear daughter is a prisoner of mine for eternity?"

I blink, trying to take all of that in at once. Eternity? Since when did I agree to eternity? But that doesn't matter as much right now. "His cancer is cured?" I ask incredulously, hope shining through my chest.

He nods slowly. "He came to me asking for a cure. He didn't even want eternal life, just a cure. I told you I don't make bargains much anymore, there are consequences for each one I do, but I decided to make an exception."

"Why did you make an exception if he's your prisoner?"

"Your father doesn't know he'll be cured," he says. "I actually didn't think of it until two seconds ago. I suppose I'm beginning to feel bad for the old wizard, with him knowing that you'll be tortured for all time. He'll know his life wasn't worth it. He'll tell you that he's old, that he's lived his life, that he's dying anyway. He will do anything to stop you from making this trade, but it's already done. You can call me Death. And I will call you *mine*."

I fall silent, stepping over a fallen log, wishing the mushrooms on it could save me from this horrible new reality I've created for myself. Of course it's going to break my father's heart to know I'll be stuck here, and at some point the truth is going to hit me too, break me into a million pieces that Death will happily eat for breakfast. It ruins me to think of my father out there, mourning me, the guilt he will feel for me taking his place.

But what choice did I have? Death wouldn't have let both of us go.

Would he have?

"How about you let both my father and I go," I tell him, trying not to sound too hopeful.

Death seems to think that over. "No," he says after a moment. "I'm not going to do that." He sighs. "The truth is, my job isn't easy and life here is almost always the same. That's what happens when you're a God, particularly one of great importance. There's very little deviation. There are eons of just... the same. I have my hobbies, I have my fights and games, I have my pets, my servants, my councilmen. I have my daughter and my son. I have my vices. I have my maidens. And I have my loyal subjects in the City of Death. But I do not have anything shiny and mortal and new. At least I didn't until your father showed up. And while he's not my first choice of company, he did provide a change. You will do the same. So I cannot let you go. One of you must stay. Do you still wish it to be you?"

"Yes," I say automatically. My heart's fucking *breaking*. "My father is a good man. A really good man. And I love him beyond measure. He does not deserve to be locked up in your castle for your amusement, to appease a God's boredom."

"And that's what you deserve?"

"Maybe." I swallow hard, the iron pressing against my throat. "I never gave much thought to what I deserve. I was just living without appreciating it, without recognizing it. Maybe this is what I deserve, for twenty-four years of just floating along the surface, not grabbing onto life while I had it."

"Mmhmmph," he says after a moment. "That's very dramatic. I can't tell if it's amusing or annoying."

I want to glare at him, but I'm still stuck on something from earlier. "Are you really going to cure my father's cancer? Torben Heikkinen? Make sure that he can live out his full life?"

"Unfortunately, yes," he says. "I regret it already, but I don't like going back on my word. I said it, so it's done."

My heart nearly bursts, even though the feeling is bittersweet.

My father's life will be extended.

I just won't be part of his life anymore.

"You could thank me," Death says. "No one ever thanks me."

"Because no one wants to die!" I tell him.

"Why not?" he asks. "If they knew what was in the City of Death, they wouldn't fear it. They might even welcome it. Even those who are damned to Inmost aren't damned forever. We have Bone Matches where the winner can live in the Golden Mean."

I stare at the black void of his face. "Don't you want to be feared? Isn't that the whole point of you?"

Another waft of dead air passes between us, sending an icy chill down my spine. In the distance, thunder crashes and the clouds grow dark.

I've made him angry again.

Death stops and takes a step toward me, leaning down, leaning in close, and all I can do is stare into the dark abyss as the abyss stares back. "Do you not fear me, little bird?" he rasps, his voice a black hand reaching into my soul. "Because I spared you on the spider's web? You don't even know what fear is, you impetuous mortal. Not yet. I will break you into a thousand little worthless pieces, I will suck your heart through the marrow of your bones, I will take your body, your memories, every ounce that defines you, and grind you into my morning coffee, so that your suffering will give me energy for the day. I will make you beg for death, and even then I won't grant it to you, all for my own fucking amusement. So go ahead and squander your fear. You'll need it later. Your life will depend on it."

He keeps walking but I feel like I'm rooted into the ground, afraid to move, afraid to breathe, the fear making a home in every corner of my body.

"Come along," he growls, yanking at the chain and I'm pulled toward him, the iron collar nearly snapping my neck. I stumble along, lost in the fear, in the loss of hope, my thoughts and emotions caught in a whirlpool of despair, until the Hiisi forest ends and we come to the desert with the weird orange haze. To my surprise, it's completely empty.

"Where is everyone?" I ask.

"They went after the redhead," Death says gruffly.

"So we're walking?"

He starts across the desert, yanking at my collar again, making me cry out in pain. "*Now* we're walking." He casts me a sidelong glance I can't see. "The nerve you have to complain about your mode of transportation."

"I'm not *complaining*," I manage to eke out, pulling the collar away from my throat so I can swallow. "I'm just surprised that we're walking to your shadow castle or whatever. Shouldn't you be riding your unicorn? Shouldn't you have a chariot made of bones, pulled by five black stallions that breathe fire?"

"You have quite the imagination. Sarvi will be back soon I imagine. The others will head to the castle. Either they find the redhead or they don't. Sometimes I think there are ways out of this land that even I don't know about."

"Who is Sarvi?"

"My unicorn."

"Do you know how silly that sounds?"

Death lets out a low growl, like a cornered wolverine. "Unicorn as a word makes perfect sense for the creatures. It's fucking fairy tales that made them into some blessed angel horse. They are anything but. Violent, bloodsucking, voracious equines with a bad attitude. I'm just lucky that they were leftovers from when the Old Gods ruled, and that they decided to serve us. They didn't have to."

"How long is the walk?"

"It will take days. Many days. Maybe even weeks because of how aggravatingly slow you are."

Great.

"Tell me about the Old Gods," I say, pulling at my collar again.

"I will tell you nothing," he says.

"Tell me how you tortured Rasmus. What did you do to him?"

"Torture? Trying to bait me with topics I enjoy?" I feel his eyes on me for a moment. "How well do you trust him?"

I balk, glancing up at his shadowed face. "Rasmus? A hell of a lot more than I trust you."

"That's a given," he says simply. "Do you know him well?"

I lick my lips, the dry air sucking the moisture from them. I'm not sure how to play this. I could lie, but that might not make a difference. Fuck, I don't think anything I do or say going forward is going to make a difference. "I barely know him at all."

"I have three sayings in life," Death says, ticking off three fingers, their intricate metal coverings glinting orange in the desert light. "Never trust the living. Never trust a God. And never trust a redhead." He glances at me. "I'm afraid you've already done all three."

I feel like he's baiting *me* now. We continue to walk, and I'm ever so conscious of the rising dust and heat and Death's commanding presence beside me, his metal and weaponry chiming with each step. Despite his size though, his movements are fluid and graceful, even if the ground shakes a little under his footfall.

"I trusted Rasmus to keep me alive," I eventually say.

"Yet you're the one who fought my daughter and killed the swan," he points out tersely. "It sounds like you kept him alive there."

"He called upon Vellamo when The Devouress was going to eat us. He told me the truth about my father. He did that ice thing with Eero and Noora, these shamans back in Finland. Saved me from them too."

"I see," he says. "Did you know his mother was a Lapp Witch? Among other things…"

"No. But so what? That makes sense that he would have some power that way, right?" I mean I don't know what a Lapp Witch is, but it sounds like a normal witch.

"Perhaps," he says. "But even Rasmus doesn't know that. He thinks his mother died when he was young, same goes for his father. He was raised by his grandmother, then in part by your father after she died. Did you know that part?"

Obviously I didn't, but I hate that Death knew of the secrets my father was keeping from him, so I don't say anything.

"Did you not wonder what happened to him in the night?" he goes on, his tone light now, as if we're having a casual chat.

I shrug. I had wondered that, of course. "Figured he went to take a piss and you accosted him?"

"He ran off and left you behind. We found him at the mouth of the Gorge of Despair," he says. "Somehow he crossed these plains and survived."

"What's so dangerous about them?"

"You don't hear that?"

I listen. There's nothing but the sound of us walking, of sand blowing in the wind.

"You'll see them soon enough," Death says. "Regardless, it's impressive. But by the time he got to the Gorge, he was stuck. We were up early doing surveillance of the area, looking for you, when we saw him. When we grabbed him, he told us he was here to do a trade. We assumed he would trade himself for your father, but to our surprise he said he was going to trade *you* for him. Must be the witch in him."

I swallow the dust in my throat. Death could be lying.

"He knew how badly I wanted my father back," I tell him. "He assumes I would gladly make that trade, and I did."

"You don't think that was his plan all along?"

"His plan was to rescue my father, to save him. He said he needed my help. If my help meant me being traded in his place, then so be it. What difference does it make now?"

"You don't feel betrayed?"

It's like he's trying to get a reaction from me, but the truth is I don't care. Okay, I do a little. Rasmus could have been honest with me from the start, but then he didn't know if I'd go through with it. It's one thing to say you'll do anything, it's another to follow through. Just as Vellamo had said.

"What are you going to do when you find him?" I ask warily. Despite Rasmus having an ulterior motive, I don't want anything bad to happen to the guy.

"Oh, I haven't given it much thought."

"Did you really torture him? He seemed fine to me."

I swear I can tell Death is smiling. "There are different types of torture, little bird."

Suddenly he stops and puts his arm out, the cloak flowing over me as I still. "Listen," he says, voice lowered.

I concentrate, listening.

Then I hear it. A long wailing sound, the same sound I briefly heard when Tellervo and I first came to the desert. It rises in tone, totally eerie and inhuman, and feels like nails on a chalkboard, making my nerves shake and twist.

"Wh-what is that?" I manage to say, the sound making me stutter.

"The Liekkiö," he says. "Spirits of murdered children."

I stare at him aghast.

He glances at me. "I didn't murder them, if that's what you're wondering," he says testily. "They are relics from the Old Gods. Like many relics here, they cling on through the ages, impossible to get rid of, like fleas on a bonerat."

The wailing gets louder, enough that I have to put my hands over my ears, the sound tearing me apart from the inside. "Fucking hell. Make it stop!" I yell.

"Can't do much about them," Death says, or at least I think he says it. I can't tell anymore, all I hear is the terrifying, persistent noise. "There they are now." He raises his arm and points in a dramatic fashion.

In front of us, flames emerge from the mist, giving off a black smoke that mixes with the orange, creating a sort of smog that fills the air. The flames come lurching forward and it's only then that I notice the bodies. The walking bones of children, mouths open in that punishing scream.

"This all used to be forest at one point," Death says, somehow his voice getting through to me. "But the Liekkiö burned it down with their rage. The Hiisi managed to put a ward up to protect this side of the forest, as Tapio the Forest

God wasn't able to stop them. That's why the Gods let the Hiisi share the forest."

I can't keep my eyes off the horrific sight, both terribly sad because these are clearly children, or were once, and terribly frightening because they won't stop screaming, won't stop staggering forward with their tiny, outstretched flaming hands and their snapping jaws.

Death steps in front of me, as if to be my shield. "They bite," he warns. "Little vampires. They won't get through my armor, but you're made of the *softest* flesh and bone."

I'm aware I'm his prisoner and he has an iron collar around my damn neck, but even so, I'm momentarily grateful for his presence. I move my head around the breadth of him to see the flaming murdered children come closer and closer, an awful stench filling the air.

Suddenly the flames are fanned as a burst of cold wind flows through us and a shadow is cast from above. I look up in time to see Sarvi in flight, huge black leathery wings, like a bat, blotting out the sun.

The unicorn swoops down, my hair blown back by the wingbeats, then dives with its horn aimed at the flames. It spears its horn through the skull of one of the children, then whips its head back, its long black mane flowing majestically, as the skeleton child goes flying through the air, landing in a heap of broken bones. The unicorn quickly does the same to the other children, spearing them in the skull and tossing them, until the flaming pile of skeletons are far from us.

"Are they...*dead*...dead?" I ask Death.

"No, they're immune," he grumbles. "They'll get up in a few

minutes. You don't want to be here when they do." He strolls toward the unicorn, who is waving its head around, snorting hot air, one white eye on one side of its face, on the other an empty socket. "In the nick of time, Sarvi," he says to it.

Then Death yanks the chain and I nearly fall to my knees again. "Ow!" I cry out.

"I'll happily leave you behind if that's what you want," Death says, leaning against the unicorn's shoulder. "You already talk too much."

"We had a deal," I say stiffly, trying to gain what dignity I can with an iron dog collar around my neck.

"That we do," he says with a sigh. "So then, you better get yourself over here."

I walk toward him, the chain clanking and then he's grabbing me, his hands completely circling my waist, and throwing me up onto the unicorn's back.

"Make a fist in the mane," Death says as he swings himself up and I find myself lodged between the unicorn's thick, partially skeletonized neck and Death's armored body. "You'll want to hold on for your pointless little life. Pull as much as you like. Sarvi can't feel anything."

Once again, sir, that's not exactly true, a placid voice with a quasi-British accent says, seemingly from out of nowhere.

I look around for the source. "Who was that?"

"You heard that?" Death asks in quiet awe.

I nod.

Oh perfect, someone else to claim to hear me and then proceed to completely ignore me, the voice goes on.

"That's Sarvi," Death explains.

My eyes nearly fall out. "The unicorn can *talk*?"

"Unfortunately." Death kicks at Sarvi's sides. "Up we go."

And we take flight.

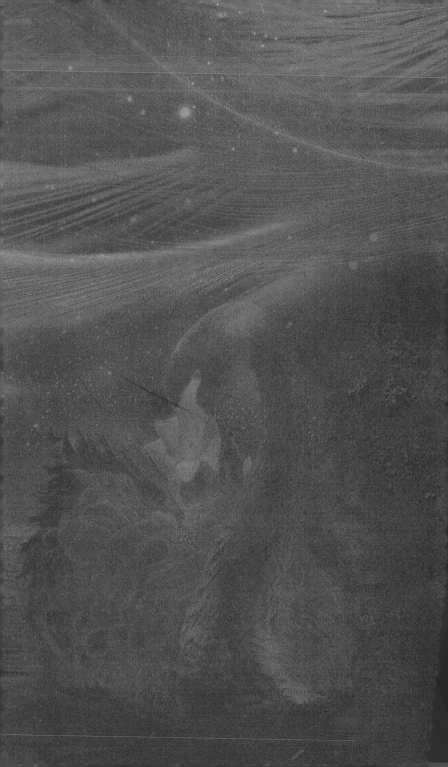

CHAPTER TEN

THE CASTLE

The last birthday I had in Finland, about a year before my mother decided to move me to California, my father got me horseback riding lessons as a present. The best present of my childhood, really. The stable was just outside of town and every Wednesday afternoon my father would take me there in his red vintage truck. I rode this fluffy white pony named Porro, but I called it Porridge, and all we did was go around the ring at a walk and a trot. Eventually I got "good" enough to canter, but I immediately went tumbling off Porridge and onto the woodchips. My instructor told me to hold onto the pony's mane next time, and I did just that. I managed to stay on that way until I had to leave Porridge, Finland, and my father behind. Once I got to California, my mother put me in dance, and riding was deemed too dangerous to continue.

Well, all those lessons are coming flooding back to me, nearly twenty years later, and maybe even saving my life. Sarvi's jet-black mane is wrapped around my hands several times over, because taking a tumble here means falling two hundred feet to my death.

Because we're flying.

We're fucking *flying*.

I'm too damn scared to even appreciate what an incredible and surreal event this is, because I've got Death's armored chest and crotch pressed against me, the front of his thighs bracketing mine, and Sarvi's shoulders jammed between my legs. The air is chilled and thinner up here and Sarvi's rhythmic wingbeats make it even colder.

If you could find something to be happy about, Sarvi says, *even for a moment, sir, it would make our journey much quicker. The clouds are holding us back.*

Death grumbles. "I would have been happy had you found that redheaded bastard."

I told you, he was long gone, Sarvi says. From what I can tell, the unicorn's voice isn't coming from its mouth or vocal chords, but somehow slipping from its brain to ours. *Kalma and Surma will double-check, but I doubt they'll find anything. They never do.*

"How can a mortal get through the Hiisi Forest that fast?" Death muses bitterly. "He's hiding."

That may be. He wouldn't have made it through the Star Swamp, I know that much, Sarvi says.

Death makes another low growling noise. With him right behind me, the guttural sound raises the hair on the back of my neck, even with the iron collar there.

"We know who his mother is. I wouldn't be surprised if she helped him," Death says.

I have questions. I have so many questions. But right now, I can't say a word. I'm too terrified to speak, like the moment I do I'll let go of Sarvi's mane and tumble through the sky forever. I've never had a big fear of heights but that will change after this.

If there is an *after this*.

She's a silent one, Sarvi says, meaning me. *I must say I'm relieved. You'll have to understand, Hanna, that so far only you and Death can understand me. The other unicorns do too, but they're not as civilized as Gods and mortals can be.*

Sarvi says this as if I should be flattered.

"I'm too scared to talk," I admit.

Death makes another low, rumbling noise behind me, reverberating through my bones. "How freely she admits it now."

We lapse into silence, though in my head I'm doing all I can not to freak out. We fly along, just under the cloud cover, the claw-like tips of Sarvi's wings scraping the bottoms of the clouds, making foggy tendrils dance in our wake. Below us the scenery keeps changing. The dry and desolate plains end abruptly at cliffs that stretch up and up, the River of Shadows snaking below it. The cliffs keep getting higher, turning to mountains that are craggy and jagged, gleaming as if made of iron, a dusting of snow on the very peaks.

Then I see something that takes my breath away.

Right in front of us is an impossibly large tower that shoots straight up into the clouds, miles and miles wide, so wide that it almost curves over the horizon. The tower is made of shining stones that reflect the sky and rises up from a walled citadel of darkness, the structures barely visible.

"What is that?" I ask breathlessly.

"The City of Death," Death says proudly as Sarvi curves around the gargantuan tower, flying at an angle that I'm sure I'll fall from, with only the G-forces keeping me in place.

I quickly glance up at the tower as it disappears into the clouds. Then vertigo sets in and I shut my eyes, no longer wanting to see the rest. "Where does it go?"

"Into the heavens," says Death. "Up there is Amaranthus. It's where the best of the best go. Below it, at the middle, is the Golden Mean. Then where you see the citadel at ground level, that begins the Realm of Inmost, where the Inmost Dwellers are beholden. Inmost goes fathoms deep into the ground, almost as deep as Amaranthus goes into the sky. No surprise, considering how many…offenders there are."

"You mean sinners."

He clears his throat. "No. Not quite. We're all sinners, little bird. Every one of us. To sin is to be human, to be human is to sin."

"But you're a God."

"Gods are the biggest sinners of them all."

"That sounds blasphemous to me."

He chuckles warmly. "There is but one singular Creator, Hanna. The word God is too weak for them. Beneath the Creator are the Gods. We are victims to the same impulses, weaknesses, and emotions as anyone else is." He pauses. "Does that disappoint you?"

"Considering I've grown up believing in only one God, whom I'm assuming is the Creator, then no. I've never given multiple Gods any thought."

"But you've thought of *Death*," he says with deliberation, an edge of excitement to his voice.

His words seem to sink into me. I open my eyes and they water as the high wind rushes into them, but the City of Death is behind us now. Ahead lie mountains taller than the ones before, covered in glaciers and thickly packed snow.

Death? Who hasn't thought of death? It's the first harsh lesson a child learns when they find a dead bird in their yard. It's the devastation of having a beloved dog be put down. It's the soul-crushing reality when a loved one dies.

There isn't one life that is immune to death.

Death is for the living.

No blizzards on Mount Vipunen today, Sarvi's voice rings out. *Perhaps you're in a better mood than I thought, sir.*

Death makes another low grumbling noise.

You see, Hanna, Sarvi goes on, *the weather in Tuonela is subconsciously controlled by Death. Unfortunately, he doesn't care about this half the time.*

"Sarvi. Shut it," Death says.

When he's happy, the clouds clear and the sun shines on the land, Sarvi goes on, clearly not shutting it. *And the more that the sun shines, the better his chances of growing certain things, such as his beloved coffee. But he's never happy, so the clouds and storms and snow persist. Personally, I don't care, but it makes flying a lot easier when there isn't so much cloud cover.*

"Sarvi," Death warns. "Just because she can hear you, doesn't mean I can't. Stop yammering about the weather and get us to Shadow's End."

Yes sir, Sarvi says after a moment. The unicorn beats its

wings faster, which causes my grip to tighten as we pick up speed. Soon we're cresting over the mountains and a whole new landscape opens up before me.

We're at the very bottom of the land. If Tuonela were a continent, this would be the Cape Horn of South America. Here there are green pastures above dark gray cliffs dropping off to a rich blue ocean below, the waves churning with kelp and lashing at the rocks. It's a formidable and harsh place where the clouds are the darkest and out along a narrow isthmus of rock and sodden pasture, lies a castle.

I have to blink a few times to really accept what I'm seeing. I don't know if I had been imagining an actual castle this whole time, but now that it's in front of me, I'm taken aback. It's a castle alright, built on a narrow peninsula of rock, a long iron road snaking along the crest of land connecting it. The castle is huge and foreboding, like something from a dark fairy tale, or a nightmare, black as obsidian, both gleaming and matte, depending on how you looked at it, as if the rocks were made of smoked crystal and iron. There are impossibly narrow towers with dagger-like turrets rising hundreds of feet above the ocean, the castle comprising of two similarly sized structures connected by walls and walkways. Everything is sharp and pointing, as if the castle is a weapon itself.

It's a place firmly rooted in the past and the future, a castle of this world and the next. It doesn't just sit on that rocky outcrop, it *waits*. Like a cat on its haunches, it's watching. Alive. Biding time before it pounces on the prey.

The question is, who is the prey?

Is it me?

Or is it everything living?

"I'll take your silence as being impressed," Death says.

I'm not proud enough to pretend otherwise. I nod, unable to find the words as Sarvi swirls down in sweeping circles, narrowing in on one turret. The pointed roof rushes up at us at increasing speed and I close my eyes just as Sarvi brings us to a stop.

I open my eyes to find us on a large slab jutting out from the tower, like a balcony with no railing. The ocean is at least a hundred feet below.

"We're home," Death says, swinging his leg over Sarvi and then holding his hands out for me, as if he were some gallant knight helping a fair maiden. I stare down at his armored hands, then glance at his shadowed face and once again I see a flash of white. Like the whites of someone's eyes. My mind puts together a ghoulish image of a bare skull with round eyeballs placed in the sockets.

The disgust must be showing on my face because he drops his hands and growls and yanks the chain. Before I can react, I'm being pulled off Sarvi, landing in a heap on the cold stone platform.

Pain shoots up through my hands and knees and I'm wondering if I have enough distance between us to do some damage. I figure I could go for it, drop kick him right off the side like I did to his daughter, and maybe the gravity of this world will help me like it did the last time, but the only thing that stops me is that I'm attached to Death. Where he goes, I go. He'll survive the fall—you can't kill a God, as far as I know—but I definitely won't.

And now he's staring down at me, the electricity in his unseen gaze felt but not seen. "I think I just saw my future in your eyes," he says quietly. "And I saw your future too. Think before you act, little bird. You're not ready for flight yet."

He raises his hand, the chain wrapped around it, threatening me.

I get to my feet, grinding my teeth. If it weren't for my father, perhaps that long fall over the edge would be worth it, even if it ended with my demise.

But my father is what matters most. He's here. He's why I'm here, why I came. And I can't fuck it all up now because I want to break Death's shiny skull with my own hands.

Careful, Sarvi says to me as the unicorn walks past me, the size of a Clydesdale. *I may have given you a safe ride here, but I serve but one master.*

Sarvi walks toward the huge glass doors into the tower, so big they must stand at least twenty-feet high. They open by people or mechanics unseen until the equine disappears inside. For whatever reason, I didn't expect a unicorn to waltz inside the castle, but at this point I clearly know nothing.

I look over at Death, who is still holding the chain in a threatening manner.

"Sarvi seems pretty loyal," I say to him. "Seems odd that you would need protection since you're a God."

He grunts in amusement. "Gods are vulnerable to other Gods."

"How?"

Again, I can feel him smiling. "And why would I tell you any of my weaknesses?"

"You don't have to. It's enough to know you have them." I give him a small smile. "I'll figure out the rest."

And then I'll kill you.

"Fairy girl," Death says, taking a step toward me. "At least see your father first before you make any rash decisions."

"You can read minds?" I sneer, feeling violated.

"I can read mortals," he says evenly. "It's my job. To know someone in life is to know them in death. I know all that you are, Hanna, all that you will be, all that you'll do. Rarely am I proven wrong."

"Is that so? You already said I'm surprising."

He laughs wickedly. "You suck up every compliment like a bottom feeder, don't you?"

I feel my face fall. I can't help it. He's got me there, one of my biggest fucking flaws, and he already knows it. This life-long incessant need to be complimented, validated, to feel I'm special in regards to *something*.

"And yes, you are strangely surprising," he goes on. "Perhaps because your entry in the Book of Souls isn't complete. Because you haven't died...yet. If you were to die at ninety, then that would give you sixty-six years to discover yourself, grow into a new person, change your ways. Right now I see you as an insignificant twenty-four-year-old, but I can't know the person you *might* become, the one waiting in your own shadows to finally find the light to grow."

He gives the chain a little yank, enough to make me glare.

"Come on. You don't want to keep your father waiting, do you?" he says.

He walks toward the open doors and I follow.

He's right. I need to keep my focus on my father, on why I'm here. I guess the reason why my mind keeps shying away from it and latching onto anger is because I'm frightened. I'm so afraid that Death won't uphold his end of the deal. I'm scared that I might not even be able to see my father. I'm terrified that my father might already be dead and I'm here for nothing.

At the last thought I have to fight the tears back. I refuse to cry in front of Death. That's something I'll promise myself right here, right now, no matter what happens. For the last week I thought my father was dead and I've had to live with that awful, life-changing, soul-crushing reality, and now that I know he's alive, that he can be cured and set free…to have it taken away again would be even worse than if I never opened that casket. To lose someone you dearly love will ruin you. To have them die and have a second chance, only to die again…I don't know what kind of person I would become after that. I think I'd become an animal, one composed of pain, to suffer eternally.

At that, Death glances at me over his shoulder as we walk across a circular room and I get another glimpse of his polished onyx skull gleaming in the light of the black candles that flicker from various holders on the walls.

"If you can put your murderous rage away for a moment," he comments, "I'll give you a tour of your forever home. This is what we call Sarvi's landing, for obvious reasons. Sarvi doesn't stay in a stable like the other equines, being sentient and all he prefers to have his own space indoors."

Despite everything going on, I can't help but be curious. I look around the room. It doesn't look like it was made for a horse. The floors are black marble, the walls a navy wallpaper with raised red filigree. There's a bunch of moss to one side with hay sticking out from underneath, trampled down until it resembles a bed, and there's a long low table made of bones lined with various large bowls. At another end is a single armchair made of charcoal leather and a small bookshelf beside it. Beside that is a stand, the kind you'd see as a teacher's podium, an open book on display.

I'm trying to picture Sarvi somehow sitting in that chair, then I realize the chair is supposed to be for guests. Human-sized guests. The image I conjure nearly makes me laugh and I realize I must be delirious. I wonder what it feels like to truly lose your mind. Would I even know?

We go down a long winding stairway lit by candles with dripping black wax, down, down, down. The air is damp in here, though it smells faintly like Death, something sweet and smoky, and the sound of his iron boots on the stone stairs echo against the circular walls, my chain clanking.

Finally, after I'm dizzy from going in circles, we stop and Death pushes a tall wooden door that opens with a loud creak.

I find myself stepping into a great hall of sorts, the ceilings impossibly high, the walls done in dark wallpaper with dripping candles, a room that's completely empty except for the five figures standing in the middle of it. Four of them are cloaked, faces hidden, bony skeleton hands gripping the man in between them.

My father.

To see him already is a shock to the system. I wasn't expecting to see him so soon, let alone see him at all. But there he is, wearing a black cloak like the rest of them, though his hood is back, and his face is clear, his hair white and balding at the top, a little long now at the nape of the neck, his beard long. His blue eyes aren't twinkling like they used to, instead they're full with both pain and with love.

But it's him.

It's my father.

"Papa!" I cry out. I can feel Death getting ready to make a move to restrain me, but I will not be restrained. I run forward with all my might, feeling an energy pulsing through me, one driven by love, and I whip the chain straight out of Death's hands.

"Papa!" I cry again, running as fast as I can across the black marble floors of the hall, the chain clanging behind me with each step. I think I hear Death yell something, and the closer I get to my father, the more the cloaked guards hold him back, but I can't stop myself.

I fling myself at him, burying my head in his neck, holding onto him even though he's not able to hold on to me.

"Hanna!" he exclaims, his voice hoarse. "My dear Hanna!"

I start bawling. The tears just flow out of me like a river, spilling onto his cloak. The smell of him! Despite where he is, and how long it's been, he still smells like home to me. He's always been my home.

"Hanna, why did you come?" he cries out softly. "You never should have come. I don't know how to protect you here."

I straighten up, my vision blurry. It's been years since I've seen him, but he looks the same as ever. Not a dying man, not a man who has been imprisoned by Death. I place my trembling hands on his cheeks. He's warm to touch.

"It's really you," I whisper. "I thought you were dead."

Suddenly I feel Death's presence behind me and my father looks up and over me with fury in his eyes. "How dare you do this to her?" he snarls at Death. "You've chained her up, you monster! Treating her like an animal?!"

Death chuckles dryly. "Because she's acting like an animal. Just as I am acting like a monster." I feel tension on my throat as Death picks up my chain. "I'll let you have your moment, but it's only a moment. Nothing more."

"Death is going to cure your cancer," I tell him. "You'll be able to live now."

He shakes his head, eyes watering. "At what cost? The cost will be you, Hanna, and it will be too much to bear. Oh my sweetheart, look at you. Look how beautiful you are, even with this thing around your neck. You wear it like a queen."

Something inside me breaks for the hundredth time. "I love you," I whisper to him urgently, my collar starting to feel like a noose, the seconds counting down. "I love you Papa, so much, and I'm so sorry we didn't get more time together, that I didn't reach out when I should have, that I thought you'd always be there, like the sun and the moon. I didn't know the sun and moon could be taken from me, but you were. You are. And I wish I could go back and make it so I stayed with you. I never should have left, I should have stayed."

"Hanna, dear," he says, trying to move his hands to hold me but the skeleton guards are strong. "You didn't stay because it wasn't your path. But I never stopped loving you, you know I didn't, and I know you never stopped loving me. Your earrings... your earrings will let you know." He looks over at Death again, a vein popping in his forehead. I don't think I've ever seen him this furious before. "You let her go. You keep me, and let her go. I don't want your cure. I'll gladly die knowing she's free."

"Mmmmm," Death muses. "How very predictable of you, Torben. But no. I'll be keeping her. She interests me a lot more than you do. You'll be going along now, back to the Upper World, and if you know what's good for you, you'll stay there. Hanna belongs with me now. She belongs to Tuonela."

"You let her go!" my father shouts. "Please, I beg of you!"

Death just reaches into his cloak and pulls out a small glass vial. In the glass vial is a writhing white centipede. I want to shrink away in horror, until I realize the centipede is meant for my father.

"You know, it was Rasmus who brought Hanna here," Death says. "It was Rasmus who had the idea to trade Hanna for your life. Hanna, of course, was willing to do that no matter who suggested it. I have to admit, I'm a little jealous of you, Torben. To have people love you that much, they would go to the ends of another world to try and save you…well, if you take anything away from this experience, it's that you're one lucky man."

Then Death removes the metal stopper and the white centipede crawls out onto his fingers. He grasps it by the writhing end, it's hundreds of tiny legs wriggling, and holds it above my father's head.

"No!" I scream, trying to fight him, but Death just holds me back with his arm and lets the centipede go. I watch in horror as the centipede crawls down over my father's face—mirroring when I saw him in the casket—and up his nose.

My father screams.

I scream.

Then my father's eyes roll back in his head and he suddenly collapses, dead weight in the skeleton guards' hands.

"What did you do!?" I screech at Death, rage tearing through me. "You promised you would let him go!"

Death is holding me back by the chain now and I'm falling to my knees, trying to crawl after my father after the guards drag him away.

"He's not dead," Death says gruffly, as if I'm overreacting. "The dreamwalker has only put him to sleep. A deep sleep that even a shaman won't wake up from, not for a few days. Gives my Deadhands enough time to take him out the way he came in and leave him in the Upper World. Where he will stay."

My heart calms, just a little, in knowing he isn't dead. "You could have just escorted him out," I say weakly.

Death lets out another dry laugh. "He's a shaman, little bird. A powerful one. Don't base all your knowledge of them on Rasmus. Your father has the ability to fight his way back here and then some. The only reason he can't use his magic in here is because of all the onyx and iron. And the wards, though I don't trust those that put the wards in place."

"He'll be back. He'll come back for me." I know I should keep that knowledge quiet, but I want to prove how strong my father is, how much he loves me.

"He won't," Death says. "And not because he won't try. He won't remember. That's the gift of the dreamwalker. All your memories from weeks prior will be gone. He'll wake up somewhere in Lapland and there's a chance he won't even remember coming here. He won't even know he's been cured from cancer until he realizes he's not dead yet."

I grind my teeth together, the anger and violence rushing through me is shocking even to me. "You extend a man's life but he won't even know it? He might spend all his days thinking he's about to die, that they're his last! You're depriving him of the gift of a second chance!"

I hear Death lift up the chain and seconds later the iron collar is pulling back against my throat. "As much as I love the sight of you chained and on all fours, ass toward me, I think it's time to show you to your room." He gives the chain another yank until I'm staggering to my feet. "And I'm not depriving your father of anything. A man who thinks he's dying, as long as his body permits him, will live out his last days by savoring everything life has to offer. Your father will go on squeezing every last drop out of his life before he finds out he has so much more ahead of him. It's just unfortunate you won't be a part of it."

"And what about Eero and Noora?" I ask.

Death walks around me and I feel his gaze as he stares down at me. I don't want to meet his eyes. I hate knowing he can see me but I can't see him. "You've mentioned them before…"

I don't want to tell Death anything else, give him any more information, but if he knows something about them, I need to know it too. "It's a long story, but they're also shamans and my father's business partners who faked his death when they found out he came here, and then lured me over to Finland with a fake funeral. When I discovered it was all a lie and my father was gone, they tried to kill me. I only escaped because of Rasmus."

A pause. "I see…" he muses. "Eero, you say? What did he look like?"

"Like my dad," I say. "I don't know if all shamans look the same, but they do. Except he looked meaner and his eyes were dark. Noora, she's blonde and short and round. Mid-sixties, maybe, for both of them."

"I'm not sure who they are," Death says after a moment, though I can't tell if he's keeping something from me or not. "But it's not my business, and it's no longer any of yours. You see, Hanna, it doesn't really matter what happens to your father after this, because you won't know about it. You will be here for the rest of your life."

He pauses and I swear he grins. "You will never see your father again."

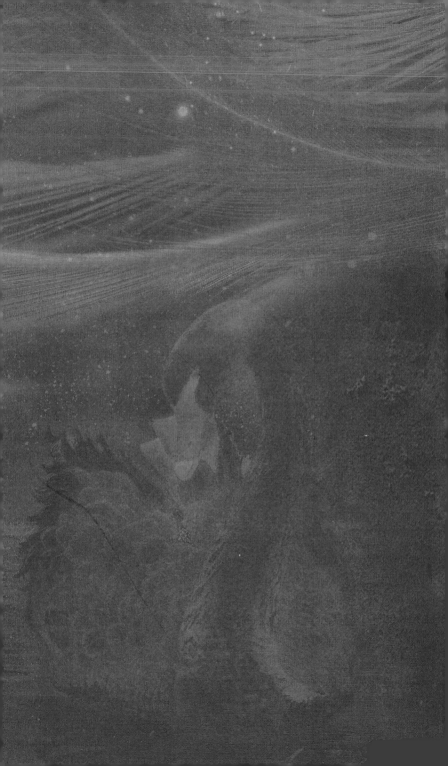

CHAPTER ELEVEN

THE LITTLE MERMAID

I wake up in a bed.

There's a brief moment when I think I'm in my room at home. The way the light is coming in on my face feels similar to how mornings hit when my alarm goes off at seven-thirty. My bedroom is—*was*—north-facing and it faces a McMansion, as our neighborhood not-so-affectionately calls them, so the light is always subdued and filtered, even at the height of summer. Jenny's bedroom faces east, so she gets the sun waking her up every morning, which is nice in theory, but I like the fact that I can sleep in if I want to.

I open my eyes but instead of seeing my popcorn ceiling—which I'm sure is full of asbestos—and the remnants of glow-in-the-dark stick-on stars left behind by renters past, I see a burgundy velvet canopy strung across black-lacquered bed posts.

I slowly push myself up on my elbows, my fight or flight instincts assuming the position. I'm in a very large, long room that looks like a Gothic combination of Victorian and Medieval. There are tall, arched windows beside the bed which look out onto…well, maybe there's usually a view but there's nothing but mist at the moment, providing just enough morning light to illuminate the space. It would be dark even with direct sunlight streaming in, since the walls are charcoal gray in color with subtle gold designs, and though there are melted candles affixed every few feet, none of them are currently lit.

The floor is a dark wood, a change from all the black marble I'd seen so far, with lush Turkish-style carpets strewn about. In one corner of the room is an iron partition, hinting at a large claw-foot tub behind it. At the corner closest to me is a wardrobe made of gleaming burgundy that matches the canopy and drapes, with a vanity desk and large silver mirror above it, the kind of mirror I'd be afraid to look into. And at another corner is a black velvet chaise lounge with a pile of old books bound in cracked leather, what looks like an iPad placed on top of them, and a very large, long aquarium. In the dim light I can't tell if it has water or anything in it, but my attention immediately goes back to the iPad. Surely it just looks like one, right?

I lift the heavy covers to get out of bed and investigate but pause in horror when I look down at myself. I'm not in my jeans and sweater, as gross and uncomfortable as they were. Instead, I'm in a black, gauzy nightgown with buttons down the middle and ruffles at the sleeves.

"Oh my god," I say out loud, my voice sounding hollow in the cavernous room. Someone dressed me? Was it Death? Was it me? My memories from last night are blank. I remember my father—oh god, Papa—and then I remember Death leading me to this room but everything else just blurs after that. Did that white centipede go up my nose too?

I press my fingers along the side of my nose, as if to find it there, then carefully swing my legs over the side of the bed. My body is sore as hell from my aching muscles but when I examine my legs and arms there are no bruises, and though my bra and underwear have been removed, I don't particularly feel like my body has been violated.

My soul feels violated though.

The floor is cold against my feet and I spy a pair of slippers near the bed. They're black felt and the soles are lined with fluffy fur but I'm entirely untrusting of this place and refuse to put my bare feet in them. Death seems like the type to put black widow spiders in there for his own amusement.

I walk around the corner of the bed.

I'm not alone.

A shadow moves off the wall and glides toward me.

I scream but nothing comes out, my breath caught in my throat.

The shadow stops a couple of feet away. It's about my height and dressed in a long black robe that trails to the floor, pooling around it like ink. The face is completely hidden by a black veil.

Do not be frightened, a voice says, slipping into my brain in the same manner that Sarvi's did. It's a female voice, young and light, and it doesn't match up with the eerie figure in front of me.

"Who are you?" I say, my voice stilted as I try to catch my breath.

Raila, she says. *I'm your personal Deadmaiden.*

"My personal *what*?"

Deadmaiden, the faceless girl repeats, though her voice

remains good-natured and sweet. *I have been waiting for a long time to serve someone, so excuse me if I seem a little excited. My last master was Tuonen, the son of Death, but since he lives elsewhere most of the time, I've had no one to tend to. You will be my first mortal, so please pardon me if I ask too many questions. You don't have to answer them.*

"Okay," I say warily. My heart is starting to slow again and I take in a deep breath. "What if I have questions? Will you answer them? Because I have a lot."

Would you like some coffee before your questions? she asks.

I'm about to tell her no, but the thought of coffee makes my body flood with endorphins, as if a cup of Joe in the Land of the Dead is going to fix all my problems.

"What's the coffee made of?" I ask suspiciously. "Snails and puppy dog tails?"

Good gods, no, Raila says, sounding aghast. *The finest Ethiopian beans. Death has others bring it back from the Upper World, though our cook Pyry struggles to grow them here. It's the lack of sun, they say. You know the master's moods, though.*

"He's not my master."

Death is everyone's master, she says cheerfully. *I'll go bring you some coffee. It's a rare treat, Death rarely shares his brew with anyone else.*

She turns, her cloak sweeping the floor.

"Wait!" I call out.

She pauses, and then turns back around to face me.

"What happened to me last night? Or yesterday? I don't remember." I rub at my forehead as if that will jog my memory. "I remember my father being taken away and then Death brought me here…were you here?"

She nods. *You were in a state of delirium brought on by stress.*

"Did you bathe me?" Please don't tell me Death saw me naked.

She nods again. *I did. It is my job as your Deadmaiden. I made you a bath, put you in it, dressed you. You shall have another bath today. You were awfully dirty, and my touch was light.*

She turns again and I watch as she goes to the wide wood door at the end of the room. When it closes shut behind her I hear her insert a key and lock it.

Figures. Maybe not all prisoners get their own servants and coffee, but the one thing we have in common is that we don't have our freedom.

Freedom. The one thing I always took for granted. Now I'm stripped of it, shuttered in another world. Come to think of it, I took my father for granted too. Now I'll never see him again.

"This has to be a bad dream," I say to myself. "It just has to be. None of this can be real."

But real or not, it is my reality now. I collapse to the floor in a fit of tears, crying for my father, for my old life, for my new one, for how quickly everything can change.

I don't know how long I stay on the floor crying, but I don't realize Raila has come back in until I see her black cloak obscuring my vision.

I brought your coffee, she says, as if I'm not curled up at her feet. *And I managed to sneak a honeycake from Pyry. It's made with Hallabee Honey, a Tuonela speciality.*

"I'm not hungry," I say like a petulant child. Truth is, I'm starving, but eating is the only thing I can control right now.

That's fine, I'll put it on the table. You can eat and drink it whenever you wish, though the coffee is better hot. So the master says.

I push myself up so that I'm staring up at the black veil in front of her face. It could be anything or anyone back there, but judging by her voice, I'm picturing a cherubic-faced blonde.

Would you like a hand? she asks, about to set down the tray on the bed.

"No, I was just having a moment," I say, getting to my feet. It's then that I notice her hands. She has black gloves on, satin with obsidian pearls.

It's good to have moments, she says, bringing the tray over to the table and setting it down. A waft of coffee hits my nose and even that makes me feel more alive. *I was told to never cry, to always keep it in, that my feelings didn't matter. I believe my life would have turned out differently had I let my emotions out. To keep them inside is far more harmful. I learned that the hard way. So did everyone else.*

I sit on the edge of the bed, unsure what to do with myself, but intrigued by my new companion. "You said you had never served a mortal before? Are you a God of sorts? Or a spirit?"

Raila laughs. It has a musical quality. *Oh, good gods. No. I was a mortal, just like you. A very long time ago.*

I frown, feeling uneasy. "So…you're dead?"

She nods. *I am. Quite dead.*

I swallow hard, suddenly afraid of what's behind her veil. Perhaps it's not a cherubic blonde after all. "How long have you been dead?" It sounds like an insane question, but I'm asking it.

She shrugs lightly. *It is hard to say. Time is different over here. It's slow at times and fast at others and doesn't obey any laws. It has to be that way, otherwise this place would be overrun by the recently deceased. In our old world, the Upper World, I believe there were hundreds of people dying every minute. That's too much for any God to handle. Here it slows down.*

"I thought all the dead were in the City of Death?"

They are, she says. *Well, not all of them. There are the Deadhands and the Deadmaidens, who serve the master and his family. Then there are the Stragglers.*

This isn't the first time I've heard the term Stragglers.

"So you died and you…have to work? For Death? Like, forever?"

She nods again. *It is an honor.*

"Is it, though?" I squint at her.

I was an Inmost Dweller before. I can assure you this life is quite the improvement.

My mouth drops for a moment. "Isn't that Hell? Or something like that?"

Yes, it certainly is.

"Why did you go to Hell?"

I killed my whole family, she says simply, and I try not to flinch. *Alas, I had to pay the price. But the master was having a contest and I won the chance at redemption by working for him here. It's the same for all the Deadhands and Deadmaidens. We've all been given second-chances at a better afterlife.*

I stare at her, dumbfounded, feeling the skin prickle at the back of my neck again. She's a murderer? Who was in Hell? And now she's my personal servant?

I know what you're thinking, she says. *I can assure you that my past is my past. I have changed and grown while I've been in the sanctity of Shadow's End, my new life devoted to serving Death.*

"What about the others in this castle? Are they as reformed as you?"

She hesitates and I both wish and don't wish I could see her eyes. *Not all. But they try. The ones in the house are mostly though. They know a good thing when they see it. Pyry is crass but she's a good cook and gardener. Harma is head of the household, and you're best to stay out of her way or she'll hit you with her femur. And then there's Avanta. She's Loviatar's Deadmaiden. She's a nice girl but she's been mute for decades. Death put a spell on her, as a warning of what happens when you don't shut up.*

At the mention of Lovia's name my heart races. "Lovia lives here? Death's daughter?"

She does. When she's not working. Her brother and her trade off in ferrying in the dead. I believe she's with Death right now, having a meeting.

"Oh fuck." I look down at my hands and start wringing them together.

What?

"I'm pretty sure Lovia wants to kill me," I say, glancing up at her and seeing nothing but the veil.

She cocks her head. *Oh? Have you two met?*

"We have. It didn't go well…something about me being not dead." And kicking her off the boat, stealing her sword and murdering the swan. But I feel like I need Raila on my good side, so I don't mention that. Even though she is a murderer and would probably understand.

I see. Raila turns around and starts heading toward the door. *Well, I shall leave you alone for now. I don't know what the master has on the agenda today, but I'll be back again later. Make sure you eat up.*

I watch as she leaves, locking me back in the room again.

I sigh and flop back on the bed. What could possibly be on Death's agenda? A little torture at eleven a.m.? A funeral at lunch? Spend the afternoon holding a job fair in Hell?

"This has to be a dream," I say again, as if that will make it true. I've felt my share of pain here and my muscles are needing an Aleve something fierce, and yet I'm still holding hope that none of this is real, that I'm back in my bed in LA, in a deep, deep sleep. Hell, since we're wishing, I'm wishing that I'm about to wake up to a Sunday, where Jenny and I will take the surfboards up to Malibu, catch a few sets, have a boozy brunch somewhere there, maybe find some guys. In the background of all this, my father will still be alive and in Finland, and I'll have never set foot in this place.

My stomach growls as I get another whiff of the coffee. Despite how tired and hopeless I feel, I'm getting up and padding over to the table, surprised to find the coffee is served in a mini French press. Beside it is a mug that looks carved from some kind of glittering black stone, with a cinnamon bun-type of pastry with a thick honey glaze on a matching stone plate.

I pick up the French press, peering at it.

Ikea. It's from *Ikea.*

"The fuck?" I mutter, but I guess it makes sense in a gonzo way. Whoever is doing Death's errands back in the normal world must have needed a coffee maker to go along with the beans and thought a quick trip to Ikea would suffice.

I pour myself the coffee, wondering how that transaction

would have gone, surely Ikea employees would be suspicious of people shopping in black robes and skeleton hands. I take a tepid sip.

Holy shit. It tastes heavenly. Or what do they really call heaven, Amaranthus? This is a beverage fit for the lucky ones in Amaranthus.

I eye the bun, or honeycake as Raila called it, from some kind of hullabaloo bee. It looks good. Really good. I reach for it but stop myself. I've barely had any food and I can feel myself slipping into old habits. Bad habits. Back when everything revolved around what I put in my body, first brought on by the insane need to be light and skinny in competitive ballet, then because controlling what I ate was the only time I had control in a world completely driven by my mother.

You deserve to eat, I tell myself. *You need to eat. You don't need to rebel, you need as much strength as possible to fight your way out of here.*

I reach for it again, but hesitate.

"It's not poisonous!" A girl's voice rings out across the room.

"Shit!" I yelp, nearly spilling the coffee. I whip around, searching for the source. Just how many people are hiding in this room?

"At least, I don't think it's poisonous," the girl adds. "You could give me some and I'll try it out for you. I haven't had honeycake in a long time."

With shaking hands I put the coffee down and walk across the middle of the room, looking around. "Where are you? *Who* are you?"

"I'm in the tank," the voice says.

"In the what?" The tank? Does she mean the bathtub? I start towards it.

"The fish tank," the woman clarifies sullenly. A splash follows.

The fuck? How could anyone be in the fish tank?

I walk over to it behind the velvet chaise lounge chair. Like earlier, it doesn't look like much since there's not a lot of light. I can see there's water in it now, some rocks, some aquatic plants that may or may not be real. It's quite large, actually, but definitely not big enough for a person.

Then I see a flash of white and suddenly there's a little mermaid pressed up against the glass, banging her tiny fists on it for a moment before popping her head out of the water.

"Here I am," she says with big aqua eyes.

I bite back a scream.

Okay. *Okay.* I know I've already seen mermaids, and seen a lot weirder, more fantastical things than that, but this little mermaid in the fish tank might just take the cake.

Again, I have *so* many questions.

"Why are you in a fish tank?" I ask when I've composed myself.

"Death put me here."

"Why are you…so small?"

"Death put a spell on me."

"Why are you able to talk?"

"I'm the opposite of the fairy tale."

It's hard to think when I'm staring at her. She's about the size of a Barbie-doll, with a shimmering white tail that flashes different colors when she moves. Her breasts are bare—no seashells here—her hair long and white. Her face is perfect, small nose, huge aqua-blue eyes that seem to sparkle, heart-shaped mouth. I suppose the other mermaids could have looked like her too, I was just in a near drowning incident at the time and hadn't been paying *too* much attention to their beauty.

"The fairy tale," she repeats, giving me a look of impatience as she hangs her arms over the edge of the tank, her tail whooshing behind her. "You know the one. There's a mermaid, she wants legs, she trades her voice to the sea witch in exchange for them. Well for me, I was finally given a voice, after Death decided to keep me as his pet. Granted, I had a voice before, he just couldn't understand what I was saying."

Suddenly Vellamo's wish pops into my brain. "You're the mermaid I'm supposed to free!"

"I hope so," she says, batting her thick lashes at me, water droplets falling off them and onto the floor. "There could be others. I hope not."

I come closer to her to get a better look. It's so fucking cool. I mean, a little unnerving and even creepy if I'm being honest, because adult humans aren't supposed to be a foot tall, so she really does seem like a doll come to life. She also has this beauty that I think is supposed to ensnare and entrap people, but so far my track record with the mermaids has been good, so I have to assume she doesn't mean me any harm. Besides, she's in a prison just like I am.

"Okay, so how do I free you?" I ask her, looking around the room. "So far I can't even free myself. Does that window open? If I chuck you out of it, will you land in the sesa?"

The mermaid's brow goes up. "No one is chucking anyone

out of a window. Was it Vellamo that you spoke with?"

I nod. "She said one of her own was taken here to be a pet. She never said anything about you being this small though."

She looks annoyed. I don't blame her. "Death has always been fascinated with us, and dare I say, we with him. Or any Gods or mortals or shamans, any men with two legs. Women too, don't get me wrong, but the men are our game. But we're also a game to Death. He's all about games, you see." That I know already. "He brought me here, promising me a new life. He kept me in the underground waterways, deep beneath the castle. There are tunnels under there, and the sea goes in and in, all the way to the Caves of Vipunen. Of course, no one would dare go that far back."

All this speak of underground caverns and waterways and I'm picturing *The Phantom of the Opera*. Without knowing exactly what Death's face looks like, my imagination wants to run away on me.

"But it wasn't long before I wanted to be out in the open sea, under the moon and stars at night, but he said I was his and that I had to stay. And so he put bars over the entrances to the underground cavern, so I couldn't swim out. I was trapped. All I had for company were the occasional fish who dared to swim that far under Shadow's End."

"So what happened?" I ask, as if we're just two girls talking about a date gone wrong over drinks.

"He would visit me of course, we would have our fun. Death is very fond of the water…" she gets an almost wistful look on her face when she says that. "But he tired of always having to travel down to the subterranean levels. He especially hates having to go past the crypt."

"I'm sorry, there's a crypt and *Death* of all people has a problem with it?"

She smirks. "The crypt is a church. For the Sect of the Undead. It's a relic, from the old days. He's not allowed to demolish it. He had to build the castle *around* it." While I mull that over, she goes on. "Anyway, one day he took me upstairs and put me in his bathtub, and I could only last a few days before it was killing me. I can be out of water, as you see I'm breathing air, but I mainly breath underwater through my gills. I can only be out of water for a couple of hours. Three at the most. Then my lungs start to cave in. Very nasty, very painful. There was just enough water in his bathtub for me to float."

The poor thing. "What an asshole."

She giggles, then covers her hand with her mouth. "I shouldn't laugh. But yes. He is. He had good intentions, I guess, because after that he disappeared into the Library of the Veils for a while and when he came out, dripped some purple wax on me and I shrank. Then he gave me a voice, and I'm sure immediately regretted it. Put me in the tank to keep him company."

"So why are you in my room?"

Her face falls. "He lost interest in me. Seems I'm not of much use when I'm this small. I should have tried to be his companion, should have pretended to love him, dote on him, do anything for him, but I was too angry. He didn't want me killed, and he didn't want me freed either, so he kept me in the tank and put me in here. I'm lucky that Lovia likes me and remembers I exist, otherwise I'd never get anything to eat and my tank would never get cleaned." She then perks up. "So, while we're on the subject of food, if you're not going to eat that honeycake…"

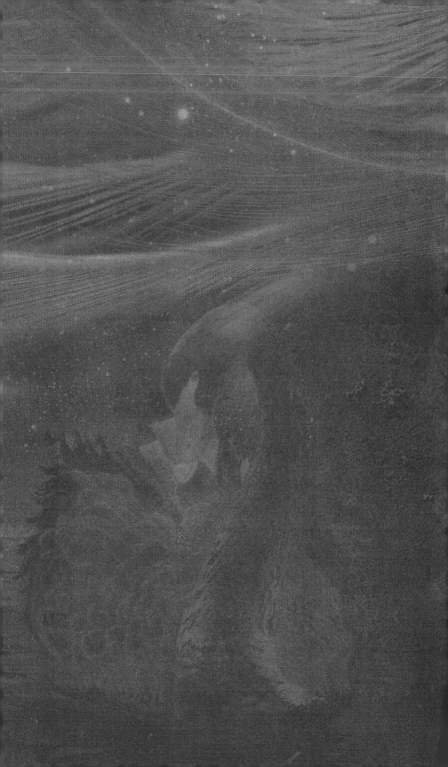

CHAPTER TWELVE

THE GAME

I go across the room to the honeycake and grab the plate, along with my cup of coffee, mouthing *holy shit* to myself because I've had a strange day already and it's just getting stranger. I'm Death's prisoner, I have my own personal servant who is possibly a monster under that veil (and definitely a murderer), *and* I have a doll-sized mermaid in my fish tank.

I walk back to her. She's waiting somewhat impatiently, tapping her hands on the side of the tank, her tail swishing back and forth. I wish I could light some candles in here because I bet her scales would reflect a rainbow of colors.

"So do I scatter it in the tank like fish food?" I ask.

"Very funny," she says.

I hand her the bun and she takes hold of it with deceptively strong arms, tearing into it. I don't know if her lower jaw unhinges from her skull or what happens but suddenly she's tearing into it like a piranha and in seconds it's all gone, only a few crumbs floating to the floor.

"Don't worry, the bonemice will get those," she says, wiping her mouth with the back of her forearm.

I don't even want to ask what a bonemouse is.

"Thank you," she then says after she swallows. "I can't remember the last time I've eaten. Lovia should have been to see me by now with some grouse or salmon, anything left over from dinner. I guess with you here, the castle is up in arms. Out of whack."

"What makes you say that?"

She lifts a shoulder in a dainty shrug. "If you haven't noticed, we aren't used to having mortals in our presence. First your father, now you."

At the mention of my father my heart pangs. "Did you know my father?"

She nods. "But not well. I only met him a couple of times, when Death showed me off."

My face scrunches up. "You mean Death was showing my father around the castle?"

"That was my understanding. He was in the same situation as you, in a way. A prisoner, unable to leave Shadow's End, but he had coffee in the mornings and roast dinners and was able to roam the halls and rooms, everywhere except the crypt and the library. And Death's bedroom, of course."

While I'm relieved to know my father wasn't treated nearly as poorly as I had imagined, I have to point out, "Except I'm not allowed to roam anywhere. I heard Raila lock me in."

The mermaid nods again. "I know. For now, you're trapped in here, under lock and key. But if you play your cards right, you'll have full rein of the castle in no time. And then, when the time is right, the both of us can escape. So what say you? Will you get me out of here if I tell you how to make this situation work for you?"

"What do you mean?"

"Well let's get my needs down first, because they're the easiest to fulfill. When the moon is full, you must take me to the Stargaze Tower. It's at the very south of the building, has a telescope and star maps and everything. You can't miss it. You'll watch through the telescope for Kuutar to appear, and she'll make sure I have safe passage to the sea. In other words, you can finally chuck me out of a window. The water is right below."

"Kuutar!" I exclaim softly. "Vellamo mentioned her. I thought it was a place."

She shakes her head. "Kuutar is the Goddess of the Moon. Anyone from the sea worships her, as she controls the tides. And because we rarely get the sun here, we bask in her light when we can."

"What if it's cloudy?" I ask. "It's always cloudy. Because of Death."

"His moods make it cloudy, but there are exceptions. When he's asleep, it clears. It's why so much of Tuonela worships the stars and astronomy. It's a celebration. When he's happy it clears too, but that rarely happens. More often than not it snows or rains or is this never-ending mist. Drives you bonkers."

"Like living in San Francisco."

She frowns. "I guess?"

"Speaking of bonkers," I say. "Where did you pick that word up?"

"Lovia," she says proudly. "When I was gifted the chance to speak, not all the translations went through properly. Lovia taught me the rest. But she also spends a lot of time in the mortal world, so she's picked up on a lot of your slang through the ages. I wouldn't know if what I'm saying is right or not."

"It's all good," I tell her. "What is your name anyway? I'm Hanna."

I smile and hold out my fingertip, wondering if this is weird or cheesy or offensive to mermaids.

But she just laughs and grabs hold of the tip of my finger, shaking it. "I'm Bell. It's not my real name, that name doesn't translate. But Death named me Bell. Well, actually it was Tinkerbell, but Lovia made him change it."

You've got to be kidding me. What is his obsession with Peter Pan?

"Anyway," Bell says, "I really appreciate you doing me this favor. Once Kuutar gets me to the sea and guides me home, I'll be reunited with Vellamo and my sisters again."

"But you'll be small."

"I'm sure it will have its advantages. After all, the giant pikes are giant, no matter if you're my size or if you're full-grown. But the sisters will take care of me." A serious look comes across her face. "But while that takes care of me, it doesn't help you much, does it? You want to know how to get out of here, don't you? Back to your homeland? The Upper World?"

I nod eagerly. "Yes. Yes, more than anything. *Please*."

If I could escape from here, I could be reunited with my father, who will be cured of his cancer. I'll have a do-over for everything. I can bring him back home with me to LA, or we could move somewhere else in Finland and I could get a new job, it doesn't matter anymore. Wherever he will be, I will be there too. I'm never letting go of our second chance.

"Then take it from me," she says gravely. "Because I've been in your shoes. Whatever Death wants, you do it and you do it with a smile on your face." My face must immediately fall because she cocks her head. "I mean it. Be as charming and seductive and willing as possible. You want Death to want you, not just physically—I'm sure that's a given there—but emotionally. That's the key. That's what I didn't have the strength or the foresight to do, but I think you could do it. You seem strong enough."

I slowly blink, my stomach sinking. "But you…originally you were into him, were you not?"

She laughs dryly, the sound echoing off the glass of the tank. "I was. I'm a mermaid. And he is the king. The ruler of the land. There is something…undeniably sexy about that."

I make a face, which makes her laugh again. "I take it you haven't seen him without his mask on," she says.

"Mask?" I repeat, leaning in. "He's wearing a mask? I thought he was just a skull."

"It's a mask," she says. "He has many of them. He wears them outside the castle to instill respect and fear in anyone in Tuonela, but especially the City of Death. After all, he has a reputation to uphold. He wants the newly dead to fear him so that they behave. He also wants the Stragglers to fear him too, but that's another story."

"What are the Stragglers? I keep hearing them mentioned."

"They're the original dead. When Death was brought in to rule the land, and lift it out of *Kaaos*, the dead had the choice to either join the new afterlife in the City of Death, or stay behind.

A lot stayed behind, fearing their lives in the City would be worse. Some of them may have been right. Maybe a lot of them, because Inmost is a horrific place, and most of them deserved to be in that place for all the things they'd done. So in other words, the worst of the worst opted to stay behind in Tuonela. Some say they're plotting an uprising against Death, some say that they're under control of Louhi."

"Who is Louhi?"

She gives me an incredulous look.

"I'm sorry," I explain. "I literally know *nothing*."

"Louhi," she says softly, as if she's afraid of being overheard. "Is the Goddess of Death. Or the ex-Goddess of Death."

"Death's wife?"

"Ex-wife. They separated long ago. She ran off to the Star Swamps with Ilmarinen, a shaman, and built a new home there. No one has seen her in years. Even Lovia doesn't see her and I don't think Tuonen, her brother, does either. Some say she's also a witch, but she's always been part demon, and that part is the one you'll know her by."

Again, so many questions, but I know I have to let some go for now.

As if reading my mind, Bell licks her lips and says, "I don't think Death realizes I'm still alive and still here, so I would appreciate it if you don't mention me. When Raila is here, don't talk to me. Or look at me. Or mention me. Just pretend I don't exist. Otherwise I'm afraid he'll take me away, or worse." She shudders, perhaps picturing herself being eaten as fish food.

"I can do that," I tell her. "I don't want you taken away. So, I can't trust Raila?"

She makes a so-so motion with her hands. "You can trust her in that she won't hurt you and she won't purposely go and tell anything to Death. But he is her master so under oath, she may blab. On the other hand, there are rumors that one of the Deadmaidens is part of the uprising. It might be her. Might not be. Best to just keep your mouth shut when it comes to important matters."

I look away at the room, at my prison for the next while. Perhaps forever. It's not *awful*. But you know, I'd rather not be here forever.

"What does Death want from me?" I ask after a few moments pass.

"I can't say for sure," Bell muses, "but I think he gets lonely."

I give her a steady look, brow raised. "Lonely? Death gets *lonely*? How could he lonely, when he's got a constant influx of people to deal with?"

"Everyone dies. Everyone goes to the City of Death. But he doesn't live there, he lives here. He's forever their ruler, their overlord. He can't befriend them. He has to make do with what he has here. I think that's what his problem is. He just has a funny way of dealing with it. Sometimes a cruel way of dealing with it." She sighs, her attention to the window, lost to her thoughts.

Finally she looks back to me. "But in the end, if you want your freedom, you have to make him love you, and if you can't make him do that, at least make him want you around. I know it seems counterproductive, but if you do, he'll give you all the freedom in the world. And I know there's some prophecy about Death falling in love again. Maybe you could play into that?"

I scoff, shaking my head. "No. First of all, I'm not that good of an actress."

"Not even if your life depends on it?"

My mouth opens and closes again. When she puts it that way… "Second of all, he's Death. I don't think Death can fall in love."

"Why not? There's no curse that says he can't. He probably loved Louhi at some time before she went full-on evil."

"Well then, they should have been a match made in heaven."

"Death isn't evil," she says.

I raise my palm. "Do *not* tell me he's just misunderstood."

She gives me a sly grin. "That's too cliché, as you mortals would say. If he's misunderstood, I think it's by mortals themselves. Lovia has told me the stories about the Grim Reaper; they all sound like fantasy to me. No, Death is just a God, like any other God. And they love and they lose and they hate and they cry. I know Death fairly well and there's no emotion that he's unable to feel…it's just that his role has made the emotion more or less obsolete."

"You mean love?"

"Something like that."

The way she says it, almost forlornly, makes me wonder if Bell had wanted Death to fall in love with her. I can't really blame her. It's a tale as old as time to have a beast fall in love with the beauty, the beast everyone says can't be redeemed.

But I have no clue how I would make Death fall in love with me, especially since I have been extremely unlucky in love. Sure, I've had my fair share of boyfriends, but nothing ever stuck, nothing ever meant anything other than a few months of fun and then boredom. I prefer the flings and the one-night stands and the occasional low-douche fuckbois, just so I can have an active sex life and work off my stress that way. It takes all the pressure off of futures and relationships and love.

So, while I appreciate Bell's belief in me, I know that's not in the cards. If I can't make a mortal dudebro fall in love with me, then I certainly can't make the God of Death fall in love with me.

That said, she has a bit of a point, one I begrudgingly admit. My first instinct is to kick and scream and fight my way out of here. But maybe that's not the best approach for this situation. I have to have an end goal and I need a strategy to achieve it. He expects me to hate him, I'm sure, so it would really throw him for a loop if I did the opposite.

I sigh, rubbing my palm along my forehead. It already seems too much to take on. Hopeless.

"Just start small," Bell suggests. "You don't want to make him suspicious anyway."

That's true. Start small. I could be nicer. I could be more compliant and less rebellious. I could do things with a smile. I have my limits, for sure, but when it comes to an eternity of this—or even worse, being shrunk and put into a *cage*—I know I could somehow get through it. The only problem is, I was stupid enough to already offer a range of services and he's already taken me up on those offers and enjoyed it immensely. *Treat me like a dog? Humiliate me?* For some reason I don't think cooking and cleaning is going to cut it for him. It's going to be *have your way with me* and or *let others do the same*.

Or, fuck. *Make me your bride.*

Why the hell did I say that?

"Make me your bride?" Bell repeats.

I look at her with wide eyes. "You read minds too?"

"No, you just said it with your mouth."

I run my hands over my face and growl. "Urgh. I had told Death earlier that he could take me in exchange for my father, and then I offered various reasons why he should. One was that he could make me his bride."

"Hmmmm," she says.

"What?" I shoot her a sharp glance.

She purses her lips together for a moment. "As I said earlier, there's a prophecy. Perhaps you could find out more about it from Raila and play into it? If you could be Death's bride…"

"I don't want to be Death's bride!" I yell.

"Shhhh," she hisses, motioning with her tiny hands to tone it down. "Take it easy, mortal girl. What I'm saying is if you could be Death's bride, that would make you the Goddess of Death. The new one. And then you could do anything." She notes the disgruntled look on my face because she quickly adds, "It doesn't have to mean anything. Have him marry you, or fall in love with you, or at least like you enough to give you more freedom. Make him happy. Do what you can to make that happen, make him want you and want to be around you. Then when you get it, you escape. You go back home. They can't get you there. That's your world, your terrain. You'll be safe. You'll be with your father, you'll get to live your life again, and none of this would have counted. *None of it.*"

I stare at her, wishing it could all be as easy as she makes it sounds.

Then the sound of the key in the lock makes me back away, the rest of my coffee spilling to the floor, and Bell ducks under the water, swimming into the back corner, disguised by an aquatic plant.

I run over to the bed and sit down on the end of it, coffee in hand, trying not to shake, just as the door opens.

The tall figure of Death strides in, a sight that makes my entire body tingle, with fear and something else, something ancient and primal.

"Good morning, fairy girl," he says in a booming voice that carries across the room. "How are you planning on annoying me today?"

Go fuck yourself, I almost say but Bell's suggestion rings in my ears. Nice. I have to play nice. No, I have to play *more* than nice. I have to act like I want to be here, want to be with him, and I have to do it in a way that doesn't read fake either.

No fucking pressure or anything.

"My, my, my," he says, folding his arms across his massive chest and staring down at me. "Those wheels are definitely turning. Plotting my demise? Have complaints about your coffee?"

I watch as he removes his hood so that his face is no longer hidden in shadow, my eyes widening at the sight. He has a different skull on today, a totally new face. A human skull with gilded teeth stretched in a macabre smile and impressive gold ram horns that curl back from the head. The gold matches the accents on his black leather gauntlets that cover his hands. The rest of his clothes underneath his black velvet robe are dark colored with leather accents at the waist and shoulders.

Somehow he manages to look both medieval and modern.

I feel his eyes burn from behind the skull as I continue to gape at him. "I take it you're impressed by my mask of the day."

"I was more impressed by the French press you got from Ikea," I remark. "What is the story with that?"

He tilts his head, and I feel him study me closer. It's most unnerving, to feel someone's eyes so clearly and yet still not see them. Since this is a mask he's wearing, I find myself trying to see into the depths of the eye sockets, to see a hint of iris or whites of his eye, like I thought I did the other day. But there's nothing but a black void.

The most disturbing thought enters my head: what if he doesn't even have eyes? What if he's wearing a mask because the thing underneath is even scarier than the masks he wears?

"You're very observant," he says in his low, silken voice. "And I have to admit, I find it fascinating that in all that you've seen so far, it's my coffee-making device that has you asking questions."

"I have more questions," I say. "You have a mask of the day. Why? You ugly or something?"

The air in the room goes still and I swear I hear Bell gasping underwater. I'm preparing for a clap of thunder, or perhaps a lashing of rain against the window, but the heavy pause ends when Death bursts out laughing. The sound is hearty and sincere, filling the room, and it makes me wonder how often he laughs like this.

"Oh, I am going to enjoy having you here," he says, still chuckling. "It's unfortunate you probably won't feel the same," he adds in a more solemn tone.

"You don't know that," I tell him.

"You're right," he says after a moment. "You might like it in the end. Oh, you'll fight me on everything, you'll hate me with all your fury. But you might love to hate me, and that will make all the difference."

"I will never *love* you," I find myself sneering.

Good job with the make him fall in love you thing, Hanna.

Another chuckle. "Good," he muses. "I wouldn't want to think any less of you. Now, get up." He reaches out and takes the coffee cup from me, which is tiny in his giant gloved hand. "Don't make me ask you again."

Or what, you'll get out the chain? I want to ask, but he probably would and my neck still feels bruised from it. So I get to my feet and stare up at him, trying to find a balance of rebellion and compliance.

Beneath his mask, his eyes are looking me over, thinking. They feel like fire.

Finally, he says. "Take off your nightgown."

My heart sinks.

Is he serious?

"Why?" I ask, trying to sound strong, though my voice trembles.

"Because I'm telling you to. Take off your nightgown."

"I'm naked underneath."

"Quite aware of that, fairy girl." He motions with a nod. "Now take it off or I will take it off for you. Which will it be?"

I swallow hard, knowing my options. There are three. I could refuse, and he could force me, which would undoubtedly be the worst. He probably gets off on the power trip. In fact, I know he does, considering how fond he was of that iron collar.

I could do it while crying, wanting to shrivel up into a ball, horrified at the thought of being naked in general, let alone in front of him. I've spent a long time, through numerous one-night stands, working on my relationship with my body, trying to find the confidence in its strength and in its flaws, trying to overcome all the years of damage I'd inflicted on it, and while I've come far, I'm not sure if I can handle this particular brand of vulnerability and humiliation.

Or I could raise my chin and own it proudly. Be strong. Refuse to give into the panic. Refuse to give him the fear that he desires from me. Refuse to be humiliated.

I choose the last one. I look Death right in those fathomless sockets, steady and calm, and I bring up the hem of my nightgown, pulling it over my head and throwing it behind me on the bed. My head is held high with nerves of steel, despite being oh so very naked right in front of him.

He doesn't say anything. His unseen eyes burn across every inch of my body, from my neck, to my breasts, to my stomach, to between my thighs, leaving goosebumps in their wake.

I swallow hard, trying to bury the terror that wants to drown me. I won't let it. I will be strong. I will not fear.

"Well?" I ask him boldly, with an expectant raise of my brow.

A low, guttural sound rumbles from inside his chest, making the hair on my body stand on end, every nerve inside me tightly wound until it feels like they're going to snap and obliterate me. Jesus. What the hell was that?

Moments pass, the tension between us growing thicker.

Then he clears his throat.

"When I was born, the first person who touched me died," he says in a rough voice, his eyes still leaving flames on my bare body. The way he stares at me feels like consumption. "It was my mother's Birthmaiden. Pirkko was her name. Though I don't remember her, I've never forgotten her name, because I killed her. My first casualty. And you never forget your first one, even as a newborn."

He turns and walks over to the wardrobe, and the moment his eyes leave my body I feel like I'm deflating, exhaling so forcefully that I almost collapse. "You see, my parents were told that one of their sons would be the God of Death, that I would be called into my role as a deity when the time was ready, when Tuonela was ready," he says, running his hands over the lacquered surface of the wardrobe. "They didn't know it was me until Pirkko died, they certainly didn't know that I would come with a price—the touch of death. My mother wanted to hold me and console me, for I was just a crying baby, new to the world, but my father couldn't let her. They are Gods, but even they didn't want to take the chance. Knowing what I know now, it was a wise move."

He sighs. "So, my father wrapped me in reindeer pelt, and it was through a lot of trial and error, in other words a lot of dead servants, that they discovered it was only my hands that caused death. After that I had to wear gloves and gauntlets all the time, but the damage was already done. My siblings stayed away from me, people and Gods alike feared me. Even my own parents treated me differently. More like a pet than a son. Always so distant."

"Am I supposed to feel sorry for you?" I ask, because one sob story isn't going to win me over.

That brings out another chuckle from him as he opens the wardrobe. "No. No one is supposed to feel sorry for Death, and especially not you. You should feel sorry for yourself, standing naked like that, all because I asked you to."

I don't know where this is going, so I decide to keep my mouth shut for now.

He carefully riffles through a drawer in the wardrobe and then brings out a white lacy thing. "Perhaps it was this that made me a better ruler for Tuonela. Because I was cruel at times, but I had empathy. Ruthless but not heartless."

I can't help but snort. *Not heartless? Yeah, you keep telling yourself that, buddy.*

He ignores me. "As you know I eventually got married. I was able to please my wife without touching her with my bare hands, I made it my mission."

"I'm not sure I need to know all this," I mutter.

"But you do," he says quickly, grasping the white dress and coming over to me. "You do. I did all I could and then some, but she said it was the fact that I could never touch her with my bare hands that made her leave me and take up with another. Frankly, I knew that was a lie, and yet I remember the prophecy that the giant Vipunen told me when I was just a young man. That one day I would find someone, the one person able to withstand my touch, a person I would then love and marry, and that an alliance would form, an alliance that would cement my position in the kingdom forever. What alliance and with whom, I don't know, and the one I am to marry? I don't know that either."

"How do you know it wasn't your ex-wife?"

He lets out a sharp, sour laugh. "Louhi? No alliance came of our supposed love or our marriage. If anything our marriage was a strategy on behalf of her father, to further fragment this world when we finally broke apart. No, it wasn't Louhi."

I feel his gaze deepening, tension thickening.

"You think it's me," I say quietly.

"It could be," he says. "I think there is only one way to find out."

He places the dress in my hands and then unsnaps one of his gloves.

I suck in my breath as terror shoots through me.

"What are you doing?" I cry out softly.

He pulls his hand out of the glove and I stare at it in horror and fascination. It's the large, lightly tanned hand of a big man. The only thing unhuman about it are the strange markings that keep pulsing with light, like someone has drawn lines all over his hand and wrist with a metallic gray sharpie, lines that keep glowing for a moment in different spots, as if lit from within. I caught a glimpse of the lines earlier in the desert, and even close up they don't make much sense.

While I'm trying to figure it out, he reaches out to my breast with his bare hand, pausing just inches away, and my body floods with adrenaline, ready to flee.

"If I touched you, I would know," he murmurs. "If I touched you and you didn't die, I would know you were meant to be mine."

I'm frozen, staring down at his hand, unable to move. "Is

that why you're keeping me?"

"One of many reasons," he says, his fingers stretching for me, closer, closer now. I swear I feel the heat burning off them, like an electrical wire on the ground, and I wish my nipples weren't getting hard at a time like this. "But then, if I did touch you, and you died, I'd lose you to Oblivion, which means I would lose you for good. There's no coming back from that— you would never be in my kingdom. And I haven't yet decided if I want to keep you or not, or what use you might be."

Slowly he withdraws his hand and my nerves buzz with relief. "So, as you can see, I'm in a minor predicament. How do I know if you're the one if I can't touch you?"

I need to tell him what he needs to hear in order to keep me. If I don't make a case for myself, at any point he could try the experiment and take off his glove and I would most likely be gone, to suffer for eternity. Because deep down, I know I'm part of no prophecy, no sick and twisted love story. I'm here because I have a loyal heart and a foolish mind, and a bit of rotten luck thrown in there.

Tell him what he needs to hear.

"Perhaps the prophecy takes time," I say slowly, looking down at the clothing in my hands. "Maybe some other things have to happen first before you're sure enough." I glance up at him in a vaguely seductive way, trying to get him to pick up on my meaning without being too obvious about it.

"You think I just need to fuck you in order to find out," he says, the word jarring me, sending an inappropriate flare of heat through my legs. "That's funny, that was my idea too."

Holy shit, he doesn't mess around!

I refuse to let this throw me off-balance, though. I straighten my shoulders slightly, maintaining eye contact. "I had a feeling. Since you made me get undressed."

Somehow I can tell he's smiling under that gruesome mask. "All in due time," he says, slipping his glove back on. "I was just taking stock of my new possession, that's all. Seeing all you have to offer." He looks me over once more. "You're more exquisite than I could have imagined, little bird."

He was right in that I always suck up compliments, but I refuse to acknowledge this one.

He nods at the white dress. "Put that on." He reaches out with his gloved hand and brushes my hair off my shoulder in a strangely tender way that makes me flinch. "With your dark hair and haunting eyes, the black nightgown was far too gloomy for a fairy girl. You should be a bright spot in Shadow's End… while you're still here, anyway."

Then he flips his hood up and over his skull head and turns and walks away, his boots echoing across the room. "We're having dinner tonight," he booms without turning around. "I'll send Raila to help you. I expect you to be washed properly, your hair done, and in a dress from the wardrobe. This is not a request."

And then he's gone.

The key turns in the lock.

CHAPTER THIRTEEN

THE DAUGHTER

After Death left, I wanted to go talk to Bell about everything she just witnessed, but I didn't have a moment to myself. I had just finished putting on the new nightgown—something white, lacy, and satiny that clung to my curves—and not because Death asked me to, but because I didn't want to be naked anymore, when Raila came inside the room. She was all a titter about the dinner tonight and getting me ready for it.

Which meant getting me naked—yet again—and into the tub she filled with steaming hot water. I have to admit, getting past the whole being-nude-in-front-of-strangers part, the bath feels wonderful, especially since she just put a whole bunch of fragrant herbs in it that seem to clear my lungs and head. An unexpected bonus is that the tub has a faucet, which means this castle has indoor plumbing. The toilet in my room is more of squat on the floor style, but at least it ain't shit into a bucket and pour it out the window style. I have a feeling the indoor plumbing thing is something else that one of Death's errand boys procured from the Upper World and once again I picture some skeleton dude perusing Ikea's bathroom department.

It's so very exciting that you get to go to dinner, Raila says as she scoops up the bathwater into a wooden bucket and pours it over my head.

The water gets in my eyes and mouth and I spit it out. She may be my exuberant servant, but she doesn't have a lot of finesse. "I'd rather stay in my room."

Oh no, you must not say that, she says, reaching for a tarnished silver jar on the wood ledge beside the tub and giving it a rough shake. Pale gold semi-translucent liquid gel comes out and she rubs it vigorously between her gloved palms. *Being invited to dinner with the master is a real honor. You are sure to have the finest food and drink in the land. It's no wonder that he wants you to look your best, he hasn't had a beautiful woman in here in such a long time.*

She applies the goop to my wet hair and starts rubbing it into my scalp, rather violently I might add. "You mind easing up there?"

My apologies, she says, the pressure lifting just a little. *My husband said I never had a woman's touch.* She laughs melodically at that, but considering what she did to her husband leaves me feeling just a tad uneasy.

It also doesn't help that I still haven't seen her face beneath that black shroud and she's still wearing satin gloves despite the fact that she's bathing me. I mean wet gloves? Ew.

"Speaking of touch," I say. "Do you have the *touch of death* too? Is that why you're wearing gloves?"

Boy, you really weren't joking when you said you'd be asking lots of questions, she says. She clears her throat, her tone more grave now. *No, I wear gloves, and this shroud, because my appearance isn't very becoming.*

"Well, that's not fair," I tell her as she continues to massage what I'm assuming is shampoo into my head. "I saw the Deadhands with my father. They were skeletons. Why are the Deadmaidens covered up and the Deadhands aren't? Seems kind of sexist to me."

You would have to ask Death, she says. *All I know is that this is the way I am always to present myself when dealing with others.*

She stops lathering my head and then scoops the water in the wood bucket, immediately dumping it over my head, the soap running into my eyes.

Close your eyes, she says cheerfully.

"Yeah thanks for the warning." I wipe my eyes quickly before she pours more water on my head, the bathtub filling with suds.

"When was the last woman here?" I ask as she starts shaking another tin jar into her hand. "You said it had been a long time since a beautiful one was here."

Well, Lovia is beautiful, but I don't think you mean her. There was Louhi of course. She was Queen. She was the Goddess of the Underworld.

"And what is she now?"

Not here, Raila says simply.

"What does she look like?"

Beautiful, in a savage way, she says, rubbing some thick red goop into my strands, making my dark hair blood-colored.

"Please don't tell me that's bat's blood or something," I say, gesturing to the lotion.

It's conditioner, she says. *I'm not sure what it does. I don't have any hair myself, but Lovia created it with the skin of frostberries. Sure does look like blood doesn't?* She says that last part almost wistfully and I try not to cringe.

"But what does Louhi look like?" I ask again, strangely fascinated with Death's ex and their messy relationship. "Can you describe her?"

Oh sure. Tall. Taller than you. Very slender. Narrow hips. Big breasts. White skin. I try not to roll my eyes, since Death seems to have gone totally stereotypical in his choice of wife. *Fangs,* she then adds. *Claws. White eyes. Several large ridged horns coming out of her head. Giant wings. Long red hair.*

"Wings?" My eyes widen. "Horns? Real horns?"

Well, she is part demon, Raila informs me. *Part witch too. Lapp Witch, the oldest and most cunning of the witches.*

The image I've conjured in my head is terrifying. "Something tells me I don't want to meet her."

I would advise against it, Raila says, pouring water over my head again while I sputter. *But she's not allowed to step foot inside Shadow's End. They have an agreement. In exchange for letting her live, she's not allowed to leave the Star Swamp. She has her lover there in her own castle, but she can't see Death or her children or interfere with the politics of the worlds at all. She had to give up her crown of crimson.*

"And so far she's done that?" I ask warily. If she's part demon *and* part witch, I don't see her giving up all her power and prestige so easily.

So far, Raila says, scooping up another bucket of water. I pinch my eyes shut and hold my breath as it cascades down again. *There. Nearly done.*

I look down. The tub is a gruesome sight, the red conditioner turning the water a wicked shade of red, like I'm bathing in blood. It makes me think of Louhi's crimson crown.

"Was it an actual crimson crown?" I ask, moving my hands under the water so that I create waves of blood. "Does she still have it?"

As I said, she gave it up. It's in the crypt. Waiting for the next Goddess, I suppose.

I think back to the prophecy. Death seems to think that whomever he's allowed to touch without killing them will end up becoming the new Goddess of Death. Is that where the alliance is formed? Between him and his future wife? Or is the alliance between other worlds or other gods?

Okay, stand up, Raila says to me, snapping me out of my thoughts.

I stand up in the bathtub, trying not to slip, fighting the urge to cover my breasts and nether region. There's no point, she's seen it all.

She's grabbing yet another tin jar and shaking what looks like brown sugar into her gloved palms. *Time for a scrub*, she says. *Lovia taught me to do this as well. She said the mortals use it for exfoliating these days. Not that I have much skin to scrub.*

I try not to make a disgusted face. I feel like Raila's happy-go-lucky attitude could turn murderous without warning, and having no hair and not much skin might be a sore spot for her. Literally.

Especially as she's applying the scrub to my body and rubbing vigorously. This time I decide to just grin and bear it, even though I feel like she may be trying to remove my skin in the end, perhaps to wear it herself.

I shake those thoughts out of the way as she finishes and starts pouring more water over my body, then slides a wet washcloth over every inch of skin. Finally she brings out a towel and starts drying me off.

There, she says triumphantly. *Squeaky clean. Now to get the powder.* She looks around her. *Oh where did it go?*

"Powder?" I ask when suddenly there's a knock at the door. Before I can yell that I'm naked, the door swings open. To my surprise it's not Death, but a striking woman with long pale blonde hair, dressed in a light gold gown that trails behind her. Even with her deer skull gone, it's obvious who this is.

Lovia.

Oh shit.

"Are you looking for this?" Lovia asks Raila as she struts into the room, her heels clicking, holding out a big black powder puff. Least I hope it's a powder puff, and not some fluffy yet deadly creature.

I was, thank you, Raila says, taking the thing from Lovia. She then comes over to me and starts patting the powder over my skin.

I have no choice but to just commit to being totally naked in front of strangers again. By the time this day is over, I think I could handle a nudist camp.

"Well, well, well," Lovia says, standing in front of the tub, her slender arms crossed. "We meet again, Hanna."

I give her a faint smile. "I think perhaps we got off on the wrong foot."

I mean, she's going to kill me, isn't she?

A wicked grin spreads across her pretty face. "I think you got off on the *right* foot," she says. "I was very impressed you were able to do that. Pissed, but impressed. And to take my sword too."

I shrug as Raila finishes powdering me, my body now slightly gold and sparkly and smelling of honey. "You can do amazing things in self-defense," I admit. "I really do apologize though. And I'm not an animal killer. I didn't want to kill the swans, it just sort of happened."

"Phhff," she says with a dismissive wave of her hand, gold bracelets made of bone jangling on her wrist. "The Swan of Tuonela has been killed many times. It always comes back. You know the relics. Or maybe you don't. The swan was the original gatekeeper before I came along. The relics don't like to let go of their roles, even when not needed. I've been butting heads with it for a long time."

I nod, unsure where this is going. It seems like she's not pissed anymore but I can't trust anyone in this castle, especially anyone in Death's immediate family.

"Anyway, normally I'd probably kill you for doing what you did," she says with a big smile, her teeth perfect and blindingly white. "I do have a reputation to uphold as the Daughter of Death. But usually it's some stupid shaman, like the one you were with, that tries to outsmart me. It's never been a woman before, let alone a mortal woman. So I've decided I don't want to kill you. I think I'd rather be your friend." She leans forward and extends her hand.

I hesitate, then shake it. Her grip is warm and firm and I

try to match it.

"Now," she says, letting go and clapping her hands together, "time to get you dressed for tonight. This is so exciting!"

I concur, Raila says as she wraps a fluffy black towel around me, another item that must have been smuggled from the Upper World. I mean, the normal world. *My* world. Fuck, am I already starting to talk like them?

"What's so special about tonight?" I ask as Raila helps me step out of the tub. "It's just dinner, right?"

Lovia flounces over to the wardrobe and opens it. Unlike the slow deliberate way that Death found the perfect nightgown for me, Lovia erratically flips through the dresses hanging in it. "Tonight you're our special guest, and it's been so long since we've had a guest here." She pauses as she pulls out a black gown and peers at it. "Although, I suppose your father was a guest. But he was never invited for dinner." She puts the dress back and continues her haphazard rifling. "I take it as a very, very good sign."

"A good sign of what?" I ask, hugging the towel close and coming over to her, the floor cold against my soles.

"That he likes you," she says, flashing me a bright smile before rummaging again.

I laugh. "Like me? I'm his prisoner. He's literally promised to ruin and destroy me for eternity."

"Ah, he says a lot of things," she says. "His bark is worse than his bite. I mean, most of the time. Sure, sometimes he'll randomly give someone," she lowers her voice dramatically and wiggles her fingers, *"the hand,"* then she smiles "but who doesn't lose their temper every now and then? Besides, you're gorgeous and you're mortal and you're the daughter of a shaman. All the things that fascinate him." She pauses, bringing out a yellow dress now, and frowns. "Actually, he hates all mortals. And all shamans. But still. If you play your cards right, you'll marry him."

I blink at her. "You actually want me to marry your father? You don't even know me."

"That's true," she says, pulling out a red dress now and comparing it to the yellow. "But it's not every day a non-dead mortal girl comes waltzing into Tuonela, especially one who can fight nearly as good as I can. It was like you were trained by Vipunen yourself. But of course you weren't…" she squints at me, "were you?"

"I don't even know who this Vipunen is," I explain.

"Didn't think so. It's an honor to be trained by him. But play your cards right, and soon you will be. No queen can live here being untrained, especially with all the rumors about an uprising. You have to be ready when the Old Gods resurface to take the throne."

She thrusts the red dress out and holds it against me, studying me like a fine arts student scrutinizing a painting. "This was mine once, but I never wore it. You're a bit thicker than I am, nothing to take personally, I know you mortal women take offense to body stuff, but I think you'll look good in it."

I'm not taking offense to what she said, I'm stuck on the other thing. "This uprising…the Old Gods are going to resurface and take the throne? As in your father's throne?"

She nods and then places the dress in my hands. It's deceptively heavy with many layers. "Hopefully I won't be here when that happens," she says.

"And where are you going to be?"

"In your old world," she says with a dreamy grin. "I want to live among the mortal boys for the rest of eternity, have fun in all the wonderful cities, eat all the delicious foods, and drive all the cars. Except I can't go now. I ferry the dead. It's my role, and though Tuonen, my brother, can handle it, it wouldn't be fair to expect him to do it all the time. But if you married my father, maybe I wouldn't be missed."

Arms up, Raila commands me, taking the dress from my hands.

I absently hand it over and raise my hands, my towel dropping to the floor.

"Don't take this the wrong way," I tell Lovia as Raila slips the dress over my head. It smells like heady perfume, gardenia maybe. "But I think you're getting ahead of yourself here. I'm your father's prisoner. He let my father go and took me instead. What he has planned might not be to marry me."

It might be to have his way with me, then place a bare hand on me and send me off to Oblivion.

Lovia thinks that over for a moment. "Well, maybe. But there's something to be said for looking on the bright side, isn't there? Now, that dress is darling on you. Really. Let's figure out what to do with this hair of yours. It's nearly as long as mine."

While she picks up an ebony comb from the vanity table, Raila starts to do up the corset at the back of the dress.

"Really?" I say, looking at Lovia expectantly as Raila cinches me in. "You've been to my world and yet you're wearing corsets down here?"

She motions to her Grecian-style gown. "As you can tell, I am not. But my father is particular about his women looking a certain way. Unless you're a mermaid." She laughs at that and Raila joins in and I'm remembering Bell again, hiding in her fish tank and watching this whole thing. Surely Lovia will remember that she's there? Then again, she did say she has a bad memory.

I hold my breath in worry, wondering if Lovia will remember and maybe take Bell away from me. But Lovia just takes the comb and starts going through my hair.

"Wish I had a blow-dryer," she pouts, braiding my hair. "I'm sure you've noticed, but we don't have electricity here. We have starstones and they can power things, but they're quite rare. Luckily, I can create fire winds."

"Create what now?"

Suddenly Lovia opens her arms, flames immediately appearing on her skin, then a giant gust of hot wind seems to flow right out of her and onto me.

My eyes pinch shut. I think I scream. It's hard to tell when you're being blown away and nearly engulfed by a fire.

Eventually though, the blowing stops and I dare to open my eyes. Both Lovia and Raila are staring at me. I can't see Raila's face, of course, but I assume she looks as amused as Lovia does.

"Magic," Lovia explains, shaking out her wrists. "I can control fire. My mother is part-demon, so she passed that onto me. My brother can control ice, but he doesn't do anything interesting with it except play hockey with Deadhands."

Raila comes over to me and starts undoing my braids. To my surprise, my hair is completely dry. And very shiny. Guess that conditioner does the job.

"Come here," Lovia says, grabbing me by the arms and leading me to the vanity desk. She sits me down and stands behind me. I look into a mirror that looks like a haunted mirror if I ever saw one. For a moment I think it might be because I don't recognize myself in it.

I don't have any makeup on, and yet I look like I do. My brown eyes are richer in tone, my lashes black and long, my lips look full and flush, stained ruby, my skin glowing (thanks to the sparkling honey powder that Raila put everywhere). My dark chocolate colored hair spills over my shoulders in shiny waves, my breasts pushed up high in the dress.

"You look like a fairy-tale princess," Lovia says. "But like a dark one. Like from a Grimm fairy-tale. Those are more up my alley anyway." She peers at our reflections, lifting the hair off my shoulders and pulling it back. "Anyone ever tell you that you have a very otherworldly face?"

I laugh. "Coming from you, that would mean I have a mortal face. But yes. I'm a bit odd looking."

"Odd looking?" Lovia says in surprise as she gathers my hair on the top of my head, and motions for Raila to hand her something. "You say that in a negative way. Odd is another word for different, that's all. You're beautiful and you look like you belong here. Well, maybe not Tuonela. But somewhere full of sun and starlight, maybe among the Sun and Moon Goddesses."

I appreciate Lovia's compliment. My mother was adopted so I don't know my family on her side, but I definitely have the high cheekbones of the Finns. Kids used to tease me and call me an "alien" growing up, because of how big and far apart my eyes are, but my face helped me be expressive during dance.

Raila hands Lovia hair pins and she starts pinning my hair up, adding in some large black feathers. I have a sneaking suspicion that those are from the swan I killed.

"There," Lovia says, placing her hands on my shoulders. "You're ready to go. And just in time, too."

I look around. There are no clocks in my room, so I've had no idea of the time, especially when the world outside the window seems to be permanent twilight. "What time is it?" I ask. "Is time even a thing here?"

She gives me a small, patient smile. "Time is a thing. Clocks are not. We have timekeeper stones, like quartz, but there's really no point when it doesn't behave in a linear fashion. Sometimes time is fast, other times it's slow. The entire world of Tuonela adjusts itself in time with the number of the dead. It's the only way we can manage it. So you'll notice when it gets lighter, well, that's morning. When it gets darker, that's evening. When the moon and stars are out, that's night. But the Goddesses will hold back the sun and moon depending on what needs to be done. Sometimes it's mid-day for far longer than normal." She pats my shoulder. "You'll get used to it. Time as you know it is only an idea. You mortals put far too much control and thought over it."

Everything she said just blew my mind. "That's easy for you to say," I tell her. "Time probably has no meaning when you're immortal."

"It'll mean less for you soon," she says, pulling me to my feet, the dress weighing a ton. "You're immortal while you're here. Ilmarinen, my mother's consort, is a mortal and he hasn't aged a day since he got here."

"I thought you weren't able to see your mother?" I ask.

Lovia's face falls for a moment but she buries it with a breezy smile. "I've seen Ilmarinen. During my job. You see a lot when you're ferrying the dead on the River of Shadows."

You mustn't be late, Goddess, Raila says to Lovia.

How can you be late if there's no time? I'm about to ask, but I think I know the answer. It all comes down to Death and you can't keep him waiting. Even I feel a strange thread of urgency inside me, like Death is driving my internal clock, though that could be my nerves.

We head to dinner.

CHAPTER FOURTEEN

THE DINNER

R aila opens the door for us and we step out into the hall. Even though I'd apparently been conscious when I was first brought to my room, everything looks new to me. Not in a surprising way, though. The décor of the hall matches my room: decadent and gloomy, like a palace for goths.

Raila and Lovia lead me down the hall, the candles flickering on the walls, oozing black wax that drips to the floor in sculptural mounds. Each wax sculpture seems to move the more I stare at it, the shape continuously shifting, and I don't know if it's a trick of the eyes or that everything in this creepy world is sentient.

The hall twists around and comes to an open area with a grand staircase that curves from level to level like a giant granite snake. I peer over the edge, counting two levels below us and two above us. A gargantuan chandelier of bones hangs just below us, lighting up the lower levels, making the shadows on the walls come alive with the flickering candlelight. I see both human and animal skulls in the macabre structure. Now *that* he definitely didn't get at Ikea.

Lovia and Raila gently guide me down the steps, and with the way that my gown trails after me, I feel like a historical romance heroine. That is, until two Deadhands pass us on the way up, their empty skeleton faces glimpsed under their shadowy hoods. Creepy as fuck.

I try to suppress the shudder running through me, wanting to appear brave but Lovia gives me a sympathetic look. I guess my disgust is hard to hide.

"I'm sure you'll get used to them," she whispers to me as we reach the next level. "I felt the same way when I first went to the Upper World, seeing all those babies and children everywhere."

I gasp. "My god. You saw dead babies and children in my world?"

She laughs, throwing her head back. "No, silly. If they were dead that would be no problem. I meant babies and children. In general. Your world is just *full* of them. They give me the creeps." She shakes her arms out in an exaggerated manner, her bracelets jangling.

"Remind me to never ask you to babysit," I say under my breath.

We head down another candlelit hall, voices and the clinking of cutlery floating toward us, then come to a large room with two skeleton guards posted on either side of the entrance holding swords. They let us pass but I can feel their eyes trained to me.

The great room has dark parquet floors and plum-colored rugs that complement the smoky purple walls, and narrow stained glass windows in various shades of gray that stretch to the ceiling as if we're in some forsaken church. Candles flicker from the wall sconces, and at one end is a huge roaring fireplace, at least ten feet long, with a tower of skulls framing it instead of stone. The fire gives off enough light for the whole room and the heat is delicious. I hadn't realized how cold I had been until now and I briefly wonder if I'm getting used to this climate already.

In the middle of the room is a long iron table and chairs with backs made of blackened bones. Two men sit on opposite sides of the middle of the table and I recognize them from the other day, both of them in robes.

One is a terrifying skeleton whose eye sockets seem to stare into my soul, even from under the shadows of his hood. The other looked like a skeleton when I saw him the other day, but now up close he appears to be more alive than I thought. He's just incredibly gaunt with pale skin, hooded black eyes, a thinning white beard and wispy white hair that comes over his forehead. He's watching me too, but it doesn't feel unkind.

And at the head of the table is Death. He's wearing a different skull for dinner—perhaps this is his formal attire. It's polished black and of the canine variety, so if he's going for a *wolfish* appearance, he absolutely nailed it. His clothes look the same, dark with some leather, except he's not wearing a robe for once so I can get a better look at his body, his broad shoulders, the width of his arms, the way his torso tapers down. He's sitting back in his chair, looking relaxed, gloved hands folded over his knee.

Watching me. Always watching me.

Smiling too. A cunning smile—I can feel it even if I can't see it.

"The guest of honor has arrived," Death says, straightening up and getting to his feet, towering over the table. "The fairy girl, the little bird, the mortal daughter of Shaman Torben. Hanna Heikkinen."

When neither of his companions rise, he clears his throat impatiently and they both get to their feet.

"Welcome, Hanna," the old man says to me as Lovia leads me to the table. "I don't believe we've had a chance to properly introduce ourselves. I'm Kalma, God of Graves."

Kalma extends his hand as I pass and I quickly shake it. His skin is ice cold and when I look down I notice his fingers are silver. His ears are silver too and when he gives me a kind smile, his teeth are the same.

"And that's Surma," Death says, gesturing to the creepy skeleton on the other side of the table. "Don't bother with him. He's not very nice."

I smile nervously as Lovia sits me down right next to Death, between him and Kalma. Surma makes a low hissing sound in response and then sits down.

"Surma is also a God of Death," Death explains. "He's just not *the* God."

"He's a relic," Lovia whispers to me before she goes to the opposite end of the table.

"Relic," Surma sneers in a raspy voice and to my horror his teeth clack together as he talks. "Your disdain for relics never fails to amuse me, Loviatar. Didn't your father tell you to respect your elders?"

"I taught her to respect *me*," Death corrects him. "And you are a relic. You're so old, you should be in the ground."

"When you say relic, do you mean an Old God?" I ask. Everyone looks at me.

"Don't tell me this wench is that clueless?" Surma says, teeth clanking, making my nerves shrivel.

"She's not a wench," Death snipes. "And while she certainly is clueless, give her some time. It's not easy being thrown into a new world, especially one so cruel."

I stare at Death, trying not to show any softness on my face. Did he actually stick up for me? In his own way, of course. He still managed to call me clueless.

"I don't think it's in good taste to insult the guest of honor," Kalma says, and I shoot him a grateful smile.

"And speaking of taste," Lovia says. "I'm starving. Bring out the food and drinks." She claps her hands together and suddenly Deadhands appear at the doorway, filing toward us carrying jugs and iron platters of various dishes.

"Surma is a relic," Death explains to me as the food is placed on the table. "A leftover from the times of the Old Gods. Like the Liekkiö, I cannot be rid of him. But he is no God. As you can see, he's very much dead."

"He's also pretty useless at a dinner party," Lovia says as a Deadhand pours what looks like wine into her iron chalice. "Considering he can't eat or drink anything."

"But I can watch," Surma says. Clack, clack, clack goes his jawbone. "And I can listen. Pardon me if I don't particularly trust the mortal daughter of the shaman that your father just let go, for no reason at all, I might add."

He twists his head toward Death now, the movements jarring. "You should have kept him, Tuoni. Or I could have killed him for you, like I used to. It was my job. Now he's back in the Upper World, and who knows what kind of magic he's taken with him there. You know more than anyone that shamans can't be trusted."

"I know that our guest needs to eat before the food gets cold," Death says just as the main course is placed in the middle of the table.

I gasp.

"It's the swan," Death says proudly. "One of them anyway. Thank Lovia for having the fortitude to pack it in the snow and bring it here."

I stare at the massive roasted swan in front of me that nearly takes up the whole table. It's done up like a turkey, surrounded by various fruits and vegetables, some strange, some familiar— like tiny apples and red cabbage. It's glazed and crispy brown and cooked to perfection and my mouth automatically waters, despite the fact that this is the holy swan I killed.

"It's the one you decapitated," Lovia says to me brightly. "I was going to have Pyry cook the head too but decided that might be a bit much for you."

"I appreciate that," I tell her. A Deadhand leans over the table and starts to slice up the swan, while a Deadmaiden starts putting various dishes on my plate. She's not Raila—I'm not sure where she went—but she's dressed in bright red robes, including her veil. It's a little unnerving that, like Raila, I can't see her face, but it doesn't kill my appetite in the slightest.

The food looks amazing. I know all I've had so far is the honeycake and coffee, but I still wasn't certain what the rest of the food in Shadow's End would be like. I'd been picturing the worst, like lots of gross raw meat and blood pudding and fish roe and that sort of thing.

This is nothing like that.

"That's the stuffing for the swan, made of grilled chestnuts, rosemary, cabbage, and smoked mushrooms," Kalma says, pointing out the things on my plate. "That's our cook's specialty, a bread made from mountain rye and birch nectar, covered in hydrangea syrup from the Hiisi Forest. Oh, and that's a mash of cliff turnips and reindeer butter, with some snowbeans that have been sautéed in duck fat, sprinkled with moonstone salt and poppy flakes."

"Don't worry, the poppy adds heat and spice," Lovia mentions. "You won't get high."

I nod my thanks to Lovia and give Kalma an impressed look. "You know your food."

"And you're in the house of a God," he says. "No one eats better than they do."

"Or drink," Death speaks up as the red Deadmaiden comes over and fills my chalice with burgundy liquid. "That's our famous sweetvine wine."

I give the Deadmaiden an appreciative smile that I'm not sure she sees, then bring the glass to my nose. It smells like red wine, maybe a bit sweeter.

I take a sip and it's like my mouth has come alive with pleasure, my taste buds buzzing.

"That is delightful," I exclaim, and Death lets out one of his boisterous laughs again.

"At least you can appreciate the finer things," Death says. "Makes me want to do this every night. We still have the other swan."

"Only on the nights I'm here," Lovia tells us. "I don't want to feel like I'm missing anything when I'm working."

"Wouldn't your brother get mad?" I ask, cutting off a piece of swan.

"Father, would Tuonen get mad?" Lovia asks him.

"He'd appreciate the food, but not the company," Death says with a hint of disappointment. I'm guessing that the father-son relationship isn't as strong as the father-daughter one.

"He'd eat it all and leave without saying a word," Lovia jokes. "You can't even get him to stay for movie night."

"I'm sorry, movie night?" I ask. "You guys have movies here?"

Lovia nods. "My father loves movies. Old ones though. I mean, figuratively speaking. He likes what you would call the classics. I think because he hates color and loves black and white."

"It's because movies these days don't know how to tell a real story," Death says, pointing at her with his fork. "The movies you watch have no heart, no intelligence. All violence and action, not character."

My brows raise, surprised to hear him say that. "And how do you watch these movies? Don't tell me you rip the dead actors out of the City of Death."

He chuckles. "No. But that's not a bad idea. Why stop at Deadhands and Deadmaidens? I could have my own actor's studio, filled with all the deceased legends."

"Don't give him ideas," Lovia hisses at me. "He'll do it, you know."

"Death often brings things back from your world," Kalma

explains to me patiently. "Oftentimes he'll bring back computer devices where you can watch the movies. The battery doesn't last long here, but it's enough for a night or two of entertainment."

Surma suddenly makes a growling sound. "I don't think any of you know how to truly treat a prisoner," Surma snivels, teeth clacking. "You don't give them grand rooms and pretty dresses, and you certainly don't wine and dine them. Tuoni, you really should leave the matter of Hanna Heikkinen to me."

There's a weighty pause in the room as everyone looks at Death for his remark. A blast of wind hits, rattles the thin, tall windows, swoops down the chimney over the fire, fanning the flames.

"Hanna is my matter and mine alone," Death says tightly. "I treat her as I see fit. She is a prisoner here in every sense of the word, she is bound between the walls and wards of the castle, she does not have an ounce of freedom to her name. She can't leave this place, nor this world, she can't be reunited with her family, nor her past life. She has truly lost all that she has gained in her meager twenty-four years, and she must comply with my orders or face the consequences of my bare hand."

His skull tilts down as he reaches for his chalice. "With all that being said, I don't know why I should make her suffer further while she's stuck in my grasp, at least not for my own pleasure. You may have once been the one who delivered suffering, but that's never been my role. I rule. I lord over. I am a God. I am the one in control, and control her life from here on out."

Well, fuck. When he puts it that way.

I lower my fork, the swan meat never quite making it to my

mouth. *Now* I've lost my appetite.

Quiet grips the room once again, the flames dying down. The windows stop rattling.

"Father," Lovia chides him, breaking the silence. She gestures to me with her head. "You don't have to be so harsh."

I put the fork down and put my hands in my lap, staring down at the food. I know I should eat as much as I can, because I don't know when my next meal will be. After all that, I'm certain that these dinners will be out of the question, especially with Surma's constant objections to my existence.

"Don't mistake harshness for cruelty," Death tells his daughter. "The truth often hurts, but it is still the truth."

More silence follows as everyone goes back to eating, the clink of cutlery on iron plates filling the space.

Kalma leans in close. "Have some more wine," he says softly. He smells like mothballs. "It will help you."

I nod and reach for my glass, downing the rest in one gulp. Then I raise the chalice, looking around for the Deadmaiden in red. She glides on over to me in a ghostly way and fills my cup. Well, if I'm going to keep being reminded of how shitty my life is going to be for eternity, I guess I can always stay drunk for eternity.

While I drink, Lovia talks to Death about something, but I'm not really listening, and I don't think he is either. I can feel him watching me, his eyes never leaving my face. I don't know what he's thinking, and I don't care to, he's already an extremely confusing person. Being. God. Whatever.

Eventually, I have a few bites of food, after I'm already feeling pretty drunk, and while the roast swan and the dishes taste incredible, I make sure not to say anything complimentary.

I motion for the Deadmaiden to bring me more wine and this time when she does, her voice slices into my head.

He likes to think he's not cruel, an old woman's voice says, *but the real truth is that he is. Death is cruel, no matter how you view it—or him.*

I glance up at her but can't see anything beyond the red veil.

Her head twists slightly to me. *My name is Harma. I'm the head of the Deadmaidens. And I am your ally, mortal one.*

Then she quickly leaves and I'm looking around subtly, trying to figure out if anyone else heard that or just me.

No one is paying attention. Lovia is eating and Surma and Kalma are talking about something. But Death, of course he's been watching me. Studying me. The hair at the back of my neck begins to rise, as if his gaze is getting more intense, then heat starts to build between my legs, making me squeeze my thighs together.

Holy shit. What was that?

I look away from Death and down at the wine. He couldn't have made me feel that just by looking at me, could he have?

There it is again. A sharp ache where all the blood is rushing to my core and I'm shifting in my seat, trying to get rid of this very unwanted rush of desire.

Death suddenly gets to his feet, tossing a napkin on the table. "I think our guest of honor may have had too much to drink," he says.

I stare at him, my body wavering slightly. Maybe I am pretty drunk. Maybe it's not him at all and it's the wine that's making me aroused. Wouldn't be the first time alcohol has done that to me.

Death walks over to me and before I can protest, he's grabbing me by my arms pulling me up to my feet with ease. I rock back and forth on my heels, wooziness sweeping over me, but he holds me in place, his grip strong.

Lovia gets up too and Raila floats forward out of the darkness, but Death just raises his palm. "I will take her safely to her room. The rest of you remain here, I'll be back in a moment."

He puts his arm around my waist and then I'm practically swept out of the dining room and into the hall. I try to fight him off, but I'm drunker than I thought.

"I'm not too drunk," I protest.

"But you are," he says smoothly, leading me up the steps. "And while I don't mind you getting out of your head for a little bit, being drunk can be dangerous here. You must always keep your wits about you."

"Why?" I ask. "Who am I to be wary of? You, or someone else?"

I think back to Harma's words. *I am your ally.*

But is she really? Or is she a trap?

I decide to not mention it, regardless.

"You should always be wary of me," he says. "But I am not the biggest threat to your life. And while I can protect you, I'm still not decided on if I should."

We round the staircase and go down the hall to my room. The further we go, the more I relax into his hold. His presence is so overwhelming, I nearly feel stunned in his grasp. Maybe I'm just drunk, maybe he's got some natural power over me, some sort of pheromones that smell like a bonfire on the beach.

Don't succumb to Death, I tell myself. *It's counteractive to living.*

He brings me to my door and unlocks it and I try to see where on his person he puts the key.

"Ah," he says. "If you're planning to steal a key from me, you have to be more subtle than that."

He pushes the door open and then presses me against the frame. I feel so tiny and frail with his huge body lording over me, that black shiny wolf mask reflecting candlelight. And try as I might, I still can't see his eyes.

"I just want to see your eyes," I tell him, my words slurring.

"Is that so?" he says in a rumbling voice. "What else do you want to see?"

I may be drunk, but I know when I'm picking up on innuendo.

"Whatever you want me to," I answer. Too boldly.

I feel the heat of his stare as it passes over my face, down my neck, to my chest. My nipples harden under my bodice. That pinch of desire hits me again and my mouth opens slightly, a small gasp emitting. Good lord, I don't know what's wrong with me. It's like I'm actually *wanting* something to happen between us.

"And what can I see in exchange?" he's practically purring now. It makes me want to shiver. "What can I have? Hanna," he whispers, drawing out my name as he reaches for my neck and trails a gloved finger down my throat, "you are playing a game with me, aren't you? I just don't know if you're ready for the game."

I swallow as he presses his thumb against me. If I were sober, there's no way I would feel so brave, would walk so willingly forward into this. There's a chance I'm drugged, that there was something in the wine, or that his mind has the power to make me feel things whether I want to or not.

Fuck, I hate it, but right now I want to.

Badly.

I squirm again.

"You can have whatever you want," I whisper, my words choked.

"When?"

"Now?"

God, I want it now.

He shakes his head and I hear him chuckle. "You don't get to decide any of this, little bird." His hand drops to my waist and he leans in close, so close that I can see his eyes beneath the mask. The whites are bright, his irises gray. They hold me in place, like I'm stuck in their gravitational pull.

His eyes are dangerously beautiful.

"Like it or not, you're mine," he murmurs, his voice thick and husky and brimming of promise. "But if you choose to like it, you might even love it."

His hands now trail up over my breasts, his sheathed fingers delicately rubbing along my hardened nipples, making my breath hitch sharply. I can't look away from his eyes, the way they shine like the moon in the dark depths of the mask.

"Now, I want you to spend the night on that bed," he says, quietly commanding. "Naked. On all fours. Your ass in the air. I will come for you when I feel like it. You will not turn around, you will not look at me. You will take whatever I give you and you will take it well. Do you understand?"

Oh Jesus.

I nod. I'm drunk, still lost in his feral stare, and I'm nodding. It scares me and it's dangerous and yet, right now, it's exactly what I want.

He straightens up, the connection between us severed, and gestures for me to go in my room. "Fly along to sleep, little bird. I shall wake you soon."

I stagger inside and then I'm alone.

I've never been more awake in my life.

The entire castle is silent, except for the occasional gust of wind against the panes, and the far-off pounding of waves against the rocky shoreline below. My own heart makes the most noise of all, like a drummer on a tangent, filling my head and ears with a shaky rhythm.

I'm lying on my stomach, on the bed, just like Death asked me to. I'm wearing the nightgown, but it's comfortably covering my ass which also isn't in the air. After he escorted me to my room and warned me what was going to happen, I've been a barrel of nerves, torn between wanting to rebel and wanting to comply. I think I've come to some place in the middle, though I don't feel good about it.

Tonight, Death showed a charming side of him. To see the way he interacts with his daughter was heartening, and I really could see the love between them. I know he would do anything for her, and even if all she wants to do is run away, I know she looks up to him greatly. And the way he came to my defense whenever Surma said anything was both appreciated and surprising.

But then all the deflating talk about being his prisoner came up.

And I got drunk and agreed to some midnight tryst, my hormones absolutely on fire and taking over all rational thought.

And now, to know that he's going to come into my room in the middle of the night and most likely have sex with me, is pushing everything onto a whole other level. I know I told him that I would do anything in order to have my father free and I know I have to uphold that end of the bargain. I just didn't think that would happen so soon. I'm not uptight about sex, I know what I want, I love the male (and female) body, I love the wanton pleasure of it all, and I love the power that comes with it, the power over someone else, the ability to make their eyes roll back in their head.

And yes, I've had sex with strangers, guys whose name I never knew, whose face I've forgotten, and it's never been a big deal. But the difference was, I pursued them. I wanted them. Right now, Death has all the control in the world, right down to the exact position he wants me to be in when he comes in.

Naturally, I took advantage of having Bell in my room and through hushed words and drunk whispers while I sat beneath the fish tank, she tried to give me advice. Mermaids take sexual freedom to a whole new level, that's for sure, and she can't really understand my problem, I guess because she knows Death intimately already. But she made sure that I knew I could still have control. I didn't have to hand all the cards to him. I could go into it wanting it.

I just don't know how that's possible now that the wine has worn off. Yes, there is a teensy tiny part of my libido that finds this all intriguing, but it's the same reason why my nipples got hard around him. He gives off this strange energy, I don't know if it's all the danger, power and uncertainty, but it crackles between us. Maybe he just smells good. Maybe he's just a big guy and while the most I've actually seen of his body is his hand…it's a good hand

Aside from the immediate death aspect of it.

Whatever works, I tell myself, fidgeting on the bed. *Whatever works.*

I'm just glad that I put a towel over the fish tank, much to Bell's disappointment. While she obviously has no problems with watching Death have his way with me, I don't want her witnessing this…whatever this is.

I move my face to the side and take in a deep breath, staring out the window. I was hoping to see the stars because that would mean that Death forgot all about me and is asleep, but it's as misty as ever.

The sound of a lock in a key fills the room.

Oh god.

He's here.

I keep my face where it is, remembering his instructions. I don't dare look over my shoulder. A faint splash of light moves across the room as the door opens and then closes, latching shut.

I close my eyes.

I hear his heavy footfall as he slowly walks across my room, his strides deliberate and purposeful, his boots echoing. He gets closer and closer until I feel his presence right behind me at the foot of the bed.

He exhales, low and deep, and I hear a buckle being undone, perhaps his belt buckle.

Oh god.

I swallow, my heart in my throat, and try my best to keep it together.

"You're not complying with my wishes," Death says in a rough voice that sends a shiver down my spine. "Perhaps I should have made it more of a command." The bed shakes a little as I know he's pressing himself against it. My mouth goes dry with fear. "I wanted you naked with your ass in the air. You're not doing either of those things."

Yeah. And I'm not drunk anymore. So go fuck yourself.

I want to turn around and try to claw his eyes out. I want to kick him where it hurts. I want to use all the fight I have in me to try and destroy him. I want to feel power that I don't possess.

But I know it will do me no good. Bell is right in that there is only one way out of this. I can't fight Death off, I can't escape from his castle—yet. It can only happen in due time, when I learn to play the game right. So far, I'm not doing a very good job of it.

And so I push up so my ass is in the air, and I pull the white nightgown over my body, slipping it over my arms until I'm completely bare in front of him.

And I wait, holding my breath, my entire body feeling frozen in place.

Death inhales sharply. I take some comfort in that, in that

he likes what he sees.

It's all that I have to barter for my life with.

I hear the metal of the buckle again and then feel him lean forward. He gently places his hands on the back of my thighs. I jump, startled at his touch. His gloves feel like leather and when he gets a better grip, they make a stiff groaning sound that reverberates around the room. It's strangely erotic, like the sound of a leather whip before it cracks.

His hands then tighten against my skin, and he's sliding them up, up, until they're cupping my ass, spreading my legs in slow increments and my eyes are pinched shut, wishing my body would just give in and relax.

But then he pauses.

A low grumbling noise emits from his chest.

He removes his hands from my thighs and then I feel him press his palm against my spine.

"You're trembling," he says in a hush. "Why are you trembling?"

I didn't even notice. I thought I was frozen in place, but instead my limbs are shaking uncontrollably. So much for pretending to not be afraid, so much for taking agency.

"Are you afraid I'm going to hurt you?" he murmurs, running his gloved hand over my spine. "Do you think that's what I want to do?"

I can't answer him. I bury my face into the blankets, wishing all of this would go away.

"You do," he says after a moment. "You disappoint me, Hanna. You think that because I am the God of Death, that it is the same as a God of Pain. I promise you, I am not here to make you hurt, little bird. Any creature can inflict pain in the name of conquest and self-pleasure. It takes no skill, no intelligence, no courage, nor no strength to only take, leaving suffering behind. To cause pain is the mark of an idiot, one without a true sense of self, a life coming together to signify nothing."

He takes in a deep breath, his fingers skirting down over my ass, his touch light and delicate. "Here I thought we were on the same page, my dear. I thought in your gumption and your boldness, that perhaps you wanted this. But no. I've caught a look in your eyes in which I am seeing only what I want to see."

I feel the heat of his body pull away and then his gloved hands leave me.

"My apologies, Hanna," he says gruffly. "You are not who I thought you were. You do not want what I thought you wanted."

Then I hear the sound of a buckle fastening, a low exhale of breath, and then the sound of his boots as they walk away, sounding less ominous than before.

It isn't until the door closes and I hear that lock and key that I collapse onto the bed, wondering what will become of me now.

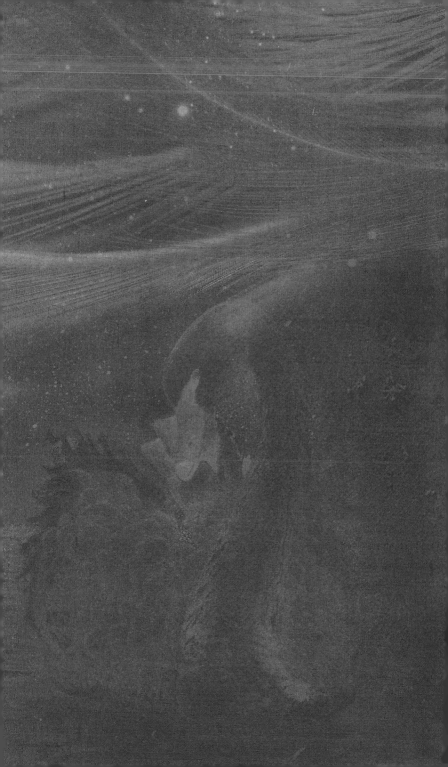

CHAPTER FIFTEEN

THE LIBRARY OF THE VEILS

"**A**nother snowstorm," Bell says from her tank, waking up for the day. "Sheesh, you really did a number on him, didn't you?"

I stare outside my window, leaning my head on the frozen glass. Outside, snowflakes are swirling violently in the sky. I can barely make out the far-off mountains, their jagged peaks faint in the blowing white, while the angry gray sea crashes against the icy rocks below, as if it's lashing out punishment.

It's been like this for days, ever since Death left my room in the middle of the night. I haven't seen him, so I can't take personal responsibility for the change in the weather, but I can't help but feel it's my fault.

Not that I'm feeling bad that I left him with blue balls. But I do feel strange about it all. I did talk a big game. I teased. I acted a certain way and then at the last minute I felt all courage and bravado leave me. In the end, I was just plain scared.

And yes, I was scared that he would hurt me. He says he's not the God of Pain, but I'm also his prisoner, everyone tells me he hates mortals, he also did threaten me with an eternity of terror, basically, so why wouldn't I think he'd physically hurt me and take whatever he wanted with impunity?

But what has me feeling strange about it all is how quickly he backed off the moment he realized I wasn't happy. I wasn't expecting that. I was expecting much worse, or at best, a guilt trip. I've been guilted by guys before when I told them I wasn't sleeping with them, and while I've been lucky that they all sulked off and managed to deal with their bruised egos and libidos in other ways, I didn't think that would be the case with Death. If it wasn't for the fact that I'm his prisoner and possession for eternity, I could almost call him a gentleman.

Almost.

"Maybe if you give him a blow-job, we can actually get some sun for a day or two," Bell chirps, drumming her tiny hands along the side of the tank. "Those sweetvines don't taste as sweet without the rays."

I sigh and straighten up off the window, walking over to Bell. I'm bored in the prison of my room. I haven't seen Death, I haven't seen Lovia. Raila comes in with my food, which I appreciate, and sometimes she bathes me, (which, I know, it's weird, but I'm actually liking it) but she doesn't stay long. It's just been me and Bell, and while I like having Bell as company, we're on totally different wavelengths. I don't know if mermaids are born with this eternally sunny disposition, but despite the fact that she herself is also a prisoner of Death, who has been shrunken in size and put into a god damn fish tank, she thinks I should be having the time of my life.

Case in point: to her, blow jobs bring sunshine.

I mean, sometimes it does.

"Hard to give someone a blow job when they aren't here," I tell her, plopping down on the chaise lounge. "And anyway, that's out of the question," I say quickly, even as a certain image floods my brain. I obviously don't know what Death looks like naked, and while he should look gruesome in theory, I've seen only his hand and my imagination is building everything based on that hand. It was strong, wide, capable, its tone honey-colored, like he spends most days under the sun. His fingers were long, quick and slender, hinting at dexterity, his knuckles big, suggesting he has the punch of a hammer. The silver lines of pulsing light etched on him just add more intrigue. Are they on his dick too?

Good lord, I need to clear my head. Apparently, this is what happens when you're cooped up in your room for too long, you start waxing poetic about a hand.

"You need to get out of this place, Hanna," Bell says. "I mean it. And unless you start playing the game—"

"He knows about the game, Bell," I interject. "You heard him the other night. He knows I've been playing it and he especially knows it now since I couldn't follow through."

"You are allowed to change your mind," she says quietly.

"*I* know that," I tell her.

"He knows that too," she says. I glance at her, and she widens her aquamarine Barbie-doll eyes. "What?"

"You are always sticking up for him. After all he's done to you."

Her little face falls and I immediately feel bad. Shit. She's in love with him, isn't she? The horny little mermaid is in love with Death.

"Hey," I add softly. "I can't pretend to know what it's like

243

to be you. You're an entirely different species, in a whole other world. We both take imprisonment differently."

She nods, worrying her lip between her teeth. "It's not that I forgive him for what he's done," she says. "It's just that I can't hold a grudge. I just can't. And I know that you're going to free me when the full moon comes, so I'm already living in the future. This already feels like the past to me."

Hell, with the way time is supposedly all chaotic out here, I wouldn't be surprised if that were true.

"Just remember," Bell says, "your future will come too. And you will want to let go of grudges, so you can truly be free. You'll be with your father again and this will all seem like some very strange dream."

My heart clenches at the mention of my father. I've been trying not to think about him, because when I do I obsess and drown in a spiral of worry. I don't know if he's in the Upper World like Surma had mentioned. I certainly hope so, but at the same time I worry about his memory of all this being gone, which means he might not know what Eero and Noora are really up to. My only hope is that Rasmus made it back home too and will help my father. I know I was just bait to him, collateral to trade, but as long as my father means that much to him, I pray he'll keep him safe.

"And if you don't get out of here," Bell goes on, "it's because Death would have yeeted you out of here. That's the word, right? Yeeted? Even Lovia wasn't sure."

Fuck. What if that's what all the snow is about? What if it's not so much Death dealing with a form of rejection, which must not happen often with a God, but that he's planning my demise? The snow doesn't mean he's upset, it could be a personification of the violence and death to come.

Suddenly there's a heavy knock at the door. I exchange a harried look with Bell and leap to my feet as she swims to the back of the tank until she's completely hidden.

I walk to the middle of the room and clasp my hands at my middle. "Come in?" I ask warily. No one has ever knocked before. They always unlock the door first and then barge in.

Now the door opens without unlocking—which means the door was unlocked this whole time—and in steps Death.

"Good morning, Hanna," he says in his deep voice, his presence flooding the room, bringing with him an air of power and death. "Will you take a walk with me?"

Oh, fuck. I'm dead aren't I? I'm getting yeeted by his hand.

I glance down at my dress. In my bouts of boredom over the last few days, I've tried on everything in the wardrobe. Not everything fits, but some things I rather like. Today I've put on a yellow dress with puff sleeves and an empire waist that looks straight out of the Regency era. Since I've been lounging, I eschew anything with a corset, which I think are unnecessary evils, a million times worse than a bra.

"You're fine," he says to me, nodding at my attire. "It's a walk through the castle. I'm afraid I can't do anything about the weather at the moment…" He lets it trail off, as if I'm able to do something about the weather. My god, what if Bell was right?

I stand there, frozen in place, staring at him. Today he's back to wearing his flowing robe and his skull is more simple, a human one with jagged bones growing out of the top to form a crown, but I can't feel his eyes the way I normally do. I can't read anything off him at all except his usual aura of authority.

"You don't have to come," he says after a moment, his tone softening. "I only figured you'd been in here for days. Not locked in here, as I'm sure you just realized, but inside this room nonetheless."

I lick my parched lips, finally finding my voice. "Why was the door unlocked?"

He folds his arms across his chest. "I wanted to see if you'd run. You didn't even try to fly, little bird," he adds in a whisper.

"It would be pointless, wouldn't it?" I counter. "You've told me time and time again that there's no way I can escape. That the walls and wards will keep me in, that the realm would probably kill me."

"Yes. But probably isn't definitely. And you're someone who will grab hold of whatever hope there is."

"You sound disappointed," I say. "I guess I should get used to disappointing you."

There. Now I feel him. I feel the change in his energy, and though his posture hasn't changed at all, it's like he slumps internally. The wind outside these walls wails in response. Death has walls just as any of us do, just as this castle does, and they aren't always impenetrable.

That little bit of information gives me a lot. It gives me the hope he just said I'd hold on to.

"You don't disappoint me," he says gruffly, his demeanor changing again. He clears his throat. "Okay, perhaps you do a little. I thought there would be more fight in Hanna Heikkinen. This is the mortal who defeated my Goddess daughter, who stole her boat and wielded her sword, slaughtered the Swan of

Tuonela. There will be poems and rune songs sung about you, like a legend. I want to see *that* girl. I want her to spar with me, to fight me, to show bravery and defiance."

He walks across the room to me, his steps slow, his boots echoing. He stops right in front of me and peers down and I see his gray eyes peering at me brightly in the dark shadows, like a silver star.

"I do defy you," I tell him, raising my chin. "But I don't wish to die. And I don't think either of us know what you want from me just yet."

"I think I've made it clear," he says brusquely.

"Then if you want it, take it," I tell him. "I can't stop you."

He cocks his head. "But you have stopped me. That's the thing."

His gaze holds me hostage and I don't know how much time is ticking past or if it's standing still, as it's known to do.

Then he reaches out and grabs my hand with his. His gauntlets look like leather, but they feel like the softest fur. "Let me take you somewhere you'd like," he says, giving my hand a squeeze I feel in my toes. "To the Library of the Veils."

Okay, now he has my interest. Truthfully, I would have gone anywhere, just to get out of my room. I realize there's a chance he's still planning to murder me, but I'd rather die somewhere different, I guess. Surrounded by books sounds like a good way to go.

I nod and give him a tight smile, and even though I don't look at Bell as I walk past, I can feel her trying to ask for more sunshine.

"I figured you like books," Death says to me as we walk out

of my room and down the hall. The castle is a little brighter than normal, thanks to the light bouncing off the white snow outside and filtering through the old windows.

"You figured I like books?" I repeat. "This is starting to sound like small talk."

"There is no small talk with you, fairy girl," he says, his hand releasing mine and sliding up to my elbow where he takes a firmer hold. "Everything you say is like a double-edged sword." His skull tilts, glancing down at me. "You know, I never thought a mere mortal would fascinate me as much as you do, but here we are. I just can't seem to figure you out. You're frighteningly complex."

I burst out laughing. I feel like I haven't laughed for days, and the sound is foreign to my ears.

"Me? Complex?" I scoff. "Right. Okay. You want to know how complex I am? I'm a social media manager for a clothing company that marks up twenty-dollar coats which I convince people to buy for five hundred. I live in North Hollywood, in a shared house, as do most other working young professionals, surrounded by succulents and surfboards. I take capoeira on Wednesday nights, I go to a local bar and drink margaritas on Fridays. My favorite food is ramen, I don't have a cat but I love cat videos, I wear all the sweaters as soon as September hits even when it's eighty degrees outside, and I don't care if people know I love pumpkin spice lattes. I watch anime but I watch anime porn more, and I scroll through TikTok to help me fall asleep at night, even though it makes me buy candles and crystals and crochet supplies that I never use. I am not complex. I am what they call a basic bitch. I just happen to be a basic bitch in the Realm of the Dead. And maybe that's what you find fascinating."

Death stops and stares down at me and I can almost feel him thinking, a pause hanging between us as he takes in all my babbling.

Finally, he says, "Basic bitch?"

I wave my free hand dismissively. "It just means I'm not special. I'm no different than anyone else. Whatever complexity you see in me, it's not there. I'm just...*foreign* to you."

"Ah," he says, slowly nodding. "I thought you meant you were not very adept at being a bitch, and I was going to say otherwise."

I glare at him. "That's funny. Did Death manage to make a joke at my expense?"

"Who said I was joking?" Then he starts walking again and tugs at my arm. We go up the grand staircase to the next level and turn the corner. There's a huge iron door with an inscription on it that I can't read.

"What does that say?" I ask.

"There was a door to which I found no key," Death reads. "There was a Veil through which I might not see. Some talk a little while of me and thee, there was—and then no more of thee and me."

I stare at the door. Not only does there not seem to be a lock, there doesn't seem to be a handle either.

But Death runs his hands over the skeleton designs down the middle of the door and then something hisses and the door opens, the air sucking us in, as if we're opening the door to an airlock.

"Welcome to the Library of the Veils," Death says, placing his hand at my back and ushering me in.

It's dark save for the grand windows that line the end of the room, done up in the circular petal designs you might find in a Catholic church, but then all at once the lights go on, illuminating how grand the room is.

No, grand isn't the right word. It's fucking *magnificent.* I'm such a whore for libraries in general—I once spent the majority of my Manhattan vacation inside the New York Public Library—but I've never seen any like this.

The library itself is at least three stories tall in places where the bookshelves reach up into the narrow circular turrets of the castle, the shelves themselves built into the iron walls. It's the library from the *Beauty and the Beast* cartoon, except gothic and foreboding. It's not just all the iron, or all the skulls and bones as décor, or the strange glass cages placed around the room with blankets draped over them, but it's this strange sense of…I don't even know if I can describe it. It's a sense of life and of death, it's ever-changing and powerful, like the atoms in the air are constantly being rewritten. It feels like there are more than the two of us in here, that instead there are hundreds of thousands of people among us, people that I can't see. I can feel them all at once, all their energy, and I'm not surprised to feel the hair at the back of my neck standing stiff.

There's also a large floating book in the middle of the room and a dog made of iron guarding it.

"That's Rauta," Death says rather proudly, gesturing to the dog. "You wore his collar for a bit. Remember?"

Rauta opens its mouth and growls at me, literal sparks

shooting out.

It's fucking terrifying, and I'm not kidding when I said it's made of iron. Part of it looks like a normal Tuonela dog, with bone and some patches of fur, but other parts look like they're welded on. Like a steampunk demon hound with red glowing eyes. Thank god that collar is back around the dog's fat neck, even though it doesn't seem to be chained to anything.

"Not a dog person?" Death asks.

"I love dogs," I say defensively. "Just not the ones that belong to Doctor Frankenstein."

Death chuckles and walks over to Rauta, crouching down to pet it. He strokes his gloved hand over the dog's head and the dog visibly calms down, its metal tongue hanging out as it lies down on the rug. "There's a good dog," he coos to it. "You're doing a good job guarding this place. A very good job."

"Is he sentient?" I ask, peering at him. The iron dog totally seems at peace now.

"All animals are sentient," Death says, straightening up. "They all experience emotions. They all have souls."

"You know what I mean. Is it like Sarvi?"

"Oh. Thank the Creator, no. I couldn't handle that."

I go back to looking around the room. It really is morbidly beautiful, and the more I stare at it, the more the details surprise me. For one, the lights that came on aren't from candles but from white lights glowing from sconces around the room. For two, the books themselves, all bound in leather and skins, seem to jostle and move on the shelves. There must be thousands and thousands of them all subtly vibrating.

For three, pretty sure I just saw a ghost glide past from one end of the library to the other.

"What?" Death asks, staring at my face.

"Is this library…haunted?"

"Oh. Yes. Very much so."

My eyes widen. "By who?"

"By *whom*, you mean? And it doesn't matter. It changes all the time. It's haunted by the dead. I don't see them anymore, though I did when I was a young boy."

"But why is the library haunted, of all places?" I ask.

"It's the Library of the Veils," he says patiently. "You know what the Veils are, don't you?"

I give him a look like *no, I don't know shit, remember*?

He grabs my hand again and leads me to the black velvet couches under a stained glass rose window. I sit down and he pulls a book off the shelf, handing it to me, the snow from outside the window causing colors of navy and eggplant to bleed through.

"This is a volume of The Book of Souls from 1946, your time, your world," he says.

I flip it open and gasp. The page is moving like I'm looking at someone's home videos played on mute, an image of a man drinking beer on the beach superimposed on the paper. The man smiles and then the scene changes to him driving down an oceanside highway, holding the hand of a pretty woman with a 60's hairdo. At the top of the page, it says Emanuel Courier: December 12th—July 8th 1965.

"Every person that has ever lived is in the Book of Souls, even if they only lived for but a minute," Death explains as I watch the scenes unfold on the page, the life of Emanuel

Courier. "When you die, your entry is complete. Nothing more to be added. You see, Hanna, when I said that I knew you, I meant it. You told me that you scroll the TikTok at night and that you like tiny prickly plants, but I already knew that about you because it's already playing in your own entry in the book."

My god. Has he really been able to watch my whole life like that? "I need to see my entry!" I exclaim. I flip through the pages but all I see are the lives of people who were born in 1946.

"Why? You've lived it, haven't you?"

"For the same reasons we take photos and videos. So that we don't forget."

"Don't you think it would be for the best if you did forget?" His voice lowers. "You're not going back to that life."

I nearly growl. I hate being reminded of that. "I want to see it."

"Maybe some other time," he says firmly. "The last thing I want is for you to yearn for what was."

"And you don't think I'm not already doing that?" I shout, getting to my feet.

He takes the book from my hands and snaps it shut. "I was just showing you something I thought you might appreciate," he says sulkily, turning around and sliding the book back on the shelf. "Each book is organized by date of birth, then by world, and they're constantly being filled and updated."

That last bit of information distracts me enough. "How many worlds are we talking here?"

"There are…a lot. Tuonela oversees them all. You think Sarvi came from your world originally? I assure you, unicorns did not. This land, this library, is the meeting place for the Veils, the thin shrouds that keep one world from bleeding into the next."

It's all too much. All these books filled with all the lives that ever lived across the universe. No wonder the damn library is so big, it's not like he's collecting all the special editions of Dickens or something. Each book, one person per page, constantly refreshing, like an Instagram story that keeps going and going, all the way until their death when there's no more life to add.

"Why do the ghosts haunt this place then?" I ask. "Shouldn't they be in the City of Death?"

"Not all that come to Tuonela come willingly," he says gravely. "Sometimes denial is stronger than death. Those spirits feel the souls in here, in these very pages, and they're somehow comforted. I try not to judge them, even though it is my job in the long run to bring them to the city. Instead, I harness their energy so at least they're good for something." He gestures to the glowing white sconce on the shelf above him. "They power the lights," he adds proudly.

I'll admit that's pretty genius, but Death doesn't seem like the type who needs his ego stroked anymore. "So, what's the floating book out there? Is that haunted? Is that the book of *your* life?"

Another dry chuckle. "The Book of Runes. The most powerful book in the realm, perhaps in all the realms."

Oooh. So *that's* the Book of Runes. I look over my shoulder, staring at the floating hardcover. Rauta is still lying on the floor beneath it, but this time keeping a red eye on me. "Why is it so powerful?" I ask.

"I'm afraid I can't tell you that," he says.

Uh huh. I think back to what Rasmus had said about the book.

"They say that some magic, in the right shaman's hands, can rival the power of a God's," I repeat faintly to myself.

"What was that?" Death asks quickly, stepping toward me.

I look past his skull sockets and into his real eyes. "It's what Rasmus told me. It's why he wanted into this place, to get his hands on that book."

The air between us becomes charged. "Ramus told you this?"

I nod.

"The boy seems to have lofty ambitions," he muses gruffly. "Wouldn't you say?"

I shrug, my eyes drawn to the floating book. Lofty, indeed.

Death goes quiet after that, stewing over something. Rasmus really seems to get under his skin, though I don't know why. I guess it's a red-headed shaman thing.

I take my chances and walk over to the book to get a closer look. Rauta, as expected, growls at me, throwing sparks that threaten to ignite the rug beneath him.

The book is black, bound in some kind of animal skin (god, I hope that's animal skin), with silver lines etched across the front, similar to the lines on Death's hand, and it practically sings to me. It's like I can hear it calling me closer, my thoughts swirling and swirling, and I find myself reaching for it.

In seconds Death is at my side, his grip firm over my wrist, stopping me from touching the book. Rauta is now on his feet and barking flames.

"What do you think you're doing?" Death asks, his tone threatening.

I shake my head and stare at my hand. "I…I don't know. I didn't mean to…I wasn't trying to touch it."

"But you were, fairy girl. I'm impressed that your boldness has returned, but try not to confuse that with stupidity."

I blink. The book has gone silent. "It was calling to me," I whisper. "It was singing, but the strangest singing I've ever heard."

His grip tightens. "What kind of singing?"

I shake my head and give him an apologetic smile. "I don't know. Chanting, maybe. It's stopped now."

He grunts and lets go of my hand. "Interesting."

"So, that's like a book of magic and spells, right?"

"That's one component of it," he says carefully. I feel him studying me now, but I just want to study the pages of the book. Even though it's stopped it's beguiling singing, my fingers practically itch to touch it.

"Perhaps you've had too much excitement for one day," Death says carefully. "You might be imagining things."

He grabs me by the elbow and starts leading me out of the library. I look over my shoulder just in time to see another ghost float past, a woman with a long gown, transparent and ethereal.

I need to get back into that library. Not just to see what my own entry in the Book of Souls says, in whatever volume I'm in, but to know why that book was chanting to me. I have the impression it doesn't normally do that. Does it want me to look at it? If Rasmus said it contains the magic for a shaman to become more powerful than a God, would I be able to use it too? I'm not a shaman, but perhaps being one's daughter might help.

We exit the library, the door closing behind us like it's sealing the room, and we're both lost in thought as we make our way down the staircase.

"Why do you think I was able to fight your daughter and kill the swans? I mean, the sword felt like nothing to me and yet Rasmus couldn't even lift it," I comment.

"I'm not sure," he says after a moment.

"Could it be the same reason why the book was just singing to me?"

"Perhaps."

It's like pulling teeth.

"Vellamo told me that she had never felt such power from a mortal before," I say innocently, gathering the hem of my dress before we head down the next staircase.

He stops suddenly, grabbing my elbow. "Vellamo said that?" he says stiffly.

I nod. "She said it was inconsistent. Like it was just waking up."

He seems to ponder that over. "Anything else?"

"That she thought it was powered by love. Love for my father," I quickly add.

He removes his hand from me, raises his head slightly. "How do you feel?"

"What do you mean?"

"Right now. How do you feel?"

I frown, trying to think. How do I feel? How do I even order those emotions into words?

"What's the problem?" he goes on. "No one ever asks you how you feel back in your world?"

Quite frankly, no. I mean I get the "how are ya?" from friends, or bartenders, or people at work. But no one asks me how I feel. About anything.

"Does anyone ask *you* how you feel?" I throw it back at him.

"No. Why would they? All they have to do is look outside." He gestures to a stained glass window at the end of the hall.

He has a point there.

"So, how do you feel? Right now. Be honest. I can tell when you're not."

I sigh loudly and close my eyes. "Right now? Annoyed that I have to answer this question."

"And?"

"And…confused. Because I don't know what any of this means. Curious, because I want to find out more."

"Think deeper," he tells me, his voice hushed. "Do you feel like you belong here?"

"No," I say immediately.

"You didn't think. You didn't feel. You only said what you wanted to hear. Do you feel like you belong here?"

"I don't want to belong here," I practically whisper.

"That's not what I asked you." He pauses, his breath raspy, smelling of mint. "Do you feel powerful?"

I swallow and find myself nodding.

"Do you feel alive?"

Again, I nod.

Because I do feel strangely alive here. I see it when I catch a glimpse of myself in the mirror. I feel it in my cells, like they're glowing. And despite the feelings of hopelessness I have over my situation, I *do* feel powerful. Maybe not to defeat Death, but even so.

"And compared to back in your old life?" he asks. "How did you feel there? Did you feel powerful? Did you feel alive? Did you feel as if you belonged?"

I shake my head, surprised at the ache in my heart. Was I just sleepwalking in my life before? Just aimlessly checking off the boxes, making sure I had everything that life expected of me without any real thought of what I truly wanted? I had spent my teenage years trying to be beautiful, trying to be the best, trying to win over the attention of my mother, for whom I was never good enough, and even though I left that behind and started anew in LA, even though I found the power I craved in capoeira, was it really enough?

Death puts his hand at the small of my back and we start going down the stairs.

"I don't know what it all means, little bird," he says to me. "But it's no accident that your father is a shaman and it's no accident that you're here. It's something I'm very aware of, and I think you are too."

We pause outside my room and Death gestures to the door.

"I'm leaving it unlocked," he says. "Your prison just got bigger."

I raise my brow. "So I can go anywhere?"

"You can try," he amends. "But if I were you, I'd keep the door locked from the inside. There are some in this castle you shouldn't trust."

"Does that include you?"

"What do you think?"

I swallow, finding that boldness returning. "I think I might keep the door unlocked tonight."

There's no way he's missing my meaning.

I hear him swallow.

"Alright," he says thickly.

Then he nods and walks off down the hall, disappearing around the corner, his robe flowing behind him.

I can't help but smile to myself, feeling a kick of power. He doesn't realize it, but I have agency now. A midnight tryst is no longer his idea.

It's mine.

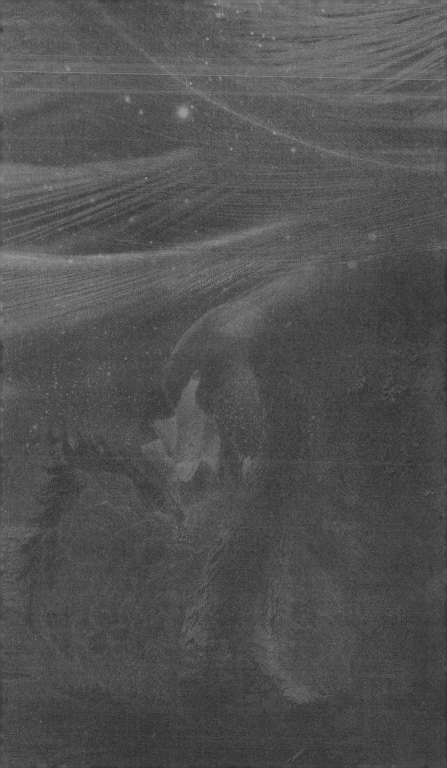

CHAPTER SIXTEEN

THE NIGHT VISIT

With Death giving me access to the castle, I spend the rest of the day roaming the halls, peeking in all the rooms that are available to me. I don't see Death, nor anyone else I recognize. There are only Deadhands marching around in unison, one arm swinging, the other gripping their swords. They don't even turn their heads when they pass me by, but since they don't have eyeballs in their skull sockets, they might be watching me all the same.

The more time I spend exploring the hallowed walls of Shadow's End, the more creepy and beautiful it becomes, both sides complementing each other, yin and yang. A castle of iron and bone filled with chilling and intricate details, furnishings that are both lush and stark. It's like being trapped in a macabre fairy-tale, where bone soldiers and servants haunt the keep. I see grand rooms for sitting and drinking, and great halls for dining, smaller libraries, some studies, a few guest rooms. There are kitchens, pantries, garrison quarters—all with various views of either the mountains or the sea.

I even find Stargaze Tower, where I'm supposed to chuck

Bell into the sea when the moon is full. The raging sea is right below, the tower rising up from it like a cliff. The room itself is a marvel, all gold and silver, with star maps and astrological drawings all over the stone walls, books of galaxies and planets strewn across sturdy wood tables. Two telescopes stand at the large windows, pointed at the clouds. Both windows open and when I test one, cold salty sea air flows into the room, invigorating me.

Finally, there is the lowest level, into the sprawling wine cellars, chain-riddled dungeons that looked primed for torture, and oubliettes that make me shudder, fathomless holes that I'm sure many have been thrown down to be forgotten about. They all seem to lead along the damp path to a black iron door with flickering candles outside. The door has strange symbols written over it. It's locked, and there's a dark, ominous hush to the area, which makes me think that the notorious crypt is inside there.

I don't stay there trying to figure it out—the place gives me the creeps. And considering I'm a prisoner of Shadow's End, that's saying a lot.

I have to say, after being given that freedom, I'm happy to be back in my room. Dare I say I'm growing to appreciate it. When Raila comes by later to attend to my needs, I request not only a warm bath with that smooth skin scrub, but a bottle of wine as well.

By the time night rolls around, the snowstorm turns to darkening mist—I'm nervous but feeling pretty limber thanks to the bottle of wine, and that nervousness gives way to strange bouts of excitement. Bell keeps trying to give me tips and pointers for my meeting with Death, but eventually I have to put the towel over her tank, shutting her up like you would a parrot. She gets the hint.

I'm about to put on the white nightgown he picked out for me (I've been sleeping in the black one), then remember his instructions for last time. I may have initiated this round, but I still want to comply when I can.

So I let myself be naked and go over to the bed, lying down on my stomach. I don't even know if he will come by, he never actually said he would, and while I feel a bit of relief at the thought, I also feel a hit of rejection.

Which is weird. Because I shouldn't be looking forward to this, not even a little. I mean, he's essentially my captor and, while I walked into this bargain, it doesn't mean that I have to like it. I shouldn't like it. I should hate every moment of it.

And yet...and yet...

I'm curious.

I can still hate this and yet want it to happen, purely because I want to know what Death has planned for me.

I want to know what he's like.

What he feels like.

The noises he'll make.

The fact that he'll come undone. and there has to be power in that.

It's my power to give.

Make him want you, make him want to keep you, make him love you.

Then fly.

I think I must fall asleep because suddenly I hear the door open, flickering light briefly slicing into the room, and then it closes.

The room is dark now, the candles having been blown out, and yet I'm tempted to turn around, to see him approach.

As if sensing this, he says in a thick, rough voice, "Keep still."

And so I do, my pulse racing so fast I think it might burst. I take in a deep shaking breath, my nerves in a frenzy, and close my eyes.

The sound of his boots on the floor is ominous as they get closer and closer, and then I feel the strength of his presence behind me. I know he's standing at the foot of the bed.

I hear the buckle being undone.

I hear his breath get deeper.

I feel his eyes as they coast over my body, leaving licks of fire in their wake, heat that starts to gather between my legs.

I swallow hard, holding my breath. Every single muscle and nerve is waiting for his touch. Will it be hard? Will it be soft?

Will it be the touch that ends me?

A low growl comes from his chest and then he's grabbing my hips with his gloves, the leather textured this time like roughed-up serpent scales. He yanks my ass up impatiently.

"That's better," he murmurs, his fingers digging into my flesh. He slowly brings his hands down beneath my ass, grabbing hold of my thighs and kneading them lightly. "Who is the last man to give you release?"

I frown, confused by his question. "Um. I-I don't remember," I say, my words shaking.

"Then it couldn't have been very good," he says, his fingers now slipping between my thighs, delicate at first.

Truth is, I probably could remember if I really thought about it, but it had been awhile and at the moment my brain is complete mush. I don't think I could tell him my name right now. I'm too focused on those roughly textured fingers slowly sliding up and up and up…

He runs his finger gently along my cleft and my breath hitches. So we're just going there. Okay.

"When I'm done with you, little bird, you'll forget everyone you ever let inside you. You'll forget every climax you've ever had. Every tongue that's licked your body, every finger that's touched your skin, every cock that's fucked your cunt. After this, there will only be me."

I gulp. Dear lord.

Death is a dirty-talker.

"I may not be able to feel you with my bare hands," he goes on, voice getting huskier, "but I promise my tongue will know every single inch of your body. What it feels like, what it tastes like. What it sounds like when I make you moan. I bet it sounds like music."

His finger runs all the way up the crack of my ass and I hear the leather of his gloves crease as he adjusts his grip, parting my thighs.

Every part of me is on fire with anticipation, my breath coming short and sharp, panting like a dog in heat. There's a possibility I might pass out.

Then he moves behind me, a rustling sound, and he places something next to me on the bed. I open my eyes, finding myself face to face with a grinning skull.

His mask. Oh my god, he's taken off his mask!

I have to look. I have to know what he looks like, if only for a second.

But before I can even chance it, he grabs my thighs, yanks me back toward him, and buries his face between my legs.

I gasp loudly, my whole body flinching from the intrusion, but his grip holds me in firmly place.

Oh my god!

His tongue assaults me, making hard passes over me before flicking my clit over and over, causing my nerves to start spinning like a pinwheel. His tongue is long, thick and strong, moving with deft precision, sliding over the exposed part of me like he's a panther lapping up blood. I don't know what I was expecting from the God of Death, but I didn't think he'd so readily devour me. Then there's the rough scratch of his facial hair against my sensitive skin, something I never imagined him having.

Death groans, the sound vibrating through me, almost making me come, then puts his lips in motion. They feel full and soft and they suck at me, his tongue lashing with so much ferocity that I'm thrust forward, but his hands are a vice and they hold me in place. It's messy and it's raw and there's no part of me that he's not consuming.

My body doesn't know what to do at first. It's caught up in my mind, which is trying to remind me that this is the God of Death, that I'm his prisoner, his captive, to use at his disposal. But then the thoughts and worries start to leave my mind and my body takes over. My hormones have been whipped up into a frenzy by Death's relentless attack and I'm starting to ache inside with the need for release. I don't think I've ever felt this way before, to have my wants and desires take such control of me.

With another rough groan he thrusts his tongue in deep and I'm clenching around him, wanting more, suddenly feeling insatiable and greedy and out of my mind. My hands make fists in the velvet blanket, as if I'm trying to hold on or hold back, I can't really tell.

He raises his head, breathing hard, and starts playing with me with his rough fingers, rubbing soft wet circles around my clit. "You taste better than honey," he murmurs. "Rich and sweet enough for my morning coffee." He pauses before flicking me. "So fucking creamy."

Oh, mercy.

My cheeks flush. My whole body feels like it's on fire.

I swear I hear him smile. A couple of fingers thrust inside me and I gasp, moaning, gyrating my hips against him to get more purchase. The texture of his gloves is rough and soft at once and I feel it all as his fingers drag against my sensitive spots. The ache inside me intensifies, my skin growing tight and hot.

"I had to get you wet enough to take me. But you'll take me now," he says hoarsely as he adjusts himself behind me and I feel the head of his cock tease at my entrance, the sound slick. He begins to push himself inside me and I'm sucking in my breath as he slowly enters me.

"Fuck yes, you'll take me," he grinds out, his fingers digging into my hips as he keeps squeezing himself in. "You'll take all of me, every thick, hard inch of my cock until there's stars in your eyes and no air left in your lungs."

I'm already there. For a moment I can't breathe, it's like he's filled up every inch of me with himself, and I'm stretched as much as I can go. He's in to the hilt.

"Do you feel me?" he rasps, stilling behind me. "All of me? Can you take more?"

The fuck? There's *more*?

I make a sound that sounds like *yes*, but before I can take it back, he pumps his hips against me, somehow driving in even deeper.

A cry strangles in my throat. Pain and pleasure blur, my eyes rolling back in my head and there's no resisting this. I succumb to him and let go. In this moment, and only in this moment, I am truly his.

Death knows it. He unleashes himself on me. With his fingers bruising my skin, he slams in and out, his cock going deeper, somehow feeling even thicker each and every sordid pump. I'm like a ragdoll, at his mercy, bouncing on the bed, lost to his punishing rhythm while pleasure builds and builds inside my core.

Then, with a low growl, he reaches forward and grabs me by the throat, his gloves gripping tight, and lifts me back toward him so I'm just on my knees and I'm struggling to breathe. With his hand pressed against my neck, his other hand slides down over my stomach and starts fingering my clit, the texture of the glove still rough despite how wet I am.

I try to talk but can't. I reach up to his fingers and try to pry them off my neck, feeling like I'm losing consciousness. At the same time, I'm close to coming and I'm realizing they're pretty much the same thing, a total submission to the unknown. Gray spots invade my vision, and I'm standing on an edge, ready to give in and take the plunge into darkness.

Then his grip lessens, and I'm gulping in air just as his fingers work me faster, the wet sounds so lewd in the dark of the room.

"Fly away with me, little bird," he grunts in my ear, stroking my clit harder and harder until it feels like the beating of wings. "Fly away with me."

Oh, *god*.

"Fuck!" I scream, the word shattering in the air and then I'm shattering too. The pressure releases, my body lets go, and I'm shot into the unknown. The whole room turns black, and silver stars fill the space and I don't even know where I am anymore, but I don't care. I don't care about anything. I'm just bliss, just a being floating through time, lost to the waves of pleasure that rip through my body, making my limbs shake, my heart pound, my cries echo…

Oh my god, I'm not dead am I?

He didn't accidentally give me *the hand*?

I blink and then suddenly the black velvet night and the silver stars fade away until they're just outside the window. I'm in my bedroom again, and Death is still inside me, his thrusting slowing, his rough gloved hands still stroking me, holding me tight.

His breath hitches, there's a gasp, then he quickly pulls out of me with a shockingly wet sound, leaving me hollow inside. I feel him come on my back in hot spurts that never seem to end, his shuddering moan shaking the bed.

The room fills with the sound of our panting breaths, my

head pounds with my beating heart. My limbs start to tremble with the strain and Death releases me, so I'm collapsing to the bed.

Good lord that was…there are no words.

I lie there, staring out the window at a crystal-clear night sky. But Death isn't asleep. He's awake. With me.

Until he's not.

He reaches forward and retrieves his mask.

I want to roll over, look at him, say something, cover up, but I'm hit with a tidal wave of exhaustion.

My eyes close just before he leaves the room.

We never said a word to each other.

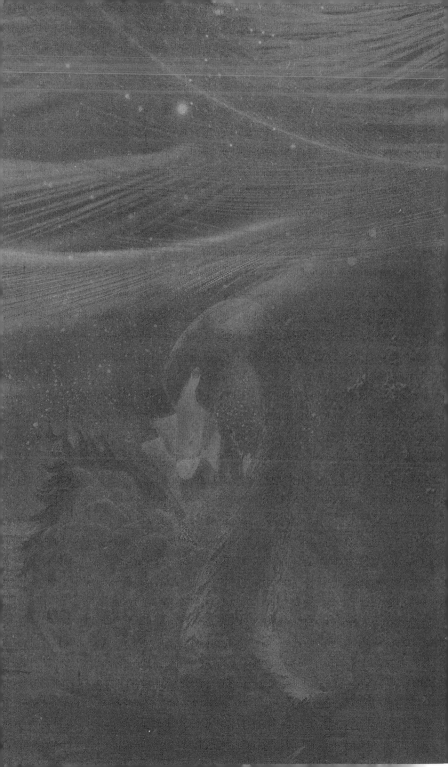

CHAPTER SEVENTEEN

THE SECT OF THE UNDEAD

The next morning Raila wakes me up.

You've slept in, dear Hanna, Raila's voice slides into my head as her gloved hand roughly shakes my shoulder. *Time to get up now.*

All the finesse of an ox this one has, I think groggily to myself. My eyes open, blinking at the light coming in the room. *Sunlight.*

It's not streaming in, but it's there. It's diffused. The morning is misted over as always, but today I can make out the Everest-type peak of Mount Vipunen. Beyond that, the sun is trying to burn through the clouds. I try and recall the name of the Sun Goddess. Is it Päivätär? So many of the Finnish names sound the same. Either way, this is the first time I've felt her presence.

"It's bright outside," I say, rubbing my bleary eyes.

Yes, it is, Raila says, sounding chipper as always. *This is good news for the garden. Pyry will be happy. She has so many things she wants to grow in the sun.*

I briefly wonder if it's my doing. I mean, I don't want to toot any horns or anything, but unless I was dreaming, I'm pretty sure Death got off on me last night. When I move, I can feel the dried places where he marked me. In a weird way, it's kind of hot, even the next morning.

But that feeling only lasts a moment. Because then the shame comes in.

I invited Death into my bed. He fucked me raw. He came on my back. He got what he wanted from the start.

Then again, I got what I wanted too. I mean, at least I got off. I can't say that I didn't enjoy the whole experience, that would be a lie. But my hormones and my emotions are all sorts of vulnerable this morning, like a nerve exposed to air. I can't say this is new to me—even when I have one-night stands, I have this oppressive feeling that sets in the moment the orgasm fades—but even so, I don't want to dwell on it.

I don't want to think about what's next.

Because that can't be it, can it?

Did Death just want a taste of me? Was I enough for his liking? Or is he still planning on yeeting me into Oblivion?

You're looking particularly well this morning, Raila says to me as I sit up. From the knowing tone of her voice, I have no doubt her face matches beneath that veil. *Are you coming around to Shadow's End?*

I've been coming alright, I think but I manage to hide my smirk.

"I must have gotten a good night's sleep," I explain.

I bet you did, Raila says, and there's more meaning in her words than normal. I wonder if the others in the castle know what happened last night. Then again, the brighter weather must be a sign, and there's no secret that I'm Death's prisoner. The writing might be on the wall.

I left your coffee and breakfast on the table, she says to me as she glides away in her dark robes. *Let me know if I can offer you anything else for the time being.*

"Actually," I say, straightening up. "You can help me."

She stops, turning her faceless head toward me. *Yes?* She sounds excited. Usually I just dismiss her quickly.

"You know that Death has given me freedom to roam the castle?"

She nods. *Oh yes. The Master told us at the morning meeting the other day that you've been freed to go where you like. I would consider it a great honor.*

"Yeah, it's something," I admit slowly. I flash her a smile. "And since there's so much of Shadow's End that I haven't seen and won't understand, I was wondering if you could give me a tour."

Me? She clasps her satin gloves together. *Well, of course I would be happy to. It is my one duty to serve you. And the Master, of course.*

"Of course," I tell her with a placating smile. "Well, let me have my breakfast and get ready for the day. Can you come back here in an hour?"

It would be my pleasure, she says with a bow, and then glides out of the room, the door closing behind her.

I exhale loudly the moment she's gone. As much as I've grown to appreciate having Raila around, she still gives me the creeps.

There's a *phhhwomp* sound from the side of the room and

I look over to see one of my towels on the ground and Bell hoisting herself half-out of the fish tank, looking at me with annoyance.

"Hanna," Bell says sharply. "Did you forget I was even here?"

"Yeah," I tell her, getting out of bed. "That was the plan."

I walk a step and then groan. My muscles ache…*everywhere*. Death wore me out last night with his exuberance. I suppress a smile at that, feeling guilty for even enjoying that thought and then delighting in it, like a novelty.

"Well, in case you didn't notice," she says, "putting a towel over my fish tank doesn't block out the noise. I heard every single thing that happened last night."

My cheeks flush. I've had sex in a public washroom before, I've had sex at a party when I knew people were outside the door listening. It doesn't bother me; if anything, it gets me off. But I'll be an old, cranky woman before I get used to the idea of a little mermaid overhearing every lustful groan and ragged breath.

"Thankfully, I forgot you were there," I tell her, going over to my breakfast. As usual, there are honeycakes, as well as some slices of grouse bacon fried in lavender syrup and the eggs of a silverloon, the yolks a bright blue, sprinkled with poppy flakes and moonstone salt. I keep the honeycakes and bacon for myself but bring the eggs to Bell. They're her favorite.

I let her grab the eggs off the plate, her tiny arms sinking into the yolks, and she sucks them down in seconds flat.

"Jesus, do you know how to savor your food?" I tell her.

"Savoring belongs to Gods and wealthy mortals. Everyone else eats as much as they can, when they can, never knowing when it will be their last."

Damn. I almost feel guilty.

She wipes her dainty mouth. "I *know* you enjoyed last night."

I roll my eyes and bite into a piece of bacon.

"It's nothing to be ashamed of, Hanna," she adds. "Death knows what he's doing."

"Okay, don't you find it weird that we've both, you know, slept with him?"

"Why is that weird?"

"Because…I don't know. Generally you don't hang around women that have been with the guys you've been with."

"Why not?" Her bright blue eyes are wide with innocence, and I know she's being truthful. But of course, I can't really figure out how to explain it.

"I don't know. It's a territorial thing. I guess."

Her brows furrow. "Did you know that mermaids are very territorial when it comes to hunting grounds? I can understand that. There's only so much fish to go around. But dick? I mean, where's the deficit?"

I can't help but laugh. She actually has a point. "Fair enough," I tell her.

"And really," she goes on, "why are you getting territorial over someone you pretend not to care for?"

My eyes go wide and I nearly drop my food. "What? I don't *care* for him. I fucking hate him, Bell. I'm his prisoner. And before you bring up the fact that you are too, just know that in my world, prison is a bad thing, power dynamics are real, and grudges are held for life."

Her frown deepens, creating a line between her brows. "Okay," she says carefully, her tone icy. "So then who cares if I've been with him? He's had a wife too, you know. There have been other mermaids, other Goddesses. He's not a God of Virtue and Abstinence. He's the God of *Death*. Death has the most power in all the realms. He does what he wants, takes what he can. Sometimes it's me…sometimes it's *you*."

I shrug. "That's fine. I really don't care. I just think it's weird to be talking about having sex with the same guy, that's all."

"Guy?" she laughs, pronouncing the word like it's foreign. "He's a God, Hanna. Not a guy, not a man, but a God. You should be receiving him with wide legs and an open heart."

I shake my head vehemently while giving Bell the last slice of bacon. "No. That's not how we do it back home. A God doesn't capture people and use them for his own amusement."

"His own amusement? I heard plenty of *your* amusement last night." She grabs hold of the bacon and wolfs it down. "And in your world, Tuoni doesn't exist," she says through a mouthful. "I don't exist. Tuonela doesn't exist. But now you know that it all does. That your world is only one of many worlds, all linked by this one. Maybe the Creator is untouchable, unknowable, but the Gods? They're just as fallible as all of us. The only difference is that they can't die."

"Well, they can, if Death gets a hold of them," I point out. "Which asks the question…what kills Death?"

Bell stares at me for a moment, as if the question takes her by surprise. "I don't know if anything can kill Death," she muses. Then a darkness comes over her eyes, turning them the color of rough seas. "Maybe love."

"Love kills Death?" I scoff. "That doesn't sound like the prophecy."

"Maybe *losing* love," she clarifies. "Maybe loss of love is what actually kills him."

I shake my head, walking across the room to my coffee. "You hate to admit it, but you're an incurable romantic at heart, Bell. If loss of love killed Death, don't you think he would have died when Louhi left him for that mariner, or whatever his name is?"

"Arranged marriage," Bell says. "He never loved her. I am sure he tried, but I know he didn't. He never even wanted to be with her to begin with."

"Yes, yes, I know. I heard. It was arranged because her father was some demon who used to rule Tuonela."

"You've never met Louhi," Bell says adamantly. "She's awful. Death was forced into that marriage because of politics, and in the end, she's the one who cast him aside. That's got to bruise the ego."

"Honestly, maybe Death's ego can stand a little more bruising," I say.

"Well, if you want out of this twisted world, Hanna, then your job is to stroke Death's ego," she points out with a sigh. "Judging from last night, you're already off to a great start."

It sounds bad, but I want to drill her about that. I want to ask her what she thought of what happened, if it sounded normal, or if I really rocked Death's world. I want *my* little ego stroked, so I know to keep going. But I manage to keep that to myself.

Instead, I give her the rest of my food and a sip of coffee

and get ready for the day. I put on a white empire-waisted gown and bring my hair up high above my head, while Bell reminds me that the full moon is three nights from now. Now that I can leave the room and I know where the Stargaze Tower is, I'm pretty sure her escape plan will go off without a hitch.

Mine, however? That's still a work in progress.

Raila comes by later for my little tour. I don't know how crafty she really is, but I don't underestimate her either. Who knows how long she's been around, who her alliances are really with, and what she really thinks of me? Because of all the unknowns, I have to tread lightly.

So, where would you like to go? Raila asks as we step outside of my room, black satin hands clasped at her waist.

"How about the Library of the Veils," I suggest.

There's a pause, as I knew there would be. *I'm afraid that area is off-limits*, she says.

"Are you sure?" I ask. "Death did say I could go anywhere."

Anywhere you're allowed, she says. *I have been given strict orders not to allow you, nor anyone, into the Library of the Veils.*

"Anyone?" I repeat.

It is forbidden.

"Why?"

There is magic in there that could overthrow the Master and upturn the whole realm, possibly even all the realms as we know them.

That much power in the Book of Runes, I ponder. If I could get that book one day, I could change so many things. I wouldn't even bother with Death or Tuonela, I would just make it so that I could be back with my father, back in the real world, and that nothing from this world, nor any malicious shaman, could hurt either of us. I know I have to die one day, and I must admit there's some comfort in knowing I'll most likely be put in the Golden Mean instead of the nebulous question mark, but I want to postpone my death as much as possible.

But that's not why I've called upon Raila today. The Book of Runes is just a shiny distraction.

"Well, that's understandable," I tell Raila. "Why don't you give me a tour of Shadow's End, from the top to the bottom then. Wherever I'm allowed to go."

I will do my best, she says.

And so I take another tour of the castle, this time with Raila's commentary.

This is the solar room, she says as she takes me into a large room with floor to ceiling windows. Aside from the iron framework, it's pretty much a solarium and right now, with the sun trying to burn through the clouds, it's bright and hot.

Usually Death is in here having his morning coffee, she says. *But he isn't a fan of the sun, even when it's his own doing.*

I take my time looking around. It really is an incredible room with a three-sixty degree view of the area. Though the mist hasn't completely cleared, it's enough that I can make out the craggy mountain ranges to the north, the sea to the south. From here it really feels like you're on top of the world and ruler of the kingdom.

But it isn't the view that has my curiosity piqued. It's the details in the room, each one telling me something about its daily inhabitant.

There's a black leather chair and footstool with an iron side table beside it, a stack of books underneath. I can just imagine Death sitting there, his coffee beside him, his feet up, book in hand, while the land stretches out beyond the windows. The image delights me for some reason and I crouch down, taking a look at his current TBR pile: *The Art of War, The Great Gatsby, Of Mice and Men, In Cold Blood, The Holy Bible*, and *Lord of the Rings*.

My brow quirks up. "Lord of the Rings?"

The Master is a very prolific reader, Raila says, watching me. *Have you read it?*

I smile. "Yes, I have."

He says Tolkien got some things right about Tuonela, like Kokko, the giant eagle, but he failed to capture the intricacies of the land, Raila explains.

I nod and look around the rest of the room. There's a wine rack, a stocked bar that has crystal decanters that sparkle like diamonds, housing jewel-colored liquids in amber, crimson, emerald, and amethyst. Then there are a few bottles of Scotch and even tequila thrown in there, obviously smuggled from my world, plus an array of glassware and iron-welded vessels.

"I have to ask, what's with all the iron?" I gesture to all the iron details in the room, which is nothing compared to the rest of the castle. I mean even his dog is made of iron.

Tuonela is built from iron, she says knowingly. *A material that created a whole world. Iron is magic and can give life to things, attract things, as well as repel. The longer you are here, you will learn to work with both iron and it's ally, silver, to your advantage. I keep an iron cross by my bedside, just in case.*

I glance at her. "Just in case of what?"

What could possibly happen to her here?

Silence. Then she says, *Old habits from the old days. Shall we move on?*

I don't want to move on, not from our conversation, but I have a feeling she won't give me any more. Why would Raila need an iron cross? I know that in some myths and superstitions they ward off fairies, but since those don't really exist here, what exactly are they warding off?

I ponder that over as Raila leads me out of the Solar Room and down the stairs, showing me the rest of the castle and giving me background information.

I have to admit, she points out some good gossip, like how one time Death was entertaining Tapio, God of the Forest, who then tried to revive all the furniture in the castle that was cut from trees of his forest, or when Vellamo and her mermaids stayed with them for a week, and the underground waterways were filled with mermaids for days on end, which attracted Gods from all over.

I have to wonder if that's when Bell was first introduced to Death, but instead I ask if I can see the waterways, knowing that they must be a level below the Crypt.

So Raila leads me down, down, down, all the way to the cellar.

She points out the various sweetvine and frostmint wines he has stored, plus those procured from my world, then talks about the dungeons, the torture chambers, and the oubliettes, really sinking her teeth into all the gory details.

Finally, we come to the crypt.

This is the crypt, she says to me. *The Sect of the Undead.*

"Can I see inside?" I ask.

She hesitates, a pause hanging between us, weighing her options.

Then she says, *If you wish to. The Master himself will avoid it completely, but he's never explicitly said that it's off-limits to others.*

"Great," I tell her, giving her an expectant look.

I swear I hear her sigh. She turns and then takes out a long key from somewhere in her robe and inserts it into the metal door. With her veiled hood, she looks extra ominous against the flickering candlelight. She turns the lock and the door opens.

We step inside.

Hell.

That's my first thought, and maybe it's a bit sacrilegious, but still.

Hell, and *snakes*.

The moment the door opens, a multitude of black snakes start slithering from the center of the room, disappearing into the shadows, hissing as they go.

I gasp, nearly jumping into Raila's arms. I think after my tussle with the Devouress, I've developed a new phobia of them.

Don't mind them, Raila says. *They are only relics. They protect the crypt.*

And the crypt itself is like an all-white tomb. There are no windows, and the walls are this smooth, blasted stone, so unlike the dark textures of the rest of the castle. But while the space is bright, the things within the space are not.

First, there is the manner in which the crypt is laid out. It looks like a church, with a few pews on either side of an aisle. But the pews consist of the type where it's all about being on your knees—there are no benches or seats.

At the front of the aisle is the altar.

The altar is made of bones, white and shining, which prop up two stands. One is empty, the other holds a crown made of black bones and red jewels. A crown of crimson, just as Raila had described to me, waiting for the next Goddess of Death.

But the crown isn't what's caught my eye, nor is it what's made my blood run cold.

It's what is lined all along the sides of the crypt, which I'm starting to realize is more of a church, a place of worship, than anything.

There are six statues, three on each side.

Four of them are of people in flowing robes, with gaunt faces, arms outstretched or together in prayer, crowns of needles or blades or porcupine quills or antlers on their heads. All of them have their eyes removed, blood or gold or tar running down their cheeks, while lit candles sit on their shoulders, the wax dripping down, making it hard to decipher what's covering their bodies.

The two other statues are in similar poses, also wearing candles on their heads and shoulders and arms, except the upper halves of their faces are covered by intricate masks, with no holes to see out of. They are essentially blindfolded, one with a mask made of gold, the other of iron, their mouths set in a chilling grin.

"What…is all this?" I ask Raila. *Fucking creepshow.*

The Saints of the Undead, Raila says, and she quickly does some kind of curtsey and hand gesture in front of the crimson crown that doesn't go unnoticed.

"And so what does it mean?"

It means... she trails off and slowly walks down the aisle, seeming to stare at the sightless statues as she passes. *It means that the Old Gods are still worshipped. You see their eyes are missing? The old believers, the real ones, they removed their eyes because they were promised riches if they did so. They were told they could gain the sight of the Old Gods if only they gave up their eyes.*

I try not to shudder. The crypt is feeling increasingly oppressive by the minute. "And the two with the masks?"

Those are the Gods, the Gods that believe, she says. *They do not have human eyes nor human sight, but to be initiated into the sect, they must give up their sight in another way. It is also the way you must approach Vipunen.*

"Vipunen is a giant, right?"

Vipunen is an Old God. The only real one we have left here. He has been here since the dawn of time, and he will remain after. No one has ever seen Vipunen, not even Death himself. He lives deep in the caves under the mountain and, because no one has seen him, there are only rumors to what he is like. But a giant he does seem to be, maybe a hundred feet tall. He's helped Death rule, he's trained his daughter and son in combat, and perhaps one day he'll train you as well, depending on what happens to you. If you were to have him train you with the sword and the blade, then you would do so by donning a mask like this one. It signifies your status, but at the same time respects the one who doesn't wish to be seen.

She looks around the crypt. *Some say that to lay your eyes upon him is to die. Even the Master might suffer that fate. The masks protect both.*

I gesture at the candles, but even that feels like I'm tempting the Old Gods to smite me or something. "So who comes down here and lights the candles? Who here worships the Old Gods this way?"

A lot of us, Raila says in a stern voice. *There are a lot of us who do. The Stragglers, the leftovers.*

Ones who have been rescued from the bowels of Inmost. Ones who wander the halls of Shadow's End without any eyes. Some of which are hidden by *veils.*

But I don't get the feeling that's Raila. Not that it really matters what the Deadhands and Deadmaidens believe— it's the least of my concerns. Then again, if they worship the Old Gods and there is talk about an uprising, well, who are the followers going to protect? It won't be Death, or his family. They'll defect.

And that's why you need to get the fuck out of here, I remind myself. *Before you get caught up in this shitty situation that doesn't concern you.*

"I think I'd like to go back to my room now," I tell Raila.

With a nod, she obliges. It isn't until I'm out of the dank depths of the castle and almost back at my room that I wonder aloud, "Let's say that I stay here forever and rule as the new Goddess of the Dead. If there was to be an uprising, how would that effect, say, my father back in the Upper World? Or any other mortal? Are there far-reaching implications, more than just what happens in Tuonela?"

Raila pauses and I can feel her stare at me for a moment. *Why, if the uprising were to happen and the Old Gods were to take over, and the Creator didn't step in, then dying itself would be punishment. It would revert to the old days, before Death was called in here, before an afterlife in the City was built. There would be no order, no judgement, no fairness, nor no mercy. It would be Kaaos forever on end. All of humanity, of creatures, of species yet discovered, would suffer for eternity.*

I try to swallow as my heart fills with dread, dark like ink.

Okay. So it seems like even when I do get the chance to skip out of here, that there's a chance that all the realms in all the universes might have to suffer until the end of time. Cool. Cool, cool, cool.

"Well then," I tell her. "Let's just hope and pray that damn uprising doesn't happen."

I give her a shaky smile but I don't think she gives me one back.

AFTER MY VISIT to the crypt, I shut myself into my room and stewed over the new information. It's just my luck that the moment I can see a somewhat clear path out of here that there's a bunch of universe-altering consequences to go with it. Not that any of this is my problem, but the fact that I even know it's a possibility kind of makes it my problem. I might be the only mortal out there who actually knows what's at stake.

This is something I want to talk to Death about. I want to know how much of what Raila said is true and how much is just rumor and hearsay. It obviously doesn't affect him as much as it does me, because if he's ripped off the throne, it's not him that has to suffer for eternity, it's everyone else that's not a God.

Then again, I don't know what the Old Gods would do to

him. I do know the relics from that era are jerks, like Surma and the flaming children and the murder swan. Then again, Sarvi is a relic too, and so far he seems pretty badass. You know, for a bat-winged zombie unicorn.

But as much as I want to talk to Death about it, I don't see him for the whole day. In fact, I get the feeling that he's doing the very human fuckboi reaction after sex, which is to avoid the woman at all costs. Maybe it wasn't quite what he wanted. Maybe I scared him off. Maybe he's already moving on by calling up every mermaid in his phonebook. I don't know.

But even so, just in case, when night comes and I go to bed, I go to bed naked and I lie on top of the sheets.

And I wait.

And I wait.

The clouds finally start to clear, showing a hint of the moon, and then the door to my room opens.

His smell, his energy, his aura fills the air and my mouth waters and my body is already squirming in place, waiting for him. Damn, he's already got some supernatural hold on me and he's only had me once. Just *once*. And yet that's all it has taken for my hormones to utterly betray me, to make me fucking greedy for him already.

"There you are," he says, his voice as rich as cream. "So obedient. So exquisite. All for me."

I feel him come to the end of the bed, his shadow looming over me, his presence overwhelming. The bonfire smell floods my senses and I'm squeezing my thighs together.

"Impatient, aren't we?" he murmurs. "How you've changed, fairy girl. So unsure at first, and now you can't get enough of me, can't get it fast enough. But I'm in control here, not you. I'm the one who decides when you'll get it."

I hear the buckle of his pants as they're undone.

"And how you'll get it," he adds huskily.

I hold my breath as I wait for his touch.

"Soft?" he goes on, his voice gentle. "Will I give it to you softly, slowly?"

I gasp as he touches me, a tentative slide of his fingertips along my waist, back to my hips, my ass, my thighs, and then back up again, all the while his breath gets shorter, louder, like he's already struggling to remain in control.

He begins to slowly massage my hips, my ass, his gloves feeling extra grippy today as he kneads my flesh, almost to the point of pain. He does this for a while, taking his time, torturing me. Then adjusts his position, and I know what's coming next.

I don't fight it.

I want it.

More than I've ever wanted anything.

I suck in my breath and feel the thick wet lap of his tongue as it slides up and down each cheek. I shiver from the sensation, wanting desperately for him to go lower, to where I already feel the pressure building. I start to move my hips back, trying to guide him.

He chuckles wickedly.

"Look at you," he purrs. "You're begging for me."

"I'm not begging," I manage to say against the sheets.

"Then what are you doing? Asking politely?" He gives me a hard squeeze until I cry out in pain. "Is this what you want?" His fingers go lower and slip between my folds, stroking them. "Is it?"

I nod, taking in a deep breath, the pain melting to pleasure.

"I need to hear it," he commands. "I *like* to hear it."

I swallow thickly. "Yes."

"Yes, my God."

Oh hell.

"Say it," he says sharply. "Yes, my God."

I nod. "Yes. Yes, my God."

He groans. "You don't know what that sounds like," he says. "Like the fucking spirits are singing just for me."

He thrusts his fingers up inside me and I gulp, my body going stiff.

"Did you think you'd be so wet for me?" he asks, briefly teasing my clit before plunging his fingers inside me again. "Does it surprise you, how much you've wanted this? Wanted me?"

Do not give him a bigger ego, I warn myself, but then my thoughts dissolve as he starts pressing against my G-spot.

Holy hell.

I need to come and I need to come *now*.

He lets out an amused huff of air, and I hear him unbuckle his pants further, hear the *thwack* of his heavy cock against his gloved palm, a most erotic sound that makes my nipples ache.

I want...I need...I'm dying here.

There's a moment's pause, and then the swollen head of his cock slides up and down my ass, and his hands go back to gripping my hips and he moves me over an inch and back into him. He eases the tip of his dick inside me and then pushes a hand between my shoulder blades so my ass is raised, the angle all the higher for him.

Death lets out a primal moan as he sinks into me, and I can't help but respond in the same way. From this angle, he's packed in so incredibly tight, nearly pressing against my cervix. It's borderline uncomfortable, but then the sensation gives way to pleasure. I've never felt so full before, like his cock was always made to fit inside me.

Like I belong.

He slowly begins to slide out and then pushes back in, holding me in place until I start to slip forward. I grip the sheets, my face pressed against the bed as he slams into me again and again.

And again.

I pant for breath, trying to hold on and wanting to let go, while a gloved hand goes for my clit, rubbing wild and messy, making me moan, while the other one goes back to my ass, searching, exploring, testing me.

Yes, yes, please.

I groan loudly, wanting more, so much more.

Who am I right now?

What have I become?

An animal, just full of base instincts?

"You like that, don't you?" he growls. "Your eagerness is showing."

He pushes his thumb all the way in and I gasp.

"If you could see what I see," he murmurs, making a raw, primitive sound from somewhere deep inside. "How you cream around my cock, how tight you grip me."

And just like that, his finger presses down in one slick motion and I can feel how wet I am and how every inch of me feels so damn full and I'm coming.

Fuck!

The orgasm rips through me and I hold onto the sheets, feeling like I'm being flung somewhere very far away, a world beyond this and the next, and my skin is blistering as the need finally dissipates. I feel reduced to nothing but a puddle, while Death is still going, still working away at me even though my body has yet to come down from the ride.

He lets out another growl, this one pure instinct and animal, and I'm not sure if he's even a God right now; I think he might be more primordial and simple than that. He fucks me like he's born to fuck me, driven to come, like that's all he ever wants to do.

The sounds are so hypnotic that I feel my sensitivity fade away, and I'm getting hot and swollen again, ready for more.

"Oh, God!" I cry out, and I can't believe it.

I'm coming yet *again*.

"Yes," Death grunts loudly. "Fly again, little bird. I want you sore in the morning."

I'm riding this insane high, panting, moaning, screaming, swearing and then his fingers dig into my skin and I know he's close, so close.

"Hanna," he bellows, his voice filling the room as he climaxes.

My name sounds amazing on his lips.

The way he comes seems violent this time, the way his body shakes, the way his cock pounds inside me until finally he slows, sweat dripping onto my back.

I didn't even know Gods could sweat, but I'm quickly

learning they can do a lot of things.

Like fuck your brains out.

He collapses against me this time and my body buckles, slamming against the bed. I'm boneless, I'm floating, I'm just a soul crushed beneath Death, and he's holding me hostage, yet he's letting me live.

He's letting me live.

This is living.

CHAPTER EIGHTEEN

THE FULL MOON

I press my fingers into my earlobes and look in the mirror, hoping to see the color change in the aurora stone studs. Ever since I got to Shadow's End, I've tried to use the earrings to find a way to know if my father is still okay, still alive. But while the rock that Rasmus had would glow like the northern lights to let us know, the studs are so small that any flashes I see might be because of the way the stones have been cut.

In other words, I have no way of knowing if my father is all right. I came to the Land of the Dead hoping to find him, hoping that he was alive. Now I'm in this land, permanently, and he's supposed to be back home and I'm still wondering.

"I wish there was some way I could know," I say to Bell, my heart feeling waterlogged and heavy in my chest. I twist around in the chair and glance back at the tank. "Are there, like, messenger pigeons in this land or something?"

"There are ravens," she says, tapping her hands against the glass like she's the drummer for Tool. "Feathers and bones, mainly, but they deliver messages between Stragglers, Gods and spirits alike. Now, they don't fly between this world and the next. The soulbirds do though, but they don't deliver messages. Not in the way you mean."

I sigh and look back at my reflection in the mirror. I look better than I've ever looked. My eyes are bright, my cheeks flushed—I have a real glow about my skin. Perhaps eating like the Gods do has really agreed with me.

Or maybe it's getting eaten out by a god, I think, trying not to smile at the thought.

"You know, when you marry Death, when he falls in love with you, he may let you visit the Upper World," Bell points out. "And if not, he may at least send someone to check on your father. Deliver messages and the like."

I give her a wry look over her shoulder. "You know I'm going to miss your confidence in me."

She shrugs and goes back to tapping her hands. "Why shouldn't I have confidence in you?"

I shake my head. She makes it sound so easy. Yes, I'm now getting fucked by Death on a regular basis, our midnight trysts where I take it from behind and he remains this mysterious force that makes me see stars, have happened for the last few nights. But that's as far as the progress goes. When I see Death during the day, it's like the whole sex thing has never happened. Our interactions are brimming with sexual tension, but we don't talk about what we do to each other at night.

"And anyway, I hope that's not all you'll miss about me," she adds with a bright smile, drumming away.

She's nervous. Tonight is the night, when the full moon will appear and I have to call upon this Kuutar to get Bell safe passage. If she has confidence in me in getting Death to fall in love (highly unlikely), I think she has a little less confidence in me getting her out of here. I don't blame her. I'm a mere mortal, I don't know what I'm doing here. But I'll follow her instructions to the letter and do my damn best. And I guess there's always the next full moon, right? Providing Death doesn't discover her by then.

"I'll miss many things about you," I assure her. "But what I won't miss is someone listening to me have sex and making notes about it to discuss with me the next day."

She laughs melodically and then goes back to tapping.

Of course the timing of everything that's been going on makes tonight's mission a little more difficult. The weather has to cooperate, which means the sky must be clear, so that we can see the moon. Which means that Death has to either be asleep, or he has to be having sex with me (or just finished having sex with me). So, when I take Bell on her escape mission, I have to wait until Death is asleep.

Now, after we have sex, he usually puts his mask back on and leaves before I have a chance to see him in his natural state, or talk to him. He's not much for the apres-fuck chitchat, and frankly neither am I. But if for some reason he were to stay, that would royally fuck shit up.

Lucky for me, I have all day to fret about it. Time passes slowly, or maybe it stands still, goes backwards, it's hard to say.

Raila brings my dinner to my room as usual—I haven't been the guest of honor at dinner since the first time—and I barely have an appetite, even though the cook, Pyry, has created yet another delicious Tuonela meal (birch-smoked pike with mashed fire pumpkins and grilled dusk lettuce leaves). I do drink a few mugs full of starwater mead—which tastes like an orange Creamsicle, and is apparently very rare—enough to gather up my courage.

Then, when night falls, the mist cloaking the castle in black velvet tendrils, I lie on my bed and wait for Death. I don't mean literally, of course.

He comes in.

Takes me.

I don't turn around, I don't see his face.

I just submit and succumb.

Oh, and I thoroughly enjoy it.

But aside from his filthy mouth, few words pass between us, and then like usual, he's gone.

Normally I pass right out into the deepest sleep, but not tonight. The moment the door closes behind him, I'm getting out of bed and slipping my nightgown back on. I grab a candle holder and light the candle, then go over to Bell's tank, peering in. The candlelight makes her white scales shimmer, the flame reflected in her aquamarine eyes.

"Are you ready?" I whisper to her.

She nods. "I'm ready."

"So how should I do this?" I ask, feeling awkward. "How long did you say you can survive outside of the tank for?"

"Hours," she says. "We have plenty of time. Just pick me up and carry me."

I have to admit, the idea seems weird. I've never picked up anyone before and carried them, not even a baby and certainly not a tiny mermaid creature.

She rolls her eyes. "Treat me like a doll if you have to."

I laugh. "Oh you don't want that. All my Barbie dolls were missing their heads by the time I was done with them." Not to mention the compromising positions I always left them in with dick-less Ken.

"I trust you won't lose my head," she says wryly, then she reaches up toward me with her arms. "Now let's get going while the Moon Goddess is still out."

I still don't feel comfortable holding her, especially since she's part fish and probably very slippery, so I go and grab my boot and then hold it to the edge of the fish tank.

"Climb in there," I tell her.

She gives me a look of annoyance but pulls herself up over the top of the boot and slides on in. I have big feet, size nine and a half, so luckily she looks pretty comfortable in it—and photogenic. If I had the artistic ability of my dad, I think I'd try and paint her in it.

With Bell in my boot in one hand and the candlestick in the other, I creep toward the door and carefully open it. I don't know what time it is in this clockless palace, but the halls feel hushed and still. Death's sleeping quarters are on the same floor as the entrance to Stargaze Tower, so I have to be extra quiet when going along his floor, especially since his guards are stationed outside his room, doing the night's watch. I don't really know why Death has so much security, since I don't think he's easy to kill, but maybe it just helps boost his ego.

Sometimes I think that's why I'm here, an ego boost. Who doesn't want a woman screaming "oh God" every night at your touch?

The entrance to the tower is on the opposite side of the floor, away from sleeping Death, and once I'm on the spiral staircase, I hurry to the top, taking the steps two at a time, careful not to trip.

I gasp. The room looks completely different than when I was here the other day. All the paintings and charts of the stars on the wall gleam and sparkle like the stars outside. There are crystals placed around the room, on shelves and desks and stands, that I hadn't even noticed before. Now they're all bathed in moonlight and glowing different colors. Jagged chunks of amethyst, spears of clear quartz, glowing towers of translucent teal, and wands of what look like selenite, glowing a faint silvery gold that matches the shine of the moon.

Because the moon is the real deal here. I've seen the moon before at night in Tuonela, quick glances out my window if I happen to wake up early, and while it's always been gorgeous, it's looked more or less like the moon back home.

But tonight, it's full, so full it seems to take up all the space in the sky. Before, if you raised your hand to the heavens, your pinky fingernail might block out the moon. Tonight, I'm not even sure my fist would block it out. I can see every single crater with such clarity that it's making me anxious and dizzy.

I'm speechless.

"She's beautiful, isn't she?" Bell says breathlessly, gazing up with entranced eyes. I must look the same.

"Is that…Kuutar?" I ask.

"Kuutar is *in* the moon," she says. "That's where she lives. Look through the telescope."

I put the boot down on the table beside a glowing cluster

of rainbow quartz, and go over to the biggest telescope that Bell is gesturing to. I peer through it and somewhere in the back of my mind I am just in total disbelief over what's happening. Am I seriously going to help this little mermaid escape the wicked castle by looking through a telescope for a woman on the moon to appear? It's amazing what your mind gets accustomed to, whether the harshest conditions or the most fantastical situations, because I'm actually getting so used to dealing with this new world that I have to step back every now and then and go *what the fuck*, is this really my life right now?

And so, when I'm looking through the telescope, I'm not even surprised to see white sand dunes. They sparkle, like each grain of sand is made of a star, and they shift under unseen winds. I have to pause and take my eye off the viewfinder and look back at the moon with my naked eye, because what I'm seeing isn't matching up.

This time when I look back through the telescope, the stardunes have shifted even more and something is starting to rise out of them, the sand moving around in a circle of sparkles.

A tall, muscular woman slides out from the sand. She has long silver hair and white skin and pale purple eyes, and has on a gauzy thin dress of shimmering stars. She's beyond stunning, and is wearing the most serene smile.

"I see someone," I tell Bell, describing her.

"That's Kuutar!" she says excitedly.

"Aren't I supposed to chant some spell or something?"

She shakes her head. "It will be fine since she knows I'm here. Bring me to the window."

I bring Bell and the boot over to the window and open

it, the cold night air rushing in. The moonlight feels like an icy caress against my skin, making my heart dance. Below the waves crash against the tower, the moonlight shimmering, making everything look coated in silver.

"Are you sure?" I ask Bell warily as I peer over the edge. "This can't be safe."

"Yeet me into the sea, fairy girl," she says with a grin. "Kuutar will grant me safe passage once I land on the moonlight."

I hesitate. I trust Bell and there's definitely a goddess on the moon, but it doesn't feel right to literally throw her out of a building.

"Please, before we lose the chance," she adds, real urgency in her voice.

"Okay," I say with a sigh. "I'm going to miss you, you know."

"You'll see me again one day, I'm sure of it," Bell says. Then she nods at the water.

I take in a deep breath, pull back the boot and then thrust it forward.

"Bye Bell," I whisper as Bell goes sliding out of the boot, diving headfirst into the water below. She's so tiny that she barely makes a splash, just a rippling of silver moonlight.

I exhale, exhausted from the build-up to this moment, but relieved it all worked out in the end. I was able to keep a promise to someone and that feels good. Better than good.

But I also know that I took a risk in doing it and that if I don't get back to my room soon, there could be hell to pay.

I pick up the candle, tuck the boot under my arm and make my way out of the tower and down the stairs, praying I don't run into anyone. I'm not sure what my excuse would be if caught.

I'm finally on my floor, creeping as silently as possible down the hall, almost to my room when suddenly a dark figure steps away from the wall.

I can't help the cry that falls from my lips.

It's Surma, covered in his flowing black robe, his tattered skull visible.

"What are you doing?" he asks in a sinister voice, his teeth clacking together in that horrible way.

I open my mouth to talk, to lie, but he's fast. He suddenly reaches out and grabs me, his bone hands crushing my wrist before pushing me back against the stone wall, holding me there, pressing against my shoulder.

"I-I thought I heard a noise," I manage to say, fear crippling me.

Oh god, he smells awful. He's what I always imagined Death would smell like, rotting flesh and meat left out in the sun. The horridness only adds to the terror.

"Lies," he hisses. "You were doing something. I told Death you had no place being in this house."

"I wasn't doing anything," I protest.

"Why are you holding a boot?"

Fuck.

"A weapon," I tell him, raising my chin in false confidence.

"More lies," he seethes. "You are no different than your father, always trying to get your hands on our secrets, and Tuoni is too trusting of you, too soft. He's made too many mistakes, granting life to those who should have died, people like your father, messing up the natural order of things. Tuoni brought this reckoning upon himself. If I had his power still, the things

I would have done to you would be too horrific to describe. And while I can't rule over the land anymore, it doesn't mean I can't do what I do best." He hisses out the last word, making my blood run cold.

"It's time for Tuoni's reign to come to an end. The Old Gods will see to it. There are so many of us who will do whatever it takes to make sure that the City of Death falls. They will place me back in the role that was always mine. But you will be long dead before then."

I open my mouth to scream but then he's covering it with his boney hand, smelling of rot, and I'm nearly choking on it. I try to summon all my strength and power to fight back, but it's like he has me completely drained.

"Do you know who I am?" Surma rasps on. "I was the one who killed. I was the Killerling. All feared me. The mold from my decaying body would make people go insane before they died. I should do the same to you, or I could make your death even more painful than you can imagine. You don't belong in this world, girl. You belong in Oblivion. Let's see if Death misses you if you're gone."

Suddenly my nose fills with the warming scent of sea salt and smoke.

"*You* belong in Oblivion," Death's voice growls from the darkness. "Let go of her, Surma."

Oh thank god. *That* God, in particular.

"Do you know what she was doing? Sneaking around in the night?"

"She is free to go where she wishes," Death says and though I can't see him, I feel his presence get closer, my skin wanting to be close to his.

"I'm just doing what you should have done to start with," Surma says to him without taking his empty sockets off me. "You never should have made the trade. You should have killed them both. That's what the real God of Death does. You're an insult to the job, Tuoni. And you know it."

"Let go of her," Death says in a menacingly calm voice. "I won't tell you again."

"Or you'll what?" Surma says, pressing his hand harder against my mouth. I cry out, trying to squirm. "You hate it when things go to Oblivion. It makes you feel weak. You are weak. You're soft and spineless."

"Is that so?" Death says, and in a flash he's taken off his glove, his hand bare, silver lines glowing in the moonlight. "You can call me soft and spineless, but I always keep my word. And my word is that Hanna belongs to me. Not you, never you. And it will stay that way."

Before Surma can say anything to that, Death reaches out and grabs Surma by the throat. He crushes the bones of his neck into white dust and Surma's awful scream fills the air and his body collapses into a horror show. Every bone is pulverized, leaking black fluid, pus, and dust, and the pain of his death is so great that I can feel it in my fillings.

It feels like I'm dying myself.

Fear floods my body, the adrenaline kicking in, telling me to run from the one that just killed someone in front of me. It doesn't matter that I know Death, it's that I just saw Death do what he does best, and that's too much for any mortal soul to handle.

So I turn and I run to my room, throwing open the door, trying to find peace, an escape from the madness.

I don't get far.

"What were you doing out so late?" Death growls, coming after me, putting his glove back on. I get halfway across my room before he's grabbing me by the arm and pulling me to him. "You know you can't trust anyone here. Why would you put yourself in that position? What if I hadn't shown up to protect you?"

I shake my head, near tears. "I'm sorry, I'm sorry."

I want to run from him and run to him all at once.

"Don't ever do that again," he says, practically barking. "I told you that you're mine—I don't want to send everyone that tries something with you to Oblivion, even if they deserve it."

"Stop saying that I'm yours, I'm not!" I yell, the adrenaline turning my fear into anger, tired of feeling like a possession, like I don't have a soul and feelings, like I'm not a person with my own agenda.

"You are mine!" he roars, his grip growing tighter. "That was what you agreed to! That was part of the deal. You're mine, Hanna, and you will stay mine for the rest of eternity, whether you like it or not!"

"Then I don't like it and I never will," I sneer at him, trying to get free of his hold. It's fruitless.

"You lie," he growls, yanking me even closer to him until I'm flattened against his chest, his other hand going to my back and holding me there. "You like it when I'm deep inside you, you love it when I'm making you come. You can't get enough of me, and you know it, and that's what makes you so angry, because you want me just as much as I want you."

"You barely want me," I tell him, feeling far more vulnerable than I should be. "You won't even show me your face. You fuck me in the dark, from behind, you have a mask on the rest of the time. You keep as much distance between us as possible. I think…" I breathe in deeply through my nose, "I think I deserve a little better than that now."

He stares at me through his skull mask, this one red with devil horns, made of some kind of stone I'm sure can only be found here.

"Is that what you want?" he says, his rough voice lowering to a hush. "To see me? Will that make you happy?"

My brow goes up. "Do you even want to make me happy?"

I hear him swallow, lick his lips. "Yes," he eventually says. Even though there was one hell of a pause there, I believe him when he says it.

"I think I'm owed that much," I add quietly.

"Fine." To my surprise he lets go of me and steps back, putting his hands on either side of the skull. "You're right. I don't like to compromise, but you're right. You give yourself to me, I give nothing back to you. I wear the mask to intimidate, to create mystery, but with you…well, I'll have to take my chances that you'll still show me some respect."

I want to tell him that I never showed respect in the first place but I keep my mouth shut.

He lifts the skull off of his head.

I gasp.

"Hideous, aren't I?" he asks with a smirk.

That smirk is there because he knows what I'm looking at,

he knows who he is.

He's the opposite of hideous.

He's fucking *gorgeous*.

And, of course, Death would be. How could anyone think otherwise? How could Death be anything else but utterly seductive?

Death's skin is tawny and smooth, with full lips that I've felt on every inch of my body, a strong jaw with a rugged beard, which I've felt too. His cheekbones are high and his eyes are mesmerizing, even more so when I can see them without the darkness of the mask. They're hypnotic-looking, deep set, with thick dark lashes rimming his eyes so it looks like he's wearing ebony eyeliner. His brows are arched and black, framing the dark gray of his eyes which seem to go from charcoal to silver to pewter all while I'm staring at him, his pupils contracting and dilating.

Then there is his hair. It's long, black, tied back in a man bun.

Death has a man bun.

Words I never thought I'd think.

He's hot as fuck.

"Yes," I whisper. "You're very hideous."

And then suddenly he's on me, covering my lips with his, and my world is blown apart because he's kissing me for the first time, a deep, searing kiss that makes my toes curl, his tongue moving into me like second skin.

Holy shit.

This is it.

The kiss of Death.

And, *fuck*, I want more.

Apparently he does too.

We attack each other. He's ripping off my clothes and I'm trying to rip off his. It's an unbalanced battle because I'm just wearing a flimsy nightgown and he has layers upon layers and I can barely get through them before I'm dropping the candle. It falls to the ground, the flames lighting the rug on fire, and then he's ripping off his shirt and throwing it on the rug to put it out.

Then he's grabbing me and practically throwing me down so that I'm on the floor too, on my back, and he's looming over me.

Like a God. Like a fucking *God*.

He grins at me, a cocky twist of his lips, a quirk of his brow, and I should have known he would have such a beautifully arrogant face under his masks.

He rips off his shirt.

Then his pants.

Until he's only wearing the gauntlets.

For the first time I see him completely naked and…

And I am speechless.

His body is magnificent, seven feet of pure muscle mass on perfectly smooth skin. I already knew that his shoulders were broad, that his waist tapered, but seeing it in the flesh is something else. His chest is sculpted and wide, his abs a washboard eight-pack, with those perfect V muscles carving a path south over his hips. His arms and forearms are massive, rippling with untold strength. Then there are his muscled thighs, full of definition. Do thick thighs save lives when you're talking about Death?

And accenting his warrior body, the glowing pewter lines are everywhere, except for his face and his dick.

Speaking of his dick, it's perfect. I knew it would be considering how he's been using it on me, but yes, it's the cock of a God. Thick, long and straight-up, his balls hefty enough to provide some counterbalance.

I can't stop staring. I might even be drooling.

"I don't blame you for taking your time," Death muses with another wry smile, his eyes dancing in both levity and lust. "I often look at myself in the mirror that way."

"What do the lines mean?" I ask when I find my voice.

He drops to his knees, his dick bobbing. "They represent everyone who has died. They pulse when a new soul leaves. They pulse all the time, and they have for most of my life. Death never, ever stops. These runes remind me of my role in this world and all the others."

He grabs my thighs with his gloves and spreads my legs wide.

"Does it hurt?" I whisper, letting him handle me anyway he wants.

"It did," he says, clearing his throat. "But you get used to things." He grins at me salaciously. "This view, however, I don't think I'll ever get used to this."

He positions himself between my thighs, slowly stroking his cock with his gloved fist, holding back. I bite my lip, watching him, wanting him. The sight of him like this, on the precipice of giving in, is something to savor.

His brows furrow, a deep crease between them, his lips curling slightly, jaw tight, and I can tell he wants to push up inside me and go nuts, that it's taking a lot of restraint for him to control himself. For once. Usually he just lets himself loose but now, with his mask off, both of us facing each other like this, naked, it feels different.

Intimate.

Vulnerable.

Raw.

His nostrils flare and his breath hitches as he guides his cock between my legs, rubbing the thick head against me, already slick with precum.

I let out a gasp. My nerves respond with shivers down my spine, my legs spreading further, craving him inside me. My hips buck up, fueled by an intense type of desperation.

The corner of his lips quirk up in a smile as his gaze skims over my body, leaving little licks of flame in its wake, a look of awe in his eyes. He shakes his head, letting out a trembling breath. "You are mine, little bird," he whispers gruffly. "No one else's but mine. You've seen what happens to those that try to take you? Try to touch you? They get touched by me."

He reaches out with his hand, a gloved fingertip brushing over my lower lip, my mouth parting for him. "Anyone who harms you will be no more, that is my promise to you."

He leans forward, capturing my mouth with his lips, and I'm kissing him back, lost to the ruthless tide as he starts to shove his cock inside me.

Fuck.

I'm already so wet and ravenous for him, yet there's a pinch of pain as he pushes himself inside, until it slowly melts away into pleasure. I'm so damn tight when he's crammed inside me like this that I feel like a virgin all over again and it's getting hard to breathe.

"Oh," I cry out through a ragged breath, trying to inhale, but the feelings are too much and I'm drowning in them.

Death responds in kind. He lets out a raw moan against my mouth before pulling back and sucking in a deep, shaking breath. "Fairy girl, your cunt is so tight, I think you might be trying to kill me."

He gazes down at me with unpolished intensity and in his carnal gray eyes, I see the Death I've always wanted to see. No mask separating us here, nothing but skin on skin and our bodies that fit together like puzzle pieces. The way he pushes his cock in, slowly, inch by agonizing inch, makes my head loll on the floor, my mouth falling open in a breathy moan.

Pure bliss. This is the most decadent, indulgent pleasure I've ever felt.

"Fuck," Death swears, his cock shoved in to the hilt. He exhales, his breath shuddering, making me shake beneath him, and he reaches out to grab my chin as he gazes at me. "This is what I've been missing. This is what I should have been seeing. This. You. Your face as you surrender."

I can't help but grin, my cheeks flushing with heat.

"Don't be self-conscious," he reprimands me, eyes gleaming. "I might have to punish you for it."

"You know I can take it," I manage to say, my voice thick, throaty, relishing the feeling of him so deep inside me. I reach down and grab his ass, all powerful muscle, and pull him into me so that he sinks even deeper.

God, *yes*.

He groans so loud that I feel the vibrations in my bones, the sound lighting me up, spurring all the desire inside me. We're moving too slowly and I'm suddenly insatiable for him. I want him to fuck me, devour me, ravage me. I'm his prisoner, I'm his captive, I'm here to be fucked senseless. This is the one time I have no problems giving up power. Hell, I don't even give it up, I readily shove it into his hands, wanting him to do his worst to me.

I want to take it all.

"I like it when you're hungry," he says in a husky voice. "I like how feral you become. There are so many sides to you, Hanna, I want to see them all come alive when I'm fucking you this deep."

He pulls back, bracketing me between his massive arms, his muscles straining as he pushes himself in again, even deeper this time.

Fuck!

I try to watch, taking it all in like a show, even though my eyes keep pinching shut with each violent thrust. He's fucking magnificent. The way his body is so perfect, his muscles larger than life, showcasing the pulsing runes of light that make him glow like the god he is.

Then his hips slam into me, hard, and I gasp, my fingers curling around the rug beneath me, and my eyes close as I let all the sensations wash over me like a tidal wave. The feel of his thickness inside me, his ragged breath as he powers through. The room fills with the smell of our sex, musky and intoxicating.

His rhythm increases, the pace getting faster, messier, his cock sliding along every coiled part of me. From the intense look on his face, his dark brows knitted together, the moans that are falling from his wet mouth, he's as lost to the sensations as I am.

He spears me with his eyes, holding me hostage in their pewter gaze, until it almost feels like staring into the sun, like it's too much for one person to handle.

Like there's too much danger at stake.

Because of course there is.

I'm being fucked by Death.

All it takes is for him to get carried away, to get careless and lose control, and for a glove to slip off.

That would be the end of me.

The thought makes me tense, fear striking me in the heart.

As if sensing this, he reaches over and gathers my wrists together, moving them above my head, pinning them there. He holds me in place with his gauntlets, grip tight, as he pistons his hips faster. They slam into me, knocking the air from my lungs, relentless. The rug starts moving backward on the floor.

"Fuck me," I whisper, breathless. I have to look away from his eyes, they're wanting so much from me right now, not just my body but my soul.

Right now, I'll give it to him.

I'll give him everything to keep feeling like this.

Through sex with Death, I've never felt more alive.

It's the act of creation coupled with the act of destruction.

It's us, as undefinable as we are.

But there is an *us* here.

My eyes fall closed, letting the fear go, succumbing to every feeling; The rough fabric of the rug on my spine, the night air as it cools my flushed skin, the sound of his raspy breath, the squeeze of his cock as he thrusts inside me without mercy, again and again and again.

"Look at me, fairy girl. I want you to know who's fucking you this ruthlessly."

My eyes open and the look on his face has intensified, his forehead creased in concentration. For a moment, I can't believe this is happening, that this man—no, *this God*—with his impeccable body, and those glowing rune tattoos that speak for all lives lost, is fucking me like this. Ruthless to the core.

"I want you to fly," Death says through a rough grunt as his body thoroughly works me, every muscle clenched and strained. "I want to see your sweet face as you spread your wings, little bird."

He reaches down between my thighs and starts rubbing my clit in rough, slippery circles.

Oh *god*.

My God.

"Don't stop," I cry out softly, my legs spreading wider for him. He lets go of my wrists and I reach up and grab his ass harder this time, until he's in so tight there isn't a centimeter of space between us.

He growls, determined to get me off, possessed by our raw desire, fingering me and fucking me with such intensity that the room seems to glow with our energy, as if we have the power of a thousand starstones.

"Oh god, don't stop," I say again. He grunts loudly in my ear and his skilled fingers play with my clit in a figure eight. His cock drives in deeper, as if he's about to impale me to the floor.

The pressure inside me builds and I feel like I'm moments from going over the edge and falling. He covers my lips with his, pulling me into a wet and messy kiss, fucking my mouth as thoroughly as he fucks me with his dick. Then he brings his head down to my breasts, licking at them, sucking in my nipples until I feel like my world is about to be blown wide open.

"Little bird," Death says thickly, just as my orgasm reaches for me. "Fly away now."

The God of Death just obliterated me.

"Oh fuck!" I cry out. I come *hard*. I'm drowning. Back arched, limbs shaking, heart trying to burst through my chest. The wave doesn't end, it just keeps coming for me, over and over again, and I can barely focus. Once again there's the slight fear that he may have just sent me to Oblivion but luckily that feeling fades and all I feel is sated bliss.

Death growls, brings his large gloved hands down to my hips, holding me in place as he fucks into his release, the movements wild and brutal. Then he throws his head back, his throat exposed, eyes rolling back, and he's coming with a long, uninhibited groan.

"Fuck," he groans, gasping for air. "You undo me, Hanna. I am undone."

I grin lazily, watching as the orgasm rips through his body, just as it ripped through mine. He really is completely undone. His muscles gleam with sweat from his own exertion, his man bun has come loose, letting his long, jet-black hair over his shoulders, his mouth open and wet, his chest heaves as he tries to regain his breath.

What the fuck just happened? We have to be thinking

the same thing, because though the sex before was amazing, it wasn't anything like *this*.

This was…soul-rendering.

With a long, slow shuddering exhale, he looks down at me, and in his eyes I see peace and I have to wonder how often he feels that way.

Then our lives start sliding back into place.

The God of Death and his prisoner.

Yet even as Death pulls out of me and I can feel the distance come between us, I know that something has changed. I don't know what it means for me, or for him.

But the game we're playing just got a little more real.

A little more life or death.

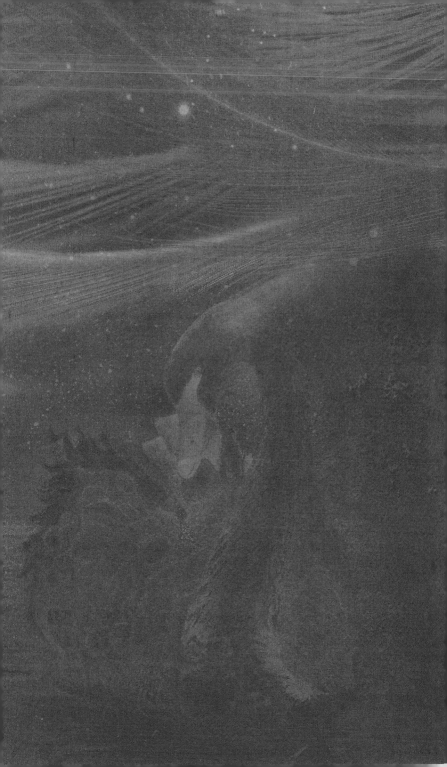

CHAPTER NINETEEN

THE GARDEN

The sun is shining.

I can barely believe my eyes. Instead of Raila waking me up, there's a shaft of shimmering sunlight on my face, coming in through the window.

I smile, my eyes closed, my sight glowing red behind my eyelids, and I'm trying to remember the name of the Sun Goddess. If she's anything like Kuutar, she's got to be beautiful. I'm picturing a woman of gold, a woman I didn't realize I'd missed until she was gone. I'm such a California girl.

Then again, this time I'm pretty sure the sunshine is all my doing.

I wake up and look over, feeling only mild disappointment when I realize I'm alone. It's not that I expected Death to stay the night with me, but after last night I thought there would be a little more intimacy between us.

Then my eyes fly open as I remember what happened.

The way that Surma tried to kill me.

The way that Death killed him.

The way he threw off his mask and kissed me so thoroughly

I thought I might die from it.

Perhaps he didn't stay the whole night, but he did let me see him for who he really is, no threatening facades. Just a deadly handsome God.

Don't get carried away by a pretty face, I tell myself. *The deadliest things are usually the most beautiful. He is no exception.*

I sigh and get out of bed. I feel invigorated from last night, from being with Death, from freeing Bell, and yes, even from Surma's death, as morbid as that sounds, and the sun feels like it's charging my bones. I go to the wardrobe and pick out a simple dress then slip on my boots. I want to be outside for this, to soak up every ounce of sunlight. I have no idea how long it will last, because I have no idea how long *I* will last here. The thing between Death and I? It could go away in a second.

Of course, I'm still a prisoner at Shadow's End, so going for a long stroll is out of the question. However, I have noticed the garden, a walled area of trees and plants and flowers between the two main buildings of the castle. I can probably go there without breaking any rules or bending any wards.

I head downstairs, passing the creepy Deadhands as I go. They stare at me and I wish I knew what they were thinking. Do they even have brains? Do they have lives? Are the same as the Deadmaidens in that they remember the people they once were? Do they miss those people, those lives? Is this what they thought death would be like?

But I don't have the nerve to try and talk to them. They might serve Death, but the last skeleton dead guy I had a run-in with ended up with him getting killed. Death was right when he said there were those that couldn't be trusted in this castle. I have to wonder who else there is pretending to serve him. Because if not him, who are they serving? The Old Gods? Louhi?

While I ponder that, I have to go through the kitchen to get to the garden, and I pass Pyry, the Deadmaiden cook in her black garb, already making breakfast.

She's not alone. Harma in her red veil is with her and they seem like they're whispering about something, stopping abruptly when they see me. If they're speaking telepathically, it's not like I'd hear them anyway.

I give them an awkward wave. "I'm just going to the garden," I tell them. "Finally a sunny day, Pyry. Hopefully the plants will take advantage."

I hope so too, dear Hanna, Pyry says with a bow of her head. They both stay silent, watching me pass with their faceless faces until I get the hint and leave the kitchen. I know Harma told me that she was an ally, but since she hasn't said anything to me since, I wonder what that exactly is, and if Pyry is in the same boat as her. Could they be like Surma, patiently working for Death while plotting to underthrow him? Not that Surma outright said he was, but he definitely wasn't on Death's side.

I try to shrug it off. It's nothing for me to worry about right now. I have other things to concentrate on, like trying to get enough vitamin D.

And no, that wasn't a euphemism.

I step through the door and into the garden, blinking hard at the sunlight while I try to take it all in.

Holy hell, it's like stepping into another world, one so different from the interior of the castle. The place is gorgeous, with rows of the biggest roses I've ever seen, the blooms the size of dinner plates, their colors lush and jewel-like, while bushes of blue and pink hydrangeas reach for the sun, and twisted vines of wisteria hang in the sky like purple fireworks. Butterflies dance in the air, their wings shimmering in shades of cerulean and marigold and amethyst, the sight magical.

Beyond the array of flowers there are tidy rows of vegetables and herbs, as well as fruit trees and a whole variety of vines, plus other plants—trees, bushes, flowers—that don't exist in the Upper World. I could spend weeks learning about all of them and still I don't think it would be enough. A botanist would have a field day here, this place being their literal Amaranthus.

And in the middle of all this is Sarvi. I don't see the unicorn that often, so to see it's big dark form in the middle of the garden takes me by surprise.

Did I frighten you? Sarvi asks, turning to see me. *I suppose you may have frightened me.*

"I'm sorry," I say. I gesture around me, hoping I'm not going to get in trouble for being here. "I'd never been to the garden before. Thought it was the best place to enjoy the sunshine."

Sarvi lifts its head to the sky, closing its one eye, seeming to relax. *It is a blessing to have Death happy enough for this to happen.* Then its eye fixes on me. *I hate to be presumptuous, but would you happen to be the cause of all this? If so, might I suggest you keep it up?*

There's a knowing tone there and I find myself blushing. Basically, keep screwing Death so we can get some sunlight. He doesn't sound much different than Bell with her talk of blowjobs and sunshine.

"I'll see what I can do," I say. I then clear my throat. "So, what are you doing out here?"

Sarvi nods at a patch of ice-blue pumpkins. *They're my favorite. Ice pumpkins. I returned from the Frozen Void a while back with some of the North's local delicacies, hoping to grow them here.*

"Does anything from the realm grow in the garden?"

The unicorn does a shrug of sorts, briefly lifting its bat wings and showcasing the row of exposed ribs below. *There is magic here, of course. Death has made the land especially fertile and Pyry has been enchanted to become the perfect cook. But when it comes to using magic, it's best to use it sparingly, especially when it comes to food and drink. Magically induced food has zero nutritional value. Over time, it may actually diminish the use of magic in the consumer.*

"Interesting," I muse, reaching out and touching the leaves of the snowbeans growing on the nearest vine.

Here, let me give you a tour, the unicorn says. We walk along the flowers and plants and Sarvi starts pointing items out with its horn, explaining what they are and where they come from. Meanwhile, butterflies continue to fly to and fro, much to my delight.

One of them even lands on the tip of Sarvi's iron horn, slowly fluttering its wings which glow blue and pink.

This is a moon butterfly, Sarvi informs me. *They only live during a full moon, so you'll see them fly around for a couple of days on either side of the celestial event, then they die.*

"Wow," I say breathlessly. "It's so beautiful."

Sarvi suddenly waves its horn, causing the butterfly to

take flight. Then the unicorn lunges forward, teeth bared, and snatches the butterfly out of the air, swallowing it down whole.

Beautiful and delicious, Sarvi says.

My eyes go wide. I guess Death did tell me that the unicorns could be nasty.

Sarvi chuckles, noting my expression. *They're a delicacy. More so than the bloodmoths, but you should be thankful I enjoy eating those as well.*

"Do I want to know why they're called bloodmoths?" I ask warily.

They're like oversized mosquitos, Sarvi explains. *And they swell up with blood as they feast. But I happen to love blood, so they make a tasty little snack.*

The unicorn licks its lips with its black tongue and I try not to cringe.

Eventually Sarvi goes back to tending to some of the vegetables, while I lean against the stone wall that surrounds the garden and close my eyes to the sun, breathing in deep, and trying to forget all this talk about blood-sucking moths.

I hate to say it but, when it's like this outside, I almost like it here. The relentless moody weather would get to me, but when the sun is out, it feels invigorating, and head-clearing. And for once, I'm not trying to use my clear head to try and plot my escape.

Then the air changes, a gust of cold along with the sun, and I know that Death is in the garden, too.

A thrill runs through me before I even open my eyes.

"There you are," Death says to me, and I look over to see him appear at the garden entrance. His face falls in the dim shadow of the castle towers, exaggerating the sharp lines of his cheekbones, the strong cut of his jaw. His beard is thicker now, somehow making him even more manly, as if that were possible. A breeze picks up, tussling his long dark hair that's loose around his shoulders, and rays of sunlight make his visible runes gleam.

Our eyes meet and he smiles at me. He fucking *smiles* and I'm suddenly struck dumb by how handsome he is. It's not just that I've spent so long not knowing what he looks like, that he's actually fucked me *good* while being completely unknowable, it's that he truly is gorgeous. A real, true God. And this is the first time I've seen him outside, a light that is sometimes unforgiving and yet here he *shines*. It's like I'm seeing him for the first time, not just as the God of Death who has taken to my bed every night, but as something more.

But then guilt drives into my heart at that thought. The idea that I could be more to him. That's what I've wanted, that's part of the plan, and yet for once I don't want to think of the plan. I just want to be here, feeling the adoration in his eyes, and the affection in his smile. I know how rare it is, rarer than the aurora stone.

"I like this look on you," he murmurs as he comes over to me, his tall, wide body looming over mine. He gently reaches out and runs his gloved thumb over my chin. Today he's wearing gloves made of black feathers and his touch is soft and seductive and my eyes flutter closed. I absently wonder if the gloves are made from the swan I murdered.

I swallow, my throat feeling thick. "What look?"

"This one." He gestures to the air around me with his other hand. "The sight of you outside here in the garden, in the fresh sea air. I don't think you've ever looked so lovely, little bird."

His eyes then darken. Literally. The gray turning a tarnished pewter, matching the color of his runes. "It makes me worry that you might catch a gust of wind coming from places unknown to you, that it may make you curious enough to try and spread your wings. That you'll fly far from here and never look back."

He cups my face now, his thumb gently brushing over my lip now. I lean back against the wall, feeling the cool air sweeping over the sides, ruffling my hair in tendrils that dance around my breasts.

"I've become quite fond of you, Hanna," he says in a low murmur, his eyes searching my face. "I'm not used to feeling anything of the sort. You'll have to forgive me if my fear makes me do foolish things."

"What foolish things?" I ask.

He gives me a small knowing smile, making him look positively roguish. "You will find out soon enough," he says.

Then he straightens up, his hand dropping to my waist, and he looks over at Sarvi who is nibbling on some grass, like a straight-up normal horse.

"Sarvi," Death says. "Would you mind giving us some privacy?"

Sarvi raises its head, then nods, tail swishing. *Of course, sir. Is there something you'd like me to do for you in the meantime?*

Another dark look passes over Death's eyes, his black arched brows furrowing. "Yes. Fly to the City of Death. To Inmost. Tell the dwellers that there will be a Bone Match next week, and for them to put forth their best fighters. There will be ten different rounds, running all day long. Each winner will receive sanctuary at Shadow's End as one of my royal guards."

Yes, sir, Sarvi says, though it sounds hesitant. *May I ask why we're having such a big competition?*

"Because I want everyone to know that I'm strengthening my army," he says gruffly, and though he may not have a skull or crown on his head at the moment, he sounds very much the king. "I want the word to spread far and wide, throughout the city factions, throughout the realm itself. I want it to reach the bogs of Star Swamp, and the shamans of the Upper World. I want them to know that any uprising will be met with a reckoning."

That little speech shouldn't turn me on but it does, heat flaring between my thighs. Apparently I'm a simp for power.

Yes, sir, Sarvi says, eye gleaming. Sarvi seems to like it too.

"Invite all the Gods and Lesser Gods," Death goes on. "Tell them it will be the first formal appearance of the new Goddess of Death."

My eyes widen. "Wait, what?"

I beg your pardon? Sarvi snorts in disbelief at the same time.

Death glances down at me, his eyes tempestuous. "You're to be my bride, Hanna. This shouldn't be a surprise to you."

Well, I don't mean any disrespect, sir, but it's a most shocking development to me, Sarvi says.

"And me!" I tell Death. Good lord. "What do you mean, your bride? Since when…we're not married. We are *so* not married."

Unless…Oh shit, is there some weird custom here that when you have sex with the king, you automatically become the queen or something?

"We will be married, soon," he says, his nostrils flaring in defiance. He looks at Sarvi. "There's nothing you need to do about it. It will be a civil ceremony, with Kalma officiating. You will be there as witness, that's all. I know Lovia will be disappointed there isn't a big party, but after Surma revealed his intentions, I don't think waiting will help anything. This world believes in the prophecy; it's the only hand I have right now."

I shake my head. This is moving fast. Way too fast. "Don't I get a say in this?"

He grins at me, looking more wicked than handsome now, a truly devious king. "It was your suggestion, fairy girl. Don't you remember what you had first put on the table? You told me you would marry me. You said I could make you my bride."

"If it came to it," I protest, feeling panicked.

"Well, it's come to it," he snaps, his eyes taking on a harsh glint. "As you know, I am not someone who goes back on my word. I let your father go, I cured him, not because I wanted to, but because I promised to. You must keep your word to me, Hanna."

"And if I don't?"

"You will," he says, his hand coming to my chin again and holding my face, his grip tighter now, his gaze hardening. "You have no choice in the matter. Unless you want me to do to you what I did to Surma."

"Are you threatening me?" I practically sneer at him. He wouldn't dare!

"Does this surprise you too? For shame, fairy girl. So much naivete." With his hand still on my chin, he glances at Sarvi. "Off you go now."

Sarvi nods. Giant black leather wings unfurl and the unicorn leaps up into the sky, flying away, leaving Death and I alone in the garden.

I watch as Sarvi's dark shape in the periwinkle blue sky disappears and then I feel truly afraid.

"You're angry with me," Death muses, his gaze roaming my face.

"I'm always angry with you." Frustration rolls through me and I try to whip my face from his grasp, but his grip is strong.

The corner of his mouth ticks up. "Not always. Not when I'm giving you release. When I'm making you come. You're beautiful when you give in, when the pleasure overrides your desire to be in control, when it makes you surrender. There's no anger there, just you at your purest self. Is it any wonder I'm addicted to making you feel that way? It's like a gift, from you to me." He pauses, giving my chin a hard squeeze. "Your soul on a platter. All for my consumption."

I refuse to back down from his eyes. "I'm not giving you anything," I deride. "Not on a silver platter and most definitely not my soul." To give him my soul…would mean death, would it not?

"You give me your body every night," he says, his hand releasing my chin and trailing down to my breast where his thumb slowly grazes across the fabric, my nipple hardening under his touch. "I don't even have to ask. You just give it to me, begging for me to take you anyway that I can. You want to be consumed, little bird. You want your feathers plucked, your wings clipped."

He leans in and kisses my neck and I fill with the smoky

sweet bonfire smell of him, mixing with the bracing sea air. "But perhaps," he murmurs against my skin. "It would be better if I did ask for your hand in marriage, instead of taking it."

His tongue licks up the side of my neck, breath hot beneath my ear, and I hate the way my body automatically responds to him, like a puppet on a string. My eyes fall closed and I try to suppress a moan, a useless attempt.

"If I did ask," he goes on, taking my lobe between his teeth and tugging lightly, his breath heavy, "would you say yes?"

"I would say no," I whisper as I try to find my resolve. "My answer would be no."

He growls, the sound making me shiver.

"Then it's a good thing I take and never ask," he snaps and suddenly he's reaching down and hiking up my dress, his hands gripping my ass and lifting me up, pressing me against the wall.

My legs automatically wrap around him, my boots digging into the firm muscles of his ass, pulling him against me. I know I shouldn't be doing this. I'm mad as hell at the idea of being forced to be his bride, no planning, no discussion. I know it was the end goal, at least the one that Bell had put into my head, but I didn't think it would happen this fast and I didn't think it would be non-negotiable. I thought there would be a proposal and fanfare, that Death would marry me because it was something he wanted, because he loved me, maybe, or at least saw me in some sort of romantic light. That there was some kind of meaning behind it all.

In the end though, it's all just a political move. I don't know why I thought it would be any different.

It doesn't seem to matter much anyway, when he's about to

fuck me senseless against the garden wall.

Death lets out a moan that I feel to my toes and reaches down, swiftly unbuckling his pants while he continues to bite and suck at my neck, leaving bruises and marks.

"I'm going to make you my bride," he says gruffly. "But first I'm going to make you come. Fuck you so thoroughly, you won't be able to walk for weeks."

He covers my mouth with his, his tongue violent and searching. His cock presses against the spot where I'm already wet, and when I shift slightly, it slides inside me with delicious ease.

God, I hate how much I love this, how much I need this.

He lets out a jagged breath and starts thrusting into me as I stretch around his thickness. I never imagined I could feel as full as I do with him, this feeling of being totally and completely whole. I moan lightly, feeling him everywhere inside me, each nerve glowing with desire.

His hips curl forward and he starts pumping into me, my back razed against the garden wall, but I don't feel any pain. Even as the pace picks up and the rhythm becomes punishing.

He's so hard, thick and stiff, shoving into a place so soft, raw and tight. Every muscle in me is tense to the point of shaking and each thrust undoes another part of me. I feel like I'm made of glass and I'm close to shattering, and that there's a chance I may not be able to pick up the pieces after this. I may not want to.

He groans loudly now as he drives himself in harder, making me choke on my breath.

"Do you know that you'll be a queen?" he rasps, delivering

another rough, bruising kiss. "Do you realize you'll wear a crown of crimson? You'll be the wife of Death, revered and feared throughout the land."

"I'm just a mortal," I manage to say through a ragged gasp. "No one will fear me."

"They will, Hanna. They will. Just you wait and see." Then he bites my neck, sending shockwaves throughout my limbs. "You have no idea what you're capable of but I'll be the one to show it to you. Show you who you truly are."

I whimper in response, my body so greedy and crazed for him and when he pulls his head back, he's staring at me with so much intensity that I know he's feeling the same way for me. He has to be.

It's almost scary how raw this all feels. We are lost to our most basic instincts, sharing this primordial, animalistic desire to make each other come like crazy, to be so deep inside each other that we don't know where one ends and the other begins.

It's only when he's fucking me that I stop feeling like his prisoner.

It's only now I truly feel free.

Each powerful pump of his hips, each time his cock drives in deeper into my slick heat, each breathless gasp I make, each hungry groan that he makes, and I'm falling.

Cracking.

Breaking.

The glass shatters.

I give in to him.

Give myself to him.

Soul on a platter.

Ready for him to consume.

"Oh fuck," I whimper as the pressure in my core tightens like a feverish spiral and my eyes pinch shut, my body pitching over the edge. I clutch him hard, nails digging deep.

"Fuck me!" I cry out and my words turn into a garbled mess as the orgasm crashes into me. My head goes back, my eyes opening to see the sky so bright beyond the looming darkness of the castle towers.

A sky of periwinkle blue.

I feel as free as that very sky.

Death is coming now too, a gorgeous, primal groan pouring out of him. Nothing has sounded sexier as he grunts into my neck, his forehead hot against my skin. His thrusts slow, then still, our chests heaving with our ragged breath.

A chilled breeze smelling of sea spray and garden mint washes over the open walls, cooling our heated skin. He pulls back and gives me a lazy grin. No, wait. It's more of a smirk. I don't think Death is ever lazy.

"There's nothing more beautiful than this," he says, brushing my hair off my face. "You'll make a lovely bride, little bird."

And then the hard, cold reality comes crashing into me again.

I'm going to be the Bride of Death.

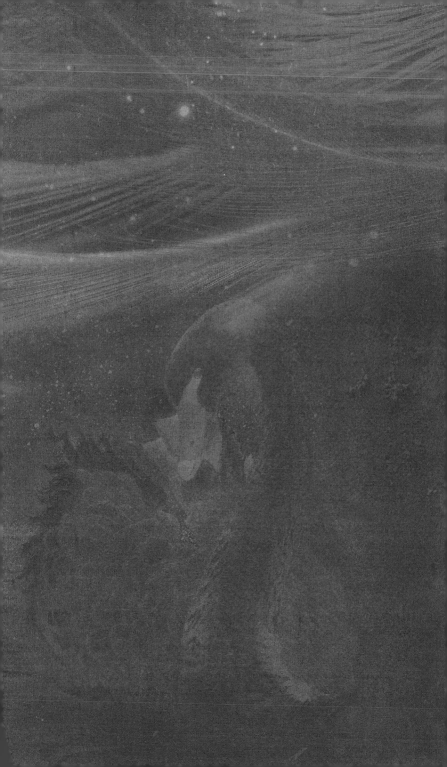

CHAPTER TWENTY

THE BRIDE OF DEATH

Despite Death's wishes that our wedding be quick and rudimentary, word of our nuptials spread quickly across both the realm and the castle. It wasn't long before others were planning the wedding for us. Or at least attempting to.

And by others, I mean Lovia.

Death's daughter was beside herself with joy, probably already picturing her exit into the Upper World, and convinced her brother to ferry the dead for the upcoming week so that she could devote all her time to me.

Which is nice and all. I like Lovia a lot, and with Bell gone, it's nice to have someone else my age (give or take a few eons) to talk to, especially someone familiar with my world and who doesn't look at you like you have two heads when you start talking about life back at home. But the more she gets excited about the wedding, the more I feel this crushing pressure, like I've been placed in a slowly turning vice.

I don't want to get married. I most definitely don't want to get married to Death, someone I can really only stand when he's shoved deep inside me. Growing up, tying the knot was never one of my goals. I mean I get it. I get that people want to be with the one they love for the rest of their years, especially when raising a family. But I guess I just never let myself even fall in love. Not really. And a family was always this wonderful thing that was meant for other people, not me.

After all, my family was fractured at such a young age… maybe I was the reason? It's a hard belief to shake, either way. Maybe all children of divorced parents think this way, but you can't help but blame yourself a little. Or a lot. Maybe there was something wrong with me, that's why they split. Hell, since I'm going down this path, maybe that thing that supposedly makes me "powerful" here, whatever that is, is what drove my parents apart.

"Why are you looking so glum?" Lovia asks, eyeing me in the mirror. She's standing behind me, trying to figure out what way to do my hair for the wedding. So far she's tried a million different options and doesn't seem satisfied with any of them. "Getting cold feet?"

That's putting it mildly.

"I'm just…I never thought my wedding day would be like this," I admit, toying with how much I should say. "Honestly, I never gave a lot of thought to it. The only thing I did know was that if it ever did happen for me, my father would be there to walk me down the aisle…" I trail off, trying to hold back the tears that are abruptly rushing to my eyes, making my nose burn.

Fuck, I am *so* over crying.

"Oh," Lovia says softly, her face falling in sympathy. "I'm so sorry. I didn't think about that."

Honestly, neither did I. Not until now. Because none of this has felt real. Maybe that's why I've just bounced along with everything that's been happening to me, going with the tide, no matter where it takes me. Ever since I stepped foot in this crazy world, I feel like everything has been happening to some other version of me. Like there's a chance that Hanna Heikkinen is still back in Los Angeles, taking pictures for her social media account, completely oblivious to what this version of myself is going through.

But this is real. Isn't it? That reflection in the mirror really is mine. This isn't some bizarre extended gothic sex dream, this is my life now and it's changing by the second.

And it hurts, it hurts so much to know that my father isn't here for these changes, as strange as they are. Hell, I even wish my mother was here. I would love to hear her commentary on what's happening, hear her criticisms over what royal death gown I'm wearing for the day, or whether I'm polite enough to the Deadmaidens.

I just feel so alone and powerless and even though the wedding isn't what I really want, it doesn't feel right to have to go into it like this. I should have a partner in all of this, but that's not what *this* marriage is all about anyway.

This marriage isn't about me. It's not even about *us*. It's all about Death. It's all about politics and tactics and appearances, everything to make him seem more formidable and in-charge, as if there's anything else more formidable than the God of Death.

To make things worse, I actually haven't really seen Death

since he "proposed." After our little session in the garden, he's been elusive and he hasn't been showing up in my bedroom at night either. The one time I did run into him in the halls when I was taking my morning stroll, and asked him where he's been, he said he's been busy and basically brushed me off. When I brought it up to Raila, she said that he was adhering to tradition, which is to not be with the future bride before the wedding. Like okay, but does he have to be a dick about it?

I have a hard time believing that, regardless. I know that Death sticks to traditions, but really, no sex before marriage? Is that a thing among the Gods? The God of Death?

Then again, Death is rather superstitious. I've noticed that he prefers things in certain numbers (in threes), that he never has his back to a door, and that he does certain things on certain days. Guess I'll have plenty of time to figure that out since I'll be fucking *marrying* him tomorrow.

"There's that face again," Lovia says. "Is it still your father? Or is it the hair? We can try a different look."

I don't give a shit about what my hair looks like for the damn wedding, but Lovia is so invested in it that I don't want to break her heart. She's probably the only person in this whole castle who is actually looking forward to this thing. I guess weddings aren't very common in Tuonela.

"The hair is wonderful," I tell her adamantly. "Really. But please, let's not fuss over me. Your father said he wants it to be as quick and painless as possible."

She rolls her eyes. "Such a romantic, right?"

"He is the king and he knows what he wants," I tell her firmly. "Besides, this is all for political gain. You know that, don't you? He doesn't love me."

I don't mean for it to come all out like that, but it does.

Lovia doesn't seem bothered, though.

"Do you love him?" she asks, and I swear she looks hopeful.

I try not to wince. "Does it matter?"

She sighs, pouting slightly with her pink lips. "I guess not. I'm just happy that he has someone."

I snort.

"Even if that someone is literally forced into the marriage?"

Her eyes soften sympathetically. "I know how this all seems to you. I don't pretend to have the answers. I just want you to know that even though he's Death, my father isn't as bad as he seems."

The jury is still out on that. The only time Death seems to redeem himself is in the bedroom, and I don't know how long I'll be able to go on that alone. I mean, it's been days since I've seen him at all. There's a chance I'll never get to sleep with him and then what do I get? Whole bunch of being the Queen of Death for eons to come with no dick.

"What about you?" I ask her as she starts taking my hair down from the updo. "When you go to the Upper World, do you see yourself getting married?"

She laughs and shakes her head, strands of blonde hair coming loose from her braid. "I am not suited for marriage. In this world or the next. There are always shamans and other Gods coming through this land trying to win my hand. It's the stuff legends are made of—the Bride of Tuonela is supposed to be *me*. But my father never wanted to give me away like that. He gave me freedom from the start to be who I needed to be, so long as I did my role."

I mull that over. Daddy Death and his daughter seem to have a pretty pure relationship, and that's something that wins him major points in my book. But the points don't add up to much when you consider the negatives. Mainly being the whole God of Death thing, keeping me as a prisoner, and forcing me into marriage.

"You *do* want to marry him though," she says, her voice singsong as she lets my hair flow over my shoulders. "You may not love him, but you do want to marry him. That much I can tell."

I'm about to protest, but then I stop myself. I have to remind myself of the truth, of the real truth. My purpose. My plan. I find it harder and harder to stick to it without having Bell here to remind me each day, but it still remains. When I marry Death, I become a queen. And while I have zero experience being a queen, it will give me power and clout. Over time, I will get used to the role, and Death will get used to seeing me in that role.

And just when it seems like he's really got me, that's when I go.

It's a long con, maybe the longest con ever, which means it has to start now.

So I just give Lovia an awkward smile and shrug. "Well, who doesn't want to be a queen?" I tell her.

That seems to please her, enough that she lets it go.

However, she doesn't let the whole wedding thing go.

The next morning, the day of the ceremony, she has Raila doing a full-on body spa treatment on me, from waxing my legs with frosthoney, to the sugar scrubs, to dustings of edible powders from herbs that only grow under falling stars. Then I'm being crammed into a red gown with a black lace veil and my hair is being threaded with crimson poppy petals and black feathers and shining rubies.

I have to admit, I do a double-take when I see myself in the mirror. I may not have a crown on my head yet, but I look like a queen. So much so that I hardly recognize myself. For once my height makes me look statuesque instead of huge, my strange face looks ethereal and wise. I carry myself differently here, wearing the clothes instead of the clothes wearing me.

You suit this place, a voice inside my head says. *You know you do. You belong.*

But I still don't want to believe it. I can't.

This isn't my place to be.

"Are you ready?" Lovia asks me. She's wearing a silver gown that's cut scandalously low and inappropriately high, her hair long and loose, carrying a bouquet of flowers that look to be made from crystals.

"As I'll ever be," I tell her, giving her a weak smile.

She takes my arm and leads me out of my room and down the stairs, Raila behind me and holding onto the train of the red gown. I actually never asked where the wedding was taking place, I assumed in one of the massive halls in the castle. But to my surprise, we keep walking down…down…down.

"Where are we going?" I whisper as we get to the cellar level, the air damp and chilled, filled with bad energy that makes me want to run away.

"The crypt," Lovia says to me.

I stop dead, Raila nearly running into my back. "What, the *crypt*? Why?"

"It's a church," Lovia explains patiently.

Yeah. A fucking creepy ass church of saints with missing eyes!

And it's tradition, Raila says. *To be in the presence of the Old Gods while a new God is sworn in. Even if you are but a mere mortal, Hanna, you become a Goddess in name when you take this crown. The Old Gods and the saints will watch the ceremony from secret dark places, bearing witness to everything n*ew.

Man, Raila has definitely been drinking the Sect of the Undead Kool-Aid, hasn't she?

"In other words," Lovia whispers to me as we approach the crypt, the candles burning outside as before, "The Old Gods will see the new queen sworn in and the prophecy shall be fulfilled. At least, that's the hope, isn't it? Anything to help stave off an uprising."

I swear to god, if I hear the word uprising one more time… I mean, what the hell is there to rise up against? The dead should be happy that they have a city to go to instead of the eternal suffering and chaos and whatever there was before. Then again, it's usually those at the bottom that want to bring down those at the top. Perhaps some will choose eternal damnation so as long as everyone has to suffer equally. A better life isn't always good enough if others have it even better.

There's no more time to ponder it. We walk through the door and into the white crypt and I'm surprised to see there's only a couple of people inside. Well, one God, and a big, winged unicorn.

Kalma is standing at the altar of bones with the crown of crimson in his hands, looking at us expectantly as we enter. Sarvi is on the other side of him, wedged between the creepy, eyeless statues, their candles eternally flickering.

"Where is Tuoni?" Kalma asks us.

"Uh, here with you?" Lovia says.

No, Sarvi says, then realizes no one understands it. The unicorn looks at me. *He is supposed to come down last. Hanna, you are supposed to wait for him at the altar.*

Oh, of course Death would make you wait for him. He has to be different, doesn't he?

But even though I'm joking inside my head, I can't ignore the kernel of unease in my stomach. That something is wrong. It doesn't help that I'm standing in the creepiest place in all the land and I swear the snakes in the shadows are hissing at me, telling me to leave.

"He better show up," Lovia says, taking me by the arm again as Raila picks up my train and we walk down the aisle. "It's rude to keep a Goddess waiting."

She gives me a reassuring smile as we get to the altar but even I see the uncertainty in her eyes.

I look over at Sarvi and the unicorn seems to shrug, albeit warily.

I then glance at Kalma and he does the same, eyes kind but on edge, and my attention is captured by the haunting beauty of the crimson crown in his hands. Up close, it's horrible and beautiful all at once, the way the black bones and ruby gems mingle with each other like blood and darkness becoming one.

The more I stare at the crown, the more that it calls to

me, in that throaty way that the Book of Runes was, and I can practically feel it hum with power. Then again, this whole crypt is like that. If I didn't know any better, I'd say that those statues aren't statues at all, but actual people and Gods who are waiting for their chance to rise. I feel like if I stare at them long enough they'll move.

I shake that feeling out of my head. It won't do me any good, I'm already as spooked as it is.

A few minutes pass. Then a few more. The energy in the room hums louder and louder and finally I have to break the awkward silence.

"Don't tell me he got cold feet," I joke.

Kalma gives me a nervous smile.

Sarvi says nothing.

Lovia frowns.

Raila, well, who knows what's going on under that veil. But she stays silent too.

I'm about to make another joke, anything to lighten the mood and dissolve my nerves that are out of control, when suddenly there's a loud BOOM and the entire crypt shakes, pieces of the ceiling crashing down, nearly hitting the statues.

"What the fuck!" I cry out and Kalma reaches out to steady me.

I must find Death, Sarvi says, and the unicorn gallops out of the crypt, hoofbeats echoing against the walls, black mane and tail flying behind it.

"What was that?" I ask Lovia as the dust settles. "Do you get earthquakes here?"

She shakes her head. "Not that I've felt."

"Not for a long time," Kalma says gravely. "Come on, we need to get out of here. The crypt might not be safe."

He puts the crown back on the altar and then takes me by the elbow, quickly leading me out of the crypt, with Lovia and Raila right behind me, carrying my train so I don't get stuck on something.

We're just past the wine cellar when there's another BOOM and everything shakes again, bottles of vintage rolling off the shelves and crashing to the floor. Fuck, Death is going to be *pissed* about that.

"Bombs?" I ask as I'm ushered up the stairs. "How about bombs? Do you guys do bombs in this land?"

Kalma doesn't say anything, though there's fear in his eyes, something I never expected to see in the wizened old man.

"Are the Realms colliding? Are we under attack? Veils flopping over? Someone tell me what's going on," I tell them as we get to the main floor. "Hello?"

"Loviatar," Kalma says to her. "You take Hanna to your father's quarters. The wards will hold there against whatever the hell this is. Make sure she can't leave, and that no one can get in. And I do mean no one."

I shall go too, Raila says, making a move to the stairs.

"No," Kalma says sharply. "No, you are coming with me, Raila."

I exchange a look with Lovia. I don't like the idea of being locked up in Death's room, but I do like the idea of being protected by wards from this strange attack on the castle. I mean, it is an attack, right? Hard to say since no one will fucking answer my questions.

Kalma grabs hold of Raila's arm, holding her tight enough that I hear the bone of her arm snap and he practically drags her away. Ouch. What the hell was that about?

Meanwhile Lovia is running up the stairs with my dress in her hands and I'm taking the steps two at a time to catch up.

"What was up with Raila?" I ask Lovia as we round the corner of one level and take the stairs to the next. "Pretty sure Kalma just broke her arm back there."

"I don't know," she says warily. "But if Kalma does something like that to you, you probably deserve it. He might think Raila is a spy behind all that's happening, whatever this is."

"A spy? She's the spy?"

"My father has a saying, never trust the dead."

"I thought his saying was never trust the living? Which, by the way, he got from Beetlejuice."

"Never trust the dead, never trust the living, never trust a God, and never trust a redhead," she adds, "which is all because of my redheaded mother."

"So basically trust no one."

"Bingo."

And as if on cue, another crash rocks the castle and both of us nearly fall over the railing of the stairs, a long way down.

"We need to hurry," Lovia says, reaching over and pulling me up straight. We run even faster now up the stairs, past Deadhands who are running the opposite way, their swords drawn as if going into battle.

Hell, I have no idea what's happening outside these walls, maybe there is some epic battle going on, an all hands on deck type of situation.

Finally we get to the top and to Death's quarters, a place
I still haven't been yet since it's been forbidden to me. Lovia
tries to push open the doors but they don't budge. Panic lines
her face and then she fishes out a set of skeleton keys from her
boobs and inserts the key.

The door opens, revealing a large lair that could only belong
to Death. Everything is black. Everything is lush and stark and
hard and soft, and a million contradictions. His private quarters
are like all of Shadow's End in concentrated form, and his
essence oozes from the gleam of the dark floors, to the metallic
black designs of the wallpaper.

But while the door to the room is wide open, it's not
easy walking through. There's a feeling of thickening air, like
something solid pushing you back, similar to the feeling of
walking through the tunnel under the waterfall.

"It's the wards," Lovia says, her face straining as she pushes
forward and finally we both go stumbling through, my ears
popping as I try not to trip over a rug.

"Father!" Lovia yells, searching the room, while I go straight
to the window and peer out to see what's happening.

Of course I can't see a damn thing. The world is covered
in the thickest layer of fog I've ever seen. I don't even know
if it is fog, maybe it's smoke. Even though he's been avoiding
me, the weather hasn't been too terrible the last few days. Not
sunny like the day he told me I was marrying him, but it's been
pleasant. But this? It's foul and I wonder if it's all his doing.

"He's not here," Lovia says, sounding panicked. "Do you
mind if I go look for him? I'll be okay out there, and you'll be
safe in here. Just lock the door behind you and don't leave this

room. Okay? He'd kill me if something happened to you."

I'm not planning on leaving, but I don't want her leaving me either.

I swallow hard, feeling so scared I might vomit.

Somehow I have enough courage to nod. "If you say I'll be fine here, then I'll stay."

"I'll be right back," she says. Then she marches over to a stand of armory in the corner, picks up a sword, twirls it around in her hand, and then grins at it in satisfaction before heading through the wards again and out the door.

I quickly head to the door and fight through the ward again to lock it. Then I turn around and face the room, wondering what the hell is going on.

Some fucking wedding day. The groom doesn't show up and then the venue gets bombed.

The little attempt at humor falls flat though when the castle shakes again, though subtle now, the boom sounding far off. Either the attack is subsiding or the wards really do have me protected.

I sit down on the end of Death's bed and try to think. Of course it's bigger than king-sized and all black satin and velvet, with iron posts and skulls in the corners. Definitely didn't get this at Ikea either.

Another distant boom sends the mirrors rattling against the walls and I get up, wondering if I should huddle under something just in case. I've had my fair share of earthquake drills, but when the actual earthquakes shake up Los Angeles a few times a year, I usually spend most of the time *thinking* about taking shelter but not actually doing it.

Another boom makes the walls tremble and my heart leaps in my chest. It's been racing steadily this whole time and I have to remind myself to breathe in deeply, in case I fall victim to a panic attack. Somehow I've survived all of Tuonela without really having one, but now I feel utterly alone for the first time.

What if everyone dies? What if this is part of the uprising?

What will the Old Gods do to me if they find me? Gouge my eyes out like the old believers? Will I be sent to Oblivion? Or to Inmost for eternity, to be turned into a Deadmaiden for them? What horrors do they inflict on mortals engaged to Gods?

Okay, *now* I'm having a panic attack.

Suddenly there's a tapping at the window.

I can't help but scream.

I whip around and look, terror seizing me, expecting to see the eye of a giant at the window, saying "Fee-Fi-Fo-Fum, I smell the blood of a social media manager."

But no.

It's Rasmus.

I don't know how, but it's fucking *Rasmus*.

He's sitting outside the window, a window that's hundreds of feet up in the air. His red hair is tousled by the high winds and he's waving at me, like he just stopped by after dinner to see if I was home, wanting a beer and a chat.

"What the hell?" I say, rushing over to him. I fling the window open, careful not to hit him with it. "Rasmus?" I cry out, blinking fast at the wind in my eyes.

"Hanna," he says, flashing me a triumphant smile. "You knew I was coming back for you, didn't you?"

I stare at him. This can't be real. I have to be hallucinating.

"How are you even…?" I begin, and then I realize he's crouched on a gargoyle of a wolf just below the window. My fear of heights kicks in and I have to grab the window frame to steady me.

"Are you ready?" he asks, then he frowns at my dress. "You look ready for something else. Catch you at a bad time?"

I shake my head, trying to form the right words, the right questions. "I don't understand. How are you here? How did you get up here? There are wards, aren't there?"

"And shamans can break through wards," he says with a cocky smirk. "The right shamans anyway. Like me."

"So, what, you can fly now?"

He frowns, his blue eyes turning glacial. "For some reason I thought you would be a lot happier to see me. I'm rescuing you. And before you try and tell me that you didn't need rescuing, you're wrong. You do, and it looks like just in time. I'm here and I'm getting you out of this castle, out of this land, for good."

"Are you doing all of this?" I ask, gesturing to the air around. "The attack?"

He gives me a secretive smile. "There will be plenty of time for questions later. If you want to leave, we need to leave now." He clears his throat. "Come with me if you want to live," he says in the world's worst Arnold impersonation.

"But how?" I ask, peering out into the thickening fog. "You got wings?"

"Just trust me," he says.

But that's the thing…can I trust him?

I don't have a lot of time to figure that out, because he turns his head and lets out a piercing whistle.

Suddenly a dark shape comes flying out of the mist, right at us.

I scream again. I can't help it. My nerves are shot.

It's a massive unicorn like Sarvi, silver-colored, beating the air with its long wings, my hair flowing back from the draft.

"You have a unicorn too!?" I exclaim.

"Actually it's your father's," he admits. "He's the one who learned how to master them while he was here."

I gasp, clutching my chest. "My father! Where is he?"

"He's waiting for you. Now come on." Another sharp look. "Don't tell me you want to stay here with Death. This isn't your world, Hanna. It never was. You belong with us. With family. Back home where you belong."

He's right. Of course he's right. This is all I ever wanted. This was the whole point of it all, so my father could be free, and so that I could escape. And now Rasmus is giving me the opportunity to do so, right here and now.

So why do I feel guilty? Why do I feel like I'm leaving Death when he needs me? And when did I start caring about his feelings like that?

"Hanna, please," Rasmus says. "You have a choice. Make the right one. Make the smart one."

I nod, swallowing the lump in my throat. "Okay," I whisper. "Yes, of course I'm going. You promise you're taking me to see my father?"

"I am," he says, motioning for the unicorn to come closer. "We just have to get out of Tuonela first. He's just on the other side of that waterfall, waiting for you."

Rasmus holds out his hand for me.

I put my hand in his.

He helps me through the window, onto the gargoyle, and then we're slipping down until we're on the unicorn's back.

I grab the mane for dear life, and Rasmus holds me from behind.

The unicorn flaps its wings and we take off like a rocket through the fog.

Leaving Death and Shadow's End behind.

But they aren't the only things that's being left in the mist.

A part of me is left behind too.

Not the end…only the beginning.

Flip the page to read the prologue for CROWN OF CRIMSON (Underworld Gods #2)—coming May 2022

EXCERPT FROM CROWN OF CRIMSON

—

PROLOGUE

THE CAVES OF VÍPUNEN

DEATH

"Have you gotten cold feet?" the deep voice of reckoning booms across the walls of the cave.

"That's a rather modern phrase for someone so old," I respond, adjusting the blind mask. I wish I didn't have to wear this ridiculous thing every time I sought out the giant, but because I can see in the dark, Antero Vipunen takes no chances. They say there's no way to kill the God of Death, but there is and he's in the cave with me. Sometimes I think that Vipunen's power rivals that of the Creator, and he could destroy this whole world if he wanted to.

As such, I wear the blind mask so I don't piss him off. Part of me feels badly that both my children had to train in combat with him, wearing this heavy bronze and iron mask the entire time while wielding the sword. But at least they're the finest warriors now.

training would be put to use, but I feel that day creeping ever so closer, like the snakes do if you stay too long in the crypt.

"Then what is it that has brought my counsel again?" Vipunen asks, louder now. In the background I can hear stalactites fall from the ceiling and crash onto the cave floor, splash into the underground lake. As it always happens when I'm in the caves, I'm brought back in my mind, eons past, to when I was just a young little shit, thrown here on my first day on the job as God of Death. I felt so vulnerable, naked and helpless then, and I despise the fact that today I feel the same.

It's a most unbecoming feeling.

"It's the girl," I tell him.

"The mortal Hanna," Vipunen muses. "Is there a problem?"

I let out a breath. Fuck. I hate how uneasy I feel. "I have some…fears about the marriage."

Vipunen lets out a low, rumbling laugh. More stalactites fall to the ground, one sounding too close for comfort. "Fears about marriage? Did you not learn your lesson the last time?"

He can't see the *fuck you* smile on my face but I hope he hears it in my tone. "Apparently not. I'm concerned that she may not be the one you prophesied about. Any chance you could, you know, clear that up a little bit? Give me something a little more to go on?"

Instead of being so fucking annoyingly vague from day one?

"To give you more information would be to interfere with your life and the natural order of things and that I cannot do," he says.

"Cannot or will not?" I ask.

A cold blast of air comes rushing at me. I'm not the only one who can influence the weather and temperature with my moods. "You dare have contempt for me?" he bellows.

"No contempt, Antero, only frustration."

"Is it not your wedding day?" he asks after a moment.

"Yes, in fact she might be at the altar right now." No doubt looking beautiful beyond words.

"Then you're cutting things a little close, don't you think?"

I sigh, adjusting the mask again. "I'm not asking if she's the one, I just need to know if I'm making a mistake. What if I marry Hanna and the one I'm supposed to be with, the one that is supposed to save my kingdom, comes along?"

Another laugh. "You think that another mortal girl will come strolling along into Tuonela like that?"

"So then Hanna is the one…" I surmise, trying to bait him.

"I will tell you no such thing. This has nothing to do with me. This is your future, Tuoni, laid out in front of you. You either take it or you don't." He pauses. "You really do have cold feet, don't you? You want a way out. An easy way out. Well, no one told you to propose."

He's right. That was all my own doing.

I just couldn't help it.

After what happened with Surma, everything changed. Hearing his intentions, his work for the Old Gods, it made me realize that the uprising wasn't just a rumor. It was real and at our doorstep. I needed to do something about it and fast. I needed to marry Hanna in hopes that an alliance somewhere would form. Perhaps just the act of marriage itself, signaling to Louhi that I have moved on, that she is no longer the Goddess of Death, would do it, or telling the realm that I am part of a unit again would make them fall in line. Either way, it was time to act.

But then there was the surprising thing with Hanna herself.

I'd been so impressed by her, in awe of her, yet I did all I could to keep distance between us. The less distance, the less control I had. The more distance, the more my power remained firmly in check.

But when I saw Surma put his skeleton hands on her, I felt a protective beast rise up inside me, one I'd rarely felt before. I wanted to kill Surma more for that than for him being a traitor to the kingdom. I realized the lengths I would go to for her, and that scared me. Moved me.

As was the way she looked when I fucked her, when she was able to look at me, all of me, just as myself. No mask. No hiding behind anything. Just me, as I am. It's not that I didn't think she'd be enthralled, it's that I didn't think I'd feel so much warmth from her. Like she was baring herself to me at the same time, like she finally fucking trusted me.

And so, after spending all night thinking about her, about my future, about strategies, I realized the time was now. We had to get married, and maybe, if we were lucky, it would be something we both wanted.

CRASH

Suddenly a loud muffled noise comes from outside the cave, parts of the ceiling crashing down.

"What was that?" I yell, nearly falling over.

"Your keep is under attack," Vipunen says simply.

Another loud explosion rocks the ground beneath me and I

press my gloved hands against my mask to hold it on.

"By who? Do you know?"

"By Louhi's son," he says.

My son? Tuonen? That doesn't make any sense, the boy's ambitions are ridiculously low. All he wants in life is to watch porn, ferry the dead, and be the referee for the Bone Matches.

"The shaman," Vipunen adds. "Rasmus."

My fist clenches. Fucking redheaded weasel. How the fuck is he attacking Shadow's End right now?

I turn to run out of the cave but the giant calls after me. "There is no use in hurrying," he says. "By the time you get there, it will be over. The attack can't do any major damage, it is only a diversion."

I come to a stop, my blood going cold. "A diversion for what?" I ask, even though I know the answer.

"Rasmus is here for Hanna," he says. "He is taking her with him."

It's like all the rage in the world starts to build inside my veins, growing tight and molten hot, ready for implosion. "Kidnapping *my* bride on *my* wedding day?" I grind out.

A pause hangs in the air, followed by a distant boom.

"She has not been kidnapped," Vipunen says after a moment. "She was given a choice. She chose to go willingly. She chose to leave you. On your wedding day." He adds that last part as if he has spite for me.

I still. My heart lurches against my ribs. The rage inside me ebbs and flows, changing and morphing. The anger goes from Rasmus, to myself, and then to Hanna.

Hanna.

"She left me," I say, practically stuttering. "She can't. That shouldn't be possible." Now my rage is directed to Vipunen. "If you knew this was going to happen, why didn't you tell me?"

"I can't affect what is already in motion."

"So what the fuck do I do now?"

My bride. My ex-wife's son has my fucking *bride*.

"I believe you know what to do, Tuoni. You do not need my counsel on that."

He is right. Hanna is mine, no one else's, whether she likes it or not. She entered into this bargain with me and it was a fair trade. She offered herself up to me in countless ways, and I was a gentlemen enough to not take her up on all of them. She is supposed to be with me, as my bride, for eternity, and she's gone back on her fucking word.

"I'm going to kill her," I seethe. "I'm going to cut her fucking wings right off."

"And if she doesn't die, it might mean she's the one," Vipunen says. "And you'll have to rule alongside her for the rest of your life, or face the end of your reign."

Fuck.

"Fuck!" I roar, throwing my head back, my yell echoing throughout the cave. I'm breathing hard, my heartbeat in my head, and I just want to rage, rip this mask right off and break everything in this cave. But Vipunen would no doubt break me first.

So I have to live with the rage for a few moments. I have to make friends with it. I have to let the red turn to black, let it settle in my bones.

And there, hidden underneath all the molten hot torment,

is the source of my rage.

It's pain.

It's a dull ache in my ribs, right around my heart.

The same kind of ache I would get when I looked at her beautiful face as she came.

Oh, I ached for her. Craved her, possessed her, relished her when my cock was deep inside, when I felt she was no longer mortal but instead part of my skin and bones.

I ached for my little bird.

Now I break for her.

I swallow it down, welcoming the anger again. The anger I can deal with, the rage I can use. I just have to learn to control it so it doesn't get the better of me. I need to wield it like a weapon against the one who spurned me.

I need to make her suffer too.

"I'm getting her back," I growl, and start storming out of the darkness of the cave, using all my senses to find my way back to the light. "I'm getting her back and I'm making her pay. No one escapes Death, not even her."

Especially not her.

EXCERPT FROM BLACK SUNSHINE

Here's a sneak peek at my paranormal contemporary
vampire romance, Black Sunshine, out now.

—

Black Sunshine

All Lenore Warwick wants for her 21st birthday is to hang
out with her friends, finish her second semester at Berkley with
flying colors, and maybe catch the eye of a hot musician playing
a show at a club that she can now (legally) get into.

Unfortunately, fate has other plans for her.

A week before her birthday, she's kidnapped by the brooding
and dangerous stranger with cold eyes and a lethal touch who
has been stalking her on San Francisco's fog-shrouded streets.
Absolon Stavig isn't your average criminal though. He's a
centuries-old vampire who's caught between wanting to kill
Lenore and wanting to save her.

You see Lenore, too, is a vampire.

She just doesn't know it yet.

Taken by a pair of vampire slayers when she was just an
infant, Lenore was raised never knowing her true nature. All
Lenore knows is that she has parents who love her, that she's
exceptionally smart, and she's squeamish around blood. But
once she turns twenty-one, she'll fully turn into a vampire, and
Solon hopes he'll be there to guide her, opening her eyes to her
deepest hunger, both sexual and otherwise.

But this turning can't be kept a secret. Soon, both slayers and vampires are hunting Lenore, with only Solon and his unpredictable motley crew of vampires to save her.

If they don't kill her first.

Black Sunshine is a dark adult standalone romance with a paranormal twist, about sex, love, secrets, and revenge, set in contemporary San Francisco.

PROLOGUE

Orcas Island, Washington State
Nineteen Years Ago

It's the snapping of a branch that gives them away.

Elaine Warwick immediately winces as the sound ricochets through the forest—a mix of cedar, Douglas fir, and alders that should have muffled the noise, in theory. But Elaine knows better.

Up ahead, Jim stops running, shooting his wife a harried look over his shoulder. He knows better too. The expression of pure disappointment mixed with fear threads through his eyes, but Elaine can only nod at him to keep going.

They're so close.

And now they've lost their advantage.

The Virtanens will hear them coming.

Even isolating yourself on an island in the Pacific Northwest, withdrawing from society in some sort of penance for your many sins, doesn't take the amplified senses out of the vampire. Once a vampire, always a vampire, until you die.

Which is why Jim and Elaine are here tonight.

To find Alice and Hakan, the famed Virtanen vampires, who inflicted centuries of pain upon people before they decided to have a change of heart — "retirement" as some in the guild called it — and put them to death.

It's going to be nasty work, and there's a chance that neither Jim nor Elaine will survive this, but it's personal. It's been personal for years, since Alice killed Elaine's sister. The guild doesn't even know that the Warwicks are here on a vengeance trip. They long ago said it was best to concentrate on vampires that were still doing damage, but Elaine hasn't forgotten, and the damage is never going away. She knows that since the guild didn't sanction this kill, there's a chance they could get in trouble for it.

Executed, even.

Then again, what the guild doesn't know, can't hurt them.

Besides, they might die here anyway.

That snapping branch didn't help.

They continue running, as soundless as possible. They've trained most of their lives for moments like this. How to be quiet and quick, especially against predators who are faster than they are. Predators who must know they are quickly approaching the property.

Elaine feels her knife burning at her calf, the energy coming off it seeping into her own skin, her own skin feeding back into the knife. The vampires won't know that knife is there, protected under a cloak of spells, buried by the sigils and fire agate threaded into her black pants. Slayers have evolved to try and trick their prey, just as their prey have evolved to try and trick them.

Jim's silhouette in front of her gets clearer, the trees tapering off, night sky peeking through. There are so many stars that it steals Elaine's breath for a moment. The moon is full, shining so brightly that her eyes burn, but even though she worships the moon, lets it influence everything she does, tonight she has the sinking, damning feeling that the glowing orb isn't on her side.

Focus, Jim's words come into her head. *We need to pull this off.*

Elaine swallows hard and nods, coming to a stop beside him, the two of them crouching down as they survey the scene.

There's a field of high grass between them and the house, the ocean behind it, the moon gleaming on it like light on a steel blade. The house is small, modest, looking like it would belong in Scandinavia rather than here in the Pacific Northwest. Moss completely covers the roof, the paint red and peeling. Elaine was never an empath like her husband, but even she can feel that there's no malice in this house, only warmth and love.

It makes her hesitate, enough that her husband puts his hand on her shoulder and gives it a squeeze. *We don't have to do this*, he says in her head.

She knows this. But she also knows it has to be done. She will find no peace until Alice pays for what she did. They say revenge is poison, but she'll gladly take it if it helps her sleep easier at night.

They must move fast. Though the house seems silent and the lights give off a warm glow, the smoke from the chimney puffing, she knows they are waiting for them. Although, something about the scene does seem odd.

It's the fire, Jim says soundlessly. *Why have a fire if they never get cold?*

Elaine nods. That's what it is. But vampires can be strangely sentimental about old ways, hanging on to their past. It's possible that either Alice or Hakan was raised around a hearth, back in the days when a fire was a house's only source of heat. While their parents wouldn't have a need for it, a child won't turn until they're older. Perhaps they keep the fire out of habit, remembering the good old days.

Elaine shakes the images of vampire families out of her head. It does her no good to view them as anything but monsters. She was born to kill them and that's what she'd do.

Suddenly, the door to the house opens and a woman steps out. They're too far to see her clearly, but there's no doubt that the vampire can see—and smell—them, like the apex predators they are.

This must be Alice.

The knife burns against Elaine's leg, coming to life, and she knows they have seconds to act before Alice attacks them. Vampires move fast, faster than the human eye can see. Luckily, being a witch, and a slayer in particular, they can track her, even when Alice uses the Veil.

But she doesn't move, not even when Elaine and Jim take their knives into their hands, the metal glinting with electric blue currents. The knives aren't as big as one would think, but they can be thrown with startling accuracy. One shot to the heart is all it takes. Of course, Jim has a machete back at home, but decapitation is a messy ordeal.

The husband and wife look at each other and, in that moment, they know they're committed.

They both run forward toward Alice, the element of surprise gone, and the risks of them dying at the hands of a vampire increasing with each and every step.

They cross the field quickly, moving soundlessly through the grass, but still Alice doesn't move. Her arms are out to her sides, but she is unarmed.

She's protecting something.

"Stop," Alice calls out, her voice melodic, but the pitch is off. Like she's uncertain, perhaps afraid.

Elaine and Jim stop. It is not by choice. The vampire is compelling them, even at this range. It won't last, it rarely does with witches, but it's enough to give Alice yet another advantage.

"Leave this place," Alice says. "Now."

Elaine breaks free from the bonds, feels them snap. "I can't," she says. "You know what you did, you know what you must pay for."

Suddenly, Hakan appears behind Alice, a tall lanky creature built for precision, and puts his big hands on Alice's shoulders. "I didn't think revenge killings were allowed by your *guild*," Hakan says in a light Finnish accent.

"I don't have to do everything the guild tells me," Elaine says.

"Turning against your own?" asks Hakan, his eyes deep gray and hypnotic. Elaine needs to keep watching them, but she's finding it more difficult by the second. "You'll be punished."

"So long as you're dead, I don't care what they do to me," Elaine says. "Besides, they won't find out. We'll make this quick and easy. Not a trace of you to be found."

Her words are strong and clear and they don't show the wildness in Elaine's heart, the fear that this could go either way. Witches have magic and the blade that can kill vampires. Vampires are predators that would love nothing more than to kill a witch, and with their strength, speed, and penchant for violence and blood, they make an equal match.

But there's something different here. Elaine knows it. There's a vulnerability to this couple that shouldn't be here. They asked them to leave. Vampires never ask to do anything. And even now, they still aren't making a move.

Which means Elaine has to make hers before it's too late.

In the back of her mind she conjures up the image of the blade leaving her fingers and going right through Alice's heart. Her intention will set the fate, unless something else intervenes.

She throws the blade, quick as a wink, the power shooting out of her fingers, guiding the knife forward. Before it can hit Alice, she's pushed aside at lightning speed as Hakan steps forward.

Taking the knife to the heart.

Saving his wife's life, but ending his own.

Hakan immediately falls to the ground, his body seized by the blue currents as it spreads out from the knife, overtaking his limbs, making them shake.

Alice cries out in horror, dropping to her knees beside Hakan.

"Why?" she sobs to him, trying to take the blade out. "Why did you do that?"

Hakan stares at her, pain engulfing him as the last vestiges of life are leaving him. It must be quite the feeling of being *almost* immortal.

While Elaine stares at the scene, transfixed, Jim points to the house, closing his eyes, and draws the fire out of the fireplace inside. Flames spread immediately, as if the place was doused in gasoline.

Alice screams. "Lenore!"

Elaine and Jim exchange a sharp look. *Lenore?*

"Go to her," Hakan says to Alice, spitting out blood. "Save her and maybe they will spare your life."

Elaine's heart clenches. *Who is Lenore?*

Suddenly a child's cry fills the air, rising above the roar of the flames, and Elaine's mouth drops in horror.

A child.

Alice and Hakan have a child.

This they didn't know.

Alice gets to her feet and runs into the house.

But Jim is fast, throws the blade so it gets her in the back, knowing the knife's power will penetrate to her heart that way, slipping past her ribs.

Alice stumbles but keeps running, right into the flames, fueled by a mother's love and protection.

Elaine looks at Jim in horror. W*hat do we do?*

We wait for them all to die, Jim says. *And we leave.*

But from the fraught expression on her husband's face, he feels as torn about the situation as she is.

And there's something more than that.

There's something that is calling Elaine to the house, the child's cry that doesn't stop is reverberating around her heart, tugging at her, making her feel. How can it not, they both know that a child is only a vampire in waiting. At the moment, the child doesn't drink blood, lives with innocence in the soul.

The child is burning to death, burning alive.

Elaine stares down at Hakan, his lifeless body, and knows the flames will reach him too.

"We have to go," Jim says. "People will see the fire, they'll be here soon."

Elaine just blinks, numb, and he puts his arm around her, leading them away from the house, the fire hot at their backs.

The child has stopped crying, which means it's dead. And it's their fault.

"Please," a tiny shaking voice says from behind them, stopping them in their tracks.

The Warwicks whirl around to see a child standing beside her father, staring down at his body. She can't be more than two, her clothes burned off of her, but the rest of her untouched. Her hair is long and dark blonde, like amber honey. "Daddy."

Elaine's heart breaks and she feels a calling to the child, like a haunting siren song that rises from the moonlit well in her gut.

The child raises her chin and looks at Elaine, right in the eyes. They're large and hazel, all the colors of nature in them.

"Please," she says again. She can't be more than two, but she's so soft-spoken.

Elaine knows she's asking for them to save her.

The fire leaps forward, licking the child's back, causing the remains of her burned dress to catch on fire and fall away, but the child isn't even hurt. She doesn't seem to notice.

This is no ordinary vampire child. Fire kills them. It kills witches too.

But it's not killing her.

Elaine looks at Jim and he nods. He knows what she's decided to do. Perhaps he can feel the child calling inside him as well.

Letting them both know that she's not just a vampire.

But one of their own.

Something that should never be.

Elaine runs forward, into the fire, scoops up the girl, the fire burning her bare arms. Elaine doesn't scream, though the pain is unbearable. She just takes the girl in her arms — Lenore — and brings her toward Jim.

Being the bigger and stronger of the two, Jim holds on to the child, and they both start running off into the woods, letting the fire burn all evidence to the ground.

CHAPTER ONE

San Francisco, California

Present Day

I think I'm being followed.

My friends have called me paranoid once or twice before, so there's a chance they might be right. But I still can't shake the feeling that someone's been following me, all the way from my apartment down in Hayes Valley, to here in Upper Haight. Doesn't help that the further up the hill I go, the thicker the fog gets, making every shadow extra ominous. That's what I get for taking the shortcut past Buena Vista Park.

I pause, coming to a standstill, and listen.

I'm a couple of blocks away from the speakeasy, in the residential area close to Haight Street, which is busy on a Friday night, and yet everything seems eerily calm. Hushed. Like the houses around me are holding their breath.

Slowly I turn around and stare back down the street.

There's a lone streetlamp on the corner, showcasing the mist rushing past it.

A shadowy figure, a man, suddenly appears out of the gray, stopping right beside the streetlamp.

Staring right at me.

Into me.

And it's like all the air is knocked from my lungs.

I'm literally gasping, my body stiffens, going ice cold.

And then the streetlamp goes *out*.

Plunging the man into darkness.

Oh fuck this.

Feeling strength returning to my limbs, I take in a sharp breath and spin on my feet, running like hell up the street. I've always been athletic and fast, despite what some extra pounds might say, and I run like I've never run before, not stopping, narrowly colliding with a couple as I sprint down Frederick until I hit Ashbury.

Only then do I stop, taking stock of the situation as I look around.

Everything seems blissfully normal here. Some people walking about, the sound of traffic filling the air. The street is brightly lit, showcasing the colorful Victorian homes on either side of the road. The entrance to The Cloister, one of my favorite bars, has only a few people in line, nowhere near as busy as it will be later. For a somewhat underground speakeasy, it's awfully popular, probably because word has gotten out that they don't scrutinize IDs.

I wonder if my mystery stalker was a cop. I turn twenty-one in two weeks, so I'm almost legal to drink, but I've been using the same fake ID for years now. Carol Ann Black, from Edmonton, Alberta instead of Lenore Warwick from San Francisco, California. The picture looks *nothing* like me either, but every person I've given the ID to has just accepted it at face value. My friend Elle jokes that every bouncer just happens to want to sleep with me, so they let it go, but either way it works.

But maybe my time is up. Perhaps the cop will show up at the bar, a total shakedown, arrest everyone. I'll have to keep my wits about me if I see the guy again.

Not that I really saw what he looked like. He was just a

hazy silhouette. Tall, at least six feet, broad-shouldered, wearing a long coat. Could be anyone, really.

I try to shake the unsettled feeling from my limbs.

It was just a cop, I tell myself as I rifle through my black studded handbag, getting out my wallet. He didn't even do anything, just stared at me. If he wasn't a cop, then it was probably just someone else out and about, nothing more than a stranger, and the light just happened to blow out above him. I'm making something out of nothing.

Cuz you're paranoid, the voice inside my head pipes up.

I shake that away, too.

I stride up to the behemoth of a bouncer and hand him my ID, doing that thing where you're trying to look bored and put-out by having to give your ID, like you do this all the time, like there's no way you could get in trouble because *of course* that's really you in the photo.

The bouncer scrutinizes the photo, then looks at me.

Looks at the photo.

Then back at me.

"Carol Ann Black?" he asks.

"That's me," I say, flashing him a smile as I stare deep into his eyes. No one with a fake ID would dare be this confident.

"Okay. Have fun," he says, handing it back to me, staring off down the street like I don't exist.

"Thanks," I tell him, and squeeze past him through the gate at the side of the building, my nerves fluttering with adrenaline. I'm so looking forward to finally being legal so I don't have to get so worked up every time I want to go out and have fun.

Not that I've been doing a lot of that lately. With my final

final exam next week, I've been doing nothing but studying. I'm doing my BA of Arts with a major in Ancient Egyptian and Near Eastern Art and Archeology, hoping to one day get my PhD and perhaps become a museum curator. I'm supposed to go to Egypt in August for two weeks as an internship (unpaid, of course, but at least they take care of the flight), on a dig, so there's a chance that my dream of working for a museum might change to becoming a hands-on archeologist. Only time will tell.

The Cloister is actually in the basement of an old church, so it's not just a clever name. Though the bouncer is stationed out front, you have to go through a side gate between the church and a blue Victorian house, then round the back and down the outside stairs to the basement. Tonight of all nights I'm still a little spooked out, and the path is extremely dark.

I stop suddenly, just before I round the corner to the stairs.

The space at the back of the church is an overgrown garden, though in the night it's just an ominous black mess. Once, I stayed at the bar until the sun was coming up and only then was I able to actually get a good look at the concrete cracked with weeds, a rotting bench overtaken by ivy, a crumbling fountain slippery with mildew.

Right now, I swear there's someone standing right in front of me, between me and the back wall of the garden. I sense them, but I don't see them — it's just black space, looking somehow denser than normal, like it doesn't stop, like it goes on and on forever, a black hole.

I supress a shiver running through me, my scalp prickling at the thought of standing on the edge of infinity with no escape, only darkness.

"Hello?" I call out, my voice sounding small and stupid.

A sharp inhale of breath comes from in front of me.

Then the door to the basement opens, illuminating the space.

I swear for a split second I see a moving shadow, red eyes, and then there's nothing at all except the fountain, the angels looking particularly warped with moss splashed across them like green blood.

A guy and a girl come stumbling out of the bar, giggling, lighting up cigarettes, hands tangled with each other. They don't really seem to notice me, disappearing into the dark of the garden, only the lit ends of their cigarettes giving them away.

The moment clears the cobwebs from my head, making me realize I need a fucking drink, and I quickly walk down the stairs, opening the heavy door into the club.

Once inside, I let out a breath of relief, Billie Eilish's "All the Good Girls Go to Hell" playing over the speakers, and start looking for Elle.

The Cloister is a cavernous space that manages to feel small, really leaning into the whole church thing. The carpet is red, the walls are dark wood, there are makeshift altars all over the place with crosses and skulls and rosaries, and the space has been divided up into seating areas by having a bunch of iron four-poster bed frames scattered around, tables and booths in the middle, surrounded by retractable red velvet curtains. Even though it's haphazardly put together, it's a little *Twin Peaks*, a lot of goth, and very, very cool. Plus, the drinks are amazing, even if they'll suck a student's budget back quickly.

I walk around, looking for Elle, and spot her at a booth in the corner. It's our favorite spot because it looks out onto the whole bar, which means the both of us get to rate every guy that walks in through the door.

I give her a quick smile and slip past the curtain, taking a seat on the hard bench across from her, a former pew chopped into sections.

"You got here fast," she says to me, sliding my drink over to me. We always have an agreement, whoever gets here first has to order the other person a drink, and the other person has to drink it, no matter what. Tonight it looks like some kind of fruity martini which is fine with me.

"I was in a hurry to get drunk," I tell her, grasping the thin stem of the glass. "Cheers."

We both raise our glasses, delicately clinking the rims without spilling.

"Well then, here's to getting drunk," she says. "And to our last exams."

I take a sip of the drink, cranberry and something, strong enough to make me cough. "Yeah," I say, trying to clear my throat. "Perhaps we should have waited to come here until *after* we're officially done."

"Oh whatever," she says, waving me away and downing the rest of her drink in one go. The girl could drink turpentine and not flinch. "You're going to pass with flying colors like you always do. You could show up to your exams drunk if you wanted and you'd still ace it."

"Right, well, I'm not about to experiment and find out."

Elle and I met the first day during our Egyptian Societies

class when she asked who my tattoo artist was, and after that we were fast friends, liking the same music, going to the same concerts, and sometimes going after the same guys (I always yield to her because it's not worth the fight…she can be a little headstrong). I never had a lot of close friends growing up. There was always something that kept me at a distance from everyone else, whether it was something on their behalf or mine, but I'm as close to Elle as I'll ever be with anyone, aside from my parents.

She brushes her short, bleached blonde hair behind her ears, the rows of earrings catching the dim light, and gives me a funny look. "You okay?"

I give her a brief smile. "Yeah. Why? My lipstick smudged?"

She shakes her head. "No. You seem a little out of breath and shaky."

She reaches out and places her fingers along the tattoo on my right forearm, the words *dreaming dreams no mortal ever dared to dream before*. I know it's cliché to have an Edgar Allen Poe quote as a tattoo, but when your name is Lenore, well, I'm like *this* place. I lean into what was given to me.

"You're cold," she says to me, snatching her hand back.

"I'm always cold," I remind her, even though right now I feel kind of flushed on the inside, like my heart is too hot. "And I'm fine. I just had a scare earlier."

"What scare?" she says loudly, her eyes going wide with excitement. Elle gets so worked up over everything.

"You're going to say I'm paranoid again."

"So let me be the judge of that. What happened?"

"Nothing happened," I tell her, tugging down the sleeve of

my yellow plaid shirt so that it covers my arms. "I thought I was being followed."

"You probably were."

"Thanks."

"I don't know why you insist on walking everywhere," she says. "Just take an Uber."

"Elle, I walked all the way up Haight." Pretty much. "It was busy as anything. I was safe. Besides, Ubers are expensive."

She rolls her eyes, her green shimmering eyeshadow sparkling. "As if you can't afford it. Your parents have told you time and time again, they'll pay for your Ubers until you get a car."

"Doesn't mean I feel good about it."

"Fine. You're getting the next round." She taps her black nails against the table, giving me an expectant look. "Since you saved some money by walking."

Now it's my turn to roll my eyes. "Fine."

"Better do it before Matt shows up."

Matt is a friend of ours. If you want to get more specific, he's my ex-boyfriend. I dated him for a few weeks last summer, totally casual. The sex was okay, and to be honest, the only reason I dated him is because he's the drummer in a White Zombie cover band, and I thought he was sexy as hell.

But, as is often the case with me, even though I'm attracted to a guy, the sexual experience ended up being lackluster. There was just no … spark. No physical connection. I know I'm probably asking for too much — Elle tells me that as long as I'm getting off I should be satisfied, but it is what it is. For a while there I thought maybe I was a lesbian, but Elle, who's bisexual, put that to rest pretty quickly. Turns out I exclusively want dick, I'm just picky about said dick, expecting my world to be blown wide open, for the earth to quake every time I have an orgasm.

I blame the monster erotica on my Kindle.

But despite the somewhat awkward hook-ups, it turned out Matt was okay with just being friends and we're so much more compatible this way. Sometimes I think it's a shame that we didn't have the chemistry I needed, but the fact that I got a good friend out of it makes it worthwhile.

"I hope he isn't bringing his girlfriend," Elle adds under her breath.

Okay, so maybe there's a teeny tiny bit of jealousy on my behalf when it comes to his new girlfriend, Beth. I know I'm the one who broke up with him, but I don't make the rules. She seems nice enough and I definitely don't want him back, but I guess deep down, the closer he gets to her, the more he might pull away as a friend. See, she doesn't like me very much. She acts like she's afraid of me for some reason, and because of that, Elle doesn't like her either, which makes our hang-outs a lot less fun.

As if on cue, Matt walks in through the door.

Thankfully alone.

I stick my hand out of the curtain and wave him over to us.

"Now you have to buy three drinks," Elle reminds me. "Should have moved faster."

Matt stops in front of our table, grinning at us both. "Okay, what are you having?"

I give Elle a triumphant smile. Matt almost always takes

care of the bill when he's here. Though he's a musician on the side, he's got a start-up going in Palo Alto with him and some of his friends, an app that tells you what TV show you should stream tonight. It's only in beta mode at the moment, but he's rolling in investor money.

"I'll have a Paloma," I tell him, looking him up and down. He's wearing a black hoodie and jeans, but his black leather high-tops catch my eye. "New shoes? They look expensive."

A flush appears across his tanned face. "Yeah," he says, running his hand through his brown hair. "New Jordans."

"Jesus, Matt," Elle says. "Your band know your shoes cost half a grand?"

He laughs, giving her a look like she has no idea. "What do you want to drink, Elle?"

"Surprise me," she says, flashing him a smile and wiggling in her seat. "I'm feeling risky tonight. Frisky, too."

Matt looks to me, brows raised, in a way that says *are we sure we should be getting her drunk?*

I shrug. There's no stopping Elle when she's in a mood.

He walks off to the bar, a line already forming, the place getting busier, half the people in here looking like they're underage. I have to wonder how long this place has until it gets shut down.

"Hey, I was thinking maybe the guy following me was a cop," I tell Elle.

"Oh yeah? A hot cop?"

I make a face. "Ew. No. I never saw his face."

"Then how do you know he's not a hot cop?" She pops the cherry from her drink in her mouth, wagging her brows at me.

"Hey, want to see me tie a knot with my tongue?"

I watch her struggle with it in her mouth, waiting to be wowed. Elle is gorgeous in this tiny little pixie way, but the kind of pixie that will bite you. Just like Tinkerbell, fueled by spite.

She pulls out the stem, perfectly tied, smiling at me triumphantly.

"How do you not have a girlfriend right now?" I ask her.

"I'd say the same to you," she says. "You know it's been a while since you went out with Matt. Maybe it's about time you put yourself back out there."

"I've been busy," I tell her.

"I know. As have I. But after this exam, you're free."

"Let's just stick to rating the guys that walk in the door."

She gives me a wry look. "You need to take chances, Lenore. I mean, look at you. You're going to waste."

I laugh. "I am not. If you're trying to make me feel old, it's not working."

"You're not old, you're hot as fuck, in the middle of your degree, at Berkeley of all places. You should be using this time to your advantage. You should be getting laid every weekend if you're not looking for a relationship."

I'm about to tell her that I'm fine, when movement by the door steals my attention.

A couple walks in, a girl and a guy, maybe the ones who were smoking cigarettes earlier, but my focus goes straight to the man standing behind them.

The man staring right at me, gaze burning deep into mine, even from across the room.

That feeling of breathlessness returns.

My skin feels too tight, too hot.

The blood pounds dangerously hard in my veins.

But instead of feeling fear, I feel complete fascination.

This is the most gorgeous human being I've ever seen.

Creature, the voice in my head pipes up. *Gorgeous creature.*

Yeah, somehow that seems more fitting, because there's something definitely otherworldly about this guy.

He's tall, broad-shouldered, big. Naturally built like a truck.

But his face is pure masculine elegance.

Square jaw, full lips, straight nose, facial hair that's artfully groomed yet scruffy. Arched low-set black brows that keep his penetrating blue eyes in the shadows. His hair is black, wavy and long, almost to his chin. He's like if Aragon from *Lord of the Rings* just walked in here wearing a three-piece black suit and red tie. His clothes scream *money*.

"Wow, I'd definitely rate her a ten," I hear Elle say.

This can't be the man who was following me, can it?

"Her?" I repeat absently, unable to look away from the man's gaze. I'm completely captive in it.

I want him to know my name.

"Yeah," she says. "What are *you* staring at?"

It takes all my effort to blink and look at Elle, and the moment I do, my blood runs cold, the connection severed.

"You don't see that man?" I whisper, finding it hard to talk.

I look back to the door, but he's gone.

"Who, the scrawny dude who just walked in with the inexplicably hot girlfriend?" she asks.

I get to my feet and step out of the booth, looking around. Where the hell did he go? "There was a guy here. By himself. I was…we were looking at each other."

"Okaaay," Elle says. "What did he look like? He must have been Oscar Isaac-worthy to get you out of your seat like that."

I shake my head, not understanding it. Not only where he went, but what came over me. That wasn't normal. I've never had my body react like that to anyone before. Maybe that's what I've been missing. It's not enough to just find someone hot or attractive, but to find yourself attracted on some other realm.

Realm? Okay, calm down, I tell myself, forcing myself to sit back down. *You're getting a bit woo-woo here.*

"Lenore?" Elle prods me. "How old was he?"

"I…I don't know. Maybe thirty-five? Forty?"

She scoffs. "You and your older men. No wonder you're so picky. And no wonder he didn't stick around. Probably stepped in here and realized we're all a bunch of youngins. The man can't party."

She's right. The mystery man probably figured out pretty fast that this wasn't his scene. I mean, yeah, it looks cool, but if you look closely you'll see how cheap and rough around the edges this place is. It's all for show.

Still, the disappointment in my chest is palpable.

"Do you think it was the guy following you?" she asks.

I glance at her. Her interest is piqued again. "I don't know. This man was wearing a suit. The other one was wearing a long coat. I think."

"A suit?" she exclaims, pressing her fingers into the table. "Since when do you go after men in suits?"

"Since never," I say. It's true. I have a very specific type. Black leather jackets, boots, white t-shirts, tattoos, maybe a bit of eyeliner. Matt fits the description to a T. This man did not.

But maybe my type's been wrong this whole time.

"I think you dodged a bullet there, Lenore," she says. "Men in suits don't usually go for girls with tattoos. Believe me, I know."

She's probably right. It's not like I'm covered head-to-toe, but I have a lot for someone my age. My parents have tattoos and they've always been strangely encouraging toward me getting them. And as long as I ruminate on what I want and what they mean to me, making sure it's something special, they've even given me the money to do it. I know it's pretty rare to have that kind of support, so I've definitely run with it. Tattoos and jewelry, those are my trademarks.

Matt comes back with our drinks, pulling me out of my head for a moment. We make a toast to the semester almost being done. Matt went to Stanford for one year, met his start-up buddies, and dropped out (which seems to be the popular thing to do around here), but he still sympathizes. Then Elle tells him all about my supposed stalker and the hot guy in the suit, and I swear I see his jaw tighten a little, like the fact that I showed an interest in another guy bothers him.

But I don't dwell on that too much. The more I think about our relationship, the weirder it gets. Better to just take it at face value.

We end up staying at The Cloister for a couple of hours, until I'm pretty buzzed. But I know I need to do some studying tomorrow, so I don't want to be totally hungover.

"I'm going to go," I say, grabbing my purse and sliding out of the bench.

Matt reaches out and grabs my wrist. "Wait," he says. "I'll walk you."

I give him a quick smile, taking my wrist back. "I'm fine. I'm going to get an Uber. Don't worry."

I wave goodbye to Elle and head toward the door, but Matt is hot on my trail.

"Don't fuck him, Lenore!" Elle yells after us. "You can do better."

Matt gives her an incredulous look over his shoulder. "Hey, thanks."

I can't help but laugh, waving her away. Way to make things awkward, Elle.

"I'll be fine," I tell him as we step out into the night. The fog seems to have thickened, the air damp, but all the spookiness is gone thanks to the crowds of people in the back garden and heading down the path.

I stop at the side of the road and take out my phone, opening the app. Matt stands beside me, hovering.

I steal a glance at him. "I'm fine. Really. No need to babysit me."

"I'm not babysitting you," he says. "I'm looking out for you. If you really do have a stalker…"

"I don't. The more I think about it, the more I think I'm being paranoid. As you always used to say." I nod at the church. "Go back inside. Don't leave Elle by herself."

"You know she's fine," he says. "But you're not."

Then, before I can move, he reaches out, cupping my face in his hands and kissing me.

Ah, fuck. Elle was on to something, wasn't she? She picks

up on shit that I don't. I figured Matt was drunk, but I didn't think he was this kind of drunk.

I press my fingers into his chest and push him back. "Stop," I say quietly, licking my lips. My red lipstick is on his face.

"Sorry I…" He shakes his head, running his hand through his hair. "I just think we could start over."

I manage a sympathetic smile, not liking where this is going. "You have a girlfriend, Matt."

"I don't have to have a girlfriend."

My expression turns withering. "If you're hoping that sounds romantic, it doesn't. Come on, man. You're drunk. You don't know what you're talking about."

"And I don't know what you want," he says sharply. "Do you even know?"

I blink at him, taken aback. Matt is always so mild-mannered and chill, this is the first time I've seen him get cross with me.

"What are you getting at?"

He takes a step toward me, dark eyes glinting in the streetlight.

"I'm getting at you," he says. "I don't know you at all. You never let anyone in. You don't even know yourself."

I feel my cheeks burn, hating how his words are making me feel. "Go back inside, Matt," I manage to say. "Before you say something even more stupid."

He stares at me for a moment before he lets out a huff of air and turns around, heading past the bouncer until he disappears into the dark.

Shit, what the hell has gotten into him?

With trembling fingers, I manage to get an Uber, only a minute away. It pulls up, and I slide into the back, trying to get some sense into my head. It was such a strange night anyway, but to have Matt get all weird at the end really pushed it over the edge.

But I'm not so concerned with what he wants from me. He was drunk.

I'm toiling over what he said.

That no one can get close to me.

That I don't even know myself.

Because he's right.

And I hate that he sees that in me, and that he used it against me.

I sigh and lean back against the seat. It sucks, but I think it's probably for the best if I don't see Matt for a while. Let him get his head on straight.

The ride to my apartment is only ten minutes and I get the Uber to drop me off on Laguna Street. Though the shops and bars of Hayes Street are just blocks away, the neighborhood is dark and quiet as usual. But I'm so lost in my head, I can't be bothered to be spooked.

I cross the road and go to my door, my parents' door right next to it. My parents actually live above me. They own the whole row house, and had it split into two residences when I graduated high school. I had the choice to live on campus, and they'd rent this out, or stay here. As much as I wanted to experience the college lifestyle, this apartment is so much cooler than a dorm, and my parents totally leave me alone. For the most part.

I fumble for my keys in my purse, glancing up at their place above. It's nearly midnight and the lights are all off, my parents fast asleep. They tend to get up at four in the morning, for reasons I've never understood. As for me, I never sleep much. My brain won't turn off.

I take my keys out when I feel a presence behind me.

I gasp, my eyes going wide, the hair at the back of my neck standing on end.

I wrap my fingers around the keys, making a fist, prepared to whirl around and stab the attacker in the eye.

"Lenore Warwick?" a man's smooth voice says from behind me.

I pause, then turn around.

There's a man standing on the curb. Tall, long dark coat, the shadows too deep to make out his face.

For a moment I think it's the man from the bar, but I already know it's not.

My stalker, however, that's another story.

"Who's asking?" I say, my voice shaking a little, my fist tight around the keys.

"Forgive me," he says, stepping forward until he's in the dim light of my front window, his face emerging from the shadows. "But I've been looking for you for quite some time."

ACKNOWLEDGEMENTS

I'm not going to lie. Out of the seventy books I've written, this was one of the—if not *the*—hardest books I've ever had to write. Which is funny, because this story has been on my brain since 2013. 2013! That's a long time to be thinking about a book, even for me.

Being half Finnish, I always wanted to do a fantasy that tackled their unique and macabre mythology, but back then I figured it would be a YA book. After all, in 2013, YA fantasy is what was selling and adult fantasy, especially sexy adult fantasy, wasn't much of a thing. And that was fine with me, I could tone it down and make it friendly for a younger audience. My agent was excited about the idea too, and I always had this project in the back of my mind, waiting for a slice of time to come along where I could write it.

That time never came. Every year I emailed my agent and asked her what my prospects were and she would cautiously encourage me, but I kept putting it to the side, trying to find space in my life that I could devote to a fantasy that would take up tons of world-building time and writing time. After all, though I've done horror romance and paranormal romance and urban fantasy, high fantasy was something totally new to me (though it had always been a bucket list writing goal, thanks to the Piers Anthony novels I devoured when younger). I wasn't sure how I'd tackle it and how long it would take. The challenge seemed daunting.

Until my father passed away suddenly in September 2021, just two months after my brother died. I was thrown into the deepest depths of grief (and still am). Because the death of Hanna's father was always the catalyst for this book, I finally felt that perhaps now I was ready to write this book. After all, I would have done absolutely ANYTHING to get my father back, including going to the Realm of the Dead, and now I could sadly relate to everything single thing that Hanna was going through. I felt her grief intimately and it gave the story validity.

On top of that, I personally had a few things to say to Death, things to reckon with, things that I know I'll never understand. If only Death was a sexy god in the underworld who would barter with me in exchange for having my family members back. But the Death we know isn't like that. Which is why it was cathartic, and at times fun, to write him differently, to make him someone whom which you could perhaps trade your soul to or reason with.

So of course, the deaths in my family made finally writing this book make all the sense in the world. It didn't make it easier, no my brain feels permanently rewritten from all the loss and sorrow. But it made me ready.

Naturally I have lots of people to thank during this most trying of times.

Kathleen Tucker, Sandra Cortez, Ali Hymer, and Kelly St-Laurent—thank you for being my cheerleaders. To all my readers and friends, especially those on IG and my beloved Anti-Heroes on Facebook, thank you for your excitement for this book and your love.

Stephanie Brown, thank you for your belief in this book, and to all at the Bookish Box team for being so supportive, amazing and talented! You really brought Death and Hanna to life in the most beautiful way.

As usual, all my love and awe goes to Scott Mackenzie (and Bruce), who had to witness the making of this book during the following: the hardships of the first birthday and holiday season without my beloved father and brother, through a beautiful but stressful, snow-packed New Year, through a road-trip we hadn't done since before Covid, which included driving on the I-5 in Washington through historic floods, a night in Newport, Oregon that turned into five plus an emergency visit to the animal hospital in Corvalis (Bruce is fine!), eight hours on the 101 heading south while trying to find Tesla charging stations in the redwoods and writing in the car, plus finishing up the book during an all-nighter which culminated with me turning it in at six am in Healdsburg, California. Where I am currently, drinking Sonoma wine and writing these acknowledgements, fully looking forward to the future adventures of Hanna and Death.

Laura Helseth and Chanpreet Singh, you may be mortal, but you are Gods to me! Thank you for going above and beyond for this book, my gratitude towards you knows no bounds during this rollercoaster of an edit and I am so thankful for you and your support of me!

Last but certainly not least, though they are no longer with us, I also want to thank my dad, Sven Halle, and my brother,

Kris Halle. You were with me every step of the way. And Papa, I'm sorry this book isn't about Norse mythology, but I've written plenty of books already about Norwegians—time for Mama to have something too.

ABOUT THE AUTHOR

Karina Halle, a former screenwriter, travel writer and music journalist, is the *New York Times*, *Wall Street Journal*, and *USA Today* bestselling author of *The Pact*, *A Nordic King*, and *Sins & Needles*, as well as over fifty other wild and romantic reads. She, her husband, and their adopted pit bull live in a rain forest on an island off British Columbia. In the winter, you can often find them in their condo in Los Angeles, or on their beloved island of Kauai, soaking up as much sun (and getting as much inspiration) as possible. For more information, visit

www.authorkarinahalle.com

ALSO BY KARINA HALLE

Contemporary Romances

Love, in English

Love, in Spanish

Where Sea Meets Sky (from Atria Books)

Racing the Sun (from Atria Books)

The Pact

The Offer

The Play

Winter Wishes

The Lie

The Debt

Smut

Heat Wave

Before I Ever Met You

After All

Rocked Up

Wild Card (North Ridge #1)

Maverick (North Ridge #2)

Hot Shot (North Ridge #3)

Bad at Love

The Swedish Prince

The Wild Heir

A Nordic King

Nothing Personal

My Life in Shambles

Discretion

Disarm
Disavow
The Royal Rogue
The Forbidden Man
Lovewrecked
One Hot Italian Summer
The One That Got Away
All the Love in the World (Anthology)
Bright Midnight
The Royals Next Door

Romantic Suspense Novels by Karina Halle
Sins and Needles (The Artists Trilogy #1)
On Every Street (An Artists Trilogy Novella #0.5)
Shooting Scars (The Artists Trilogy #2)
Bold Tricks (The Artists Trilogy #3)
Dirty Angels (Dirty Angels #1)
Dirty Deeds (Dirty Angels #2)
Dirty Promises (Dirty Angels #3)
Black Hearts (Sins Duet #1)
Dirty Souls (Sins Duet #2)

Horror Romance
Darkhouse (EIT #1)
Red Fox (EIT #2)
The Benson (EIT #2.5)
Dead Sky Morning (EIT #3)
Lying Season (EIT #4)
On Demon Wings (EIT #5)

Old Blood (EIT #5.5)

The Dex-Files (EIT #5.7)

Into the Hollow (EIT #6)

And With Madness Comes the Light (EIT #6.5)

Come Alive (EIT #7)

Ashes to Ashes (EIT #8)

Dust to Dust (EIT #9)

Ghosted (EIT #9.5)

Came Back Haunted (EIT #10)

In the Fade (EIT #11)

The Devil's Duology

Donners of the Dead

Veiled (Ada Palomino #1)

Song For the Dead (Ada Palomino #2)

Black Sunshine (Dark Eyes Duet #1)

The Blood is Love (Dark Eyes Duet #2)

Nightwolf

River of Shadows (Underworld Gods #1)

God of Death (Underworld Gods #0.5)

Crown of Crimson (Underworld Gods #2)

Printed in Great Britain
by Amazon

79184506R00246